Promises of Like Souls

Val Conrad

Black Rose Writing

www.blackrosewriting.com

ISBN: 978-1-61296-149-1

PUBLISHED BY BLACK ROSE WRITING

www.blackrosewriting.com

Printed in the United States of America

Promises of Like Souls is printed in Times New Roman

FORWARD / ACKNOWLEDGMENTS

Writing has been something I've done as long as I can remember. When I was about seven, my parents bought me an electric typewriter (no more breaking my fingers on that old manual Smith-Corona). Being a writer, whatever that meant, began at a tiny little desk under a goose-neck lamp. This was way before computers became household items, but I remember pretending I could type in search words and get results from all sorts of places – libraries, companies, police departments, something magically all-inclusive like Wikipedia – more or less everything that I can sit here with my laptop or my phone and do today. I *wanted* there to be an Internet long before I had any idea there might ever really be such a thing.

I also remember writing stories as a youngster, though I remember little of it and have none. But I was an avid reader, and looking back, what I read then heavily influenced what I write today.

That's sort of how I began with this series. *Blood of Like Souls* took me about sixteen years from its first two pages in a completely different storyline to actually being happy with it after I got to "The End." Writing the second in the series was much easier, without as much hesitation to say to others that I was writing, or I had written. But I hesitated to call myself a writer. However, I have to thank my number one fan, Peg Sottile for her confidence. She celebrated with me when I got my first contract, and when the book came, and at the book signings, then we celebrated again with the second book. She tells complete strangers about my books. Bless her, she's been a devoted publicist, more than I could ever pay someone else to be so excited about what I write.

Back to this book. Thanks to Suz Anne Kurten for her read-through and edits. She's been waiting a long time for this. Also to Tonie Bolin, because a librarian is a powerful friend in a small town. She's been an avid supporter and friend who offered her time to read and edit as well, though I thought at one point she was going to drive to my house and throttle me for something I wrote in this book.

When I got to the point I needed to pick a title and design a cover, I did something different than before – I asked Jim Bridwell, owner of Jim's Diamond Shop at 519 North Main in Borger, Texas, to create for me the rings pictured on the cover. (www.jimsdiamondshop.com/) Took a bit of explaining that I really did want the rings to be linked, but he did so and created a wonderful pair that I photographed for this book. I think the rings were perfect, and lunch was in no way enough gratitude for his work. If you're shopping, browse on by and tell Jim you saw his work on a book cover. I think he'd be tickled.

In this story, there is a scientific dilemma for which I had to chase down professionals to find an answer. I will not spoil the story here, but I would like to offer my appreciation to the following people for taking the time to provide me information to use in that portion of the book (and the next):

Drew Atkinson, Forensic Specialist IV – DNA Section, Kansas City Police Department Crime Laboratory;
Daniel J. Wescott, PhD., Associate Professor, Director, Forensic Anthropology Center, Department of Anthropology, Texas State University, San Marcos, Texas.

Any mistakes regarding evidence or DNA collection and use are strictly my own. That apology, of course, goes to all the police procedures and other laws of man or nature I may have bent or broken in the story, as I'm sure I've far exceeded someone's rules, but this *is* fiction.

Thanks to my husband for believing in me, for understanding when I spend so many of my nights writing instead of sleeping. He's been a devoted supporter of my writing and the best best friend I could have. There's only one place I'd rather be than writing, and that's my favorite place – next to him.

And to those fans who've passed on a good word or a book to others – no thanks will ever be enough.

Promises of Like Souls

CHAPTER

1

Not every bride gets to move into paradise – a cabin in the hills of Washington State, surrounded by green trees and fresh air.

Paradise, except alone, without my groom to make it perfect – Zach Samualson.

The alone part came after our small wedding and reception in Albuquerque, after which Zach continued working with his team in the Drug Enforcement Administration until his transfer to Portland could be finalized. Meanwhile, I'd returned to Michigan without him, resigned from my position as medical examiner investigator, boxed my belongings for movers and packed my Suburban with personal belongings I didn't trust anyone else to move, and donated a ton of stuff I didn't use or need anymore. But saying goodbye to the friends I'd made there over the past four years and leaving my job with Dr. Gerald Katz was difficult, even though the decision to get married and move to Washington had not been.

Zach promised to be there with me at the cabin as soon as he could.

Two days after I'd arrived, the moving company unloaded its truck and left me again in the peaceful quiet. I breathed a sigh of relief that my traveling and the move were over. Making my way across the northern part of the country in March had not gone without incident though nothing disastrous, despite a snowstorm and other issues. For the long drive from Traverse City to our new home in Washington, my only companion was Laser, the police dog I'd been asked to retire by the Grand Traverse County Sheriff after his handler, Matthew Shannaker, had been killed.

I tried not to think about how he'd died.

Once the boxes had been delivered, I felt no rush to unpack them and find places everything – I'd have weeks to sort and organize before Zach arrived. The tranquility of our cabin was nearly perfect, feeling more like home than any city where I'd lived as an adult, I thought as I gathered another load of clothes to throw in the washer.

Paradise was interrupted by the ringing of a phone.

"Julie?" The familiar voice came from over a thousand miles away. My husband.

"I didn't think I'd hear from you until later this week, Zach," I said.

"Yeah, well, um. . . " He cleared his throat. "I know you had to pack by yourself and you've driven all week." This time, he paused, and the lengthy hesitation was so out of character for Zach that I stopped what I was doing. "Can you come to New Mexico? I need your help."

"What's wrong?" I asked, fearing the implications of last sentence. "Are you okay?"

"I'm fine, Julie. This isn't about me." He took a deep breath. "Not exactly. Remember one night in Hawaii, when I told you about my first time, having sex with Amy Donlon, Zoe's best friend?" Another pause that made me suspect that he was fidgeting like a kid being forced to confess gluing the teacher's desk shut.

"Yes, you said she was mad at her boyfriend, the captain of the football team," I offered.

"Amy's family moved away that summer we became juniors, after we . . . um, you know. Zoe might have known, but I swear to you, Julie. I never had any idea that Amy was pregnant."

The reaction he apparently expected from me was not how I felt at all. His news was a surprise, but I wasn't angry.

"That's quite a revelation, Zach, but why does it necessitate me coming to Albuquerque?"

"I guess you could say that's the good news," he said, sounding as if he were still braced for an impending explosion on my part. "Amy's missing. Her daughter, Amber, called the police two days ago when Amy didn't come home from work. It took them all day yesterday to track me down."

"What do they expect you to do?" Missing persons was not in the purview of the DEA.

"Amy's separated from her husband, and no one knows where he is. Amy's mother, Agatha Donlon, is in a nursing home. She can't take care of the girl, so she asked them to find me and have me take Amber temporarily." He inhaled, waiting. "Because I'm her father."

Perhaps Zach thought I missed the obvious conclusion about Amy having been pregnant when she moved away. I hadn't, yet I still wasn't angry. However, I was a bit skeptical. "I don't mean to sound insensitive, Zach, but are you sure this girl is yours?" I asked.

"She's got my green eyes," he said, as if that explained everything, and I got the feeling he'd already considered all the possibilities. "Yeah, I'm sure. Look, I'd help, even if she weren't. And I wouldn't involve you in this except I'm supposed to leave for El Paso tomorrow to work, the next day at the very latest."

"Already?"

His DEA team had another lengthy operation at the border, but he hadn't been scheduled to leave for two weeks. In fact, he'd hoped the transfer to the Seattle division would be done before he had to go south.

"You can thank Domino Hurley for this little change of plans. He's been a busy man while I've been away." He paused. "You're not upset?"

"No, Zach, I'm not. There's nothing either of us can do to change what happened, and being mad wouldn't accomplish anything."

"I love you, Baby. You're the greatest," he said, his voice sounding relieved. "Can you be here tomorrow, and maybe plan on staying a week or so? And bring the dog?"

"I'll be on a plane as early as possible," I said, needing no further explanation. If he wanted me there, I'd go, even if he hadn't said exactly why yet. "What's the story about Amy?"

"From what I could get from the Albuquerque police officer who located me, Amy worked late Monday – she's a hair stylist. Her last client, an older woman, was a regular customer for whom Amy made late appointments often," Zach explained. "Apparently they left the building together when she closed up. Amy's car was found in front of her business which is in a strip mall. No security video."

"So it's not likely she left that parking lot on her own," I concluded.

"No," he said, sounding defeated. "Look, if I could get out of this assignment, I wouldn't leave Amber. If the circumstances were different, I'd have my mother keep her. The truth is, I'm afraid that Amber needs to be with someone who can protect her, and you should come prepared to do that."

"Protection from who or what?"

Now we're getting down to the real issue.

"I don't know. The husband is always the first suspect. Greg Hennessy was Agatha Donlon's guess, too."

"Have you talked to Amber about Greg?" I asked.

"She remembers her mother and him arguing a lot, but I don't get the impression he ever hurt her or Amy."

"That's a good thing. He wouldn't want to be on your shit list for that," I said. "What're the chances of finding Amy at this point?"

"There's no obvious crime scene, no place to search. We both know how this usually plays out after 48 hours," he said with little hope in his voice.

Without any ransom demand or a crime scene, the chances of finding a victim alive after two days went nose-diving from slim to none so fast your ears would pop.

"Must have been a little overwhelming," I said, "walking into this blind."

"Certainly wasn't the way I envisioned finding out I was a father," Zach confessed. "I'm kinda numb to that news right now. Aggie didn't tell me about Amber until after she introduced us, but I knew in my heart, just seeing her. Aggie said she's always known." He sighed. "She wants to keep Amber, but she's pretty much at the end of terminal lung cancer and just can't."

"What a nightmare."

"I'm really sorry. I'll make this up to you," he said, quiet again. "I don't know how, but I will. Somehow."

"No need to apologize to me. You'll owe Laser more for this trip. He thinks this place is heaven, and now he gets stuck back in a cage for another plane ride," I said, trying to lighten the conversation. "Where will you be tomorrow? Can you pick us up?"

"I don't know. If I can't arrange to pick you up, you may have to rent a car, something big. Maybe an SUV," he said. "Bring your guns."

My guns?

"Damn, Zach, are you sure I'm what you need?"

"Hopefully this doesn't have anything to do with Amber, but I'm not willing to take that chance, whether she's my daughter or not," he said. "I don't mean this to sound crass, Julie, but knowing what you're capable of doing to protect someone else's child is all that matters to me right now. I couldn't ask more of anyone else."

Zach meant that I'd killed Matt Shannaker in cold blood to save Dr. Katz's teenage daughter, and he found that to be a desirable trait on my resume.

First time I'd thought of it as a compliment.

"Also, if they find Amy dead, I think you can relate better to Amber about a parent being murdered."

"I don't know about that, but I'll do what I can."

"Listen, I need to go," he said. "There's a briefing I have to attend. I'm sure everything will be fine, but I just didn't want you to be unprepared."

"I'll page you with a flight number and arrival time later," I said.

"Thank you with all my heart, Julie. You'll never know how much this means to me. I love you."

"I love you, too. See you tomorrow."

We hung up.

I stood there in the kitchen, doing the math and then wondering what I'd say to a young teenager, the daughter of my husband. Then it struck me – that sort of made me a stepmother.

And where would I really fit into that relationship, one that hadn't actually existed before a day ago?

Laser trotted into the kitchen for a drink and noisily lapped up water from his dish.

"Looks like you'll be adding to your frequent flyer miles."

I called the airline and booked a flight for mid-morning for me and the dog, with an open return. At least I hadn't gone grocery shopping and bought a bunch of fresh food to spoil while we were gone.

Then I paged Zach the flight number and time in an eight-digit number, a sequence I knew he'd understand.

Dragging in the suitcase I'd tossed into the garage just hours ago, I began sorting clothes from the dryer, picking what I'd take versus what I'd fold or hang up. I'd lived more out of my luggage in the last three or four months than I had my house, but I refused to let my mind wander through the reasons why, only remembering I moved across the country for the man I love. There'd be plenty of time for retrospection on the airplane tomorrow, or when I couldn't sleep tonight.

I tried to unpack more boxes, but I couldn't concentrate, so I headed for the shower. As the hot water cascaded down my back, I thought of the missing woman and her daughter – Zach's daughter.

I hope I can keep the A names all straight – Agatha, Amy, Amber.

A thirteen- or fourteen-year-old girl. Wow.

Questions fell through my mind like the water drops that splashed around my feet.

What was Amy like? How had she raised her daughter? When had she married, and why had they separated?

When Zach and I were in Hawaii, I remembered him telling me how Amy had invited him into her bedroom one afternoon and kissed him, and then she peeled her shirt over her head as further incentive to a sixteen-year-old boy.

Had Zach ever thought about Amy being pregnant?

And I wondered what he would have done if he'd known she was pregnant then? What does a teenage boy do in that situation? Getting married was no solution. Being Catholic, I wondered if he would have fought her if she'd wanted an abortion?

What would Zach have done if Amy had come to him with a daughter she said was his?

I wasn't sure, but had he known about Amber in the last few years, I suspect he'd have done something for her, especially given his inheritance. And though I wouldn't object, I had to wonder what he'd do for them now.

If Amy was still alive.

CHAPTER

2

Thinking about Zach's situation, the hot water hadn't calmed my nerves as I'd hoped.

I stepped out of the huge shower Zach had designed, and rubbed down with a towel most five-star hotels would envy – that was the sort of luxury he indulged in. Lotion all over, a little hair mousse. No need for makeup – no one would see me today. I felt properly pampered but jangled with anticipation.

With hours to kill, I took my guns out to the makeshift target range Zach had created down the hill from the cabin. He'd piled dirt in a ten-foot embankment backed by railroad timbers, complete with target stands and a shooting bench, which turned out to be a very nice place to shoot. After an hour's worth of practice in the crisp winter air, I cleaned my pistols and locked them into cases that would go in my suitcase when I packed tonight.

Still, I had a lot of day left to ponder the possibilities.

After five o'clock in Michigan, I picked up the phone and dialed the Katz's home number.

Gerald Katz had been my boss in Grand Traverse County. His wife and two daughters had made me a part of their family from the beginning, and I treasured the friendships.

MaryAnne answered.

We spent fifteen minutes catching up although it had only been a week since I last saw her. I detailed how the move had gone without Zach, including the flat tire on my truck just outside Butte, Montana.

In a snow squall at 2 a.m.

"I knew I should have stopped for the night," I confessed.

"See? Even fate thinks you should sleep," she agreed.

"MaryAnne, I have a problem I'd like to discuss with your girls." I explained about the kidnapping of a high school friend of Zach's and that he'd asked me to come and stay with her daughter during the investigation. I left out the part about Amber being *his* daughter or that my directive was to keep her safe. And that no one expected to see Amy alive again. "I'm hoping Kim and Kayleigh can give me little advice on what a teenage girl might be like, what sort of things she'd be interested in. I need a lot of coaching, I think."

MaryAnne laughed. "Don't we all?"

Kimberly and Kayleigh each picked up a phone extension so we could chat.

I explained again about Amy being missing.

Both Katz girls had lots of advice for me. With my prompting, they provided a list of teenage trends, movies they had seen in the last year, and a brief lesson on girls' attitudes on boys, which the sisters disagreed about due to their ages.

From the mouths of babes, Kayleigh shared the one gem I probably needed most.

"Just be honest about what's happening," she said. "When you're a kid, no one wants to tell you anything bad. Like when Mom got cancer. You just get the news after it's all over."

Honesty. I hoped I could manage that.

The next morning, I drove to the Portland International Airport and parked in a long-term lot after offloading the dog cage at curbside service to hold. Laser and I returned on the shuttle.

Bless the dog's silly heart. Even when I put him in the large crate, he still seemed excited to be traveling.

His needs took more space than my own, but he'd become a good companion, and I trusted his instincts and senses. I just hoped I wouldn't need them.

As always, the time before boarding was a mix of mind-numbing boredom and unwelcome observation of those with whom I'd be sharing recycled air for the next few hours. Watching these people around me, I knew that with very little intention or concentration, I could become a full-fledged obsessive-compulsive maniac who must boil my toothbrush or wash my hands after touching anything in public. If I continued that line of thinking, I decided, I'd never get on the jet.

Those waiting for the plane included an irritating group of rowdy young adults with a nauseating variety of dirty punk clothing, nasty-looking dreadlocks, body piercings and piss-off-the-world attitudes. They had been successful in angering a good number of passengers long before we boarded the plane, mostly with button-like clickers and foul language. Oh, and of course, there was the one who wore a lemon-yellow ten-gallon hat that Dr. Seuss would have been proud to rhyme about, except it was crowned with an adult diaper.

I remarked to the woman next to me that this must be because the wearer was so full of shit that it tended to overflow. She laughed.

Once at cruising altitude, I alternated between naps, a paperback I'd picked up at the airport bookstore, and watching the landscape slide by beneath me, especially intrigued by the mountaintop snow, which looked like whipped meringue on a chocolate pie.

The expansive geography made me feel insignificant, which only made Zach's situation more surreal. I struggled to make the connections benign, but seldom does something so complicated turn out to be a series of coincidences. Dozens of unanswered questions jumbled around in my head. I went back to reading a hot romance novel to escape.

We landed in Albuquerque just after 2 p.m., having lost an hour to the time zone. As soon as the plane turned on the taxiway and the flight attendant said cell phones could be used, I dialed Zach's number.

"Hey, Babe, hang on a second," he said after one ring and returned to another conversation with a tone of authority and impatience. "No, that's not acceptable. I told you, I don't *care* what it costs. Just do it. Call the bank, I don't care. Absolutely. That's terrific. She'll be here to sign in thirty minutes. Just keep working on that contract."

I waited my turn, wondering what he was doing.

"Sorry, J'," he finally said back into the phone. "You haven't changed the name on your driver's license, have you?"

"Not yet, why?" I was waiting to get one in Washington.

"Change in plans. Dom will meet you at the luggage pickup and bring you here. He's with a couple of Feeb's."

No details were forthcoming, for whatever reasons, but I had no doubt they were all taken care of by Zach and anyone he'd wrangled into this mess. Including the FBI, it seemed, if they were with Domino.

We disconnected.

After collecting the dog and my bags, I stood at the luggage carousel, waiting. I didn't see Domino Hurley, but then I remembered maybe I shouldn't look for how Domino normally appeared.

Sure enough, with one more casual sweep around me, I saw him standing near a bank of courtesy phones. When he saw I'd picked him out, he nodded and headed out the door to short-term parking, not waiting on me.

No problem. I can wrestle all this by myself.

Maneuvering the luggage and rolling dog crate, I followed him across the street into the parking structure.

As I walked through a row of vehicles, a man stepped out from behind a white van in front of me even though Domino had continued walking past it.

"Mariah?" the man said just a little too loudly, making eye contact worthy of a five-minute penalty in the NHL. He wrapped his arms around me in a hug I barely had time to react to, and whispered, "I'm Special Agent Rollin Turner, FBI. Please let us get you loaded. Agent Hurley will return as soon as we have you out of sight."

I looked over his shoulder and saw Domino nod his head without looking back at me.

"It's so good to see you," Turner continued loudly after releasing me. "We were just getting ready to come inside. Your flight must have been early."

"Uh, yeah. Nice tailwind, the captain said." I smiled. "You look great. This warm weather must be good for your health."

What the heck. I can act, too.

Another man appeared from the driver's side, and they loaded up the dog crate and my luggage in a matter of seconds, scooted me through the side door into a seatless interior, and closed it up.

They both got back into the cab.

I heard one of the men say, "Package arrived. Clear for pickup two." The driver started the engine and backed out of the space.

"Ma'am, if you would please move away from the door," Turner said from the front. "We'll be picking up Agent Hurley on the way out of the parking structure. Also, if you have your weapon packed, I would suggest you get that out of your luggage now."

I scooted over the carpeted flooring to my suitcase and from it, slid the aluminum case out into my lap.

Sure enough, the driver slowed and the sliding door opened. Domino rolled in as we accelerated around a corner toward the exit, and the door closed again.

"Hiya, Sweetheart!" he said with a smile almost hidden in a bushy moustache and beard. He leaned over to kiss my cheek. "Sorry for the welcoming committee."

I finished retrieving and loading both the Glock 26 and the Smith & Wesson Airweight .38 and holstered them on my belt and ankle respectively. I left the larger Glock inside the case.

When I was done, Dom took a phone from his jacket pocket and dialed a number, then handed it to me. "Secure line," he said.

"We're ready," Zach said when he answered.

"It's me," I said. "I'm on the way."

"Okay. Thanks for not quizzing me before."

"So what's the plan?"

"When you get here, you'll sign papers on a new vehicle. Pick a color."

"Blue, the darker the better. Black if necessary."

"Take the black one. It has a much better sound system. Besides, you didn't really have a choice – they've almost finished installing the tracking device. Amber is packed and ready to go. We're in the service department out of sight. You sign a bunch of stuff. Amber gets in, the dog gets in. Someone throws in your luggage, I kiss you goodbye, and five similar vehicles pull out of here at the same time in different directions." He paused again. "Hey Eric, good to see you. She'll be right here."

"Rader?" I asked. My voice cracked.

"Yep. He has papers for you to sign to reinstate your

commission."

Reinstate me to the state police?

"Why?" I squeaked, sounding more like a twelve-year-old boy in puberty each time I spoke.

"Because a badge can open doors, and you might need to exercise some authority."

"They can't just hand back my badge," I argued.

He laughed at me. "Seems Eric can do just about anything he wants. Reinstatement was his idea, not mine. I asked for help because I know you trust him."

"This is out of control, Zach," I finally said, regaining my breath.

"Yeah, it is. Dom and I are headed south, like I told you, so El Paso is not a choice. Pick a large city destination and then find a hotel, not something near the freeway. Phoenix, Oklahoma City, Denver, Dallas, I don't care. Make 300 miles today if you can. Keep going tomorrow if you feel you need to. They have satellite tracking on the truck. Someone with the FBI will be nearby wherever you go. Give your cell phone to the driver."

I pulled it from my pocket and gave it to Dom to hand it forward.

"Is all this really necessary?" I asked.

He ignored my question. "You'll have a scrambled phone like the one you're using, with several preprogrammed numbers. Don't call anyone from it unless it's an absolute emergency. Buy cheap calling cards to use pay phones if you need them."

While we talked, Domino opened the dog crate and let Laser out. A string of quiet "good buddy" greetings was finally answered by a loud bark. Instant friendship, bought with a handful of doggie treats that looked like bacon and smelled so good I almost shook hands for a strip.

"You're here," Zach said and disconnected.

Having grown up in Albuquerque, I recognized the auto dealership sign through the windshield as the driver slowed to turn. Within seconds, the van pulled into the shop area and a door rattled down behind us.

"All clear," voices said outside the van.

The van's side door slid open, and there stood my husband of less than three weeks, looking like he carried the weight of the world on his broad shoulders.

"I'll take the dog for a quick walk," Dom said, hugging me. "You take care, Julie."

Laser went with him, more treats being dispensed.

Zach took Dom's place inside the van, and the door closed behind him.

The two men in the front got out.

"I think we're alone now," I whispered to the tune of the Tommy James song.

Zach smiled in spite of his worries. "As much as I'd like to take full advantage of that," he said, leaning forward for a kiss that left me breathless, his green eyes locked with my own as he held me close for a moment, "I think they're still listening."

I rolled my eyes.

"Three things have happened since I talked to you yesterday. First, in the middle of the night, Aggie Donlon, Amy's mother died. No surprise medically, but on top of everything else, it'll be hard for Amber."

I nodded.

"Next, we found out Amy wasn't alone when she was abducted. She was doing a favor, letting her last client's granddaughter spend the night while the girl's mother was recovering from some dental surgery or something. Amber didn't know the girl would be with Amy, and no one suspected this girl Wynter Hammond was missing until she didn't come home from school yesterday. Whoever took Amy probably also nabbed her."

"Did they think it was Amber?" Rhetorical question but dismal news.

"Exactly. And third, this morning, the police tracked down Amy's husband, Greg Hennessy, who is and has unquestionably been on an offshore drilling rig in Croatia, Caledonia? Hell, I don't remember. Timbuktu for all it matters. But he couldn't have grabbed Amy three days ago."

"That's good news, isn't it?" I asked.

"Depends. Not ten minutes after detectives talked to him, a woman called the police department and told the detective she was Greg's girlfriend and that he'd asked her to pick up Amber and keep her until he could get back to the states," Zach told me.

Good news that faded to black.

"While she was on the phone, another detective called Greg back to verify, and he claims he doesn't have a girlfriend and didn't call anyone," Zach continued. "Tracing the number came up to a burn phone, somewhere in downtown, which made it impossible to track down. When the cop told him Amber was with me. He said he was fine with that. Amy had apparently told him I was Amber's father before they got married."

"There's more to this, isn't there?" I asked. I took a deep breath, facing a fear I'd ignored over the last twenty-four hours. Fear of the one monster left from our pasts. "Please don't tell me this has something to do with Pauly Brodenshot."

So he didn't, but he held my stare.

"Zach?"

"I've received hang-ups on my phone since we headed to Hawaii. It's more than an odd coincidence that somehow Pauly walked out of a Florida jail five days ago and disappeared. Someone called me last night and asked how I'd feel about losing my family."

"Great. You could have told me he was free five days ago," I said with a groan.

"I didn't know. On the road, you were as safe as you'd be anywhere. Then this happened. It could be totally unrelated."

"Right. It could be, but neither of us believes in coincidences of that magnitude. But what kind of connection would he have to Amy?" I frowned. "How would Pauly know about Amber if you didn't?"

With a heavy sigh, Zach said, "Pauly was the captain of the football team, the boyfriend that Amy was mad at."

CHAPTER

3

My heart fluttered as air wheezed from my lungs, leaving me speechless at the revelation that the man who'd become Zach's biggest enemy had also been the boyfriend of the girl Zach got pregnant. Suddenly all the connections snapped together in my head.

"I'm sorry, Julie," he said, taking my hand. "You've been through hell already without my demons chasing you, too. I've been a wreck since I called you yesterday, hoping I'm doing the right thing. For both of you. But he's the one link that makes this all something very different than a random kidnapping."

"I understand. I'll take care of me and Amber; you just take care of you, okay?"

He nodded but didn't look convinced.

Me, either.

If someone would kidnap Zach's biological daughter and her mother to get to him, why not his mother, or mine? Lots of easy targets besides me to worry about.

"I just put our mothers on a plane for a vacation," he said, reading my thoughts. "You missed them at the airport by about an hour. The deal was they told no one where they're headed, not even you or me. They'll call Eric in a week to check in. Mom brought me this." He handed me a large manila envelope. "New pictures of your colt. He's a feisty critter."

I took it but didn't look inside.

"There's also ten grand in cash. Do not use your bank accounts, credit cards –" He swallowed hard. "You know the drill. I'm handing you two off to the FBI, which I don't think I could do if Forrester hadn't arranged it personally."

"You got Nolan involved in this, too?" I'd begun to wonder if the governor wouldn't be there to see us off.

"Well, yeah. You have better contacts than I do, you know that?" He winked then shook his head. "I'd walk away from this job if I could protect you by not going."

I wondered whether there really was no other option, but it wouldn't matter. "So you're going to be the bait again," I concluded. "It's a good time to visit a zoo, I think."

Without hesitation, he nodded. He knew where I'd taken the zoo photo that had been on my wall. "I don't want to know anything else."

I wanted to ask why not, but he dismissed the conversation by opening the van door, then kissing me one more time.

He helped me scoot out and get to my feet, and reached around to pat my right hip under his favorite denim shirt.

"I thought you –" The panic in his voice was sharp as the holster he felt for wasn't there.

"Holstered at my back and ankle," I said. "I'm prepared, like you said."

And, of course, he had to slide his hand around my waist casually as we walked into a hallway, just to check.

"Julie," a voice called from behind us. Eric Rader, who had been my commanding officer when I worked for the state police in Alamogordo.

"Hello, Eric," I said, turning to extend a hand to shake, which he ignored to hug me.

"I wish I could be doing this under more pleasant circumstances, but I'm glad Zach called. You need to sign about a hundred pages – remember the drill?" he said, dumping a stack from an envelope onto a tabletop. "The usual hiring stuff, W-2's, insurance and such. The name is still Madigan," he pointed out as I got ready to sign the first form, "rather than trying to get personnel to change everything on short notice. Hope you don't mind. Payroll might have been a problem if the name didn't match on all the documents."

"Payroll?" I said, astounded.

"Can't work unless we pay you," he said with a smile. "Gotta love the government. The state never received your resignation, so you were simply on long-term leave of absence. My deepest apologies for that – I must have misplaced it."

I rolled my eyes.

"Check in at least once a week, directly to me. You've been assigned to Internal Affairs."

"Great," I moaned. "A perfect place for me, right?"

"Actually, except for your rank, it was. So I promoted you," he said as I flipped pages and signing my name for the tenth time.

I stopped cold.

"Zach," Rader said, "may I present to you Lieutenant Julie A. Madigan, Internal Affairs, New Mexico State Police."

"Sweet, I always wanted to sleep with an IA officer," Zach said, stepping out of reach of my not-so-playful slap.

"Your badge, Lieutenant," Eric said, holding out a gold shield and ID. "Sorry, had to use your old photo, too. Now to swear you in."

"I swear to get even for this someday, Rader."

"That's good enough for me." He leaned down and kissed my cheek. "I've gotta run. Call if you need anything. My cell number is on the card. Be careful, wherever this takes you, Julie. Keep in touch." He marched down the hall to the showroom floor, waving when he got to the door.

"I'm jealous," Zach ribbed. "I'll never make lieutenant."

"You might not be sleeping with one if the jokes continue," I warned. "I don't find this humorous in the least."

"The badge offers you credibility to detain someone until local authorities can. The promotion is his way of keeping you under his wing."

I shrugged. "This is getting out of hand, Zach."

"I know. Look, I'll try to call you every morning between six and seven, or when I'm able. Keep the phone handy when you can." He also handed me a new pager. "In case I can't call, I'll check in. Don't return any calls from it unless there's a code with the number. If you get any other calls or pages, any at all, you let Nolan know."

Tears flooded my eyes.

Zach took my hand and kissed my palm, then held it to his cheek.

"You don't know how much this is tearing me up. I pray to God I've made the right decisions today, but I know you'll be fine. I love you, Blue Eyes." He pulled my face close to his again and whispered, "Amber has another envelope for you with more instructions. I don't trust anyone but you. Trust Eric Rader or Nolan, but no one else. Especially anyone from the DEA. Take the money and disappear."

"How will I know when it's safe?"

"Eric will know. Don't come back for anyone else. Not even me, Julie," he said. "Do you understand?"

I didn't like it, but I understood. "I love you."

He stole one more soul-shattering kiss and wiped the tear that trickled down my cheek.

"Let me introduce you to Amber," he said and reached for the door. "I haven't told her that her grandmother died last night, either. Sorry."

"Is there anything about this I'm going to like?"

He leaned down to my ear and whispered again. "Yeah, going to Pauly Brodenshot's funeral."

In a small office area, two men stood guard next to a dark-headed girl in her young teens, who sat, reading a book in her lap.

"Amber?" Zach said from the doorway.

She looked up, a mirror of his green eyes. It was almost unreal how much she looked like Zach.

There was no doubt who her father was.

I understood now how Zach knew the first time he saw her.

Zach walked over and pulled the chair next to hers out at an angle, then motioned for me to take it. He dropped to his knees in front of her.

"This is my wife, Julie," he said to her, as I sat down.

"I'm Amber Hennessy," she said in a quiet voice. Her face remained as stern as she could make it. "Do you know my mom?"

"No, I don't."

She nodded, but I could see the sulkiness behind the intentional neutrality of her expression.

"I know this is all overwhelming," Zach said, "but I need to make sure you're safe. Julie is a New Mexico State Police officer. She's going to take you out of Albuquerque until we find out what happened to your mom."

She only nodded.

"There's more bad news," Zach said, putting a hand over one of hers that gripped a book. "You knew your grandmother's lung cancer couldn't be treated anymore. I'm sorry, but Aggie passed away last night."

Silently, the green eyes spilled tears down her cheeks, shattering the calm. "Mom's dead, too, isn't she?" she blurted out in anger. "No one wants to tell me anything, but she's dead, too, right?"

Zach looked stunned by her reaction, so I answered.

"Amber, you probably feel like no one will tell you what's been going on the last few days. Once we leave, I'll tell you. You deserve to know the truth because everything that has and will happen affects you, too. It affects you the most," I said. "But to answer your question, we don't know about your mother yet."

She sniffed and pulled a tissue from her pocket to wipe her nose. "Why is this happening?"

"Why is a very important question for everyone," I said. "The point is that we can't guess right now what that answer is. We can and should hope she is alive. But because a young girl was also kidnapped with her, the kidnappers may have thought she was you, making it crucial we protect you."

She watched me speak, listening carefully.

"I will do everything in my power to make sure you are safe, but I need you to trust Zach and me to do that."

Biting her bottom lip, she nodded slightly.

"Do you have any other questions for Zach before we leave?" I asked.

"What about my dad, I mean, you know, Greg?" she said, struggling with what to call him, now that she had a new "real" father, obviously something she hadn't known before.

"The detectives talked with him this morning. He's on his way back to New Mexico, but it will take him almost two days to get here," Zach said. "Meanwhile, we're going to get you two out of town now."

She shoved her book into a satchel and stood. "Fine, I'm ready."

Domino came into the building with Laser trotting beside him.

"Is that your dog?" she asked with a cold attempt not to sound interested.

"Yes. Laser's a retired police dog," I said.

"I used to have a dog when I was little, but it ran away," she said. "Is he friendly?"

"Especially if you have a pocket full of treats," I said. "Hit Domino up for his leftovers."

"Julie can tell you about him once you hit the highway," Zach said, interrupting the beginning of a conversation. "As much as I don't want to send you two on your way, you should get going."

I nodded and stood up. "We'll be fine," I said, touching his sleeve.

I'm not sure either of us believed those words.

CHAPTER

4

We made our way through the maze of walls back into the service area.

"That's your new vehicle," Zach said. "Hope you like it."

He'd picked a black four-wheel drive Chevy Suburban with tan leather seats and dark tinted windows. The options alone probably cost more than my first car.

"Stunned with your flare for the absolute over-achievement of my satisfaction," I mused, shaking my head. "As always."

One of the sales staff came and presented me with another forty pages to sign.

After signing those necessary to register the vehicle – title and insurance papers, and such, Zach motioned him and his papers away. "I paid cash – the FBI is covering the paper trail. She's not signing all that shit for your dealership," he said, dismissing the younger man who still held dozens of pages.

With hurt feelings, it appeared, the sales person slunk off down a hallway.

"I packed a loaded 30.06 with plenty of spare ammo for it and for your handguns," Zach began. "A box of food and bottled water, in case you get stranded. Blankets, coats. There's a cooler with drinks and snacks and stuff to keep you rolling for a day or so. Dog food and a couple of gallons of water for him, too." He walked around the truck, showing me its features and pointing out the surveillance equipment, including the panic button. And then silently, but making sure he'd made his point, he showed me how to deactivate the beacon.

I nodded, thinking he'd prepared me for a war.

What the hell am I up against, Zach?

He mouthed one word again. "Disappear."

"You're sure?" I asked.

"Absolutely. Whatever it takes, Julie, no matter what. Promise me."

I kissed him to seal the deal.

Done with his tour, he handed me the key and remote lock fob. "I gave Amber one spare key and Nolan the other."

Someone gave me a dealership cap. I tucked my hair up and put on a pair of aviator sunglasses from the lost and found box. We put Amber in the middle row of seats and had her lie down under a blanket. Laser hopped in the back, obscured by the dark tinted windows.

With one last kiss goodbye, I followed one Suburban out the bay door, with several more trailing my own – decoys. The first vehicle turned right toward the freeway, I opted for left to a different access point.

I didn't look back, no matter how much my instincts screamed I should stay with Zach.

After a route through a neighborhood to look for a tail, I drove east on Interstate 40, mostly because that direction had the best variety of exits actually going somewhere – westbound, the interstate goes to Gallup before intersecting any highway to a destination short of nowhere. I intended to turn north at Cline's Corners or Moriarty to Denver, where I'd implied I was going, but I could easily go eastbound into Texas or south toward Vaughn.

After I'd passed the Tramway exit, I told Amber she could sit up and buckle her seatbelt until I could stop.

"So tell me about the dog," she said, turning to rub his ears as he draped his head over the seat for the attention.

"I used to work for the medical examiner in a Michigan county. The deputy who worked with Laser was killed, so the sheriff asked me to adopt him," I said, unable to tell her exactly my part in Matt Shannaker's death.

"What happened to the bad guy?" she asked, more interested in the criminal than the victims.

Was I the bad guy?

I hesitated, not wanting to talk about people dying. "Police shot him in Florida." I glanced at her in the rearview mirror, hoping she wouldn't ask how – I didn't want to explain that Zach had been involved.

"Have you ever been shot?" she asked, as if this were a virtue.

"No, I haven't," I replied.

Without further details, her attention turned from me back to the dog and the scenery outside the passenger-side windows.

I wasn't sure if the subject matter bothered her or maybe she was extrapolating an ending to the situation she faced today. Nothing about her emotional state had been what I expected – she didn't seem to be frightened or grief-stricken. She almost seemed to be acting like an adult, which concerned me even more.

We rode in silence for another fifteen minutes before she spoke again.

"Did Zach love my mother?"

There was no traffic around, so I asked her to climb into the front seat. She did so without effort, and Laser jumped forward a row as well, not wanting to miss out on the pets this new person was giving.

"I told you I'd be honest, right?" I asked, and she nodded. "Amy was best friends with Zoe, Zach's twin sister, but Zach was just friends with Amy. He didn't know she'd had a baby until your grandmother told him a few days ago."

"Oh, so he didn't love my mom," she said. "She lied about that, too."

Great. Biology on top of everything else. Not the sort of conversation I'd planned.

"Your mother probably didn't want you to know what happened, Amber. And I wasn't there, so maybe you should ask her or Zach."

"I was an accident – that's what happened," she blurted with acidic sarcasm.

Arguing with her wasn't going to change her mind, I decided, so I didn't say anything.

"It musta been pretty weird for him, finding out about me," she eventually said. "I know I freaked out when Mom told me Greg wasn't really my dad."

"I'm pretty sure Zach was surprised, but he's not disappointed."

"Really?" she asked, weighing my statement for the truth.

"You look very much like him and Zoe with your green eyes. Zach said he knew right away that you were his daughter." Truth. It sounded sappy, unless maybe you were a distressed fourteen-year-old.

She seemed to like the news. Or maybe talking beat listening to the voices in her head. "What's he really like?"

"Zach? He's smart," I said. "He likes horses and fast cars. He's a very good artist. We should have him draw a portrait of you. In fact, I'd be surprised if he doesn't draw something while he's in El Paso."

She nodded.

"He's honest to a fault and a man of his word."

"I hope I'm really tall like he is. He's a lot better looking than Greg, too," she said. "He's kinda ugly, you know?"

"I haven't met Greg, but Z' is nice to look at." I could see the question in her eyes about his nickname. "I don't know if there's a story to why it's just one letter. How much shorter can you make a four-letter name, right? He calls me J' sometimes, too."

She considered this. "I don't think I want to be an A'."

"Fair enough. Do you have a nickname?"

She wrinkled one side of her face in disgust. "Mom calls me Punkin, but I don't like it. Sounds like I'm still four or something. I'm fourteen now."

"Maybe you can think of something you like better while we're traveling," I suggested.

The freeway traffic began to break up as I passed Moriarty, and I pushed past the speed limit another five miles per hour.

"Zach said you'd tell me about your father," she said, opening a new topic.

I took a deep breath. I'd rather have let her talk, but I hoped the story was a way to make a connection to build her trust. "When I was sixteen, my father was murdered, so it was really difficult for me."

"Do you really believe my mother is still alive?" The question came from behind Zach's serious green eyes.

"I do think there's a chance, yes. That's why getting you away and safe is so important. It's possible the man who kidnapped them thought the other girl was you," I said, hoping the honesty bought me something, as terrifying as it might have been to her. "He may have wanted you more than your mother."

"Kidnap *me*?" Her voice broke.

I nodded and continued, "Police don't know for sure. But that's why it's safer if you are nowhere near what's going on."

"Who would want to kidnap me?"

Despite my promise to tell the truth, I didn't exactly lie – I just didn't answer her question directly. "It's still just a theory."

No way could I bring myself to explain that her newfound biological father might be the primary target of this crime. If Zach's fears were right, Amber was the sacrificial pawn. Hurting her or her mother was a way to get even for standing up to a fellow agent gone bad. And after sitting in a Florida jail for almost four months, Pauly was someone who might still hold a grudge that his high school girlfriend's child was Zach's, on top of everything else.

"We're going to stop soon, do you want anything?" I said, seeing the signs for the exit ahead.

"I need to go to the bathroom," she replied.

"Okay. Deal is, wherever we go, we need to stay together. Not side by side, but within ten feet or so."

She tilted her head.

"For instance, inside this store, you should be aware of your surroundings – is anyone paying special attention to you, getting a little too close? Someone who seems to be herding you away from me or toward the door? That sort of thing. Keeping you safe is my responsibility, but you have to participate, too."

"Is this kinda like *The Bodyguard*?"

I couldn't remember – did someone die in that movie?

CHAPTER

5

"Yep, kinda like Whitney Houston and Kevin Costner," I said.

At the Highway 285 exit, I decided indeed to go north and eventually meet back with Interstate 25 north or actually east of Santa Fe, instead of taking Highway 3. I wanted to get to Denver and spend a day or so before I ditched the FBI tail.

The weather was good and was supposed to hold, so the roads and skies were clear. For the third week of March, it was warm, but I'd seen heavy snow this time of year, too.

I'd left Oregon in similar warm weather but with frequent rains. Fortunately, our property hadn't suffered any real damage from the heavy downpours that washed out so much of the snowpack, causing rivers to run over their banks in the Portland region in the previous weeks.

The sun dropped behind the Sandia range shortly after I exited the interstate, and the temperature began to drop, according to the thermometer display on the rearview mirror, which also served as a compass and who knows what other options.

Options. I didn't have many, but the Suburban had everything GM could put in a vehicle and a dozen things I didn't know a driver could possibly need. The manual would be necessary to figure out some of them.

And the vehicle had a sound system that could levitate it right off the ground at about half its potential volume. Zach, true to his music-driven soul, had tossed in his case of CDs for me.

"Where we going?" Amber finally asked.

"First to Denver. From there, I'm not sure. We probably won't stay anywhere very long. Is there somewhere you would like to go?"

"Can we go snow skiing?"

Felt pretty crappy to shoot down her first idea, but I did. "I'm sorry, Amber. I recently had surgery on my shoulder, so I don't think I ought to try that. And since we ought to stick together, you really shouldn't ski alone. Do you like zoos?"

She shrugged.

"The zoo in Denver is great. I think that would be a nice day's activity, if you like. I've been there several times, and it's my favorite."

"Are there lions and tigers? I like the big cats," she said, then apologized to Laser, who literally stuck his nose into the conversation as well.

"I think we can probably find some big cats there."

"What's your favorite animal?" she asked.

"I like the cats, too, but my favorite there are the polar bears and other water animals, like otters and seals. I could watch them play for hours."

The zoo seemed like an acceptable alternative to skiing. She picked out one of the magazines she'd bought.

In the tourist shop where we'd stopped half an hour before, I'd told her she could get anything she wanted, which apparently no one had ever said to her before.

She looked at me suspiciously. "Anything?"

"You should be reasonable, of course. I don't think you should buy things you don't really want, and we are sort of traveling light. Is that fair?"

Amber had chosen a bottle of apple juice, a couple of magazines, then asked if she could get movies to watch in the Suburban. I'd said yes, so she picked out two.

When she finished flipping pages in silence, she tucked the magazine into her backpack.

I reached into the center console and pulled out the manila envelope Zach had given me and found the photos of the horses his mother had brought him. There were a couple of other smaller envelops I didn't mess with, one fat one which was probably cash.

"I think these are pictures of a mare Zach bought last year with her new colt."

She opened the processing envelope and took out a set of prints.

I glanced as she crooned at the black leggy colt in the bright sunshine near the barn.

"What's his name?" she asked.

"I didn't think to ask. The mare's name is Julaquinte."

She kept shuffling through the pictures. "They're prancy. What kind of horses are they?"

"Friesians," I said, which explained all I knew about breeds. "Z's the expert. Do you like horses?"

"Sure." She sounded a little defeated. "But Mom doesn't want me around them."

"Maybe we can work on that. My mother keeps her horse at Zach's mom's ranch, so I bet we could all go for a ride."

"I love horses." And she went off into a lengthy description of different breeds she liked and why.

I listened, thinking this was a lot like if I'd told her about my favorite guns – some of it was just plain foreign. But it gave me an idea.

"Do you know anything about shooting?" I asked when her horse stories wound down, and she leaned back to feed another treat to the begging monster beating his tail on the leather seat like a drum.

"No. My mom said having a gun was asking for trouble."

"People who don't like weapons shouldn't have them, I agree," I said, trying to cross that anti-gun sentiment. "But like horses, if you're with someone who works with them every day, they aren't so dangerous. Maybe we can find an indoor shooting range, and you can have a lesson," I said.

Again, she just shrugged, which I interpreted as a teenage equivalent of ambivalence that tried to hide the fear I sensed running just under the surface.

"I have my guns with me, Amber. I'd like you to know something about them so you know how to handle them."

I didn't say the next three words that popped into my head.

Just in case.

CHAPTER

6

North of Santa Fe on I-25, I picked out the FBI tail in my rearview mirrors. I didn't attempt to identify the car directly, but there was only one going the same excessive speed I was, yet not coming any closer when I slowed down. Perhaps the lack of highway patrol speed traps was their doing. I didn't care if I got pulled over or not. Doing so would likely force a car following to pass me.

We pulled off the freeway in Trinidad, Colorado, for dinner at my personal choice, BlackJack's, a local restaurant where you shucked peanuts and threw the shells on the floor, complete with a white buffalo head mounted above the bar.

This was an easy decision after Amber declined the available choices of fast food. I wasn't about to argue if I could get the steak I'd been craving. She ordered grilled chicken and a baked potato.

Our initial getting-acquainted conversations in the truck had faded to silence before we crossed the border into Colorado, and Amber had started watching a movie on the video player from the back seat, Laser by her side like a new best friend.

At dinner, the conversation returned.

"Zach told me he doesn't live in Albuquerque anymore."

"He built us a cabin near Portland, Oregon," I replied, showing her on the US map I'd bought at the truck stop. "I just moved there from Michigan. We both grew up in Albuquerque though. Our moms were friends."

"So did you play together as kids? High school sweethearts and all that?" she asked.

"No, I'm seven years older than Zach, so we weren't friends. When he was your age, I was in college."

"A younger man," she observed with grave maturity and an impish smile.

I leaned toward her and lowered my voice. "Everyone called him Cubby when he was little because Zoe couldn't say 'Zach.'"

She laughed.

"I only remember seeing him once, at my dad's funeral." Zach had been almost as tall as me then, though I put on another two inches before I quit growing. He'd added a whole foot in the next five years or so. "He was nine."

Amber made a sour face, then smiled.

Our meal arrived, and we began eating.

"How did you get that scar on your neck?" she asked.

For the first time I could remember, I didn't feel the need to reach up and cover the mark across my throat. "About five years ago, the man I was married to attacked me. He also threw me down a flight of stairs and broke my neck."

"I thought you died when your neck got broke," she said, wrinkling her brow.

"Sometimes, depending on how badly and which of the bones is broken," I explained. "My fractures didn't cut the nerves in my spinal cord, which is what causes people to be paralyzed. You know, like Christopher Reeve. I'm pretty lucky."

"What about the guy that killed your father – how many people did he kill?"

I wondered where this line of questions was headed.

"We were never really certain, but about twenty over the years."

"So why do people kill other people?" she asked, concern dark in her eyes.

"A lot of reasons. Might be an emotional outburst, like extreme jealousy, anger, hate or even love. So-called crimes of passion," I said. "Some people kill for power or money or greed. Some are mentally ill and don't understand the consequences of their actions. And some are simply evil and kill because they enjoy hurting others."

Like Anthony Bock.

"Oh," she said, taking another bite of her chicken.

This was a young girl on the cusp of figuring out the world wasn't all safe and happy, despite her mother trying to protect her. Whatever exposure she'd had to violence in her short life before, this was extreme and very personal.

I understood that, and I suspected her fear would jump exponentially as she learned more about the situation.

She pondered that and then nodded. "Why would someone kidnap Mom and me?"

"Kidnapping has two general purposes. One is to move a victim somewhere," I said, thinking how this type of kidnapping was usually to finish the attack in privacy. "The second reason is when the kidnapper uses the victim as a hostage to get someone else to do something, such as to give him money."

"So my mom," she said, "which was it?"

"I think that this kidnapper wanted to demand something of someone else, which is why I think your mother is still alive."

"Oh," she said, digesting the information along with her dinner.

What I couldn't bring myself to tell her was that this kidnapper would not be satisfied with the wrong kid. I told her I'd be honest. I didn't say I'd tell her every suspicion that crossed my mind.

After eating, we headed north again. Amber sat in the back to finish her movie, leaving me to my thoughts.

If Pauly Brodenshot was behind this kidnapping as Zach suspected, what reason would he have to keep Amy alive? I wasn't as sure as I'd been several hours ago. Amber was the blood link to Zach, so what would Pauly do when he found out he had the wrong child? He'd have no use for hostages, so he'd kill them and move on to something else.

Pauly's intention was to make Zach suffer, so killing him would not be the primary goal. But I had been involved in breaking up the drug-dealing scheme, too. If Pauly couldn't get Amber, I'd be the next choice. Did Pauly have the information and resources to link me with Amber and track us now? Was there someone else in the DEA or the Albuquerque Police investigation working for him? I shuddered, wondering if I could really trust Domino.

Could I really trust anyone?

Not that I was worried Dom would intentionally betray Zach or me, but he also had a family to protect. I was proof that people can do a lot of unpredictable things to save those they love. In fact, I recalled Domino saying before I joined him going to Florida that if someone wanted to get to Zach, I would be the perfect target.

Following my headlights through the darkness, possible answers to these questions made my steak rumble uneasily in my stomach.

It was after midnight when I finally chose a hotel on 17th Street in downtown Denver. Amber had fallen asleep an hour or so before, bored with the night, out of questions, or probably plain exhausted.

I woke her, and she followed me in a sleepy silence inside where I registered.

"With the proper deposit," the clerk sighed. "Doesn't matter whether or not it's a police dog."

I paid cash, then got a cart to fetch luggage and animal, Amber dragging reluctantly along with me. I'd just closed the back door when another dark Suburban pulled into the lot and parked just a few spaces away.

"Honey, take the leash and follow me now," I said, not using her name but getting her attention.

She did so without argument, and we were almost to the hotel door when I glanced back to see the driver get out and turn so I could see his face clearly.

My paranoia turned to relief.

Nolan Forrester. Alone.

He couldn't be part of the tail working by himself, could he?

Other than a slight dip of my head in acknowledgment, I made no other indication that I recognized him, and we went on inside to the lobby and elevator.

I intentionally stopped back at the front desk and asked the clerk if he had a razor available – something the hotel might offer but would not put in each room. I overheard him mumbling some obscenity under his breath as he turned to go to a small side room. Obviously I was interfering with the late night television blaring from the small office.

He brought back a package and slid it across the counter.

Nolan entered the doorway behind me and was close enough

when I asked the clerk again if it was room number 323 or 232, apologizing for being so sleepy.

This time with an undisguised roll of his eyes, he repeated the number, pointed to the elevator, and told me to go to the second floor, get off and turn left.

I thanked him and put my hand on Amber's shoulder as we moved away from the desk and Nolan replaced us, either getting an earful about women in general, or suffering more sarcasm when his registration also interfered with the clerk's television show.

As we waited at the elevator doors, I leaned down and asked Amber to take a good look at the man checking in.

She turned slightly and looked, then nodded.

"He's the only other person you can trust if something should happen while we're traveling. You should be suspicious of anyone else, but Nolan is one FBI agent I know we can depend on, okay?"

She just nodded again.

On the second floor, walking slowly, messing with the dog and the bags, and having turned right intentionally instead of left, by the time we got back to our room, Nolan was stepping out the doors of the elevator.

Again, I made a barely perceptible nod to him.

"I need to get some ice when we get into the room," I told Amber as I dug for the key card in my pocket and Nolan passed us. "Do you want a soft drink or anything?"

"No, thanks."

"You must be pretty tired," I continued as I opened our door. "I'm beat."

She yawned and mumbled something sleepy as I closed the door behind us, then smiled. "This is like being a spy or something," she whispered.

"In a way, it is," I agreed, grabbing the ice bucket from the little bar. "I know this seems unnecessary, but would you please wait for me in the bathroom with the door locked?"

"Not a problem," she said, dumping her pack next to the dresser. "That's where I have to go anyway."

I let myself back into the hallway, making sure the door closed and locked behind me, taking the bucket to the ice machine near the elevator.

And of course, I bumped into a fellow traveler in search of late night junk food.

"Long day, eh?" I asked.

"Mm, I thought I'd never get here," he said, feeding a drink machine quarters and hesitating. "Crap, this stuff is expensive. I need change," he said, pulling a ten-dollar bill out of his wallet.

The machine took one's and five's, so I figured he wanted an exchange.

I took two fives from my change purse and offered them to him.

He handed me the ten, hiding a key beneath. "Thanks. In case you don't like black."

Our eyes met.

"Polar bears, 1300," I whispered.

Nolan nodded that he understood I meant the Denver Zoo at one o'clock.

I smiled. "Watch the door while I walk the dog?"

CHAPTER

7

The secure cellular phone rang at exactly six o'clock the next morning.

"Hey, how's it going?" Zach asked.

"Well enough. She's a smart kid," I said, hoping she was still asleep.

He sighed. "God, I hate this. They found the girl's body last night."

"But not. . . " I dared not finish.

"No, not Amy. And I'm supposing you'll say that still supports a possibility she's alive?"

I considered this briefly. "Not long though."

"You're both okay?"

"Yep, just where I wanted to be today."

"Okay. We should keep this short, but I'll try to keep you posted."

"Please be careful, Z'. I love you."

"You, too, Blue Eyes."

Amber wasn't awake yet. After dumping crunchy nuggets into Laser's bowl and checking the chain on the door as well as the chair lodged under the knob, I slipped into a long hot shower where the world disappeared in the fog for a brief moment of sanity.

Reality reappeared when the mirrors cleared.

When I came out of the bathroom, Amber was sitting up on the bed, some morning network show on mute. When I said good morning, she only mumbled a response before sliding off the bed and disappearing into the bathroom.

Half an hour later, she marched out, hands on her hips.

"Zach called this morning, didn't he?" Not so much a question as a statement.

I nodded without time to explain before her next verbal accusation, but I could see where this face-off was about to go.

"You said you'd tell me everything," she challenged, now crossing her arms.

"I didn't tell you about Zach's call because I thought you were still asleep," I replied. "And I said I'd tell you the truth, even if it wasn't good news, not that I would tell you everything."

Semantics didn't fly, even if the intention was to protect her.

I sighed. "Yes, Zach called this morning to say that the Albuquerque Police found the girl who was with your mother. She had been killed."

Her pretty young face twisted, anger dissolving into guilt as her eyes filled with tears. "Because I wasn't with Mom."

"This is not your fault, Amber," I said, reaching out to touch her hand, but she yanked it away from me and bent over, maybe attempting to hide her face.

"But if I had been with Mom –"

"Amber, stop," I said gently. "All the what-if's in the world will not change what has happened. It's okay to be angry or sad or anything else you feel, and you can express that to me however you want, but none of what's happening is your fault."

She inhaled deeply, and stood up, walking back to the bathroom. I heard her blow her nose behind the door, maybe trying to compose herself.

I don't know what I would have done in her shoes. Nothing in my past prepared me for what she faced.

Finally she came out and got dressed without any more conversation, and we walked to the restaurant across the street.

At breakfast, I was relieved when she slipped back into her own personality instead of the best-behavior grownup act. I was concerned the adult facade that she'd put up for most of the day before was something she felt she had to make permanent, but this didn't seem to be the case. She broke into a string of stories about her friends, favorite movies and actors, and a description of professions she might consider.

Being a cop wasn't on the list, though knowing my own roots, I thought, no one would be surprised if that's where she ended up, following in her father's footsteps. I wondered if she'd try to solve this crime over and over subconsciously.

"I get the impression you could be just about anything you wanted," I told her. "Shall we visit the zoo?"

As we left, I identified an overly-average dark green sedan in the parking lot, occupied by two men, one asleep against the window. I looked away immediately, not wanting them to know I'd made them.

There was no question I was right when they followed us into the parking lot at the Denver Zoo.

They were supposed to tail us, but I wasn't sure how closely, so I set out to determine whether they were going to follow us inside or just wait us out in the car.

Once Amber and I made our way through the gates, I checked the park map and chose a route to take enough time to put us in the arctic animals about ten minutes before one.

Amber morphed into a true kid as we strolled through cages and around pens, chatting non-stop, silly to irritation at times to someone who hadn't been around children very much.

Trying to remember she wasn't an adult, I tried to enjoy the park from her perspective, too, but I found that to be difficult in full-alert defense mode, carrying two guns and checking to see who might be following us around.

We bought drinks at The Hungry Elephant, then we headed toward the polar bears.

There were two people inside when we arrived, but they didn't linger.

Amber was immediately amused with the bear playing with a basketball, tossing it, then jumping after it. She stood right at the glass and watched, giggling.

I stepped back to better observe the overall enclosure and its entrances.

Only a few minutes later, an elderly woman entered, dressed in a bright silk jogging suit, the Kodacolor female human equivalent of the peacocks we'd seen.

On second glance, she was very tall and straight for a woman who appeared to be in her seventies.

Nolan?

I almost laughed aloud, disguising my chuckle with a polite cough.

After observing the bear a few minutes, the woman moved toward me casually.

"I never know which is more fun – the children watching the animals or the animals watching us back," the woman said in a voice so very Boston I could only nod, biting my lip.

The voice changed to a lower timbre and back to something a little more Middle America. "How are you doing?"

"Oh, I think we're okay," I offered, suspecting that wasn't quite what he meant. "I got news this morning. Why do I get the feeling this is going to get ugly?"

"You're a realist, and it's already way past ugly," he said. "In my Suburban, tucked into the springs under the passenger seat, are directions to a place you can go. It's my first wife's parents' home, so there is a wide gap in names and times if someone was looking for connections to find you. They will take care of her."

"Why would I need someone to take care of her?" I said, not liking the possible reasons that zinged off in my head like a roll of exploding firecrackers.

"Because you can't lie well enough to make me believe you won't go to Zach."

I felt like he'd slapped me.

"I understand," he continued. "I'm not here as an agent, Julie. We're friends. I'll help you however I can, officially or unofficially, but as far as this little trip, I'm on vacation."

"I didn't know you were married," I said, changing the subject.

He smiled, showing a bit of lipstick on his front teeth. "Not currently. I hear I'm hard to live with."

"Could be the cross-dressing," I offered. "Red's really not a good color with your skin."

He laughed.

"Here's one more number," he said, handing me a business card. "It's toll-free, so you can call it from anywhere, and it's forwarded to my personal cell phone."

Amber turned toward us.

"We'll go see the cats in just a second, okay?" I said, seeing the polar bear had exhausted her interest. I'd promised we'd see the cats last so she could spend as much time there as she wanted.

She nodded, rolling her eyes at the wildly-dressed woman next to me as she turned away.

"Amber was pretty upset this morning when I told her about the other girl. She feels guilty. I wish I'd taken more child psych," I said quietly. "This is over my head."

"Get your head out of academia and follow your heart, Julie. She doesn't need therapy yet, just someone who cares."

I knew he was right, but the logical part of me wanted a better foundation to deal with the situation – that's how my bricks were stacked. Not understanding children was something that terrified me about the possibility of having any of my own. Some people are born to be parents, but I thought maybe I missed that gene along the way.

"Keep me posted, no matter what you decide to do. I won't be far away, but I won't keep popping in, either. As far as Batman and Robin out there," he said, "it would be helpful if you could give us a good night's sleep occasionally when you can. This may be a long assignment, and they're both okay guys."

"Sorry. I just wanted to get into the city last night," I said.

"And if you feel you need to drive all night every night, you do what you must. There's two of them. Sleep is as much for you and her as anyone else."

"I could sleep for a week, I think."

"Why don't you find a nice hotel with a restaurant, lots of amenities, stuff nearby to do, and stay put a few days?"

I nodded.

"I'll be right around the corner."

"Hell of a way to blow your vacation," I said. "But thanks."

He laughed again. "You two have a lovely time," he said with the old woman's voice that reminded me of Robin Williams playing Mrs. Doubtfire.

Amber and I walked out of the exhibit, leaving him with the next wave of zoo-goers, which included the two men he'd referred to as Batman and Robin, the FBI agents.

We made our way to the cats, which included leopard, jaguar, Siberian tiger and South African lion exhibits. Amber walked from one to the next, reading all the posted material and asking questions I mostly couldn't answer.

She was entertained for over an hour, moving from cage to cage and comparing animals, but eventually hunger got her attention, and she asked if we could go have dinner.

"Of course," I said, walking with her toward the exit. "The zoo will be closing in a little while anyway. What would you like?"

"Could we have pizza?" she asked. She asked as if it were a real treat for her and not the main staple of her diet, like mine.

"Absolutely. Laser likes pizza bones."

"Pizza bones?"

"Umhmm, the crust."

She laughed again and repeated this over and over until I thought I'd go nuts, teasing Laser with it when we got into the Suburban in the parking lot until he began leaping back and forth over the back of the middle seat like a gazelle.

I had to do some driving around to find one, but eventually we found a local pizzeria instead of a chain restaurant. The dining area wasn't crowded, and we took a booth near the corner rather than sit in a table in the middle where we could be surrounded by people. Normally paranoia doesn't demand I sit facing the entrance, but this was different. I wanted the best view I could get.

I saw the anonymous sedan park, and both of the men came in. I got a much better look as they ended up seated within my view, just past Amber's left shoulder.

One was a younger man, maybe early thirties. He had short spiked hair and bizarre neon blue eyes. A good-looking kid who looked like he'd be more comfortable in his well-worn Levi's and a red and blue rugby shirt than he would be in a suit.

His partner was a middle-aged man. Though I couldn't see much of his face, he had big ears under salt and pepper hair. They had an almost father-and-son appearance, similar postures, as if they'd been together sitting in a fishing boat on a quiet mountain lake.

"Who were you talking to at the zoo?" Amber asked after we'd ordered.

"That was the man I pointed out at the hotel last night," I said quietly. "He's pretty good at disguises, huh?"

Her eyes got bigger as she nodded. "Can we do disguises?"

"What would you be?" I asked, trying to sound neutral about the idea, but it did have some merit.

"If he was a woman, I guess my only choice is a boy, isn't it?" She sounded disappointed in the conclusion.

"We can work on that tomorrow, but you do have other choices. The idea is to change not just your appearance, but who you present yourself to be." I winked. "I could see you being an old woman, too."

She nodded and emptied her red plastic glass of water, having again declined getting a cola of some sort. This surprised me enough to ask why. She hadn't ordered a single soft drink since we were together.

Amber blushed. "My mom is kinda heavy. I figure if I watch what I eat now, maybe I won't get fat. I don't drink pop or eat a lot of junk food. I mean, it's not like I'm starving myself or anything."

Apparently, she'd had to defend her choices before.

"That's very sensible, Amber. I wish I had that kind of willpower," I said, holding up my soft drink. "I live on fast food."

"I don't think you'll get fat, no matter what you eat. Mom wouldn't like you because you're so thin," she stated.

I hope she gets the chance to hate me.

Our pizza came, and conversation gave way to cheese and pepperoni.

"How about we go to the mall when we're done," I suggested as the meal wore down, wary of the feeling of being watched.

Of course, I knew we had the FBI escorts, but this felt different.

CHAPTER
8

Amber changed focus from eating and followed me to the checkout, having saved the pizza bones for Laser along with two leftover pieces.

We hit the nearest shopping mall at about six o'clock. Amber's attention differed from mine, and I had to keep reminding myself we had no agenda. She needed to wander like a kid, and I needed to watch her, which meant adjusting to her detours when she slowed to browse at something.

I was hoping to make another connection with music, so I nodded I wanted to go into a store specializing in CDs and videos, but she just hung around me without looking at anything. The indifference she portrayed struck me as strange.

"What kind of music do you like?" I asked, aware of her boredom.

"Nothing particular. You?" she asked politely.

I was scanning the newest releases, including one by a good-looking Louisiana boy named McGraw, who'd likely follow the successes of George Strait and Garth Brooks. "No rap. I don't care for blues or soul in general, but some of it is okay. Any music you want to check out?" I asked, trying again to engage her in conversation.

She shook her head and turned her back to me.

"Music's good for your soul. Some rhythms make you relax; others make you think more clearly. Some makes your body just want to move."

She shrugged, uninterested in anything in the store.

A kid who doesn't like junk food or music – that didn't fit what Dr. Katz's daughters had told me when I called to ask for pointers. At least there were movies.

Giving up on that topic, we moved back into the mall.

The next stop was a department store, where I bought us each a bathing suit since we were missing out on hotel pools. She chose a pair of jeans and several shirts. I bought a belt and a pair of jeans as well. I paid for our purchases in cash, and we went back to the Suburban.

I'd just buckled my seatbelt when the satellite phone rang.

"Yes?" The very idea someone was calling zinged my nerves.

"Are you somewhere you can talk?" Zach asked, not knowing how relieved I was just to hear his voice.

"No." Not sure what he meant, I guessed he wanted to know whether Amber was nearby.

"Have you read any of the letters in the packet I gave Amber?"

"No, we've been out, and I forgot about it. Sorry."

"Read the first one. It has your name on it," he said. "Sometime after eleven, call the fourth number programmed on your phone." Ominous sounding.

"Okay," I disconnected. "That was Zach. He asked if I'd read the stuff he gave to you for me."

"I left it at the hotel in my backpack," she said.

"That's okay." I started the truck. Changing the subject, I asked, "How tall are you? About five-four, right? How would you like to look older instead of like a boy? You could be my niece, if anyone asks. " I'd brought along the spare green contacts I took to Florida. If nothing else, those would make me look more like Amber, maybe enough to be her mother, but I didn't want to go that far. An aunt would be close enough.

"How much older could I look?" she asked, the idea piquing her attention.

"Three or four years, if we work at it. Maybe change your hair, add a little makeup, and touch up your clothes by a year or two. Let's aim for eighteen."

"Sure," she agreed. "Where'd you learn this?"

"From Domino, one of the DEA officers who works with Zach.

He helped me change my appearance. We cut my long hair and dyed it dark. I used colored contact lenses to make my eyes brown, changed the way I dressed." I didn't tell her I'd gone slumming around in bars looking for bikers.

"That's awesome. Can we lighten my hair?"

With that, the plans for the next day were made.

By ten o'clock, we'd soaked in the hotel hot tub until we were both wrinkled. She showered and went to bed after giving me the waterproof envelope from Zach.

I spread them out on the desk and started with the handwritten letter on top.

Hey Blue Eyes,

First, let me thank you again for coming to help me. By the time you're reading this, I've probably already gotten to El Paso and am working. I hope you're far away and lost to anyone looking.

Here's what I know is going on. Our bad guy in question got processed out of lockup just before he was to be transported to a federal courtroom for indictment. No one can explain how the release paperwork appeared legit, but it happened five days before Amy's kidnapping. While I don't think he actually did this – he doesn't do any of his own dirty work – I suspect he had a local officer involved. Where there's one, there may be many. That's why I told you not to trust anyone but Eric or Nolan. You have a previous alliance with them that is above suspicion.

You've probably guessed by now that my concern is that this is meant to target me. I understand a lot better how you must have felt as Bock chose people close to you. As I told you before, I know you'll do the right thing. Getting you two safely out of town was the primary goal. Distance is safety – I don't think he can chase us both, but he obviously has more help than we thought.

There is a guard at my mother's ranch in Albuquerque – to feed the horses and cattle. I didn't put anyone at your mom's house. Don't go to either of them or to Michigan. I did call Brandan so he'll keep an eye out for Dr. Katz and his family. He said to tell you hello and congratulations, though at the moment, I'm sure you're wondering what the hell for.

If you haven't run into Nolan yet, you will. Don't hesitate to use whatever options he may offer as you find necessary, but he's doing this off-duty, so try to stay below the FBI radar. This whole operation is so out of the ordinary that people will be talking, and someone is listening. If you feel you need to ditch the tail, do it, then disappear.

I've enclosed a copy of my will. Please don't be mad for me being pessimistic. You might need to have it without going back home or wondering where it was. There's an attorney's name inside. He can help you long distance, if needed.

Holy crap, I thought. Zach doesn't think he will survive this. The very thought of losing him took my breath away.

I've also enclosed some bonds, should you need more money than the cash you have. I wish I could have arranged to get you out of the country. You might could get into Canada but not with the guns. Mexico wouldn't be as hard to enter, but getting out could be a problem without Amber's birth certificate. The best alternative was simply for you to be invisible.

While I'm making wishes, I hope you won't be angry that I'd like us to consider taking custody of Amber if this all falls down around her. If you say no, I'll understand, but I'm asking you to think about it. If something happens to me, you will both be taken care of the best I know how.

I felt a tear roll down my cheek as the fear burned in my chest.

I've already made arrangements for Aggie's burial and Amy's, too, if it comes to that. I feel responsible, if only by the connection that brought them into this mess.

As for you . . . I miss your smile, your arms around me, and your sweet voice. You're the very best thing in my life, and I'll do everything possible to come home to you, I promise.

Forever and always, my love,

z

There were several other sealed envelopes inside the outer wrapping, contents marked in his neat printing. I tucked them into my bag to read later.

I took the phone out onto the balcony and dialed the number programmed in the phone.

"Hey," he said after two rings.

"Are you okay? I read the first letter, and I'm worried about you."

"I'm fine for now. I'm sorry, Julie. You didn't sign on for any of this."

"I'm doing it because you asked me to," I said. "Nothing in the note surprises me. I don't have an answer to your wishes yet, but I'll think about it. We'll be moving tomorrow."

"Just don't let down your guard because you're hiding, no matter where you go." He paused. "Now for the bad news. They found Amy tonight. She died . . . " He swallowed and inhaled. ". . . just like Zoe did."

His voice sounded strangled, as if hands were wrapped around his neck.

"Oh no." The news would be devastating to Amber, of course, but I also knew how badly his twin sister's death hurt him. Then the connection between the two women clicked, and I felt my heart rate jump. "You don't think he . . . I mean, could he have been involved with Zoe's death?" I stammered, trying not to wake Amber.

"I don't think so, but he knew the details," he said. "This settles it. Go buy yourself a beautiful, expensive dress for his funeral, Julie. Something gaudy and strapless and wildly inappropriate. Something people will gossip about for weeks."

"That would be fun," I said ambiguously, glancing through the patio glass at the child across the room.

I tried to remember how they broke the news to me about my father, but I'd already known the truth, I thought. Amber had suspected her mother wasn't alive when we started our trip, but that's a million miles from hearing the words.

"If you have to," he said, "wear something sexy and wildly inappropriate to mine, too."

"Don't tempt me, Samualson."

He actually laughed, but I really didn't find the possibility humorous at all.

"I'd like to tell Amber about her mom."

"She's already asleep," I said, hoping he didn't want me to wake her.

"Okay. I'll try to call a little later in the morning than normal. I'm sorry I have to do it and leave you to be with her."

"It's okay. That's part of why I'm here." To pick up the emotional pieces of a young girl whose world just shattered, as well as to protect her life from the same threats.

After we hung up, I opened the next envelope, marked 'personal.'

Immediately I knew this letter had nothing to do with the case or our present predicament. He'd written it just hours before Matthew called me to the barn that Anthony Bock blew up around me.

Saturday morning, September 2, 1995 – 4 a.m.

I snuck into your house just a few hours ago, and now I'm waiting for a flight out again. After almost four years, you still tremble when I surprise you, even after you realize it's me and that I won't really harm you. You always give yourself completely to the moment and succumb to the feeling, knowing it's a game we play. I have some inkling how it makes you feel, but do you ever think it feeds something primal in me, as well? It's like owning something forbidden, sneaking away to play with it when no one is looking. Knowing I can do anything to you. . .

So last night when I peeked into your bedroom, I was surprised to see that silk scarf I'd tied over your eyes the last time – covering your face, your hand softly caressing it against your cheek. You always amaze me.

When I came in, I turned on the light over the stove, knowing it would be just enough to illuminate the hallway but not into your room at the end. I stood at the bedroom door and watched you sleeping. You didn't wake up when I slipped in through the garage door and into your kitchen. I knew you wouldn't hear me. I've been in your house so many times, waiting for you, I know every creaky board, every whisper of the carpet as I move. I've practiced these steps so I could watch you all night, if I wanted to, even moving into the bedroom and lounging in that chair in the corner without waking you. I know because I've done it.

I doubt you ever question my return, but I knew you wouldn't be expecting me again so soon.

The scarf thing baffled me. . . As much as you'd fought me blindfolding you, why did you have the scarf against your skin now?

It didn't appear to be tied, just draped over your face. What had your fantasy been before you slept?

This game we play, it's killing me. I sneak into your life every few months, and I feed this desperate need you have to be afraid and satisfy the enormous need I have to touch you. Then most of time I sneak away instead of staying to enjoy time with you in the daylight, which is what I want.

God, I love you with all my heart and soul, and if this is all I can have of you, I'll take it for now. I can live with this until . . . Until.

I didn't want to crawl into your bed unannounced this time, didn't want you to feel I took you against your will. I wanted you to invite me, to hold me and . . . Julie. . . what I want most is for you to say you love me. I'm afraid someday you'll tell me not to come back again, that the game is over. So I play carefully, trying to balance your fears against my love. We are both desperate for something we can't have. I wish I could tell you how I feel, but you don't want to hear that I love you.

Or is that maybe the biggest fear of all for you?

I slipped off my t-shirt and jeans. When I sat on the edge of the bed, you stirred. "Shhhh," I whispered. "Julie, it's me."

"Zach?"

My name she says. I smiled.

"Yes." I touched the silk across your forehead. "Can I kiss you?"

"Mmmhmm," you moaned and rolled back a little.

I didn't lift the silk. I just touched my lips to yours over it, feeling the warmth of your breath against the fabric.

"Come to bed?" you asked softly.

My heart skipped a beat, hearing the invitation. I didn't come to surprise you this time, only to spend a few hours close to you.

"Don't move the scarf. Not yet." I hesitated. "No games. I just. . . " Just what?

I slid beneath the covers next to you, scooting near until my legs and chest touched you, propping up my head on my hand so I could look at you in the shadows.

"I didn't expect you so soon," you said. "Is something wrong?"

"No," I lied. "I just wanted to see you." I touched the loose end of the silk on your pillow, and you reached to touch my hand.

I wanted to know about the scarf. Did it make you think of me?
Had it been comforting or did it bring back the fear I've delivered?
"Why?" you asked.
"You know why," I said evasively.
Please don't make me say it – neither of us can take it.

The words in this letter were so raw. And suddenly I felt the emptiness of knowing he had not put this letter in with those hundreds of others in the Christmas box he'd given me just months ago. This one had been kept separate, unshared. I could only guess it was because he still tried not to make me feel responsible for so much wasted time.

I ran my fingers up and down your arm next to me, feeling goosebumps rise to my touch.
Nudging you onto your back, I lifted your left arm and put it behind my neck so I could put my head down on your shoulder, like you've slept next to me so many times. The tenderness of you wrapping yourself around me so close...
Damn! I didn't want to cry. . .
"Kiss me again," you whispered and turned my face toward yours.
This time I lifted the silk slightly and touched my fingertips to your lips to kiss you, softly, tasting you, inhaling every molecule. I let my hand caress your face through the silk, and with the touch, your response increased. Your body turned toward mine.
"You taste like whiskey," you whispered.
"Stopped in the kitchen for a drink," I answered.
You licked the remaining taste from my lips.
My very soul aches for your touch, your kiss, but until the moment you can say you love me, my life will remain empty.
I left the scarf in place so you couldn't see the tears.
I keep returning to you, stealing kisses and touching you in the dark, even though it rips my heart out that the only thing to penetrate the walls around you is fear. It tears me apart, coming so close to hurting you, knowing it's a fine line between what turns you on and going too far. And it astonishes me the pleasure each of us finds in it –

it's not just you anymore.

Still, I slip away in the night when you are sleeping so you don't see me fall apart after we've made love. I feel helpless, selfish, cruel to be torturing us both like this. But I can't stop.

Our bodies respond to one another, chemistry and physics and biology I doubt we could alter. Magnets drawn together to become one, stronger together than apart. I let you move at will, slowly waking to my intrusion, to my wanting you again.

And I do want you. One night so long ago, you told me you didn't want someone to love you. You needed someone to want you.

You must know by now how much I want you, but you pretend that you don't know I need you so much it hurts to breathe, that I miss you when you're gone from my sight, even when I only close my eyes. But I love you, too. I can't help myself, Julie, and I'm sorry. Please forgive me. Saying those three words aloud would be as bad as physically breaking your arm; it would be irreversible and terminal.

So many times before, I've led the dance. This time, you touched me.

You may simply drive me out of my mind. . .

Until I felt your tears against my skin, without telling me why you shed them.

Unable to control my own, teardrops squeezed from my eyes into my hair. Hopefully without a sound, I mouthed the words I've been dying to say out loud for so long. "Julie, I love you. I love you. . . "

His letter explained so much about what had happened that night, but it left so many questions unanswered. Giving it to me now, I understood Zach wanted me to know how he'd felt, as if it were his way of saying goodbye now.

CHAPTER

9

Just as reading the letters and notes in the box he'd given me at Christmas had made me see how my choices affected us both, Zach's words about being apart broke my heart again.

I'd spent almost four years of our lives running, hiding, pretending. Throwing away precious time when I could have been feeling like he made me feel – whole and loved. Unbroken.

So many what-if's.

I was too distracted by Zach's letter to sleep, so I wrote back, shaking my head at the irony that just hours after he wrote those lines, while he was on a flight to who-knows-where, I was standing on a bomb in a barn.

Zach,

You've never said why you came back that night, what was wrong. I knew you'd lied to me about it being nothing, and you knew that I didn't believe you. But this trip was different from the others, and as your tears mixed with mine, (and I did know you were crying,) there were no words between us, only comfort. Whatever it was, I hoped just being there with me somehow made it better for you. My tears were for you.

To answer your questions from the first letter, I know you will take care of what you need to for your daughter and her family, especially now. Of course I am open to discussion about what all that may entail after Amy's death, but honestly, I wasn't anything but

*surprised when you told me about Amber. Please don't think I harbor
any resentment or anger that you have a daughter.*

*Your daughter. Having spent just these few hours with her, there
is no doubt in my mind she's yours. Not just the green eyes, but the
way she sleeps, sprawled across a bed, almost snoring but not quite.*

*She's been a champion so far, but I don't know how long a kid
can go before too much is just too much. I'll pick up the pieces the
best I can.*

*And one more thing, I'll buy a strapless black dress for Pauly's
funeral. If you make me come to yours, I'm wearing something blood
red.*

I love you, Z'... Forever.

I stuck all the papers back into my briefcase, queasy at the
thought Zach might never read those words. Stretched out on my bed,
with the light off, I listened to a smaller body breathing in a deep
sleep that sounded just like her father's. I wondered just how many
other things she inherited from Zach without having known him.

The situation had escalated, not just to murder, but something
deeply personal to Zach, and I was worried. He might not tell anyone
else, but I knew he believed the only way to catch Pauly was to be the
bait unless somehow the criminal got caught in some wild twist of
destiny before.

Stretched out on the sheets, I stared up at the little red smoke
detector light on the ceiling for another hour before drifting off to an
unrestful sleep.

When the phone rang the next morning around 7:30, I'd been awake
since six, up and showered, trying to steel myself for what would
happen. I answered, talked only briefly to Zach, then motioned to
Amber.

"Zach would like to talk to you," I said, extending the phone to
her.

She took it, taking a deep breath before speaking. "Hello?"

I stepped away to offer what semblance of privacy one could get inside a hotel room. I didn't think Zach would make a lot of small talk, but she answered that we'd gone to the zoo and then done some shopping yesterday, then paused again.

Although I couldn't hear more than an occasional buzzing sound from the receiver she pressed up against her ear, I could tell from the change in her posture and expression that he had moved right on to the bad news.

She shook her head back and forth as he talked, the motion exaggerating with each cycle. Then she began to punctuate it with a pitiful "No, no, no. . . " that I'd expected to become a shriek before he finished. But she just kept whispering it until she finally dropped the phone and collapsed on the floor, hiding behind her hands as the news overwhelmed her.

I went to her and put my arms around her, and she clung to me, sobbing. Then I picked up the phone and said goodbye again to Zach and disconnected.

Like Nolan had said, I didn't need a college degree to understand that two arms to rock her in my lap, to try to make her feel protected, were what she needed at the moment.

I pulled a bedspread off to wrap around us and let her cry.

Finally, tears slowed enough we could talk.

What does one say to a fourteen-year-old who found out her father wasn't who she thought, whose grandmother died of cancer, whose mother has been murdered, and who was being dragged around the country by a woman she barely knew from a danger she could not fathom?

What would I have wanted someone to say when my dad died?

Somehow, I found words. I couldn't make it better. I only promised she could walk through this, one small step at a time, with new people in her life to help.

She had some questions I hadn't gotten answers for from Zach. I didn't know where they had found Amy's body, and I didn't have any specific details how she died. I didn't want to make any assumptions about his reference to how Zoe had been killed. "I don't know," seemed enough.

"Zach said he will take care of all the arrangements for your mother and grandmother, but the funerals will wait until you get back home safely," I told her.

"Home?" Her voice croaked, angry and raw from crying. "I've got no home now."

"What about Greg?" Stunned, I realized how wrong what I'd said sounded.

"I'm not his daughter, and he's always gone. He won't want me," she said with defiance that attempted to disguise hurt but failed.

"We'll work this out. I'm sure it's not a matter of Greg wanting you, Amber, but you'll have a home where you'll be safe and feel wanted. You have Zach's word and mine."

In that moment, I made the decision Zach had asked me about.

✄

Even though I'd let her crawl back in bed to sleep a while longer, by noon, I decided Amber needed to escape the four walls surrounding her, to divert some of her attention from the grief. Facing a fine line of letting her stay cooped up or putting on a front to go out, I encouraged our plans to get her haircut – I needed to see that she could keep functioning because of our circumstances. When that was done, we returned to the hotel where we lightened her hair to a wheat blonde that made her skin a warmer tone.

Although she'd been quiet, once her hair was done and styled again, she asked for a lesson in acting older.

"Sure," I agreed, happy she asked.

I gave her pointers about makeup and expressions, letting her perform each step and then evaluate how it changed her appearance.

"How about if I looked older and you looked younger?" she suggested, looking at us both in the mirror.

"Okay, give me some advice," I said. I didn't want to tell her that the sadness in her eyes made her look older than the makeup ever could.

"More makeup," she said. "Maybe some highlights for your hair, too."

We decided on another trip to the store later so she could do something with my hair.

"So what's so hard about this disguise thing?" she asked, her voice dull as lead.

"The idea is not just to look like someone else but to use all of their personality," I explained. "You don't want to attract lots of attention, but you don't want to be someone who is hiding, either."

"Like how?"

"Old habits can give you away. For example, if you browsed a stack of magazines at the salon, your new character might choose *Cosmo* rather than *Teen*. You'll have conversations with people who are much older than your actual age, so you need to speak as if you're eighteen," I said. "That means different slang, references to your new age, like what college you're going to, what your major might be, the guy you're dating, and so on. You start with appearance, but building the new character takes planning and practice so you're ready for anything."

She ran her fingers through her new blonde hair.

"That," I said. "That's a good move. Do it again."

She repeated the motion. She didn't look twenty, but with the right makeup and clothes, a solid seventeen was plausible.

"Say you're at a doorway in a store," I continued coaching, "and a man stops and holds the door open for you. What will you do and say?"

"Just go in, I guess," she said.

"The older you should smile, make eye contact, and say 'thanks.' Nothing fancy, but remember, men are more likely to take a second glance at you," I said, turning her to face the mirror, "and you don't want to give away that you're pretending, even to bystanders. Walking around adults as if you're eighteen, nodding at people in greeting and meeting their eyes when you talk, a smile here and there. You think you're up for this?"

She sighed. "I guess. What if I goof it up?"

"Ever played basketball or piano? Anything you get good at, you do by practicing. Eventually, no matter how much you rehearse alone, you have to put on your game face and perform your first recital or take that shot, regardless how nervous you are."

She nodded, then sat down heavily on the bed, shoulders sagging. "Julie, I'm scared."

"There's nothing wrong with that. A lot of scary things are

happening around you right now. Hold on to what your mother gave you – her love, her strength."

"Do you think Mom can still see me?"

"I believe my dad watches over me, all these years later. Sometimes, I go somewhere quiet, just to talk to him."

"You do?" she asked.

"Because I was there when he was shot, it was really hard for me. I wanted to stay with him, but he told me I had to leave. To get help, to get away from the man who killed him. So I ran, but I felt guilty that I didn't save him," I said. "Finally one day, I actually spoke out loud as if he could hear me, telling him how much it hurt that he made me leave him alone to die, and then it didn't hurt quite so much anymore."

"I don't think this will ever stop hurting." Hers was a much more mature observation than that of many adults I've known.

"It doesn't ever stop, Amber, you're right. But one day, you'll think about it, and find out it hurts a smidgen less." I held my finger and thumb just barely apart. "That's the best we can hope for, that it doesn't hurt quite so much tomorrow."

CHAPTER

10

I called the desk to say we'd be in the hotel another night, hoping that not relocating would make things easier for Amber. Later in the day, the walls seemed to close in, so we loaded up the dog and went to find a park to play in the sunshine. We stopped at a grocery store for picnic supplies and another box of hair coloring.

Both girl and dog burned up some excess energy romping together, playing fetch and tug-of-war. I had a lot of stressful energy that needed to be used, too, but what I wanted to romp with was more than six hundred miles away, working undercover.

Amber came over and sat down next to me, her bottom lip sucked between her teeth as she searched for a way to express her feelings. "It feels wrong to have fun when Mom and Grandma are dead," she finally said. "Like, sometimes I forget, and I shouldn't play."

"That's part of grief. Nothing feels right when you think about losing someone you love. You have to keep being Amber, though," I tried to explain. "Do you remember when your dog ran away? At first, you thought a lot about it being gone. After a while, you'd think about other things. Eventually, you thought about it being gone less."

"It's not like that," she argued.

"No, of course not, but losing someone you love is a similar adjustment. Mothers and grandmothers don't want their loved ones to hurt, whether it's a scraped knee or a broken heart, so it's okay if you feel better some moments than others. They know how hard this is, and they wouldn't want you to be sad all the time."

"You're sure?"

"Positive. I thought I'd be sad and miserable forever, thinking that's what I ought to do. But it didn't take long to begin remembering good times with my dad, realizing that he wouldn't want me not to have fun just because he was gone."

I handed her a bottle of orange juice while she was thinking about all that.

"It just doesn't feel real," she finally said, her seriousness suddenly fitting her older appearance. "Like I'm at camp or something and it's a bad dream. Last night I dreamed I cried and cried and cried, but when I'm awake, I just can't."

"Tears will come, too," I said. "I remember dreams like that."

As we snacked on apples and slices of cheese, the breeze began to cool off.

"Maybe we should find something indoors to do for this evening," I said, beginning to pick up. "How about a movie?" I suggested.

"Julie, can we go to mass today?"

"Of course. I'm sorry, I should have thought about that."

Geez, Madigan, just because you don't believe. . .

She was Catholic, like Zach. No surprise.

Finding a Catholic church wasn't likely to be difficult, and perhaps if she could speak to a priest, it would be better than just talking to me.

But could I trust that no one would think to follow us there?

"How about we go wash up a little and drop off Laser, then go to a Saturday service?" I suggested.

"You don't believe in God?" she asked, though it was really a statement.

"Well, I have a hard time believing in God the way most people do," I finally answered.

The tilt of her head asked why, but I didn't want to discuss my lack of faith with a fourteen-year-old Catholic when I couldn't even discuss it with her father.

I picked up the bags and the blanket we'd been sitting on and started toward the Suburban, surveying the parking lot for the green sedan that had followed me the last few days. It wasn't there, but there were a couple of other vehicles I didn't recognize. Parked unnecessarily close to my vehicle and occupied.

One Caucasian male in each.

Not my FBI guys from Pizza World.

Where were they?

"Amber, I want you to look around and see if you see another truck like mine," I said softly, stopping to rearrange the load in my arms so I had one free. "The one the FBI agent was driving."

"Why?"

"Amber, please just do what I ask," I said seriously.

She took the ball from her jacket pocket and made a nice throw for Laser which gave her an opportunity to take a look around us. "Fetch!" She spoke without turning toward me. "Yeah, that man from the hotel is to your left where the ball landed."

Laser came back with the slobbery tennis ball, and Amber took it.

"So throw as hard as you can that direction again after I tell the dog to stay, okay?"

"Um, okay," she said, unsure.

"Laser," I said firmly. "Stay."

His ears perked, turning toward me, expecting a command. I don't think he was ready for the cue to sit and stay, but he met my eyes.

"Now," I said, not looking away from the dog.

I have to give Amber credit – it was a World Series outfielder's attempt to throw out the winning runner.

Laser tensed to give chase, but I repeated the command and made the visual hand cue. If looks could bite, he'd have taken a hunk from my calf.

The look Amber shot me wasn't much nicer.

"Tell him to fetch," I coached.

She tried, not understanding what I was trying to do.

But the dog sat, torn between orders.

"Oh, let's just go get it," I said, tossing the blanket to her. "Laser, heel."

We all turned to wander toward the vehicle she'd picked out.

No longer facing what I'd assessed as a threat, I told her under my breath that I wasn't sure about the cars that had parked near where we'd parked.

"All right, but why not just come this way anyway?"

"Instinct, I guess. So pick up the ball," I said, looking toward Nolan, who was sitting in his Suburban, eating a hamburger, like I've done a hundred times. A cool spot in the shade, away from the noises of the office and a fast food restaurant.

I hitched up the load in my arm again, and reached to rub my eye with two fingers, pointing my thumb to my right.

Nolan reached for a drink, nodded his head once, and stowed his burger as Amber, Laser and I turned back toward the parking lot on the other side.

The engine started up after I'd taken fifteen steps, so he could time his arrival to that area with ours. I imagined that he had unsnapped his holster, maybe even drawn his weapon, resting it beside his thigh within easy reach. I wanted to put my hand on my own gun, but having a free hand was the best I could manage. Reaching around to the small of my back would only serve as a warning to someone watching that I was alarmed and armed. While not all civilians would notice the motion, anyone who carried a gun would identify it as "petting."

In my peripheral vision, I saw Nolan's vehicle come into the lot where I'd parked. He pulled up beside a pair of garbage cans, apparently gathered up his trash, and stepped out as we reached the curb.

Using the remote to unlock the truck as we got to it, I then helped Amber put the stuff we were carrying inside and had Laser jump in.

"In here," I said to her, opening the passenger door behind the driver, nudging her inside.

"I don't want to sit in back," she said, but stepped up anyway when I wrapped my hand around her upper arm.

Not a good time to argue, I clicked the lock button on the remote fob. The doors had all locked, and now I clicked the unlock button once, for only the driver's door, which I opened. I saw through the windows out the other side a man in a nearby coupe swing his legs out of the car and stand. White male, mid-forties, casual dress, leather bomber jacket, dark mirrored sunglasses.

My heart sped up. Instinct made me want another look.

But what if the obvious threat was really only a decoy? It made perfect sense, and I turned to scan the area again as I stepped my right leg into the running board.

Sure enough, another man had gotten out of a car behind me, but on the side where Nolan was, and Nolan called out to him as a distraction.

I climbed on inside, locking the doors again. "When we start moving, get down on the floor flat until I say it's okay," I whispered. I slipped the key into the ignition, started the engine, and shifted into reverse, trying hard to look casual and calm. I left Nolan engaged with the man and the other walking to the sidewalk in front of where we'd been parked.

After pulling out of the lot and driving ten minutes, I told Amber she could sit up, but then I spent the next hour trying to make sure I wasn't being followed. Three men could trail me from quite some distance and knew where our hotel destination was, and somehow, that wasn't nearly as comforting as it should have been.

During this detection and evasion drive, we passed a large Catholic church with a nearly full parking lot for the Saturday afternoon service, which according to the sign, had begun almost an hour before.

"This is a good place to stop."

"Whatever," she said as I pulled into the lot closest to the church and found a slot.

In the rearview mirror, I could see her sitting with her arms crossed, lips crunched together in anger.

"Amber, your safety comes first, above all else. I don't always have time to stop and explain why I'm doing something. It's not always a game."

"Yeah, I know," she said. "Whatever."

"Look, I understand you're angry with me. You can tell me why or not. But we need to be able to communicate. If you don't want to go in now, we can come back in time for the next service. But for now it's a good place to park and see what happens, even if we don't go inside."

Her face turned red in pre-tears.

"I don't want to play this spy game anymore," she wailed. "I want to go home!"

I climbed out of the driver's door and into the second row of seats to be closer to her.

"This isn't a game. It's for your protection."

"Why?" she sobbed. "Why does it have to be me?"

Out of less terrifying options, I didn't know what else to do but tell her the ugly truth. "The man I believe kidnapped your mother and that other girl wouldn't just kill you, Amber. He would hurt you in ways you can't imagine in order to hurt Zach. That's what we think this is about."

"What did Zach do?"

"He refused to join their drug smuggling ring in Florida. Because of Zach, this guy was arrested, but he escaped a few days before your mother was kidnapped." I weighed whether to tell her the rest of the truth, as stunned as she already appeared, but I needed to make her understand the enormity of the threat. "If he finds us, he'll do whatever he can to make Zach pay for that."

"He'd hurt you, too?" she asked, more alarmed.

"Yes, he would. That's why we're out here together."

Despite the explanation I gave, or maybe because of it, Amber finally pulled herself together a little bit, deciding she really would rather not go inside.

We sat in the parking lot another ten minutes until the majority of the congregation had left, a crowd all the better to hide in.

"So how about an early dinner now?" I asked.

"Can we just go back to the hotel?" She sounded like a much younger child. "I'm not hungry."

"Of course."

Back in the room, Amber fell asleep almost immediately, something else she either inherited from Zach or had been driven to by complete emotional exhaustion.

Time for dinner came and went, but she hadn't stirred, so I let her sleep.

On the other hand, I had an abundance of physical energy with no way to burn it off. I couldn't leave Amber, not even to go to the pool. I resorted to the bits of yoga I'd learned from Jeremy McNeeley.

A couple of lessons and a book were probably not the best way to learn yoga, but I'd found it calming in the last few months. Anything would help for the night.

I put on my sweat pants and a loose t-shirt. Having just sat at the foot of my bed on the industrial-grade carpet, I saw a shadow pause outside the door long enough to shove a piece of paper beneath, so I got to my feet to go get it, holding it in the light of the bathroom.

"Need to talk – 15," the note said in a first-grader's perfect print.

I put my jeans on again and added a sweatshirt then slipped on my shoes. Before I left, I tucked my Glock into the sweatshirt pocket, grabbed my change purse and the room key, and let myself into the hallway to go to the vending machines. I was still starving.

I stood, feeding quarters into a soft drink machine for a bottle, then turned to the snack machine.

Chocolate.

I hadn't had chocolate in weeks, it seemed, and I could hardly wait to get the wrapper off to take a bite of a plain Hershey bar.

When Nolan rounded the corner and found me, I had my mouth full.

"PMS can be such a nasty thing," he said, chuckling. He inserted coins to buy himself a bottle of juice. "You did have some company at the park today. Very good eyes, but I only got the one. The other took off after you did, in a different direction. I assume he either didn't follow you, or you lost him."

"Didn't see anyone behind me after we left," I said. "So who's the guy you got?"

"Wouldn't talk, so he'll sit for a day or two in county jail until someone figures out there's no paperwork to keep him – at least till mid-day on Monday. Probably long enough the Air Force will consider him AWOL," Nolan said, raising one shoulder to show his lack of concern. "Professional courtesy and a huge abuse of the American justice system."

Craving a big glass of ice-cold milk with the chocolate, instead I washed it down with cola, then took another bite.

"I suspect he's just a closet pervert of some kind – pedophile, cheater. He was all kinds of defensive about what he was doing. I'm not convinced that him watching you two had anything to do with Brodenshot."

After swallowing, I asked the question that had bothered me ever since we left the park. "Where were the guys who are supposed to be tailing me?"

"I don't know," he said, rubbing his temple with a thumb. "And that worries me. Even though they can tail your car by ten miles or so doesn't mean they shouldn't have had visual contact with you in the park. They are back at the hotel now though."

"That's it," I announced. "Amber's asleep, but first thing tomorrow, we're leaving and I'm ditching their surveillance. I don't need help I can't depend on."

Nolan sighed. "Did Zach show you how to disable the beacon?"

I nodded. "They've been sleeping in the car, so I can't just go raise the hood and turn it off here," I said, then took another bite.

"They got a room tonight. An alarm signals them when your engine starts," he said, "so they only need fifteen or twenty minutes to get out the door to stay within range. They apparently think the satellite tracking is close enough when you're driving."

"If I disable it sitting here, they'd think I did it on purpose," I said, thinking through the options. "So let me lead them out of town first. A technical glitch will be more convincing if they lose me on the move. I could do it at a traffic light just off the freeway, turn around and take side streets for a while, and they'd be sunk."

"Your call – if you do it here, you could be several hours ahead of them." He held up his hand in surrender. "I don't care which. Just let me know where you're headed so we can meet up tomorrow if you still want me involved in this."

"Yes, I do, Nolan. I know I can trust you."

Throwing away two candy wrappers, I almost felt ashamed I'd practically swallowed the contents whole without tasting them during our conversation. I went back to the room for the night, my nerves screaming on caffeine, sugar and adrenaline.

It was almost midnight when Amber awoke. We ordered late night pizza delivery, and she used the kit we'd bought earlier to frost my hair with a similar ripe wheat color, which made it look lighter without being all one color. She did a great job on it, I thought.

I wondered if it was a skill she'd learned from her mother.

CHAPTER

11

Despite not sleeping most of the night, I was awake the next morning at 5:30, wanting to be coherent when Zach called. Questions. I had so many questions. A quick shower and a cup of the nasty stuff that dripped from the coffee maker in the room, and another chocolate bar, and I sat propped up in the bed, waiting.

Nolan had offered me a place to shelter Amber, away from any possible connection to me or to Zach. That meant I could go to El Paso, if I only had some idea what was really going on or how to help. Was Zach still the target, or would Pauly run since the kidnapping failed? If the goal is to hurt Zach, wouldn't it be better if I were the bait?

Either way, I thought, putting Amber somewhere safe would be better than dragging her around with me. I was already torn, ready to ditch federal officers I should have no reason not to trust except their absence when I needed them the previous day. Now I worried myself sick whether someone working with Zach had turned on him and was tracking us all.

But as I watched the digital clock numbers change to 6:00 and then to 7:00, that sick feeling went from simmer to a low boil as the phone continued to sit silent beside me.

I woke Amber half an hour later.

"We need to leave here this morning," I explained. "Can we go next door for breakfast then get packed up?"

Nodding, Amber didn't ask why or where we'd go next. She just shrugged and began gathering her stuff to dress.

On our way by Nolan's room, I slipped a note under his door. It simply said Shy Mountain Lions, SBT/SBC. *Same Bat Time. Same Bat Channel.* It had been his reference to Batman and Robin.

She didn't speak until we got to the restaurant. I tried to get a conversation going, but the emotional toll was beginning to catch up to her ability to outrun it.

Over waffles, she told me she was worried about falling behind in classes, but I assured her we'd get it worked out. I kept her talking about school and friends, but her heart wasn't in it.

We walked back to the hotel, but I didn't see Nolan's Suburban in the parking lot where it had been. Hopefully he'd found the note and beat us out of the hotel.

I finished packing up my toiletries as Amber brushed her teeth.

"Does moving around like this bother you?" I asked. "I can find us somewhere we can stay longer, but I don't know what might be nearby to do. It could get boring after a few days."

"No, I like hotels," she said. "I'm just sad."

"Anything I can do to help?"

She looked up at my reflection in the mirror. "It's hard to breathe," she finally said.

"That's exactly how it feels."

She nodded and a tear slipped down her cheek.

"I don't know how I'm supposed to act," she added.

I hugged her. "I don't want you to think you have to act grown up and tough. Especially for me. You may be sad or angry or a hundred other things. Just be you, okay?"

We loaded the luggage and the dog into the Suburban, and drove back to the freeway and went north. Speeding up, I moved through traffic for about six miles before taking the off ramp to an exit where I knew I could turn around and get right back on the freeway southbound. I pulled into a gas station on a corner, got out and turned off the GPS unit.

Someone didn't spare any expense. It looked like a NASA lunar module component.

That someone had been Zach.

". . . disappear. . . " he'd said.

Poof! Disconnecting a wire, we vanished from FBI surveillance.

✂

Taking a wildly out-of-the-way route to get there, three hours later I paid admission for Amber and myself at the Cheyenne Mountain Zoo in Colorado Springs. From the entrance, we took the tram to get to the primate exhibits on the west side of the park.

Amber watched the orangutans and gorillas, taking almost half an hour. Then we walked back toward the center of the zoo, stopping to see the birds of prey.

Maybe it was the piercing calls that set my nerves on edge, but I suddenly felt we were being followed. I spent more time looking at people around us than at the animals, and I lost touch with the enjoyment I'd previously felt.

The weight of my Glock rode against the small of my back, but it felt too far out of my reach.

Moving on, we entered the lions' den alone. Amber wasn't as excited about the huge cats as she had been in Denver, but she studied them as they paced, lounged behind the barriers, cleaning themselves with tongues as wide as my palm. I stayed close as she moved from one cat to another until I saw an older man enter from the other doorway.

"Don't go out of my sight," I warned her quietly.

She nodded and turned back to the lioness grooming a cub.

The man, easily recognizable as what I'd expect Nolan's father to look like, walked by, excusing himself as he passed in front of me.

"Pardon me, sir? Do you have the time?" I asked when he was a few steps away.

He turned to me, looked at his watch, and said, "It's getting later every minute."

I must have made a face at this, and he smiled.

"I thought this would be a good touristy spot." I shrugged. "Lots of attractions."

"Great clue," he said. "Are you going south for a reason?"

I looked over my shoulder at Amber, torn between promising Zach I'd protect her and my need to be with him.

"Umhmm. I thought so," Nolan warned me. "Just don't let predictability work against you."

Didn't know how to answer that.

"The surveillance team reported they lost you this morning. To their credit, they only delayed that bad news about an hour while they looked. Neil is pissed. They must be tearing up the interstate searching," Nolan said. "But I can't very well ask where they were yesterday instead of being at the park without revealing I was there. Not now anyway, but I'll get to the bottom of that."

I nodded.

"It's kind of a reverse backward non-logic that you wouldn't go south, I think, but at least now we're all confused. So you're free of everyone but me." He wiggled his eyebrows. "Oh, and I put new license plates on your truck last night, since you really don't want to be found. It's now registered in Utah."

I hadn't noticed the plates, but I was comforted the surveillance tail was gone.

"You know, I have an idea what you're thinking of doing, and for the record, I don't like it. If I had any sense at all, I'd take you both to a safe house in Minnesota and lock you up." He smiled. "But I'd rather tangle with that cheetah there."

I shook my head. "That's a mountain lion."

"Might as well be a man-eating tiger I caught bare-handed. I'd find myself wondering how the hell to let go."

"Which experience makes you think that about me?" I asked with an innocent smile.

No answer was forthcoming.

"I really don't know what to do, Nolan. At least right now, I have to presume Zach's all right, and my first responsibility is to her." I nodded toward Amber. "But I'm open for suggestions on how to do take care of them both."

"Let's have dinner tonight, and we can discuss it," he said, handing me a small envelope. "I took the liberty of reserving us all a suite. A family will attract less attention. I like the hair thing you both did, too." He winked. "See you around six."

I nodded, and he wandered away, appearing to enjoy the animals every bit as much as Amber.

Personally, I was beginning to lose my enthusiasm for zoos.

Amber and I arrived at the hotel several hours later, a much grander place than I had chosen in Denver. No one gave us a second glance as I rolled in my luggage and led Laser on his leash, with his head hung low to show his indignation about it.

In the room, we found Nolan working at the desk.

I formally introduced Amber to the FBI agent, and she shook his hand politely and excused herself to the bathroom.

"Is this okay?" he asked, motioning to the suite, complete with a connecting room. "I figured you two could share the big bedroom, I'd take the other one."

"It's great, Nolan. She's just a little overwhelmed, you know?"

"Aren't we all?" he asked, leaning back in the swivel chair. "So how's married life this go-round?"

"I'd like to tell you, but given the circumstances, I'm a little short on data," I said, dropping onto the sofa. "I went back to Michigan, put my house on the market, and moved out to Washington while Zach stayed in Albuquerque to work until his transfer. Now this."

"Rumor has it he's an exceptional agent."

"So they say," I replied, nodding. "I've experienced some of his surveillance tactics firsthand, and I'm glad he's on my side."

"You'll go, won't you," Nolan said, not bothering to make it a question. "Like you did in Florida before Christmas."

He meant when Domino had come to me, fearing Zach was in trouble. We had gone, and we had saved Zach.

Nolan stared at me hard, weighing more than my words.

"You know I will," I finally said.

"Then we should make a plan. After dinner," he said and handed me the room service menu. "Unless you'd like to go out?"

We agreed on staying in for the evening. Amber ordered chicken fettuccine, much to Nolan's surprise when the menu included hamburgers and chicken strips. Nolan and I ordered steaks, baked potatoes and salads. He also ordered us a bottle of wine, and milk for Amber.

After we ate, Amber asked if she could watch television in the other bedroom while we talked.

She settled on the bed with Laser, remote control in hand.

Nolan and I stretched out in the living area.

"Just for the record, if this is who Zach thinks it is," Nolan said, "and I have no reason to doubt that, Pauly Brodenshot knows how to play you both. He's known Zach for years, worked with him. He knows your weaknesses, too."

"You mean that I'm predictable?"

Nolan only nodded and lifted his wine glass. "More?"

I held up my glass for him to top off as he continued.

"Worse than predictable, you proved you'd do damned near anything to save Zach. That you'll kill a man to save a child. That's powerful stuff to a sociopath," he said, holding my argument at bay with a hand in the air. "And make no mistake – he's been paying attention. Whatever you do has to be a huge variation from that theme if it's going to be a surprise."

"How do I change who I am?" I asked.

"You went undercover in Florida. No one expected that."

"I'm supposed to become someone he would trust?"

"Someone he would trust, that would be difficult," he said. "But how about someone he wouldn't look at."

"He knows what I look like, Nolan. It's not like I can just change the color of my hair again and use hazel-colored contacts to be different." I was flustered.

"That's just appearance. Think about Zach. He can never be any shorter than he is, right? But he can blend into the wallpaper like a chameleon from what I've heard. How does he do it?"

"He's followed me, and not only does he disappear, he's quiet as a snake. But I don't *know* how he does it."

"Think about when you saw me at the Denver Zoo. What was your first impression?"

"You were dressed like a peacock!"

"Sure, and not at all what you expected. If you were looking for a middle-aged man who didn't want to be seen, why would you consider such an outrageously dressed elderly woman to be a threat?" he explained. "I've read Brodenshot's arrest records. He's a dedicated, world-class homophobe. If you have to be invisible to him, the best thing you probably could be is a wildly gay man. He would go out of his way to not pay attention to you."

I laughed. "You've got to be joking."

"No. It's not perfect, but it's certainly an option if you need it."

❈

Another early morning, I waited for Zach to call, fighting concern festering into panic. By eight o'clock, I'd resigned myself to another day without hearing his voice. I tried to reason away the dread, but knowing that Brodenshot was involved, I couldn't make headway in it. Every thought I had about Pauly put him closer to the category of evil I'd previously reserved for Anthony Bock.

Nolan woke early, too. I heard him moving around in the room next door, then the shower.

I wanted to shower, too, but I couldn't walk away from the phone. Just couldn't. So I waited for Nolan to show himself for breakfast.

A while after he'd finished in the shower, I could hear him talking but not exactly what he was saying. When I was sure the call had ended, I knocked.

"Zach didn't call again this morning," I whispered when he opened the door.

He nodded then waved me inside the smaller room. "Neil Tanner, one of your escorts, just called. I told him to go back to Albuquerque and stay put until further notice, no exceptions. For the record, Tanner could be helpful in El Paso."

"I don't know for what," I argued. "I still don't know anything about what's happening down there. Not where Zach's been working, who his contacts might be. Last time, I had Dom to tell me who the players were, walk me through their little neighborhood of hell. Now I know nothing. Worse, I have a badge again."

"Oh, that's what that was about," Nolan said with a nod. "I wondered why Zach had called Eric Rader."

"A badge and a promotion to lieutenant in Internal Affairs, for crying out loud. I can't very well go rogue now. I didn't like it to start with, and now I feel trapped."

"Use it to your advantage. And Neil has contacts."

"Damn it, Nolan. I'm surrounded by cops I don't know if I can

77

trust," I said. "Zach said he couldn't trust anyone but me, and I could only trust you."

"Okay, so trust me. Let's drive Amber to the place I mentioned. I'm a hundred percent sure about it being safe. Then I'll go with you to El Paso."

"I won't let you throw your career away," I stated.

"Julie, I told you that you weren't so broken I wouldn't work with you, and I meant it. I can't get you a federal badge, but I have one, and together we have a lot of resources."

"You can't do this!"

"Most of my career has been investigation of crimes after the fact. I'd like to actually change the outcome of something instead of trying to piece together the puzzle afterward."

"You're insane."

"That's what my ex-wife told the divorce judge, and he agreed, so it must be true," he said with a grin.

CHAPTER
12

"Amber, I told you I'd be honest," I said, watching her dig through her bag. "We need to consider changing the way we're thinking about keeping you safe."

She stopped, raising her head to stare at me as if I'd turned green.

I kept talking. "We believe the person responsible for kidnapping your mother is someone who knew her and Zach before you were born. They all went to the same high school. This man was dating your mother before she got pregnant, and then her family moved away, which is why Zach didn't know anything about you. But this other guy, Pauly, he probably did, or maybe he found out since."

Amber nodded, her expression moving from acceptance to anger.

"He worked for the Drug Enforcement Administration with Zach, but then Pauly turned to dealing drugs," I said. "He killed one of their team and would have killed Zach, but he got caught. Somehow last week, he made an arranged escape so we know he has people helping him. He's proven he'll do practically anything, including kidnapping and murder, to reach his goals, and we need to make sure you're safe. Does this make sense?"

"No, none of this makes any sense!" she said, slamming her books into the suitcase.

I couldn't argue with that.

"What I'm trying to say is that I think you and I are in more danger being together than if I could find you somewhere safe to stay. Pauly will most certainly be looking for us as a pair. Whether it's

Zach or us, whoever he catches first, he'll use one of us to get to the other."

"So you're going to just dump me?" It was a cutting accusation.

"No. I'm asking if you would be willing to stay with someone Nolan trusts, someone I've never met, making it impossible to link them to me or Zach, until this is over. I believe you'll be safer if I let Pauly chase me and not put you in danger." I hesitated. "But I'm giving you the choice. I will stay with you and protect you, or I can try to help Zach. But I can't do both."

Amber's skin turned pale. "Zach told me you saved his life in Florida," she said.

"We sorta saved each other, but that's why I went, to find him when he disappeared."

"And he said you killed a man to save some other girl?"

Thanks a lot, Zach.

"That's true, too. I'm actually the one who killed the deputy who worked with Laser. He was a good friend of mine. Matthew would have died, regardless, but the murderer made me do it to save the teenage daughter of the medical examiner I worked for in Michigan. I did what I did to protect her. I'd do the same for you."

I wondered if she was having difficulty thinking about me killing a man I called a friend.

"If Zach can't stop this guy, how can you?" she asked.

"I don't know," I said, shrugging my shoulders. "This is your decision. Your safety is the very most important thing to me and to Zach. I won't leave you if you say no."

She squinted at me. "You mean you'd stay with me even if it meant this guy could hurt my fa-. . . I mean, Zach?"

"Amber, you can call him your father. And yes, that's exactly what I mean."

She thought about that, hard enough she had to sit down, but the look on her face truly indicated some lengthy extrapolation of the situation's options and consequences.

I looked up to see that Nolan had heard enough of our conversation from the doorway to question the sanity of letting a fourteen-year-old emotionally distraught girl make such a decision. I gave him a stern warning glance not to intrude, and he backed into his adjoining room without a word.

"What if something did happen to my father?" she asked, finding a void in her future she couldn't fill.

"What do you mean?" I was confused as to what she really wanted to know.

"I'd like to live with Zach," she announced, "but if –"

Wow, Julie. You should have seen that coming.

"Amber, Zach and I would welcome you," I said. "I don't know if you have any other family that might want to have you live with them, or what Greg Hennessy has in mind. A judge might have the final say, but you're old enough to decide."

"But if . . . if Zach dies," she really struggled with saying that part aloud, "could I stay with just you?"

I took a deep breath and hoped something good would come out of my mouth. "I'd be happy to have you live with me."

Amber's eyes suddenly looked very old. "I've never met people who love each other like you and Zach. I'll go wherever you say so you can help him. On one condition – you teach me to shoot."

✖

One indoor range in the area. For two pretty impressive badges, they made exceptions to almost every one of the rules. No guests, no kids, no shoulder holsters. But midmorning on a Tuesday, there were no other members to complain. I bought target ammo for my guns, hearing protectors and safety glasses for us all, and rented a .22 revolver for Amber to start with. And I promised I'd come back and look for another holster when we were done. Dropping a couple hundred bucks on accessories made up for our inconvenience, I figured.

Nolan and I began the weaponry education of a fourteen-year-old, despite his weary looks about the whole idea throughout my shopping spree.

"First rule is that a gun is a weapon, just like a knife. It's not a toy," I told her. "You don't play with it, and you always assume it's loaded, so you never point it at anyone unless you mean to defend yourself." I showed her the .22 and .40 caliber bullets, noting the difference. "Don't let the size fool you," I said. "It might look half the size, but this bullet is just as capable of killing as the larger one."

I let Nolan go through handling the revolver while I set up a couple of targets for us.

"Okay," he said. "I'll fire the first six, so you can hear and see what it's like. Watch how I hold the gun and how I stand."

We donned the ear protection and glasses, and she studied him as he gripped the pistol with both hands and fired.

I retrieved the target and found a fair group, but all high and right. Consistent, anyway.

He ejected the brass and then took her step by step through the process of aiming the gun empty. When she was comfortable holding it, he had her dry fire it to get the feel of the trigger, and finally he directed her how to load it.

"Now, think about what you're holding, where it points, and always make sure your target area is clear all the way to full left and right. Something that's to one side can quickly move into your field of fire when you're concentrating on the target. Aim, both eyes open," he said, leaning down to help her steady the gun, "and squeeze the trigger."

The first shot barely clipped the paper target at 15 feet, but she had a huge grin on her face. Five more shots and each got a little better, certainly good enough to wound a standing human target.

"I'm going to shoot some, too, while you practice," I said as she reloaded. "My gun is a lot louder than yours, so I'll move down a few lanes."

I took my three guns out and put them on the deck in front of me, wondering again what I was getting myself into in El Paso, whether I was going to be able to pull something off like I had in Florida.

Then again, looking back at that trip objectively, it wasn't much of an achievement. I'd found Zach, yes. I'd been able to get several people arrested, but I'd been more or less responsible for the deaths of several others. I struggled with calling it a triumph. But Zach had come back with me alive – that's all that mattered.

I wonder if Zach regretted not killing Pauly in that warehouse where he was arrested.

Slipping on my ear protection, I picked up the five-shot .38. I leaned back and indicated to Amber and Nolan I was about to fire.

Five shots. Put it down and pick up the 9 mm, fired sixteen. Put it down, and with the .40 caliber, I fired ten more. I dropped the empty and replaced it with a full one, then I reloaded the Glock magazines first, then the .38, before I pulled my target back.

"Very nice. You can shoot from behind me," Nolan kidded.

His compliment was a little sideways, like telling a mortician he's good enough to work on you. You'd like the very best, but you don't want to be in that circumstance, regardless.

I'd guessed at least 26 hits were inside the black 8-ring, it was sorta hard to tell with all the holes, but there were five in the 7-ring at 25 feet. I needed more practice.

Amber brought her target to compare to mine after she fired 20, and I got a high-five from her, and we laughed.

I put up a new target and fired another 15 rounds one-handed from the 9 mm and retrieved the target again.

"Can I shoot one of yours?" she asked, looking at them on the firing deck.

"I don't care if you do, but they are a lot different."

She pointed to the compact .38 revolver.

"In this case, size of the weapon is deceiving. Actually because it's so small and lightweight, it really kicks," I said, picking up the Glock 26. "Why don't you try this instead?" I dropped the magazine to start a brand new lesson on a semi-automatic.

"Gee, can I shoot the other?" Nolan asked playfully.

I nodded for him to help himself and let him have the lane so he'd be near the ammo. I took Amber back out in the hallway where she might have a chance to hear me while he fired, and I showed her the Glock and explained how a semi-automatic differed from the revolver she'd shot.

We went back into the range, where I helped her load the magazine and let her pull the slide back to chamber the first round.

Nolan stopped what he was doing to watch from a distance as we put on our ear coverings.

She carefully picked up the Glock and cradled it with both hands like I'd shown her. The same way Nolan had, I put a steadying hand under her arms. She took a breath and squeezed, jumping slightly when the gun fired.

She turned her head to me and smiled.

"One at a time, fire them all. Take a breath between each."

She fired the second round, and I felt her shoulders relax a little, so I eased up my support for the third, then stepped away for the rest.

"When you fire, you have to anticipate that it will be noisy," Nolan offered when she was done. "You can't help but blink, but try not to flinch." He made a face to show her how she was reacting, but explained it was good that at least she wasn't doing it before she pulled the trigger.

Amber loaded again, and we watched her fire 15 more without any assistance.

When she was done, putting the gun back down, she shrugged her shoulders. "Wow, it gets heavy."

We pulled her target and showed her the more consistent pattern of low and right, but out of 30, she had put 23 on the target and 14 inside the black.

Nolan unholstered his Sig Sauer for her to look at, explaining the slide safety, a major difference in the two models. He offered to let her shoot it, but she declined.

I took him up on the offer and emptied the magazine, making a fair showing.

"I like girls who can shoot," he said as we wiped down the guns. "You did great, Amber."

She glowed with pride.

"You are in a very precarious situation," Nolan said. "If, God forbid, you should have to point a weapon at someone who means you harm, consider this: You may only get one good aimed shot, so make it count. The very fact you *will* pull the trigger is your best offense. An adult might not hesitate if he believes you won't fire for fear of getting in trouble."

I finished for him. "If you use a gun in self-defense, shoot to kill. Do you understand?"

The smile had faded from her face, and in that moment, I saw not only Zach's green eyes but a little bit of his soul, as well.

CHAPTER

13

Going west out of Colorado Springs on Highway 24 before noon, Nolan drove his Suburban. Following him, Amber and I tried out her sightseeing game – taking turns pointing out interesting things by consecutive letters of the alphabet.

"Julie," she finally said as we had begun to give up on finding something that began with the letter Q. "Zach's gonna be okay, right?"

"All I can say is I hope so." I wished I had a better answer.

"I'm really scared."

I looked over, only to face a frisky dog's nose on my cheek. "Nothing wrong with being scared. I am, too. How about I leave Laser with you for company?"

"Really?"

"As long as it's okay with Nolan's friends," I said. "We don't want to impose a monster slobber-dog on them."

Laser looked insulted. Wet-nosed, yes. Slobbering, never.

The highway crossed the continental divide. The afternoon was perfect for a long drive. I wished I'd been on the motorcycle.

Nolan pulled into a scenic lookout, and we all got out for a stretch.

Laser and I took a walk over to some interesting grass, and I heard Nolan speak to Amber.

"We're taking you to where my first wife's parents live."

Her shoulders sagged at the thought of hanging around with

people even older than us.

"But I think you'll like them," he continued. "Grace is a part-time ski instructor at Aspen. Moses plays in a band at one of the resorts. They're actually pretty cool folks."

I shot a look at Nolan as I joined them.

"Moses Webster is a retired Air Force colonel. Grace is a pediatrician," he offered for my reassurance.

"Maybe I can learn to ski after all," Amber declared, then looked at me for approval. "If it's okay?"

"You can do anything they allow," I said. "Just be reasonable in what you ask of them, though."

She nodded.

The 160-some miles took us about four hours, but we weren't pushing.

Grace and Moses greeted us at the front gate and ushered us into an A-frame set on what I guessed to be at least twenty acres of open land surrounded by forest. Through the front door, the atmosphere was cozy, comfortable. Venison or maybe elk, and other wonderful odors wafted from the kitchen – making my stomach rumble.

"I hope you'll stay for dinner. Stroganoff will be ready in about an hour. How about something to drink?" Grace led Amber and me into a kitchen outfitted for someone who took cooking very seriously. "Would you like juice or something, Amber?"

"Juice, please," she said, perching herself on a stool at a breakfast bar.

"A glass of wine, Julie?" she asked as if we were old friends, already pulling down two glasses from the oak rack.

I was amazed, doing the math. She had to be my mother's age and then some, maybe. But with the exception of some silver laced into her long dark hair, she didn't appear much older than me. Medicine had been very kind to her.

From the living room, I heard laughter from the men.

When I turned back, I saw Grace nod about the question in my eyes, about who Nolan really was to them to ask such a big favor for a stranger.

"Amber, we have a hot tub and pool. Would you like to try them out before dinner?"

That must have been the final selling point, as she went racing out to the Suburban for her suitcase.

Grace and I followed, and I begged an invitation for the dog as well as the child, feeling I was taking advantage of the hospitality of people I didn't know well, but then, Grace no longer felt like a stranger.

Of course the dog was welcome, she said, ruffling Laser's ears.

Back in the kitchen, I listened as Grace showed Amber where to change into her suit just off the den where the hot tub and pool sparkled.

"Gosh, maybe I'll stay, too," I kidded Amber as she waved through the sliding glass door wrapped in a bright beach towel, headed toward the hot tub.

Grace motioned for me to sit while she got our wine. "We can keep an eye on her from here, but still have a chance to talk alone," she said, returning and settling into her chair, pulling her legs up beneath her.

"You can't imagine how much you keeping her means to me and my husband," I tried to start, but she waved my gratitude away.

"It's a nice change to have a child here. Gina and Nolan didn't have any, so we have only two teenaged grandchildren who live in Utah. I wish we had a dozen more. I love being a grandmother," she said with a smile.

My confusion must have shown.

"Gina had a massive stroke the third year they were married," she said, stopping to sip her wine. "She lingered nine weeks in a coma. It broke Nolan's heart to have to make a decision about discontinuing medical care, and finally God must have intervened. She slipped quietly away one night."

"I had no idea," I stammered. "I'm so sorry. Nolan never told me."

"Doesn't surprise me. He doesn't talk about her often because it hurts him so much," she reflected, swirling her wine in the glass. "He's always been part of our family, even after he remarried, although I suspect his second wife was just a desperate escape from the loneliness."

"I don't know much about his personal life," I said. "But he's been the sort of friend that's very rare."

"He's an unusual man," she said. "Nolan told us some about you, what's happened to your family. He said you're a lot like Gina – gutsy and determined. We're happy to help. I can't imagine what Amber's been through, but I believe that somehow God brings lives together for a reason."

I only nodded, wondering, if such omnipotent power could bring people together, why did it also pull them apart?

Nolan and Moses joined us just before dinner, still discussing music. Moses played guitar on weekends in a pop-country band at a local bar frequented by tourists. I had heard him play a few samples from the den and liked it.

The braid of gray hair Moses wore halfway down his back surprised me, considering the military rank Nolan had mentioned. Not what I expected.

Obviously my recent speculations and assessments of men had been so far off mark I was lucky to get gender right three out of four guesses.

"Nolan tells me you taught the young lady a little firearm handling today," Moses said, topping off my wine glass and sitting down next to me on the sofa. "That's good. I don't expect any problems, but I want you to know I'm prepared, too."

"Like I told Grace, you can't imagine how much I appreciate you doing this for us. I don't want to leave her, but –"

"Julie, we don't need explanations – you do what you have to do," he said firmly. "We're happy to help."

We finally coaxed Amber out of the pool to dry and dress for supper, sitting down to a hearty feast of slow-cooked elk, homemade noodles, bread fresh from the oven, and a salad with botanical samplings I couldn't identify but grazed eagerly.

Nolan and I both refused more wine, knowing we'd be on the road again soon, but the food itself was as comforting as the company.

Even Amber had seconds, which I had not seen previously on her sensible diet.

Before we left, I went to see Amber's bedroom, decorated in a similar theme as the rest of the house – contemporary wilderness.

"The Websters will do everything they can to make you feel at home here. I'll try to call every few days, but don't worry if you don't hear from me, okay?"

"I don't want you to go. I'm afraid you won't come back, and I'll be completely alone." She slumped to the bed.

Her honesty was as gut-felt as mine had been.

I sat down beside her. "I asked Zach once what his favorite love song was, and he told me it was from *Robin Hood*, you know, 'Everything I do, I do it for you.' Zach sent you with me because he knew you'd be in danger with him. I'm leaving you here because I love you both and I don't want you to be in danger being with me. We all want this to work out right, but you being safe is all that matters to us."

"Please be careful," she said, wrapping her arms around me, "and come back. Both of you."

❇

"I sure learned a lot about you today," I said to Nolan as I drove us back toward Colorado Springs in his Suburban, having left mine in a shed behind the bar where Moses sang. At least it would be away from their home and would not be a target for FBI agents searching for me.

"I'm sure very little of it is true," he said in a mixture of sarcasm and smugness. "I'm nothing like Grace's impressions of me."

"She told me more about who you are than I ever found out from you."

"Funny, that's how I got to know you, too," he said, more serious than before. "What was it you said about talking to your neighbors? You can't believe everything they say, right?"

"Right. I'm curious, Nolan. Did you steal my blueprints for that wall you built around your life or did you draw your own? It's not very aesthetic, but it's certainly effective," I teased, trying to keep him from retreating further.

He sat in a silence that must have been uncomfortable because he began fidgeting.

I just let him bump around in it, feeling the edges of a shattered heart. If he wanted to tell me more, I was within arm's reach to listen.

89

"Their daughter, Gina, my first wife," he began a while later, still struggling to say the words. He turned to wipe away a tear that slipped down his cheek. "Falling in love with her was the most beautiful thing in the world, like it seems to be with you and Zach. Losing her changed everything."

"Of course it did. Watching her hang on in a coma must have been devastating."

"You didn't fall apart when your husband died," he said.

And you didn't shoot your wife in self-defense.

I didn't want to knock down his grief, only the self-pity of still being a grieving man after so many years, but I wasn't sure what to say.

"Or Dr. McNeeley," he said.

"Don't think I didn't crash and burn over Jeremy. I didn't have to struggle with the decision to let go of him, either."

"But with the deputy," he said, not wanting his words to be an accusation, "you did what you had to do. I couldn't let go of Gina, couldn't let them take her off the machines. She was already dead inside, but. . . I couldn't do it."

"When he was sixteen, Matthew Shannaker learned his father had been diagnosed with a brain tumor. He asked Matt to shoot him," I explained, "to make it look like a hunting accident, rather than let a slow death ruin his family. In the end, Matt understood that more torture would come before Bock would let him die. He told me that if I had any options, to do whatever it took to get out alive. For myself, I wouldn't have done it. For Kimberly, I'd have done that and a lot more, probably."

"That's what I mean. I couldn't even do it for Gina or her parents."

"Do you think I could let go of Zach and not be wrecked?"

"You'd be wrecked, but you'd do the right thing."

"What's the right thing, Nolan? I don't believe there's something better after we die, a place we meet back up. I believe we get one shot at a decent life, and many of us screw it up anyway. Why is it wrong to hold on to the one person in your world who makes you feel whole? To question if it's the right thing to let go?"

"It wasn't that. I just didn't want her to ever know I gave up," he finally said.

"Would you have died in her place?" I asked.

"A thousand times," he said. "Sometimes I still feel like I'm dead, but my body just keeps going through the motions like hers did."

"Trust me, I understand that part," I said. "Grace told me you'd remarried. Why?"

Nolan looked at me. "People kept telling me to get on with my life, that I should find someone else to love. I guess I tried to do it."

"I can't imagine Grace saying that. I'd have told you that someday you might find someone else you *could* love when you were ready to look. Not the same as you loved Gina, but maybe as much."

"I didn't want to love anyone else." He sighed. "I still don't."

"I know all about that, too, Nolan." I smiled. "You must have felt something for this other woman, though."

"Wasn't love, I assure you." He pointed at the sign for the next highway intersection where I had to turn.

"What made you love Gina?"

"Everything," he said. "She was a psychologist. Smarter than anyone I'd ever met. A sense of humor and wit that made me laugh."

"So when she died, you became a workaholic agent, plodding through the last fifteen years, heading to a quiet retirement," I said. "Why are you sticking your neck out for me?"

He stared at me for a long moment before speaking. "Because you're the only person in all those years who hasn't felt sorry for me, didn't excuse my behavior based on my past. You've shown me that worse things happen to people all around me and most are survivable."

"That sounds a little like pity for me."

"No, it's respect," he said. We rode in silence for a while before he spoke again. "You and Zach can't have had much of a relationship before, living so far apart and him working like he does."

"It wasn't a relationship like you'd imagine. He was in love. I was living in the castle behind walls with gigantic 'No Trespassing' signs all around, just like you. He kept climbing over to sneak inside until one day I began expecting him to be there."

He nodded.

"Jeremy McNeeley and I had dated a long time ago when I was in college, and then he suddenly broke it off. Then, I found out I was pregnant. Within two months, I'd lost them both. I buried myself in work until I got transferred to Alamogordo. I dated David for a while. Getting married seemed to be the next thing to do."

"So you married someone for the wrong reasons, too?"

I nodded. "But after what he did to me, I didn't want any more emotional ties to men. Twice burned, it was easier to be alone than careful."

"Does finding out that Anthony Bock had involved your husband when he attacked you change how you think about David?"

Blinking didn't make the flash of Bock's face disappear from my memory, and I still felt anger about David cutting my throat, regardless who or what had driven him to do it.

"He's dead, so it doesn't matter," I replied, trying to dismiss the question because I didn't want to answer it.

"Doesn't it?" Nolan persisted.

I looked out the window and sighed. "Made it easier to try and forgive him."

"You didn't like doing it, though, did you?"

"I've had to forgive a lot of people. It's not something that comes easy for me."

"Did you get around to forgiving yourself, Julie?"

✿

Nolan and I arrived back in Colorado Springs before midnight. Not sleepy, we stopped for a drink at the hotel bar, finding a quiet booth in the corner away from the television blaring some west coast basketball game.

"Why won't you consider working for the FBI?" he finally asked over his Scotch.

"Because I'm allergic to metal, Nolan. I'm really tired of being shot at, cut up, and sewn back together," I said. "Why on earth would I want another badge just to end up on someone else's shit list? I'm obviously more than capable of doing that by myself."

"Looks to me like you're drawn to law enforcement," he

observed with an unnecessary smirk. "As much as you may not like it, may even hate it, you're a survivor. I'd give anything if we could teach that instinct, like weapons training or first aid," he said. "It's not a skill. I don't know how to describe it except for stubborn determination, but you have it. And you have other skills to back it up."

"It's been barely enough most of the time, I assure you. I'm not sure it's going to be enough now." Having considered all the options for going to El Paso, I'd yet to find one I thought might be successful.

"If we do this smart, it'll be plenty. Neil thinks he lost you going north in Colorado, but he didn't mention that he thought you did it on purpose. They think it's technical," he said. "I encouraged his notion that I believed you'd keep going north, and if you made Wyoming, you probably wouldn't need surveillance anyway."

"You think they didn't notice you hanging around me?"

"Neither of them has ever met me face to face, Julie. I'm a voice on the phone." He smiled. "I even chatted with them at the zoo in Denver, and they didn't have an inkling."

I took another sip of amaretto, a double shot straight in a small snifter. Smooth and sweet, it left a warm trail inside.

He picked up his glass, then paused. "Can I ask you something personal?"

"Sure, why not," I answered with a raised eyebrow.

He hesitated, swirling the half-empty glass of Lagavulin, a scotch that was old enough to vote, he'd commented when it arrived. "Last year, in the locker room, when I came to get you to fly to New Mexico, you said something I've always wondered about," he said, referring to when he agreed to help me find my mother, who was being held hostage by Bock. "You were angry enough to scratch my eyes out, I know, but you threw down the towel and told me to take a good look at all your scars."

He hadn't asked a question, so I waited.

"Is that how you think I see you, how other people see you?" he asked.

I took a sip before answering. "Every day, for the last five years, I've looked in the mirror at the scars – across my throat and elsewhere. I see people glance down from my eyes, then look away in shame. Scars are just visible proof of what some man or another has done to me," I said. "I slept with Zach almost two years before I let him leave the lights on when we made love. Yeah, Nolan. That's how I think people see me."

"Might I say that, given a fair chance to see everything that day, I didn't notice any scars." He bit his lip to conceal a grin. "Just as an objective observer."

I wasn't sure how to respond.

"What I'm saying is that I respect you for who you are, not what you look like. I don't see the scars. I guess I never have." He took a sip of his Scotch. "Seeing how much loving Zach has changed you, you make me think that maybe I could love someone again. Some day."

"I'll cross my fingers you find someone. It's hell living in a castle by yourself."

"That's not what I wanted to ask, though," he said, waving his hand through the air as if to erase our previous conversation. "What possessed you volunteer to bait Rory Stewart?"

Muscles in my chest tightened. "Is there supposed to be some connection with that to seeing me in the shower?" I challenged.

"No, not really. The image of you stomping across the room naked said you were a force not to be reckoned with," he said with a shrug.

"What do you know about Stewart?"

"More than you probably think. Before I came down here, I talked to Brandan Callaghan. We've become pretty good friends."

I tilted my head.

"Just friends, Julie. I'm not his type." He smiled. "Brandan voiced vague concerns about putting you under pressure. I had to pry the story out of him." He held up his hands in defense. "He wouldn't tell me everything. Some I just put together from the pieces. Part of it I asked Zach before we left Albuquerque."

I emptied my snifter and said nothing.

"Did you intend to shoot Stewart that night?" he asked.

"Oh bloody hell, Nolan, what do you think?" It was no answer, and we both knew it.

"Part of me says no, or you wouldn't have taken the tape

recorder. But the part of me that knows about those scars has to wonder."

"I thought you didn't notice them."

Nolan said nothing, left no trace of emotion on his face but he did not look away from me.

"If he'd just –" I stopped when my voice cracked. *If he'd cut me up on the outside instead.* "Stewart left me with scars no one can see. So yeah, that part of me wanted to shoot him." I stared at Nolan, rolling my empty glass between my hands.

Plain brown eyes that showed no pity looked back at me.

"None of that is what you really want to know though, is it?" I asked, putting the empty glass back on the wooden table.

"No." He studied me. "I'm trying to figure out how you're going to kill Brodenshot," he said, emptying his glass. "But I'm pretty sure there's no part of you that will let him walk away this time."

CHAPTER

14

I stretched out on the bed, smelling the crisp bleached hotel sheets, but mostly feeling the emptiness beside me.

Nolan's questions about what I'd do when I got to El Paso left me unsettled, uncertain, and unable to sleep.

I was angry he'd been digging into my past and madder still that Brandan felt the need to warn him about what happened with Rory Stewart. Yet given Nolan's commitment to my endeavor, I didn't begrudge him needing to know.

But needing to know what? I was unsure what conclusion he'd drawn from Brandan's warning and my own answers tonight. Would Nolan still stand beside me?

My thoughts drifted back to Zach.

Where was he and why hadn't he called?

"Crap!" I sat upright in a panic, having forgotten all about the pager he'd given me – it was in my Suburban, now sitting halfway across the state. I cursed myself for being so stupid. Why hadn't I been carrying it? I hadn't even checked it in two days. What if he'd paged instead of calling? What if. . .

Looking at the red digits on the clock next to the bed, I realized it was too late to call the Websters. I rolled over and punched my pillow in frustration.

Trying to relax one muscle group after another, I wished I'd had another drink or two when the phone in the next room rang.

Nolan's attempt to be quiet was short-lived when he let loose a string of profanity. I didn't make out all the words in between, but the message was clear enough.

Trouble. Whatever it was, it was deep trouble.

"Where the hell did that happen?" I heard more clearly as his voice rose in volume and pitch. "Both of them?"

I got up and rushed to the doorway separating the rooms, banging on it when I found his side locked.

"Just the people next door, complaining about me yelling, I guess," I heard him say to the caller, but he got up and unlocked the door, putting his finger to his lips as I pushed my way in.

Barely contained, I nodded and dropped onto the foot of the bed but couldn't remain still. At one point, I realized I was shivering.

Nolan continued his call, taking notes on a legal tablet, rubbing his temple between scribbles.

My heart galloped in my chest. I paced, hoping the news wasn't about – well, I didn't know who I wished it about more or less than anyone else, and so I gave up on that thought. Finally, my eyes locked on Nolan's, and my stomach dropped.

He hung up, looking for a place to start with the bad news.

I just hoped there was some good news, too.

"That was Neil Tanner. He got an update in Albuquerque about the situation in El Paso. Police found Domino Hurley." Nolan didn't have to say Zach's partner was dead. The strained tone he struggled to keep under control told me that Dom was dead.

Nodding was the best I could do, feeling like I'd been punched in the stomach.

Nolan's skin was pale, and he gulped air before continuing. "And Zach's missing." He swiped both hands over his face, still puffy with sleep. "They were supposed to meet a contact at a strip club. That's the last report anyone got."

My knees quivered as I stood, a huge sour lump in my throat. "I have to call the Websters," I said, turning for the phone he'd just hung up.

"Julie. I'm sure they're just fine –"

"No, Zach gave me a pager, to drop messages if he couldn't call. I left it in my truck. It may hold the only clue we have."

Nolan nodded.

"Let's hit the road," I said. "I don't trust the phones here. In fact, I don't trust anything right now. We can find a pay phone."

As I packed, I let my tears drip unchecked. I thought about Veronica Hurley, opening the door to the brass who would deliver news about her husband. She'd know, without words. Domino once told me Zach had sworn him to the task of telling me, so I could only presume Zach would have promised to tell Roni.

Nolan came into the main room, waiting as I zipped closed my suitcase.

"Nolan, you're not married now, are you?"

He raised an eyebrow. "No, why?"

"Because I'm really tired of spending time with other women's husbands before they end up dead."

✂

"Moses, it's Nolan. I hate to wake you up, but I need another favor. We left a pager in the car in the little cubbyhole between the visors," he explained. "If you can go fetch it, I'll call you back in half an hour."

That was apparently agreeable, so thirty minutes later we stood in a convenience store, the third one we'd tried before finding one with a working pay phone.

"Okay," Moses said, finally back on the line.

Nolan gave me the receiver.

I explained how to retrieve each message, plus the time and date of the call.

Moses looked at the screen and said he'd have to get his glasses. What probably took him thirty seconds to do felt like two hours to me as I stood, rocking from one foot to the other.

Finally he returned and read off two messages. Lots of numbers that I jotted down as he called them out. When he finished, I thanked him, then asked him to call Nolan if any other messages came through.

We got back into Nolan's Suburban and headed south with all my electronic equipment turned off. I'd pulled the battery from my satellite phone at the same time I disconnected the locator on my truck – nothing to trace, nothing to follow. As far as I was concerned, everyone could think I'd disappeared into outer space.

Nolan drove while I used a flashlight to read the numbers and try to make sense of the messages. The first was simply a 143, the 'I love you' message, sent Sunday night after he'd talked to Amber.

The second took a bit of trial and error to make sense of the numbers. Finally, it read: "Nick Helle, Sunalnd Pk" – obviously a misspelling – plus the security authentication.

I repeated it for Nolan, then snapped off the light.

"Sunland Park?" he offered.

"Yeah, but the city or the race track?" I asked.

He shrugged. "Neil said they found Hurley down near the river. I've never been there."

"Neither the town nor the race complex of Sunland Park is in El Paso. They're both in New Mexico," I said, my mind whirling. If the crimes took place on New Mexico soil instead of Texas, I'd have more authority. This left more questions than answers. "There's a thousand places to hide a body. What if dumping Domino in New Mexico was intentional?" I thought aloud. "What if Brodenshot knows I've been reinstated and wants to get me down there?"

Nolan's head nodded in the pale light of other headlights on the interstate. "Looks like he'll get his wish."

CHAPTER

15

We rode for a while without talking, options and bad news bouncing around my brain. "Did they torture Domino?" I finally asked, watching the twin light beams slice through darkness ahead of us.

"Oddly, no," Nolan answered. "Single shot to the head. He was left where he'd be found."

I wrinkled my nose in confusion. "What about Amy Hennessy?" Zach's only description, that Amber's mother's death had been like his twin sister's, had been sufficiently vague.

"Different story altogether. It was ugly," he said, sparing me the details I imagined. "She was dumped in an alley behind a row of stores."

"But both were left where they'd be found," I concluded. "Pauly doesn't like to do his own dirty work. He wanted Amy to suffer and for it to be obvious. No sense torturing her if Zach wouldn't find out. But killing Dom was different. Why?"

"It's a message to you," he offered, trying to sound detached. "That he could do the same to Zach."

"He could do to me what he did to Amy, making Zach watch." I sighed. "Yeah, he bloodied his hands with a motive in mind."

In Santa Fe, we grabbed a drive-through breakfast before sunrise. I got an extra coffee and drove while Nolan dozed. In Truth or Consequences, we traded again.

"Try to get some sleep," he said. "I'll wake you in Las Cruces."

With the caffeine, I felt so wired that I doubted my eyes would close at all, but I curled up on the second row of seats and covered up with my jacket, intending to start with the same mental relaxation exercises I'd been trying when a phone call interrupted our night. Soon the gentle rocking and highway humming beneath the tires did the trick. Or maybe it was the new-car fumes.

The driver's door opened, waking me from crazy dreams I didn't want to remember. Already daylight, I stretched, a dull headache slowing my intentions to climb out and face the morning.

When I turned to look, Nolan was headed toward a grocery store, so I took my time putting on my shoes and unfolding stiff joints before I finally stepped outside the truck.

Nolan returned, holding up a sack. "Got us some bottled tea and deli sandwiches. Restrooms are to the left inside the doors." He pointed over his shoulder with a thumb at the store.

The coffee and orange juice from breakfast had settled uncomfortably into my bladder, so I hurried in the direction he'd indicated. After washing my face and running wet fingers through my hair, I returned to find he'd set out lunch for us in the cab.

"Glad you got some rest," he said.

"I could always sleep in the car when I was a kid. Same with airplanes usually," I replied and took a bite of ham, cheese and bacon on a croissant, then wiped my mouth with the back of my hand.

Nolan handed me a paper napkin, apparently offended at my lack of social grace.

"We're eating in a car, for crying out loud," I said. "How much etiquette is really necessary?"

He smiled at me as he chewed.

"What?" I demanded.

"You. You're just so . . . you."

I rolled my eyes.

"I've seen you in some real highs and lows, and you always exceed the requirements of the situation to most everyone's amazement," he said. "But when you think no one's looking, you are just you."

"Think so?" I asked.

"Sure. You don't try to impress anyone. You're not a snob with your money."

"Running my financial statements now, are you, Nolan?" I asked, dabbing my mouth daintily with the rough recycled paper product meant to be a napkin. "I've been meaning to ask, speaking of money. Did Zach pay for this one, too?"

"The truck?" he asked, almost innocently. "No, we made a deal. He covered a down payment, I'll make the monthly. I had no idea how much one of these can run."

"Wait till you hit the gas station," I said. "You may need financing for that, too."

"I've experienced fuel shock already," he agreed. "But I don't have a lot of expenses otherwise, so I think I'll manage."

"Yeah, until you get fired for helping me," I groused.

"I told you, I'm in this for you and Zach. To do what's right. If that doesn't work for the bureau, screw them. I've been in thirty years already."

"Really? You don't look that old," I mused.

He didn't. I'd have placed him at about forty, maybe forty-five, not fifty and change.

"Maybe I aged well, but I'm old enough to be your father," he said.

"Great, so I'll fix you up with my mom," I kidded.

He smiled kindly. "Dagmar's a terrific lady, and she did okay with you. But I'd have to ground you for this if I were your step-father," he said with a mock stern voice. "Your behavior is entirely too risky for anyone in my family."

"If you only knew," I mumbled. My past riskiness rattled in my memory, threatening not to stay behind me. I stuffed the last bite of sandwich into my mouth.

We swapped places so I could drive, and we arrived in the El Paso area around noon, opening our discussion where to begin.

"Zach's message indicates this Helle guy," I said. "I say we find him."

"How would you find Zach if you didn't have this name?" Nolan countered. "I'd suggest we wait to see if we need to make that contact."

"What if that contact has information we already need?" I asked. "Zach wouldn't have sent it unless he knew I'd be coming down here."

"You being here is such a big surprise," Nolan said with wild sarcasm. "And what if the message is a setup?"

"It's not. It was not only coded, it had a preset authorization number only Zach would know. There's even a code for a message sent under duress."

"You two have quite a system."

I shrugged. "I want to do the right thing, but we have little information and no trustworthy connections."

"There is Neil Tanner," he offered. "I told him to head down here this morning."

"You said you've never met Tanner face to face. How can you trust him? Just because you believe he's clean. . . " I'd taken a deep breath, ready for a major argument.

Nolan raised his hands in surrender. "Julie, I'm here to back you up, not to lead you or make decisions for you. All I ask is that you consider my suggestions, fair enough?"

"I'm sorry," I said, taking a deep breath. "I'm out of my league. My knack has always been understanding how people think under stress. How and why they make choices."

"Like why you came to El Paso. It's how someone who is used to controlling things would respond," he said. "That only makes you more predictable."

"So what makes Pauly Brodenshot predictable? He doesn't kill for himself when there's nothing to be gained. It's personal with Zach or me, and it's rage." I watched the pavement pass while I thought. "But he also chooses not to kill – why not? Does some part of him change because he can't escape being a victim himself?"

"But how would that would apply to Brodenshot?" Nolan asked.

"He acted normal to fit in because keeping his job was important to maintaining his status, but he only operates within the borders of normal socialized or professional behavior when necessary. Otherwise, he's a sociopath with no conscience," I said. "But he has other people kill for him – why?"

Nolan shrugged.

I nodded. "Something altered his ability to react either normally or abnormally to killing. Probably during his career or he'd never have made the agency to start with," I speculated. "Can you get his psych records from the DEA?"

❋

At the track, Sunland Park's horse racing season was underway for the winter months. There were hundreds of cars.

We walked into the security building.

"Excuse me," I said to the top of a head hidden behind a high counter. "I'm looking for Nick Helle."

Platinum blonde no human's hair could mimic tilted to show a gaunt, wrinkled face that would likely be a plastic surgeon's fantasy. She looked up from a stack of papers and studied me. "He's not working again until Saturday," she said in a gruff attempt to dismiss me.

With a gracious smile, Nolan stepped forward. "Ma'am, it's important we reach him. Could you phone his home so that I might speak with him?"

"Personal information cannot be given out," she stated without hiding the roll of her eyes.

Leaning over the narrow counter, Nolan produced his gold badge and subtracted his previous courtesy. "I didn't ask you to give me his number, only to dial the phone so we might speak with him about an urgent matter. Or perhaps I should ask your supervisor instead?"

Flaring her nostrils, she made a nasty *hmmmph* sound and looked up the number in a rotary file. She dialed the phone, going to great lengths to make sure we couldn't see her fingers, and then introduced herself to the person who answered. After a brief conversation, she handed the receiver to Nolan, who only nodded at me to take it.

I put the receiver to my ear. "Is this Nick Helle?" I asked.

"Yes, who is this?" the irritated voice demanded.

Trying out the new credentials, I said, "Lieutenant Madigan with the New Mexico State Police, sir. I'm here at the racetrack with FBI Special Agent Forrester, and we need to discuss an ongoing investigation with you."

"I don't know anything about any investigation," he barked.

"Sir, as a courtesy, we would like to meet you somewhere besides your home, but if necessary, the FBI will produce a federal warrant to pick you up and hold you for questioning," I lied, I think. "Your cooperation would be appreciated."

Apparently the bluff worked.

"Meet me where?"

After discussion, we agreed on the food court in a nearby mall in an hour.

"Thank you so much for your assistance," I said with a syrupy smile, handing the receiver back to the woman behind the desk, who slammed it down on the cradle hard enough the pens in her holder rattled.

On the way back to the car, I jangled the keys, still broadly smiling, and Nolan shot me a quizzical or perhaps irritated look.

"I think we should visit Mr. Helle's neighborhood," I announced as I unlocked the truck doors. "Another of my nifty talents – I can read upside down."

Taking Sunland Park Drive northeast back into El Paso to where it became Shadow Mountain Drive at North Mesa, then right on Thunderbird toward the Coronado Country Club.

"You know your way around here better than I thought," Nolan observed.

"Some of David's friends lived just off Thunderbird, so I know this part of town." I pointed as we passed Helle's house, which had been easy enough to find. I went past, then turned around at an elementary school and parked a few houses away.

"Interesting," I said, wishing for binoculars.

Out the door, a man followed a tall blond woman who stormed outside to a car. He seemed to be yelling at her right up until she got in and slammed the door, backed out and squealed the tires as she sped away.

"Now who do you think that was?" Nolan asked. "His wife? A lover?"

"It took us twelve minutes to get here. Could he have called to get someone to cover him at our meet?"

"They didn't look like they parted company amicably," he said, shaking his head. "I'm guessing she was already here when we called. He was getting rid of her."

Helle went back and locked his front door. Two deadbolts, different keys. Then he got in a ten-year-old sedan, taking the same streets I'd driven to his home out to a main thoroughfare.

I waited ten seconds then followed him past Shadow Mountain to North Mesa where he turned right. In less than fifteen minutes, he'd found a space at Sunland Park Mall near a main entrance.

Nolan got out as I pulled close to the building, so he could follow while I parked. I met him just inside the doorway.

"He went into the restroom in the food court," he said. "I waited so you could get a good look at him before we split up."

I nodded as we strolled.

"That's him," he said with a nod as Helle came back into view.

Nick Helle was about my age, very blonde, over six feet. He hid his eyes behind a pair of tinted lenses, just reflective enough to obscure his gaze.

Nolan detoured to move behind him, as Helle wandered to find a table away from most everyone except girls gossiping over fries and soft drinks.

I went directly to him and sat down across the table. "Nick, thank you for coming," I said, surprising him. "Julie Madigan."

"You're early."

"Well, so are you," I observed. "So let's get this over and done."

He sighed and ran his hand through short, almost-white hair.

"You seem nervous," I said. "There's no reason to be. I need your help. I'm Zach Samualson's wife."

If he'd been anxious before, the sheen of sweat that popped up on his forehead gave away near-panic.

I waited for him to speak, but he sat frozen like a rabbit in a spotlight. When I began to doubt he was even breathing, I spoke. "Nick, Zach's in trouble. I already know that. He sent me to you."

"I can't help you," Nick replied, sounding like a child whining.

"But you know him," I persisted. "He's been targeted by Pauly Brodenshot, who was arrested for smuggling drugs in Florida before escaping." I let that sink in. "Then he kidnapped and killed a child he mistakenly thought was Zach's daughter."

Fear shown in his wide eyes through the blue lenses.

"Now Zach is missing, and his partner is dead."

"D-Domino?" The stutter was pure anxiety.

I didn't know the name of this song yet, but I'd definitely struck a chord he recognized. "Police found him last night with a bullet in his head. Domino was a friend of mine, too," I said, hoping to sound less authoritative and more sympathetic. "Zach sent me to you, Nick. I need your help."

The man appeared to sit still, though I could see his eyes dancing behind the lenses.

For a moment, I thought he would try to bolt, but Nolan was standing nearby, so I didn't act spooked. Nick was smart enough to leave his hands on the table between us, and I left mine there as a show of trust. After a few moments, though, I was less sure this man might not spontaneously implode rather than just run for a door.

"What's the connection? Why would Zach send me your name?" I repeated.

"It's not me," he blurted in a 12-year-old's voice that he tried to clear with a cough. "It's my sister."

"What do you mean?"

"I went to college with Domino. Introduced him to my sister, who's been working for him as an informant for a couple of years. We had it worked out so she passes some of her information to me to share with him, for her own protection. Zach wouldn't know who Dom's source was, just my name."

"Would she be the woman who just left your house?" I asked.

His eyes jumped from me and looked around the large open space, and I knew he felt like I'd just slapped a target circle on his forehead.

CHAPTER
16

"Nick? I'm not here to get you or her involved, but I don't know where else to turn," I pleaded.

"You're not here alone, are you?"

"My partner is behind you, covering us. He's FBI, like I told you on the phone." I nodded behind him. "I have no authority in Texas, which is why I agreed to meet you here."

He nodded.

"Look, we're trying to take down the man responsible for killing Domino and Oz," I said, referring to one of Zach's partners, who had been murdered in Florida, "and the mother of Zach's daughter. Please help us do that."

After a deep breath, Nick nodded. "I'll set something up."

Nolan and I grabbed fried rice and a couple of egg rolls from a fast food place, leaving Nick to make arrangements in private.

In less than half an hour, Nick Helle came to give us details. He'd arranged for us to pick his sister up at eight o'clock at "work."

But that left us with more than six hours, so Nolan called in a favor to his supervisor, asking him to contact DEA and get us access to Brodenshot's personnel file. The result was a meeting with someone who could produce Brodenshot's work history and hiring records – the best that could be done on such short notice. We were to meet our contact at an almost deserted bar at four o'clock.

Finding the contact wasn't difficult – he was probably the only person in the building who paid retail for his clothes instead of shopping at thrift stores. The Italian loafers were a dead giveaway in a room where dusty boots were the norm.

He didn't bother to stand, so I slid into the booth opposite him. "I'm Julie Madigan," I said, flipping open my badge, then added, "Internal Affairs, New Mexico State Police."

I was beginning to like that title, after seeing its effect on people.

His expression changed from one of weary dismissal to one of deep trouble. "Martin Jasper." He didn't offer a hand to shake.

Nolan introduced himself and scooted in beside me.

"No one said there'd be two of you," Jasper said, pounding out his cigarette.

"And you didn't see either of us," Nolan prompted.

Jasper stared at him for a moment, then nodded.

"Pauly Brodenshot escaped from a Florida jail a week ago," I said.

"No one's convicted the man of anything, yet," he countered with a scowl.

I cut my eyes at Nolan and back. "The fact is, he's not in jail where he's supposed to be, which is pretty much a crime he can't debate," I stated, knowing that getting Martin to help wasn't going to happen if I kept pushing so hard. "Think of what we're trying to do as good for Pauly, if you want. I'm just trying to keep him from killing another one of your agents, since apparently shooting Oz and Domino wasn't enough."

"He killed them both?" Jasper tried to swallow, but his mouth had gone dry.

"Zach told me he watched Pauly shoot Oz," I answered.

"You can tack on killing the mother of Zach's daughter and the child he mistakenly thought was hers, too," Nolan added. "Do we have your attention now?"

Jasper's tanned face paled in the dim yellow light, but he finally nodded. He reached down beside him to produce a folder and slipped it across the wooden table.

Nolan nodded for me to take it. "Your idea."

Inside, there were stapled sets of hiring and initial evaluation forms for Pauly, including a brief history about his family in Albuquerque.

Typical stuff, I thought, as I turned the pages. Pauly had a working mother, an over-working father, a younger brother. His parents apparently divorced sometime after he'd been hired at the DEA. Nothing outstanding.

I kept reading. Incident summaries came next, and eventually one caught my eye.

Six years previous, Pauly had been assigned to a different team in south Florida, working drug running and distribution. This incident stood out because of a formal reprimand, written after Pauly was AWOL for five days. There was no explanation for his absence attempted, which earned him a thirty-day suspension.

I scooted the file toward Nolan.

"If no one knew where he was, there's no proof he wasn't turned by money or power or whatever during that time," Nolan concluded. "Might have been held captive and turned."

"Actually, I'm more concerned that he might have already been involved," I said, flipping through more pages, becoming more engrossed.

Music played at a volume just below too loud, but at the sound like a gunshot, all three of us reached for our guns before realizing the bartender had only dropped a glass. The sigh of relief was audible at the table.

"There's an audio tape recorded while Domino and Zach were on a stakeout, a couple of days ago," he said, turning his attention directly to me. "I don't think it will help you find them, but it's about you, so I thought you might want to hear it anyway."

When he produced a small cassette device with ear buds, I pulled it toward me and nodded. "I'm going to the ladies' room where hopefully it's quieter."

Inside the wooden door, it wasn't quite as noisy, only by cutting out the background chatter. I inserted the earpieces and hit play.

"How do you like being a married man?" Domino kidded Zach.

"What do you think?" Zach replied.

"I think you look like a kid on Christmas morning."

"Yeah? Feels a thousand times better than that."

"I'm glad you finally got the girl. She's been under your skin a long time."

"Since I was nine years old," Zach said, letting the reference go unexplained.

Dom laughed. "I think you were born loving her."

"Maybe I was."

There was almost a minute without them talking.

"Would you ever have told me what happened that night we picked her up at the bar in Albuquerque?" Dom asked. "If I'd asked?"

Zach gave no audible answer.

"Good, 'cuz I'd have been pissed hearing it from you."

"You've got no idea how pissed you'd be," Zach muttered.

"She told me enough, thanks." It sounded like Dom took another bite of something and chewed for a few moments. "I don't suppose you'd tell me why she really left you in Washington either?" he asked with his mouth full.

"It's not on the top of my list of things to discuss."

"I called her, after I told you I'd go out there. She begged me not to let you work, but she wouldn't say why. I was afraid you'd hurt her somehow, but when I asked her, she just said no and hung up."

Zach sighed. "At first, I didn't understand why she was leaving, even after she got on that jet. I thought it was my fault, too, whatever the reason, but I didn't hurt her. You know I wouldn't hurt her." There was a long pause. "You'd have to know Julie a lot better to understand some of her demons."

"I stayed by her side for three weeks. I couldn't get to know her much better and keep my pants on," Dom said. "She's a damned good cook when she wants to be. Did you know that?"

Zach apparently turned toward the microphone, his voice louder when he laughed. "Well, no, I didn't. I do most of the cooking."

"Wow, that secret will cost you twice. Why the hell are we eating pizza every night if you can cook?" he asked.

"Don't push your luck, Dom."

"So tell me what happened in Washington."

Zach hesitated. "This Bock guy shot her father. She tried to help him, but her dad made her leave. When she ran toward the exit to get help, Bock got his hands on her," he said. "Julie repressed the memory of seeing Bock. Of what he said to her. But subconsciously, she began to believe his words – that she'd grow up to be a killer just like he was."

"Geez, what a monster," Dom said with disbelief.

"Then she shot David Wesley but didn't know or remember Bock was there, either. When she had to kill the deputy in Michigan, I guess that ripped open all those feelings. On New Year's Day, when she cut my arm, even though it was an accident, she told me that something in her just snapped."

"Holy shit," Dom said. "So her leaving had nothing to do with the drugs?"

"No. I wish it'd been that simple. Something she could have blamed me for."

"But it worked out for you both that she left in the long run, right?"

"I got clean and she got . . . You know something, I really don't want to discuss this anymore," Zach said, ending the conversation.

His words echoed in my head, but I finished the sentence mentally. "I got clean and she got raped."

No way I could believe that it didn't still bother him.

❦

For our arranged meeting with Nick's sister, Nolan drove; I sat in the back to be invisible.

I had to suppress a laugh when he saw he was in a part of town where women walked the streets, advertising in skin a commodity no laws had ever successfully banished.

"Oh great," he grumbled, fidgeting with his shirt collar. "How will I find her out here?"

"I get the feeling she'll find you, if you'll just slow down a little," I said, spying a woman dressed as Nick had described, walking down the sidewalk. "Pull over here."

He did. The woman who crossed the street in high heels with a long easy stride reminded me of someone who could run the hundred-meter dash well. She passed by a couple of other cars that had slowed down to gawk, head high.

She came to the passenger window, which Nolan powered down.

"Hey, Sugar, you looking for a good time tonight?" she said, leaning on the door with her elbows.

"Nick sent me," he said in a low voice.

Instead of answering, she opened the door and slid inside as if the seat were greased. She pushed the button to raise the window and said, "Go."

Nolan accelerated away from the curb back into traffic.

"Left at the next light," she directed, not looking at either of us. After several more turns, she pointed to a low-rent apartment.

Nolan parked, and they opened their doors.

"You," she said over her shoulder to me. "Follow in about ten minutes. Room 212, up the stairs and turn left."

She got out and wrapped herself around Nolan's arm, and they went through a glass door that hadn't been cleaned in a decade.

I waited until I saw a room light come on. Checking to see that no one had followed, I got out and went through the door. Up the steps, thinking how much this sleazy place reminded me of the low-rate hotel where Domino and I had checked in while in Florida.

At the door she'd indicated, I hesitated, listening for trouble inside. It opened without me knocking, revealing a room that was not a reflection of the dinginess of the building.

"Let me see your ID," she said, closing the door behind me.

I pulled out the badge and identification Eric Rader had provided and handed them to her.

She took a look, handed them back.

"You must be Zach's wife," she said, looking me over, head to foot and back. "He mentioned being married, but I thought he was joking."

"You know him?" I asked, hoping the answer was no, given her profession.

She laughed. "Well, I hope the video tape shot last night is convincing I know him Biblically as they say, but you'll have to take my word for it – and his – that it didn't happen the way it looked."

CHAPTER

17

"What video?" I demanded. "What the hell are you talking about? Who are you?"

Sure, I was angry, but I recognized jealousy fueling those flames, as well. I'd never feared losing Zach to another woman, but hearing her words about my husband yanked my chain hard enough I considered pulling my Glock and shooting her.

"Look, I don't really know Zach personally – I'd only seen him a couple of times before with Dom," she said, sitting down in a comfortable-looking chair opposite us. "Let's start at the beginning. My name is Sabra Helle. I dance at The Ranch, and sometimes I freelance for extra cash – mostly for high-end clients, almost never walking the street."

"So you are a prostitute?" Attempts to control my emotions were not working well.

"Most of my clients are arranged by a service, but yes, more or less." She shrugged. "I've also been an informant for the El Paso County Sheriff's Department almost five years, and then for Domino when Santiago started moving drugs at the club." She leaned back, obviously unconcerned about telling us anything. "A few nights ago while I was dancing, I saw Dom at The Ranch and the big guy with him. Zach got up and headed toward the restrooms. Santiago, the owner, came and sat down with Domino. The next thing I knew, both agents were gone. The next night, I got wind of Santiago wanting to 'entertain a guest.' I traded places with the girl he was going to send. I got to the warehouse early. Inside, I heard men talking. One played a recording for Zach from some guy who promised to do really ugly things to his wife and a little girl."

I cringed, imagining what Pauly could threaten.

"When I saw Zach, he was tied to a metal chair. He finally looked up at me, but I could tell he was half-blind with the pain. I propped my foot between his thighs, and he looked down at the black boot, snug over my calf and up beyond the knee, ending beneath a matching leather miniskirt. No panties, he could tell." Sabra looked at Nolan and smiled. "And yeah, I'm a true blonde."

She was tall, Scandinavian with spiked blond hair too perfect to have come from a bottle of peroxide. Blue eyes. Good teeth with a wicked smile.

"You're every bit of Zach's fantasy woman, then," I said with a shake of my head.

Sabra nodded. "That's kinda what he said - 'You know, if I weren't married. . .'"

That would be Zach's reply, yes.

She explained how she leaned down and tilted his chin up with her fingertips, and then brushed her lips across his, careful of a swollen split. She'd nibbled her way to his earlobe, then whispered, "There is a camera behind me, Zach. This has to look good. I can't get you out of here tonight, but I will help you."

I nodded, waiting for her to get through with this story so I could do something – adrenaline screamed through my bloodstream.

"With this little stiletto tucked in my boot, I cut away his jeans and peeled the layers of fabric out of his lap." she stated with an impious smile I wanted to slap off her face.

My agitation must have been palpable, because Nolan put his hand around my arm to keep me in my seat.

"I told him the camera was straight behind me, that what I was doing had to look legit," she told me in a matter-of-fact voice.

"Where was he?" Nolan asked.

"In a warehouse off Doniphan Road." She hesitated, not providing an address. "Santiago set this up, so there are bigger considerations. You can't just waltz in there and cut Zach loose."

"Try me," I scowled.

"Listen to her a minute, Julie," Nolan said harshly from his corner of what was about to become a boxing ring.

"Whatever it takes to get Zach away from there," I said, turning from him back to Sabra, "I'll do it."

"I convinced Mia to let me go again tonight, that I really liked it." She winked. "I'm sure I would have, too."

Resisting the urge to throttle her, I said, "So I go instead."

"If the camera feed is live, and I suspect it is, then you risk them catching you together," Nolan stated.

"If they are expecting you to go back, they will be watching," I argued, "then Pauly will show up if he realizes it's me."

"Sugar, if they find you there instead, you're both dead," she replied. "Who is Pauly?"

Nolan explained, and the three of us came up with a theory how he fit into the drug world Sabra had been observing for so long – Pauly was the supplier for The Ranch's cocaine business, and his recent imprisonment in Florida had severely impacted the sales at the strip club.

Despite detours into a dozen arguments, we put together a plan. By ten o'clock, we'd gone through Sabra's wardrobe, looking for something suitable, and she began dressing me to look like her.

"Take off the underwear," she instructed as I zipped up a red leather skirt that I wouldn't have worn twenty pounds or ten years ago. "Are you really blonde?"

I remembered that Amber had lightened my hair just days ago, but nowhere near as light as Sabra's. "What the hell does that have to do with anything?"

"Curious. Keep the skirt on – just hike it up when you . . ." She didn't even try to hide her smile. "Of course, you can really get it on with him, can't you? Lucky woman."

I winced at the thought that an exotic dancer and part-time prostitute wished she could have a go at my husband.

I can't blame her, though.

"Haven't you ever wanted to do something else, Sabra?" I asked. "Besides dance?"

"Dancing pays well. And escorts bring home loads more than what you make."

No doubt – I didn't have a job at the moment.

"Sex for money can't be your life's ambition," I countered. "How about going to school?"

"For what?" she laughed. "First, you think I do this a lot – I might work six nights a month, and I don't work for a pimp or for drugs – I'm clean. Second, I work at a radio station during the day, a job where no one sees me, and I enjoy what I do. And third, you're a college girl. What did you have when you were 30 years old? I could retire tomorrow on what I've invested."

Her candor didn't make me want to change professions, but I envied her foresight.

When everything was ready, Nolan had made plans with the local FBI. I took Sabra's car, a ten-year-old Honda Accord – no frills and no payments, she promised. The Honda blended in well enough as I made my way across town, following the directions I'd memorized.

I wasn't wearing enough clothing to conceal more than the five-shot .38 Smith & Wesson tucked inside the thigh-high red leather boots I'd borrowed from Sabra's collection. She'd showed me the tiny pouch where she kept a stiletto hidden, and I'd taken it, too, but tucked it along my left wrist under the black lace gloves.

The warehouse was one of several along a nearly abandoned area of the industrial zone near the railroad tracks.

Must be something secure about warehouses, since Pauly liked to operate out of them.

I parked and stepped out of the car, hoping to stay upright on the spiked heels of boots two sizes too big for me as I walked through the gravel to the building.

An open padlock hung on the staple, though when the hasp was closed over it, even a bent nail could easily prevent an escape from inside.

I pulled the door open. Without hesitation, I walked toward the light, slowly but steadily. Ahead, what I saw wasn't anything like what Sabra had told me. Zach wasn't sitting in a chair bolted to the floor; he was flat on his back in front of it, his arms pulled over his head and hands cuffed around one metal leg and crosspiece. A dirty blanket lay beside him.

Even in the summer, the concrete floor could drain a person's body heat quickly.

Fluorescent lights hung high in the metal trusses, casting lots of shadows.

As I came closer, Zach's breathing changed, perhaps as he recognized the footsteps as female again. I walked straight to him, then stepped over his chest to straddle his body.

Looking far worse than Sabra's description, it looked like he'd been beaten again. His eyes were swollen nearly shut, lips cut and bloody. The shirt was ripped open, and chest marked with bruises, mostly boot-shaped.

"I thought I told you not to get yourself killed," I said in Sabra's higher voice.

He opened his eyes as best he could to look at me and raised his head.

"You again. You'll forgive me, I don't think I'll be as much fun this time," he said, letting his neck go limp.

"Damn," I said, bending down to turn his chin further toward the dim light. "I was so hoping to get my hands on you again."

His eyes jerked open wider as he realized who I was, and he opened his mouth to speak.

"Shhh," I said, placing a finger lightly on his lips. "Sugar, we'll make it all right; you'll see."

I knelt, straddling his chest, and slipped my hands up along his arms until I dropped a handcuff key into his right palm, but he didn't wrap his cold fingers around it until I closed them. Moving around and over his body, I finally worked the .38 out of the boot and put it on the right side of his chest, but I doubted he could use it if his hands were numb. At least it was where I could get to it.

The knife was still secure in my lace glove.

Slithering up his chest, smooth red leather skirt between us, I leaned carefully over his battered body again.

"Someone's in here," he whispered.

Bad news, but that was what I'd hoped – but not so soon.

"Unlock one cuff to get free but don't move."

He groaned as I licked his earlobe.

"Come on, Cowboy, I know you can do better than that," I taunted him, wiggling my hips.

"He'll kill you," Zach groaned as I shifted my weight.

"Element of surprise; he'll think I'm Sabra."

"How did you –" he started to say, but I shut him up with a kiss as I heard the door open. "I love you, baby."

I smiled. "My .38 is next to your hip. I love you, too."

Boots clomped heavily toward us. "Ah, Señor, a man has needs, and I see this lovely filly is taking care of yours while you are away from your wife," the man said, standing just outside the light.

This wasn't the man I'd hoped. Worse, I had no idea how Sabra would normally respond to him, whether he knew who she was. I turned slightly to hide the gun closer beneath Zach, seeming to pull down the leather skirt over my hips.

"Sabra," he commanded. "Move away so I may talk to our friend without your delightful distractions."

I stood up to step into the shadows toward the camera, turning away from the man.

"She's quite good at what she does, don't you think, Mr. DEA?"

Zach didn't reply or even look in his direction.

"She's not who I sent to entertain you, but you appear to be enjoying yourself," he said with a heavy Hispanic lilt. "You deserve the very best in the stable, my friend. You can think of this as your last supper, and all you get is dessert."

I heard Zach sigh, as if bored with the one-way conversation.

"As for you," the man said, taking another step closer, "since you are neither Mia nor Sabra, I think I'll have to break you in for my stable myself when I'm done with him."

In the dim light, he pulled his hand from his pocket.

I barely had time to scream before the stun gun zapped me, and I hit the ground in a pile of spasming muscles as the current pulsed through my body, but I was far enough from Zach that when I fell, I took down the camera and tripod, too.

Glass and plastic shattered.

"You bitch!" the man yelled and then converted to a string of profanity in Spanglish I might have been able to translate except for the pain.

I wasn't even sure I'd quit screaming yet or if that sound was just echoing in my head like the stars bouncing in my vision. As normal sensations began to return, a new pain exploded as a pointed boot connected with my left flank and again in my abdomen as I doubled over, gasping for air.

If Zach hadn't picked up the gun by now, I decided he probably couldn't. My choices were to either stay on the ground and get the shit kicked out of me, or to fight back, despite the pain. Wrapping my fingers around the thin handle of the knife, I rolled between kicks to make one swing at the man's groin, the only critical target within reach.

Based on the wounded-bear howl that escaped his lips, I knew I'd connected with his genitals, over which he clamped both hands, then dropped to his knees, blood soaking through his jeans around his fingers.

I managed to get to my feet, despite the damned high heels. Even with busted ribs on the left, the adrenaline level was so high, I hardly registered the pain.

Zach was trying to pick up the gun, but he would not shoot this direction with me in such close proximity unless he had more control of his muscles than I'd first thought.

At least I hope not.

I stumbled the first step toward the man I'd stabbed, still on his knees.

He reached to his waist for a gun, and I made an awkward but effective kick to the side of his head, knocking him face-first to the concrete with a sickening sound of his jaw breaking as he landed, unconscious.

I reached down and jerked the gun from his waistband, and kicked him in the ribs one more time just for grins since he seemed to be out cold and I could return the favor.

It hurt me worse than it hurt him.

I drew a ragged breath that felt like fire in my lungs and stepped toward Zach.

Slow applause echoed through the metal building, coming from high above. "That was some show, Julie," a familiar voice called from the shadows. "I expected you to kill him though. Drop the gun."

I did so only because I had no idea what direction to shoot, tossing it away from the Hispanic man.

"You'd almost convinced me you were the other dancer, until you called him Cowboy. Brilliant performance otherwise," he said. "I was so looking forward to watching."

"Of course you'd watch, you cowardly son of a bitch," I yelled, reaching down to yank off the boots, only to find my left arm wasn't working very well. "You wanted me here. Come and get it, Pauly."

"Where's the girl?" he asked.

"What girl?"

A bullet whizzed by, rattling my nerves but giving me an idea where he was.

I stood my ground.

"I'll shoot him next," he teased. "Maybe start with your favorite parts of his body."

"You don't get it, Pauly. He doesn't know, and I swear to you that you can't hurt either one of us badly enough to make me tell."

"I don't believe you, Julie." He fired another shot.

I didn't flinch as the bullet exploded on the concrete just a foot or so behind me to the right. I concentrated on pinpointing the muzzle flash.

"And you're not a very convincing shot, Pauly," I replied, crossing my arms over my chest, as much to help me breathe and stabilize my left arm as in defiance.

His next shot hit the concrete between my bare feet, and hot shrapnel struck both ankles.

But this was followed by two shots from my left, as Zach fired toward where the muzzle flash had been. One struck metal and ricocheted; the other must have hit Pauly, based on the groan.

Scrambling for Santiago's gun, I scanned for cover, but there was none. I dropped the magazine to check to see it was really loaded, then slapped it back, pain arced lightning through my left arm, which then turned to numbness. I couldn't pull the slide back to see if a round was chambered – so I pointed toward where Pauly had been and pulled the trigger, relieved at the shot.

"I'll kill you both," Pauly moaned from above, his next shot going wild.

Zach struggled to get up, so I fired four rounds into the rafters as I helped him to his feet.

When more gunfire came from above us, I shot out the fluorescent lights, dim as they were, leaving us in sparks and raining glass, but enough darkness to get to the door. I emptied my gun blindly behind us as we hobbled.

Outside, I found an interesting conglomeration of law enforcement personnel waiting for us, including two SWAT team members who quickly escorted us to cover.

Nolan rushed to meet us, screaming for a medic as he and Zach helped me to the ground.

"I'm not hurt," I tried to argue, knowing I had some bruises and cuts to my feet from the broken glass. Probably a broken arm. "You need to take care of Zach," I kept trying to say. "There's nothing wrong with me."

Until I looked down and saw – all the blood was mine.

CHAPTER

18

Looking up at the black sky and the panicked faces, I heard distant voices, felt hands moving – oxygen mask, IV. Everything around me reeled slow and hazy, then it just faded away.

Next time I opened my eyes, the sounds of intensive care – beeping and whooshing and hushed voices – almost overwhelmed me, but I couldn't even remember what city I was in.

I tried to turn my head, despite the pain. The next breath hurt enough I heard myself groan. The smells of disinfectant and alcohol and blood made neural connections to so many bad memories in my brain, nausea began to squeeze my stomach.

"Julie," a voice said quietly from nearby. "I'm here."

I opened my mouth to speak, but I didn't know what to say.

A large hand wrapped around my own, warm and gentle.

"Zach, are you okay?" I finally asked, making another effort to turn my head and open my eyes to see him.

"Not too bad," he said, not raising his voice. "Broken nose, banged up ribs. No holes."

He looked better than the last time I remembered seeing him except for the black eyes.

"Did they get him?" I croaked, speaking taking more effort than I expected.

"Pauly died at the scene." He reached to touch my cheek. "So did Santiago."

"And Amber's okay?"

"Yes, she's just fine."

"What about me?" I asked, knowing the news wasn't good if I was in ICU.

"Broken ribs, wrist," Zach started, then paused, turning away.

"What else," I asked, wincing at the pain it caused.

"You got shot and lost a lot of blood. They had to do surgery."

"Surgery?" I echoed.

He wiped a tear that slid down his cheek away on his shirt cuff before he looked back at me. "Did you know you were pregnant, Julie? Did you put yourself in harm's way, knowing –" he stopped when his voice cracked.

"I had to do it, Zach," I said, trying to hide my surprise – even had I known, it wouldn't have mattered. "You know I had to come for you."

Silence filled the space between us as he tried to hide something he didn't want to say.

"Tell me what you're thinking, Zach."

"After the surgery, the doctor said you can't ever get pregnant again." His voice trembled.

That left me speechless.

Overwhelmed, I tried trying to think of something to say and gather the energy to voice it past the lump in my throat, but Zach let go of my hand and rushed out the sliding glass door and down the hall out of my view.

"Zach!" I called, splinting my ribs, difficult because of the cast on my left arm. "Please come back." I made a brief attempt at sitting up, but realized that the ribs weren't the only place where pain limited my motion.

A nurse came in, carrying a replacement IV bag, unaware of what had just happened.

"Don't try to move around so much," she cooed, trying to rearrange me to be more comfortable. "How are you feeling?"

"Like I was run over repeatedly by a bulldozer."

She looked a bit startled by my answer. "Do you need something for pain?"

"I *need* to talk to the attending who admitted me," I said. "Or better yet, the surgeon."

"I don't know what time he'll make rounds this morning," she said with diplomacy that went unappreciated.

"Then call him," I said. "I want answers."

"Physicians usually don't –"

"I don't give a damn what they usually do," I said, growling with the pain it caused. Passive consolation was not going to work with me, no matter how badly I was injured. I took another painful breath and blasted her. "If there isn't a doctor here in the next hour, you can bring a release because I'll walk out of here!"

Screw the pain, I thought. *I can get out of this bed and walk out now if I have to.*

"Mrs. Samualson, you're in no condition to –" she began again.

"Don't patronize me," I warned, but the sound of the name caught me off guard. Samualson – we were married. Married, pregnant, and now infertile. Tears filled my eyes as anger and emotional turmoil battled in my chest. I was struggling again to sit up when Zach's broad shoulders filled the doorway.

"Julie, please stop," he said, wiping his eyes.

I relented more in agony than surrender.

The nurse hung the IV solution and restarted the pump, stepping away before Zach came to the bedside.

"I'll place a call to the attending to let him know you need to speak to him," she said as she reached the doorway, then slid the door closed and left us alone.

"I'm not mad at you, Julie. Sounds silly, but I didn't want you to see me cry." He sat down close to me, his eyes still watery and red. Warm hands wrapped around mine. "After all this, I'm devastated that he ruined one more thing between us."

"I had to come, Zach," I repeated, hoping I wouldn't start crying, too.

"And you did," he said. "You can't imagine how much it hurts to see you in another hospital bed because of me, but you saved my life."

"I recall you saved mine once," I said, trying to lighten the tone.

Zach nodded. "Besides, it's embarrassing when a tough guy like me needs a woman half his size to bail him out of a jam." He smiled, just a little. "Twice."

"A woman with a lot of help."

"Yes, there was a lot of help. Nolan said he'd be by later. He gave me the number so I could talk to Amber and tell her we're both okay."

"Are we?" I asked.

"Absolutely," he said, kissing my fingers.

"Good, because I think we've become a family anyway."

CHAPTER
19

Recovering in the El Paso hospital was no different from any other place I'd been admitted. This time, however, Zach sat with me for hours at a stretch, often not saying anything. Still, just his presence was comforting during the grief we each walked through.

We lost both a child together and any future possibilities of another, which in some ways I found easier to accept than Zach did. He wanted to be supportive of me, but still I could feel his anger and disappointment at the circumstances, not just his sadness.

Also difficult to grieve was Domino Hurley's death. Hard for me because I'd spent weeks with him, during our trip to Florida to find Zach. His laughter still echoed in my head when I thought of him. So did his words about his wife – that they'd been high school sweethearts and that he'd never been with anyone else. I'd only met Roni once, but the idea that she'd lost that sort of faithfulness, in a profession so thick with divorce, was hard to fathom.

But I knew Zach's feelings of loss were much deeper than my own. They'd been partners almost since the beginning of Zach's career with the Drug Enforcement Administration, which despite attempts at keeping their worlds separate, was much like being brothers.

I insisted Zach go talk to her and attend Domino's funeral. "Veronica needs you," I said. "More than I need you to sit here and hold my hand, she needs you."

"What do I tell her?" he asked, wrinkling his forehead. "I don't know what to say."

"You've heard people try to say things that end up being wrong." I squeezed his hand. "The fact that you are there, even if you say nothing more than you're sorry, will be enough. I promise."

With a little more coaxing, he caught a morning flight to Albuquerque, then returned to my hospital room late that evening after the service. The hug I got from him told me how much his heart was broken.

"Roni seems to be holding up," he said, finally letting go of me and pulling a chair toward the bed.

I was out of ICU but my hospitalization would last several more days.

"And his kids?" Although I hadn't known till Zach told me, the Hurleys had two sons and a daughter, ages sixteen and under.

"Hard to tell about them. His older son latched on to me, asking all sorts of things about Domino."

We both pretended his voice didn't squeak when he said Dom's name.

"How are you?" we asked at the same time.

I went first. "Still sore, but I've been walking. Back on whatever they call real food here."

"Probably not up for a big platter of fajitas yet, are you?" He laughed when I nodded my head eagerly. "Amber's okay. I talked to her again this evening while I was waiting to board. She really wanted me to come on up and get her, but I told her we needed to get a few things settled."

Seeing that he intended to ignore my question, I repeated it. "And you?"

Eyes down, he shook his head. "I still have trouble believing he's gone."

I ran my fingers through his thick hair. "It's not going to be easy."

"No, it's not. But I keep thinking about what I'd do if . . . How I'd have nothing if it had been you," he said, tears glinted in his dark lashes, just before the wall finally crumbled.

When I tried to sit up on the side of the bed to hold him, I was surprised that he nudged me over and crawled onto the small mattress beside me, his head on my shoulder, and cried.

I couldn't stop the tears either, so we held each other until they were gone.

Much later in the night, I realized I'd never seen Zach cry like that before, and I wondered how he made it through his twin sister's murder, knowing she hadn't fought back. Between the two of us, we'd felt the loss of so many people.

But looking ahead, he had gained a daughter, and we'd agreed to open our lives and home to Amber if that's what she still wanted. Our fathers died when we were young, and we both knew something about losing a loved one to crime, which would hopefully help us offer emotional support for the losses of her mother and grandmother.

I hoped Amber could see that she'd also gained a new family – not one to take the place of her old one – but one to be there instead.

Two days later, Zach helped me move from the wheelchair into the second row of seats in Nolan's Suburban.

Another friend I could never thank enough, Nolan Forrester had provided me with the strength to leave Amber where she was safe and the support to find Zach.

He insisted on driving Zach and me from El Paso to the Websters' in Colorado to pick up Amber, Laser, and my Suburban. Another FBI agent would be bringing Zach's vehicle to Albuquerque.

From a seat behind them, it was nice to hear the two men, from different government agencies, talk to each other about their jobs and their lives. Surprisingly, Nolan told Zach about losing his wife and how it became a brick wall he hid behind for so long.

As I pretended to read a magazine instead of listening, I couldn't help but believe that Nolan's words were a story of his survival, the climb up instead of the fall.

Zach's mood lightened a bit as he told Nolan about the setup that had taken them to Florida before things had gone all to hell. "Living in a waterfront mansion, fast cars, huge boat and never-ending parties," he said, as if he ought to miss them. "Hard to believe sometimes the illusion we create to blend in."

"Never worked undercover," Nolan replied.

Both men must have thought the very same words about my undercover activity, because they each looked away and became quiet.

No way I could forget Zach's words after Rory Stewart had been led from my bedroom in handcuffs: *Did you like working undercover?* Nor could I forget Nolan's confession that he'd talked to Brandan about the same incident before he came to New Mexico to help me protect Amber. That sting operation to catch Stewart had gone horribly wrong.

Although it had affected me – sometimes in ways that surprised me still – being raped by a Grand Traverse County deputy had been a point where Zach and I had been unable to meet. Initially, neither of us understood how the other felt, so assumptions of anger and blame led to withdrawal from the bond we'd developed.

The silence in the vehicle was too loud for the space.

"Come now, gentlemen," I said in a mock English accent. "You've better things to talk about than the past."

Apparently the levity was sufficient to start their conversation again, almost like filling a gas tank just as the engine begins to sputter.

"You'll like the Websters' place," Nolan said as he drove. "You two should take a little time to explore, hike around. It's a good place to get better acquainted with Amber."

"I still get this tight feeling in my throat when I think about having a teenage daughter," Zach said, then chuckled. "We should hope she didn't inherit her adolescence from me."

✂

On our way through, we stopped in Albuquerque for a few hours to discuss the custody issue with Greg Hennessy before going on to Colorado. Greg's career revolved around offshore drilling rigs all over the world. While I had no doubts that he'd have given that up and kept Amber if there were no other option, neither of them would have been happy about it. He asked if he could stay in contact with us and offered to contribute to a college trust fund or something similar for Amber, to which we agreed.

Having all the decisions made beforehand, there would be little dispute when we sat before a judge for disposition of Amber's custody. Zach called to have his attorney draw up documents for a hearing when we returned the following week.

Once we were back on the road to Colorado, conversation hit a lull, and I fell asleep. Not until we turned off the highway toward the Websters' A-frame did the bumps wake me. Inhaling, stretching, the air felt lighter, cleaner than I remembered.

When the truck came to a stop in front of the house, dog and girl came bounding out the door through the gate. Amber wrapped herself around Zach when he stepped out first. I opened the door to an equally exuberant dog who'd forgotten his training and manners and jumped up to nuzzle me for more pets. Finally able to push him down, Amber came and more carefully hugged me.

"Thanks," she whispered. "For bringing you both home."

CHAPTER
20

One look around the Colorado mountains, and Zach agreed with Nolan's suggestion that a few days together in such a peaceful place would serve as an icebreaker to the new family we'd become. We found a rental cabin not far from the Websters' house, though they opened their home to allow Zach and Amber use of the pool one evening, then served us all a magnificent dinner. He and Moses took Amber snow skiing while Grace and I spent an afternoon together.

With the dangers surrounding the crimes resolved, Eric Rader had contacted my mother and Zach's – they'd gone to San Antonio for all its tourist sites and great food – and they were back home before we left Colorado.

When we returned to Albuquerque, my mother told me that while we were all welcome to stay at her house, she thought it would be better for Amber to be out at Vera's, to get to know her real grandmother first.

"Mom, that's terribly generous," I told her, "but for all the changes we have to make, including me and you as part of this new family is important, too."

We compromised, and my mother stayed out at the ranch a few nights while Vera went to work.

"Your mother has a funny accent," Amber whispered one evening as my mother cooked supper.

I laughed. "She grew up in Germany," I said. "Still speaks German occasionally when she gets excited. My father met her overseas at a military hospital, and they eventually got married. I was born there, too."

"But you don't talk funny, except that 'eh?' thing you forget and say once in a while."

A habit I'd picked up in Michigan. "That's good to know, eh?" I said, pronouncing the vowel sound more like *hay* than *bed.*

Zach's attorney had scheduled the court appearances and memorial services. After the legal proceedings in Albuquerque and the funerals for Amy Hennessy and Agatha Donlon, we helped Amber sort her belongings and close up the house where she'd lived. Ten days later, the four of us drove back to the cabin in Washington as a new family.

The loss of a spouse or a parent, job changes, serious personal injury or illness, and loss of pregnancy are among the most stressful events an individual can face. Each of us had suffered major losses, some of which weren't even listed in the top twenty-five most stressful events on the scale I'd once seen.

"I guess whoever wrote that list didn't think about things like killing a good friend to save a child, being tortured and watching a best friend being executed by someone you once trusted, or discovering the man you thought was your father was really not," I told Zach one evening as we fixed supper together.

"Maybe not, but we've got each other."

We did shore up each other as we adjusted to being together and learning to deal with the past and a present that none of us had imagined just a few months back. There were few secrets between the three of us, and that honesty was helpful.

In addition to finishing my own interrupted unpacking from my move, we got Amber settled into the cabin.

"I want the bedroom at the far end of the upstairs hall," she announced. "That leaves more walls to muffle sounds."

I wasn't sure whether she meant we might hear her, or whether she didn't want to hear us. Nonetheless, I set up my desk and computer to share the room where Zach had hung his favorite drawing of me, making it officially the office.

Getting Amber enrolled in the last two months of the school year took more effort than Zach had expected, but she finished the year without any below-average grades, despite the fact none of her new teachers made it easy to catch up. Their expectations made the time she spent studying more valuable to her than if they'd just given her an A for pity.

The climate in Washington really bothered Amber.

"You must be allergic to green," Zach said with a laugh. "You've probably never seen grass and trees like this."

True enough, Amber had never been out of New Mexico, so the sneezing and itchy eyes made her irritable until we found an antihistamine that worked for her.

I slowly recuperated from the physical injuries throughout the summer. When the cast on my arm came off in the necessary six weeks, the immobilization left me weaker than I expected. The new scars just added to the collection. But losing the baby left emotional fallout neither Zach nor I anticipated, and I continued counseling because Zach had asked me to. We all did.

Zach took extended leave from the DEA to take care of things at home with a new teenage daughter adjusting to a new family life, and a wife needing to heal. He didn't talk much about Domino Hurley or what else happened when he went to tell Veronica Hurley about her husband. I didn't need to hear those details, but it was important to me that Zach knew I would listen when the time came.

I wouldn't be getting back on a horse any time during the early summer, said the doctor who followed up on the surgery. As the ribs and abdominal muscles healed slowly, I had no reason to argue, but I missed riding much like I missed working.

Being unemployed through the summer had been relaxing and yet empty. My focus in life needed constant adjustment, away from work that served strangers to serving the needs of a new family. What was hardest for me was the loss of privacy with Zach.

In May, for his birthday, I gave Zach a Kimber .45 caliber semi-automatic pistol, a new release from a company renowned for its craftsmanship of rifles. For mine, he bought me a custom saddle and started a barn to put it in.

With a little help from Delbert Clinton, the neighbor up the road, the barn was framed in record time, but Amber and Zach worked together on it while I watched from the deck. One evening a week, he took her to the Clintons' ranch to ride, and from their conversations, I gathered she was becoming quite an accomplished horsewoman.

One weekend in June, Amber went to stay with a friend, and Zach drove us into central Oregon to a place in the Cascades I'd picked to hike and camp for the weekend.

The forest was quiet except for our footsteps and an occasional bird in the distance. No breeze rustling leaves. No traffic in the distance. Not even the sound of the creek we'd crossed an hour back. The stillness made the wilderness almost seem surreal.

And yet the silence was not as perfect as it had been the previous night when we'd driven to the top of a ridge just to see where the road went, and found a dead end above the clouds we'd been hoping to escape. We had pitched a tent as the sun set and watched a full moon rise over the mountain ridge. Then, like a lake filling up, the clouds floated up from the valley to engulf us in an eerie dense shroud of absolute silence and darkness.

In the daylight, we hiked through areas of forest that by today's standards would be antique, though not rated as old-growth timber. A few signs of a forest fire several years ago were visible as we walked – scorched logs, bare spots, lots of young ferns.

"There can't be another human being within ten miles of here," Zach said as he walked behind me through the forest.

I thought it was funny that he'd whispered.

"At *least* ten miles," I agreed.

He reached forward and took my hand, pulling me to a stop in the middle of the trail.

"I don't think the birds will mind then," he said, gently wrapping his hands around my face and kissing me. "Do you have any idea how much I miss having you all to myself?"

I felt my knees quiver and my heart race. "Yes, I do."

CHAPTER

21

In early July, while we were planning to go back to Albuquerque to pick up the horses, I got a call from Connie Thompson, the secretary at the Grand Traverse County Medical Examiner's Office.

"I told Dr. Katz I'd let you know. His wife MaryAnne lost her fight with breast cancer last night," she said. "It metastasized to her lungs and didn't respond to the chemotherapy."

So instead of going to New Mexico with Zach and Amber, I flew to Michigan to attend her funeral. Zach offered to go with me, but MaryAnne wasn't dead because of me, and I felt no remorse, only intense sadness because I'd lost such a dear friend.

"Not that I wouldn't appreciate the company, but I think it's more important for you to spend time with Amber," I told him. "I'll be okay."

"You know, you've been the foundation for so many people," he said, wrapping me up in his arms. "I just don't want you to think you have to do this alone. I'm here for you, too."

To me, just hearing his commitment was support enough.

He and Amber dropped me off in Portland at the airport then headed south.

This time, I caught a flight with tears in my eyes for a different reason.

MaryAnne's was one of the hardest funerals I'd attended in a long time, but then I hadn't attended services for a number of people who'd died in the recent past. When Amy and her mother were buried,

I went to support Zach, who was trying to make things as right as possible for Amber, but I knew it hurt him. Amy was dead because her killer had wanted him to pay for his choices – and Amber would have been another victim, had another young girl not been kidnapped by mistake. Keeping my thoughts hidden, I suspected Zach would have done anything to save Amber, had that been the situation.

✂

"How's the colt?" I asked, calling Zach at his mom's ranch from my Traverse City hotel three nights later. The day had been warm, breezy, and tearful, but I did not want to talk about funerals.

"Feisty as ever. He's grown a lot. When are you going to name him?"

"Me? How about you get him home first?"

"Home. That sounds like a wonderful place to be."

"Good," I said. "I'll see you there in a week."

"Before you hang up, can I ask you something?"

For Zach to ask if he could ask a question was out of character and boded bad news along some channel or another.

"Of course."

"In all these years, you've never told me anything about David," he said, hesitating – maybe to see if I immediately slammed the door on that discussion. "Will you?"

"I've never been able to keep secrets from you," I replied. "I don't talk about him because I don't have much to say."

"You married him," Zach challenged. "Surely in the time before he assaulted you, you felt something."

I leaned back into the overstuffed hotel pillow and considered the statement. Inhaling, ready to make a long explanation, I found it absent.

"We don't have to do it on the phone," he said, interrupting my thoughts. "I just wanted you to know I was curious enough to ask."

"Actually, I guess this call is a pretty good analogy of my relationship to David," I said. "It seemed real in one dimension, but really it lacked intimacy and emotion of being together. We met in class, and one thing led to the next until we'd been going out a year

137

and decided to get married. Being a couple was an answer to the social expectation that people our age settled down. I liked him, but looking back, I'm not sure there was more."

"Did he love you?"

"We cared about each other. I don't think either of us was in love."

"Okay," he said, sounding satisfied I'd answered his question.

"Letting the relationship with him go so far had more to do with rebounding from Jeremy than it did my feelings for David. Maybe even at that point, I only wanted to be wanted."

"Even five or six years later?" he asked, surprised.

"At first I didn't date when I got into the state police because I didn't want anyone to think I'd slept my way into a position. Once I transferred to Alamogordo, I spent almost as many hours in classes as I did working, so I didn't have time for a relationship initially."

"If I might make an observation," he said, "it sounds like you never gave this much thought while you were recovering."

Damn, he could be so blatantly honest.

"No, I didn't. All I could focus on while I was in the hospital was rage." I paused. "And after that, I didn't care about me, much less him. Then you came along."

In October 1996, I flew back to Michigan to sign papers finalizing the sale of my house to Olivia Palmeri, the lab technician who had been living across the street with her mother.

I'd introduced Olivia to Nolan Forrester after MaryAnne's funeral, because I wanted him to meet the woman who had helped us without even knowing how. Because of her eidetic memory, she remembered the license number of Bock's car, and we'd not only identified him but also saved my mother's life in Ruidoso.

Once the sale of my house came up for discussion, I wasn't sure that I didn't see a tiny spark between them then.

So four months later, I was happy to hear she was still seeing Nolan.

"Neither of us is ready to make a commitment yet," she told me as we each signed a stack of papers. "We keep discussing the age difference – it's almost twenty years. He's getting ready to retire, and I've got a toddler."

"Age is trumped by being happy together," I replied. "Follow your heart."

❈

That evening, I had dinner with Gerald Katz and the girls.

"I got a call from the Skamania County Sheriff about you a few days ago," Gerald said as we sat down to the table in a house that just felt emptier and less energetic without MaryAnne. "He'd like you to take a position there similar to what you did here."

"Fix his computers so they can play Solitaire?" I teased.

"And then some, I'm sure," he said, passing me a hefty dish of lasagna that Kimberly had made.

What a lovely young woman she had matured into, I thought. Aged by circumstances no teenager should ever have to face, but alive and vividly so.

"That sounds really awesome, Julie," she chimed in.

"I'm not sure I'm ready to go back to work yet." I scooped out the meaty lasagna and passed the dish on to Kayleigh. "I'm still recuperating."

Gerald served himself salad and passed the bowl to me. "Just do me a favor and give him a call when you get home. Doesn't pay much, but there's apparently not much call for solving murders there. Must be a rather peaceful change of pace. If you don't, maybe I'll take the job," he kidded.

Death had overwhelmed his life, just as it had mine.

Serving dishes settled to the table, and we all picked up forks for the first bite.

Kayleigh's voice cracked as she threw down her utensils and scrambled away from the table, screaming, "It's not like Mom's!"

I saw Gerald and Kim exchange looks, like this had happened before.

"How about I go talk to her?" I asked, which received enthusiastic nods from them both. I got up and followed Kayleigh down a hallway I was as familiar with as any home I've lived in, and yet the emptiness still touched me. The home was missing its mother as much as its occupants missed her.

Knocking quietly on the bedroom door, I heard her sobbing.

"Kayleigh, can I come in and talk to you?"

"Leave me alone! No one listens to me anyway."

"I'll listen, I promise."

The door opened, and I stepped inside where MaryAnne's thirteen-year-old daughter crashed into my arms and cried even harder.

I waited as she wept, her tears soaking into my shirt. My own, though not as abundant as hers, were wiped away on my shirtsleeve. I recognized the agony of holding back the sadness because it seemed no one listened. Truth was, after my father died, I figured out that no one really knew what to do to make it better.

She had something to say that she didn't think anyone else heard, and this was her chance to say it uninhibited. Having lost a parent, too, I'd had so many things I'd wanted to say aloud, but felt I wasn't supposed to put in words because they would upset someone else.

I coaxed her to the bed and let her cry herself out.

"Why did she have to die?" Kayleigh finally whimpered. "It's not fair!"

"No, Kayleigh, it's not fair. I don't know why it was your mother and not your best friend's mother, or my mother. People die. We try hard to fix their bodies, but sometimes we can't."

"She left us, and I hate her," she declared, "and I hate God."

"Your mother didn't want to leave you, and she fought very hard so she could stay with you for a few more years or even just months," I said. "It's okay to be angry, but are you sure it's really her you hate? Or do you hate the way it feels because she's gone?"

She sniffled and then shook her head. "My friend Mindy says it's a sin to hate God."

"I think God will understand right now."

"Daddy just acts like everything is fine now when it's not."

"Would you feel better if he broke down and cried every day, or if he was angry like you sometimes feel?"

She thought about it, then shook her head again.

"Kayleigh, don't be upset if he doesn't cry in front of you or that he doesn't look like he's upset or angry, because he is."

She shrugged her thin shoulders.

"Can you tell me why are you upset about dinner?" I asked.

"Kim keeps trying to fix stuff like Mom did, but it's never right. She's trying to do everything, to replace Mom like we didn't need her!"

"Think how hard it is for Kim to be the new cook for you and your father – she either fixes food like your mom made it, or tries something different. Either way, it's just not right to you, is it?" I asked. "But trying to do things that your mom did doesn't mean you and Kim and your dad didn't need your mother. But there's still cooking and laundry and vacuuming that has to be done."

"No one misses her enough." Plain truth. That's what she thought no one was hearing her say.

I pulled her back to me. "No one misses her the same way you do, Kayleigh – that's unique. Your father lost his best friend after twenty-five years together. Kim lost her mother, too. I lost a good friend, and I miss MaryAnne very much," I said. "But there is no such thing as missing someone the same. There is no 'enough' or 'too much.' Everyone feels loss differently, and it's not a contest to see who feels more pain or who feels better first or worse last."

"Sometimes I can't remember her right," she said, tears streaming over her lashes again. "I don't want to forget her." She held on to me, squeezing.

"You won't ever forget her. Until you have children, there's no one so close to your life – you came from her. There will be days long in the future when you'll think of her, and your heart will ache just like it does now, but you'll remember everything good, too. Including how her lasagna tasted. And maybe someday, yours will taste the same."

CHAPTER

22

Motherhood, I discovered, especially step-motherhood, sometimes reared and kicked like a wild stallion as the summer turned into fall that first year. While I didn't expect Amber to be a perfect teenager, her occasional hormonal outrages sometimes left me speechless.

Seemed benign enough to say, "Can you pick up your clothes so I can vacuum in your bedroom?" but this set off a bizarre verbal rebellion, attacking both my lack of a hereditary link to her and her right to live the way she wanted, even if that happened to be chaos. With a shrug, I simply left the appliance outside her door and walked away. At supper, she apologized, having cleaned up both the mess and vacuumed the floor.

"She'll get past it," Zach soothed me later as I described the dispute while we cleaned up the kitchen together. "This hasn't been the easiest year for her to face," he said, "even without adolescence."

"Yeah, but –" I started to argue, only to have fingertips touch my lips.

"Tell me that living around you the year your father died was something your mother enjoyed," he said with a raised eyebrow. When I shook my head, he nodded. "We have a little latitude here that will benefit us all in the end."

I didn't answer.

"Trust me. She'll grow out of it," he assured me.

When I turned away, I muttered under my breath, "In about seven years."

Zach wrapped his hand around my arm and turned me to him, face stern. "See? I was thinking more like twelve."

We laughed.

He pulled me close and held me, a near guarantee that Amber would pop around a corner and make some exasperated sound regarding our frequent displays of affection.

Maybe she didn't think I'd noticed that when she was out at the barn, Zach would cheer her on about a horsemanship achievement or thank her for helping him with some chore, often with a physical sign of his approval – a hug, a hearty pat on the back, or a high-five she had to jump to reach. And while she didn't always show him she liked it, I'd seen her turn from him and smile.

Even though the step-mother reputation was hard to live down some days, I could see that Amber's responses to me were for the most part positive, and often her extremely negative outbursts had more to do with things I did or said than with me personally, which I understood to be emotional reactions culminated by age, hormones and circumstances.

"She's still so angry about what happened to her mother," I told Zach as we whispered in bed one evening.

"Don't you think she deserves to be? The difference is," he replied, "she lets you see her anger, even when it's disguised as something else. But she never shows it to me. She believes you understand her feelings. You're neutral, at least to her. You have similar experiences, so you listen and empathize without being affected by her pain."

Wow, I hadn't realized that before.

"I wish this were easier," he continued, pulling me tighter against his warm body. "None of us came out of Pauly's attack unscathed. I'm hoping that getting her focused on the horses will give her a better outlet."

"What about you?" I asked. "You never talk about Oz or Domino."

Silence held a while, then he shook his head. "I think I understand now what you meant when you told me you couldn't talk about being raped. No matter how much it hurts, there are just no words."

❉

School started for Amber in the fall, but she'd made friends in our rural neighborhood during the previous spring and over the summer break.

When we shopped for school clothes, I noted that she'd stretched upward another couple of inches and leaned out a bit more. She found this growth spurt to be exciting news. Her goal was to be taller than me by the time she got her driver's license – four more inches in seventeen months, she informed me. I more than expected it would happen, considering her father was six and a half feet tall.

Knowing I'd have more free time once Amber was in school, I made an appointment to meet Skamania County Sheriff Wade Fordham, who had called in late summer to discuss a job proposition.

In his office the next morning, he shook my hand and waved me to a chair while we waited for the medical examiner to join us. "Given your experience, it just makes sense to invite him," Fordham said. "I don't think we've had a dozen murders in the eight years I've been sheriff, and most of those were domestic related."

"That's something to brag about," I concurred.

The sheriff's description of the county crimes was interrupted by a knock at his office door as the ME came in, introducing himself to me, then taking a seat.

"I was tickled when Wade called to say you were coming in to talk. We're thinking that you have a unique qualification for helping us," Dr. Boyd Bishop stated. "While the actual murder rate is pretty low, there are still other deaths I have to attend. My office serves Skamania County as well as bordering areas of Klickitat, Lewis and Yakima Counties best accessed by Skamania County, about two thousand square miles," he explained. "Most of the deaths I investigate are of natural causes from age, but in those few others, it would be nice if someone who has an eye for both crime and medicine evaluated them."

"Well, I do have priorities," I explained. "My husband's daughter lives with us now after her mother was kidnapped and murdered, and I might not always feel I can leave her alone yet when Zach is gone.

She's fourteen, but it's been a tough year."

"Mrs. Samualson," Dr. Boyd said, "if you only went to one call out of every five I have to take time out of my day or night to attend, my office manager would declare you a saint, as would my living patients."

Wade kicked in that the doctor's office manager was also Mrs. Bishop.

I pondered that. "Okay, but would I be a county employee, on contract, or what?" I asked, hoping to clarify whose office would own me.

They exchanged looks, and Dr. Bishop shrugged. "She'd have more authority as a deputy, and you could use a part-time hand, too," he offered. "I'll foot the salary if you'll cover benefits and training."

The deal was struck, but I felt like I'd been drafted into a professional sport somehow.

"Officially, I'm still on the payroll with the New Mexico State Police," I explained. "I need to terminate that."

Fordham's rise from his seat stopped midway. "You're what?"

Visions of a deal-breaker flashed before my eyes. "It's a long story," I said, hoping to avert disaster. "I started out with the NMSP in 1984, got injured, left on medical more or less, and went to Michigan where I worked in the medical examiner's office. When my husband got involved in a case in New Mexico, my previous supervising officer reinstated me into internal affairs." I showed him the badge and ID.

"What's that mean, Wade?" Dr. Bishop asked, one eyebrow up. Both of us were confused whether my background was a good thing or a bad thing

The sheriff smiled broadly. "That means I don't have to send her to the academy, which helps our budget a long way," he said. "Not that you're not worth it, but I can't imagine we could teach you much nor that it's an experience you want to relive."

I shook my head. No, I didn't want to run, wrestle, shoot, and sit in classes for weeks.

"You're hired," they said together.

✂

"Are you sure that's what you want to do?" Zach asked me that night while we got ready for bed.

I shrugged. "I feel useless not working, and I think I'm okay as far as the physical effort, especially since I don't have to go to the academy. This is just an on-call sort of thing, maybe a dozen shifts a month. I can refuse if I can't leave Amber when you're away."

"Yes, Julie. That's all very convenient," he said, solemn as a banker. "I asked you if that's what you *want* to do."

"For now, yes."

"Then congratulations. I get to sleep with the internal affairs officer one more night."

CHAPTER

23

A week later, I had new uniforms, ID card and badge, shiny polished boots, and a new pager and radio. Same old gun and holster.

"Great. Now I'm *really* going to be an outcast at school." Amber actually groaned at dinner. "Dad being with the DEA is bad enough, but a deputy, too?"

Coming from most any other teen, this would have been the worst kind of parental embarrassment possible. Despite her mood swings, Amber's smile indicated she was only joking.

Dropping the sarcastic tone, she informed us, "No one will dare mess with me now."

When Zach had registered her at school the previous spring, Amber took a brief tour of the facility. Waiting outside, standing beside his truck, he'd been talking to Carolyn Weaver, the principal. When the bell rang, a hundred noisy teenagers spilled out the doors to freedom for the day. According to Zach, silence spread so fast he thought his ears had popped. From the crowd, Amber had marched right up to him and turned to her new classmates with him as her defense, which earned her friendship of several people, including the sheriff's daughter Savannah Fordham, who suffered the same stigmata of a law enforcement family.

Amber's new friends had become an important part of her life, which I believed to be healthy. However, in a year or so, when it came to dating, I could imagine boys taking one look at her father before they turned and ran.

"Hey, Dad," Amber asked as she passed him the potatoes. "Can we go riding this evening?"

"Have you finished your chores and your homework?"

"I just have one chapter to read in biology, but I can do it before bed. Please?"

Trying to hide a smile, I knew Amber had shown no mercy when wrapping her father around her little finger. But she was good to her word that she'd only need an hour, and she'd have it done by bedtime.

Sometimes I wondered what alien species she really was, given horror stories of other teenagers with drugs and stuff. Other times, her human emotions echoed through the house as she screamed in bursts of temper just short of peeling paint from the walls.

I kept hoping Zach's promise that she'd grow out of it would happen soon.

✄

Christmas as a family was a first for both Zach and me. Somehow, not getting to start with a baby seemed odd. Still, it was a lot of fun, a pair of us shopping for the third person in secret.

Amber selected a new roping saddle for Zach, as well as new blankets for all the horses, and as always, more ammunition. I bought him a new four-horse trailer.

Amber picked out earrings for me, as well as a slow cooker and cookbook for days when I worked, though we all knew that Zach would use it most. He bought me a GPS unit, an expensive and unusual gadget, to say the least.

But the best surprise was the Trakehner-Quarter Horse gelding Amber'd ridden during the early summer before she went with Zach to bring our horses up from New Mexico. Zach and I bought him and another from the Clintons. Unable to tuck horses under the tree, this particular present to her was boxed as a pair of muck boots and a "go try them out in the barn" card.

I'm sure the neighbors a mile away heard Amber's squeals before she wrapped her arms around Rainier's neck for a photo.

Although he didn't give it to me when we opened all our gifts on Christmas morning, Zach also bought me a locket with an antique floral cameo – the sort of thing one doesn't wear every day. He had it wrapped in a box he brought to me in bed Christmas night.

"What a unique gift," I said, holding the locket into the light. "Where on earth did you find something like this?" Unusual and beautiful as it was, without a key, I couldn't get it open.

❈

As a deputy, I only covered two shifts a week, but when I was working, I often responded with the ambulance to lend a hand.

One such incident in mid-April of 1997 took me to the home of an elderly man who failed to answer his door for a grocery delivery.

"We've never been here before that I can remember," the older of the EMS duo said as we approached the house together.

Ringing the doorbell didn't elicit an answer, so we went around and peeked in the kitchen window. Mr. Sells lay on the floor between rooms. He waved his arm when I knocked. When we found the back door locked, too, I took out my Maglite and broke a pane of glass in the door to gain entry.

Finding William Sells was not difficult, but getting to him through the heaps of food piled on the floors was. EMS concentrated on getting him strapped to a backboard and out the door. I wandered around the three-bedroom house that had mounds of packages everywhere, some thigh-high on me.

Apparently Mr. Sells had fallen. Tripped, he explained to them, though that would have been anyone's guess. He'd been on the floor for three days with nothing to eat.

The EMT looked at me, not believing his ears – the patient had been in a mountain of potato chips and cookies and crackers. Not one package was open.

When asked, Mr. Sells produced his wallet from his flannel shirt pocket.

The medic opened it, looking for a Medicare card, and rolled his eyes.

Holding it away from his body as if it stunk, he said, "Deputy Samualson, would you please take this?"

I did, flipping it open and pulling out the folded contents, including checks from an investment company – nine of them totaling over forty thousand dollars. There was also a large amount of cash in every denomination and no order. The wallet did not contain any other emergency contact information, only a driver's license that had expired seven months ago and a Medicare card, which I gave to the medic.

"Mr. Sells, I'm going to take this down to the station and lock it up for safe keeping," I said, digging an envelope out of a jacket pocket.

"Just keep it," he said, sounding a bit drunk. "I don't have any use for it."

The response still took me by surprise, even if I wasn't sure he understood what I meant.

All three of us worked to carry Mr. Sells on a backboard over the food outside to the gurney. The medics got him loaded and ambulance left the scene, headed for the hospital.

Dispatch cleared another unit from a traffic stop, so I asked if he could rendezvous with me at this location. Ten minutes later, Deputy Mitchell Seaver parked his cruiser beside mine.

"What's up?" he asked as I walked over to his car.

"Ever been here before?"

Seaver took a look at the house. "I don't think so. You got a crime?"

"Probably." I scrunched my face. "But not the sort you're thinking." I waved for him to come with me to the back door.

From the porch, he peeked inside. "Wow, that's –" The sight left him without a proper description.

"Yeah, and then there's this," I said, showing him the evidence envelope with both the cash and checks fanned out to show the enormity of their worth. "Now that's a crime."

Whistling, he nodded. "So what do you want to do?"

"There's no next of kin listed in here," I said, holding up the bagged leather billfold that was probably older than either of us. "But maybe we can find something in the house. I just didn't think I should go back in there by myself."

Seaver nodded appreciatively at the paranoia.

"Also need to get someone to fix the window I broke out to get inside."

He made a radio request, while I stepped carefully through the door, avoiding the broken glass.

The house didn't stink like some places I've been. There was an odor of urine where Mr. Sells had been, but if he'd been down for three days, I thought, it could have smelled worse. The overwhelming smell was of sugar. Cookies – mostly the kind with two waffled layers and white filling in the middle, cheap store brand kinds, two for a buck.

In the kitchen, when Seaver joined me, we concluded that Sells probably never ate any of the stuff collected throughout the house. The trashcan was only partially full, but it had no packages from what he'd amassed. We found an empty half-gallon milk jug, a couple of unmarked window envelopes with nothing inside, and two empty soup cans that he'd thrown away. The refrigerator was almost empty, save more milk, unopened, and a few condiment packages like food service uses – mostly mustard. The freezer held three corndogs in a box, so at least the mustard made sense.

And I thought my kitchen used to be bare.

The shelves held a neat but dusty assortment of dishes and glasses. It appeared that he used only a few items – a mug, dinner plate, miscellaneous utensils, and a worn non-stick skillet and saucepan.

In the bathroom, I only found half a package of cheap toilet paper, a new bar of soap in the bathtub, and a couple of bottles of cleaners. The razor and shaving cream on the vanity shelf were dusty.

"Must have quit shaving months ago," I observed, mostly to myself. "He had a full beard."

"Here," Seaver called, and I stepped out of the bathroom. "Maybe this is what you're looking for." He held up an address book from a nightstand drawer.

I took the faded red leather book and flipped through the pages, which were mostly empty. "Sells," I said. "One listing with that name. I'll start there." The number was for Portland. I checked my cell phone and had good service, so I dialed.

Four rings, a message began. "You've reached Bob and Della's residence. We're not home right now, so at the tone, please leave –" A loud click. "Hello?"

The machine had answered the call first, followed by a real person.

"This is Deputy Samualson in Skamania County," I started. "I'm looking for Robert Sells?"

"Oh, yeah, sure," the female said, sounding both out of breath and disappointed. "Daddy, it's for you," she yelled.

Another click, and a male voice came on the line. "I got it. This is Bob."

I explained again who I was, and that I was looking for next of kin for William Sells in Carson.

"I'm his son," he said. "Is Dad okay?"

"The ambulance took him to the hospital. I don't know the full extent of what happened. He fell at home and couldn't get up. Three days ago." I looked around the house again, shaking my head in disbelief. "When was the last time you were here or saw him?"

"I don't know, several months ago. I called him at Thanksgiving, invited him to come be with us, but he wouldn't. I've been meaning to drive out there, but I've been busy," he said, already sounding like he regretted his decision.

"Mr. Sells, I think you need to meet me here at the house after you go check on him at the hospital. Things are probably much worse than you realize."

"Worse?"

I gave him the number for the dispatcher and asked him to call when he was ready to see the house, and he said he'd be over in a few hours.

Disconnecting, I shook my head again. "No way."

"What?" Seaver asked.

"Could this have all accumulated in a few months?" I asked, looking around for keys to the house and finding them on the kitchen counter, where I'd put them if they were mine, I thought.

Seaver looked around the living room, digging toward the bottom of the mound for a cookie package with a date. "This one isn't expired. Maybe," he said. "You got me."

I chuckled. "This stuff might not ever expire, given the sugar content. I can't believe the mice aren't fat and fearless."

Replacing the address book, I was about ready to leave when a soft knock came at the front door. "We should go around," I said. "But I guess we're done here."

Walking around the house from the back, I encountered a short woman of about sixty on the front porch. Again, introducing myself, I told her we'd left the front of the house locked.

"Is Mr. Sells okay?"

"He went to the hospital," I said, not revealing anything she didn't already know.

"I'm Beatrice Townsend, his neighbor. His wife Crystal and I were good friends before," she lowered her voice to a whisper, "before the cancer got her."

I nodded.

Seaver veered off toward his patrol car, and I waved goodbye.

"We've been worried about Bill. He gave up without her," she continued, bringing me into the rumors spread about him. "Last Halloween, when a group of kids went to his door, he scared them. Can you imagine?"

I shook my head, but I really could imagine.

"He refused to leave the house anymore. Wouldn't answer the door. It's as if he lost his will to live," she continued.

Or lost his mind, I thought.

Maybe he'd had a mental break and begun hoarding food, though the choices of chips and cookies confused me – a preparation for something in the future, not things he would eat to save himself. Perhaps it was just to fill the emptiness that his wife's death had left.

Someone had to be delivering this massive amount of junk food over the last few months if he wouldn't go out. Wouldn't it be obvious that something was wrong? I'd have to find out who had been bringing this stuff.

The glass man Seaver asked dispatch to send to fix the back window pulled a well-used van into the driveway.

I thanked Mrs. Townsend and excused myself to take him around, but I made note which house she went back to, in case I needed further answers.

Her information about the elderly man only added to my questions. The fact he fell beside a mound of food but had not eaten any of it in three days baffled me. That he carried thousands of dollars in undeposited checks and cash in his wallet and seemed unconcerned about the money made even less sense. Together, I worried that this would not turn out well.

CHAPTER

24

Bob Sells waited for me in the small lobby at the sheriff's department at six o'clock that evening. His paunchy build seemed a size too large for his frame, causing bulges in his worn sport coat and over his belt.

"I went to see my father at the hospital." He hung his head. "Now I'm afraid to see the house."

"His neighbor said your mother passed away about a year ago," I said. "I got the impression he took that very hard."

"You mean Crystal? She wasn't my mother," he corrected me. "My mother died in 1994, and Dad married her."

Bob said this very factually, not trying to hide the disapproval in his voice.

"I see."

His expression changed. "No, I doubt you really do. I have four siblings, and Crystal was younger than all of us. I'm the only one who'd speak to him after he married her."

"But you did?"

"Someone had to step in and make sure he didn't just sign over everything he owned to her," he said. "Even still, she cleaned out photos and antiques from the house, things that we kids wanted. Getting rid of junk, she said."

"I'm sorry, Mr. Sells. That must have been very difficult for you all," I said, trying to sound sincere. "If you're ready to see the house?"

"What's it look like? I mean, you were sort of cryptic on the phone."

What did it look like – a garbage dump.

"There are large mounds of packages throughout the house – cookies, crackers, chips. But there's no evidence that he'd opened any of them, even after he fell right beside the piles," I said, holding up my hand to show how high the food was stacked, which made Bob's eyes widen. "And we found both cash and unprocessed retirement checks in his wallet."

"Money?"

I nodded.

"I don't understand."

"Frankly, Mr. Sells, neither do I," I stated. "You should see."

I followed him over to his father's house and used the keys I'd found earlier to unlock the front door, then handed them to him.

Bob Sells stepped inside and stood, mouth slack, trying to take in the magnitude of what he saw and smelled.

"We were a little overwhelmed, too," I offered.

"Why would . . ." Words failed him, and he walked back out the door.

On the front porch, we stood, breathing fresh air.

"My father was a plumber," he said. "Not well-educated, he was still a smart man who liked his job and was good at it. Retirement didn't come easy for him, but he quit when Mom got sick. Stayed by her side throughout her cancer, fighting when she fought, and holding her hand when she gave up. Then he went back to work." With a weak smile, he said, "As old as this house is, he probably worked on the plumbing here a lot."

I nodded, following him inside into the kitchen.

"He began dating Crystal just a few months after Mom died – she was one of my mother's home health nurses."

An idea occurred to me. "Your mother died of cancer, and so did Crystal?"

"Yes."

"And he was a plumber," I repeated. "When was the house built, do you know?"

A shoulder barely lifted. "Sometime in the late forties, I'd guess."

"Did both women have a similar type of cancer?"

He shook his head. "Mom had lung cancer from smoking. Crystal had some sort of kidney cancer – that's what my father said, anyway. What are you getting at?"

"Paint in a house this old may have been made with lead," I said. "Lead itself isn't a direct cause of cancer, but it can be a contributing factor." The women's cancers were not the issue writhing in my head. I turned to face the house, thinking. "Perhaps your father was exposed to lead in his line of work and here. His behavior could have a neurological history."

"If he had lead poisoning, how did he outlive two wives?" He stole a look over his shoulder at the door.

"Just statistical bad luck that he met two women who developed cancer first."

Bob Sells shrugged, picking up a pottery coffee cup with the words "Favorite Grandpa" on the side. "What do I do for my father?"

Coming from me, the next two words sounded foreign, but I said them anyway. "Forgive him."

✂

"You mean food just piled all over the floor?" Zach asked when I elaborated why I was late getting home.

"Yeah, cheap stuff, like two-for-a-dollar cookies and such."

"No wonder I can never find any good junk food to eat around town," he teased, offering me a baby carrot. "Wanna go for a ride after supper?"

"Sounds good."

He called Amber down to eat, and she came bounding down the stairs to the kitchen.

"I talked to Mr. Clinton about the summer trail rides," she said, starting a new topic of conversation, "and he says I can be one of his guides."

School hadn't even been going for two months yet, and she was making plans for a job next summer. I wasn't sure if that was good news or bad.

This was one of those topics where Zach might seek my input later, but the permission loop did not include me directly.

157

"That's a lot of responsibility," Zach told her, passing me a bowl of salad. "Can you handle your horse and someone else's?"

"Yeah, sure. And there's a trip planned into the Menagerie Wilderness in July, he says. It's five days long and –"

Zach just held up his hand to stop the sales pitch. "I'll talk to Delbert tomorrow." He spooned me a serving of roast and potatoes from the pan.

Amber didn't pout, though her silence showed how much she disliked being stopped mid-sentence.

When the rest of the food had been passed around, Zach said a quick prayer before we started eating.

"I'm thinking about taking an undercover slot soon," he announced.

No doubt he timed that statement so that my mouth was full.

Amber's wasn't. "I think you should."

Zach and I both turned our heads to look at her, unsure if we heard correctly. Apparently Zach was prepared for an argument from both of us.

"You do?" he asked.

"Sure, then I could get my license to drive early because of Julie's job and –"

"No."

I forced myself not to giggle when he shut that idea down even quicker than the one about her getting a summer job.

"I think we could work something out if you were gone more," I said after I swallowed.

Zach took a bite of salad and nodded.

"When does it start?" I asked, hoping to continue a discussion before Amber found another great benefit of him going away for long periods.

He swallowed. "I don't have the details yet. I wanted to discuss it with you two first."

Zach had not worked undercover for almost a year – since transferring to the Portland unit. Instead he'd dealt with the move, my recuperation, and building a barn and a relationship with his teenage daughter.

I understood his need to do what he did so well, surprised he'd gone this long. On the other hand, I'd gotten used to having him around most of the time and didn't want him to be gone for work more than he already was.

CHAPTER

25

Early in May 1997, as the high snows started to melt, I responded as an medical examiner investigator to a body thought to be a hiker, on the north side of Skamania County, possibly even in Lewis County – the deputy hadn't been exactly sure, based on the directions he'd gotten from the ranger, now passed on to me.

Though the weather was clear and warm, I made sure my down jacket, gloves and fur-lined hat were in the truck, just to be cautious. High country weather could turn nasty in mere hours, regardless of the forecast.

I drove toward the southeast slope of Mt. St. Helens, making a mental note to ask Zach and Amber if they'd be interested in a weekend climb up before all the snow melted.

More than an hour later, I found the deputy's car in the parking lot and followed the trail half a mile before detouring along the marking flags deeper into the forest until I found Mitch Seaver and another man, standing twenty feet from a deflated-looking set of clothes.

Deputy Seaver introduced me to Drake Lawrence, from the National Forest Service.

"Been here a while," the deputy explained. "Not a lot of skin left."

"I see that. We may need to come back after the snow thaws and look around for more evidence. No sense digging now." I pulled the GPS Zach had given me from my coat pocket and logged the latitude and longitude coordinates for future reference. Then I pulled two plastic tent stakes from another pocket and stepped on them to bury them, one at each end of the body for a permanent marker to indicate how the body was oriented.

I snapped a couple of photographs of the area, then turned my attention to the remains.

The body was face down. Dark brownish shoulder-length hair tucked into the synthetic fabric of the light jacket. Blue denim jeans, with a wallet line on the right pocket suggested gender and age, but no wallet. Women and younger men would be less likely to carry a wallet long enough to cause fade marks. Heavy hiking boots, though they didn't look expensive.

"Any missing persons reports match what we can see?" I asked.

"No one has looked yet," Mitchell said, possibly insinuating that was my job, or the more obvious – *I've been here waiting for you, when would I check missing persons?*

Fair enough. "Just thought you might remember something," I said.

I pulled out a handful of purple nitrile gloves from a pocket to share with my living companions, then fished for a body bag in yet another coat pocket. Neither of the guys looked thrilled.

"You can help, or we can all stand out here for another couple of hours while I wait for Dr. Bishop," I suggested. "Recovery doesn't get much nicer than this – it's old, it's cold, so it's not likely to be smelly or buggy."

Lawrence nodded. Mitchell surrendered.

I spread out the bag, and we rolled the body over on to it.

As I'd suspected, there was no snow beneath, but the ground was damp as if there might have been at some recent time. Evidence of insects was visible on the bare earth below but not the sort to indicate decomposition. No plants, no obvious signs of criminal activity. I zipped up the bag, which Mitchell offered that they carry out to my vehicle, if I no longer needed them. I agreed and tossed him my keys. "There's a Thermos of coffee while you wait for me," I told them. "I'll be there shortly."

A polite way of saying, 'Please don't leave me here.'

They left, crunching through the snow, leaving me to the silence of the forest.

I walked around, gathered samples, and took more photos.

When a gust of wind rooted down my collar, I realized I'd been collecting dead bugs and prodding the dirt and snow around where the body had been found for nearly thirty minutes, without finding anything of interest. I pushed myself up from the cold ground, stretching before the hike back to the parking area, when something caught my eye.

I snapped a couple of photos before pulling out an evidence envelope to tease a twenty-dollar bill from the dirt at the base of a tree about ten feet from where the body had been. It was soiled and looked old. I slid it into the evidence envelope and sealed it, tucked it into my pocket.

Money, but no wallet.

No more currency caught my eye, so I headed to my truck.

The two men had put the body bag into the back and finished their coffee before I'd returned. I thanked them for their help and for waiting, then followed the patrol car down to the main highway before turning east on Highway 14 toward the hospital.

From the time I'd reached the site to the single table where Dr. Bishop performed autopsies at the hospital took more than four hours. The room was not a morgue, and remains could not be stored there, but he'd agreed to meet me before going home for the evening.

After a quick examination, we agreed that the victim was an adult male, though the time of death could have been anywhere from three weeks to three years, depending whether the body was in unmelted snowpack the whole time. My best guess was a few months, which would likely have to include a weather graph I'd put together.

I took the body to the morgue cooler before heading to the sheriff's office to log in the other evidence and drop off the photos for processing before going home.

Through the garage door, I entered the cabin to find a symphony of smells for supper, and my husband mastering them all like a conductor.

"Gotta have a shower," I said, undressing and tossing my clothes in the washer where I stood in the foyer.

He sniffed in my direction, wrinkled his nose and nodded. "Ten minutes, okay?"

I went upstairs, stopping by Amber's room to say hello, but she wasn't there.

The hot water felt wonderful, although I'm sure I spent more than my entire allotted ten minutes before crawling out and pulling on a sweatshirt. I was putting lotion on my legs when I heard Zach behind me.

He'd wanted me to know he was there so I didn't have a heart attack, intentionally making noise when entering the bedroom.

"Interesting case today?" he asked.

"Might be. Body in the national forest area toward Mt. St. Helens."

Nothing interesting about that, his expression said.

"We'll have to see about the identity, but I found a loose twenty nearby. An old one. And no wallet."

That earned a raised eyebrow. Money had always intrigued Zach. He knew things about a dollar bill and its intricate artwork that I couldn't even see.

"We'll find out. Starting tomorrow." I smiled and went to him for a kiss, which I'd foregone when I came in. I'd smelled, and I knew it.

Zach wrapped his arms around me and kissed me like he didn't have dinner waiting downstairs.

Like there was no one else in the house.

"Wow," I said.

He picked me up and laid me on the bed. "Amber's staying at the Prices' tonight with Kara," he explained, reaching under my sweatshirt to bare skin. "And dinner won't be ready for an hour yet."

"Oh my," I whispered. "So why did you only give me ten minutes for a shower?"

He grinned. "Because I didn't want to waste a moment of this."

CHAPTER
26

Despite the best that medicine could offer, including a transfer to Portland for hospital dialysis, William Sells – the man from the house full of cookies and chips – died nineteen days later of kidney failure. Because of the fall, he'd developed rhabdomyolysis, where the muscle tissue breaks down from injury and cellular starvation, leading to those larger protein molecules clogging up kidney filtration.

Bob Sells wrote me a note to say how much he appreciated those few days with his father. He knew that responders could easily have not bothered to look through the house for an address book until it was too late. In the end, forgiveness had made Bob feel better. I hope it had given something to William. I wondered if any of the other kids visited him before he died.

Meanwhile, identification of the body from the forest stalemated after repeated failure. No cause of death could be determined. We found no match to missing person reports in an expanding area, including the surrounding states. Blood type A-positive didn't help much. Lack of dental work or surgical implants shut down that avenue without any leads – it wasn't as if we could ask doctors and dentists across the country to give us identities of average males with no outstanding dental records. DNA would take about six months for such a low priority case, then it would be a fantasy to match it. The county didn't have funds to waste on rebuilding a face from the skull, but I imposed on a friend of Zach's from Albuquerque, begging a free basic sketch from a photo of the skull from a forensic artist.

Squinting just right, the resulting image sort of looked like the realtor I'd used in Michigan, except my house was sold by a woman. The pair of Jockey shorts on the remains had pretty much sealed the body's fate as male.

I even asked the Department of Treasury to examine the twenty-dollar bill found at the scene. Two months later, an agent told me it was legitimate currency, and it had never been part of a ransom. Not much help at all.

So the case gave way to other more pressing issues – not forgotten, just with no clear next step to take.

Dispatch called me in from home one July morning to meet with three officers from the Portland Bureau of Police, members of a task force following an illegal shipping ring that had come to their attention via a private investigator.

I was a little confused why anyone would want to talk to me since I worked only part-time and didn't think any of the cases I'd worked on would be of interest in Oregon.

Lieutenant Layne Sebastian stood and introduced himself and his two partners, Xavier and Vincent.

The sheriff in turn introduced me, and we all took our seats around a crowded conference table in a room so warm and humid the glass window began to fog.

"Sheriff Fordham," Sebastian began, "Thanks for meeting us on such short notice. We're running down leads about fake merchandise and guns, drugs and money. One of them brought us all the way out here."

He had my attention, but I didn't know how anything I could offer would help him.

"Millions of shipping containers a year from both national and international sources pass through Portland," Sebastian explained, in a calm voice that had probably told the story dozens of times. "There's no way to search them all, and the criminals know that. But in the last year, we've traced some illegal items coming into the shipyards and money going back to a Los Angeles port."

Wade nodded, as if he knew what was going on.

"Portland is a shipping destination for all sorts of counterfeit purses, shoes, t-shirts, wallets, you name it – knockoffs of expensive name-brand merchandise, pirated CDs and such. Although we care this stuff is coming in, it's what goes back out that concerns us more. We opened one outbound shipping container at the dock and found hundreds of automatic weapons, and millions of dollars in drugs and money."

I couldn't stop my question. "Why isn't the DEA involved?"

Sebastian smiled. "It is, and the FBI and ATF – all the alphabet agencies. And honestly, we can confiscate a container or a dozen, but they find another shipper or just make up a fake company name. We have undercover people working in LA and out at the docks in Portland."

"Had," Vincent corrected. The single word came out like vomit on the table.

"We had an undercover cop in place, working at the port. According to him, we should have been near an arrest point," Xavier continued. "But in February, he disappeared and all our surveillance hit a wall. No one's heard from him since."

"But that doesn't explain why you're here," Fordham said.

Looking at the two men accompanying Sebastian, I got the feeling they didn't know why they were so far from their investigation either.

"I heard about your John Doe through the grapevine," Sebastian explained. "Thought it would be worth a look at your findings off the record."

After they provided physical details of their detective, I excused myself from the room, squeezing out behind several chairs and going to my desk to retrieve a notebook. When I returned, I had everyone's attention.

"Detective Sebastian," I said, flipping open the book to the sketch. "Is this him?"

The guys from Portland traded looks. "It's not exact, but yeah, that's our guy."

"If he disappeared in February, that's within the window of estimated time of death," I stated. "He was found close to Mt. St. Helens on forestry land. No ID, no wallet, nothing."

"Shit," Vince muttered, looking away. The response said they'd been friends.

Not a good way to find out someone you know is dead.

"We didn't issue a missing person report because we didn't know for sure and didn't want to jeopardize his undercover identity if we were wrong," Sebastian said.

"I'm sorry. How can we help?" Wade asked.

"Can we talk to your coroner?" Xavier asked. "Find out what else was at the scene, try to identify who killed him?"

"Even better," Fordham said, standing up. "Julie's your gal. Everything you need, she has or can get. If you need anything else, I'll be in my office."

I looked at the three men at the table, their anxiety and expectation palpable. "He means I doubled as the deputy and the medical examiner investigator who investigated the case."

All three men had questions, and it was like fighting off a swarm of mosquitoes as I tried to answer them. I finally waved to make them all stop.

"No cause of death was determined because there was so little tissue left after three months. No slugs, no obvious damage – but he could have died of a dozen other things such as suffocation," I said. "However, I doubt that it was natural, given the setting and your history."

"Out," Sebastian told the other two. "Go find something to eat."

Vincent and Xavier exchanged looks again but did as they were told, leaving me face to face with their commanding officer, alone.

"Now," Sebastian said, leaning back in his folding chair and crossing his arms. "Tell me what you think."

"The body was face down, no identification –" I began.

"You told us the facts. I want to know what you think," he repeated

"If this is who you believe it to be," I tried again, "I think he was tortured, using electricity. Bones and teeth show cracks from pressure. More than a seizure would cause. Then I think they made him walk into the forest, because it was certainly too far to carry a body, and in his last dying moments, he pulled a twenty from his pocket and let it go."

"Wow, that's something." Sebastian studied me for a long moment before speaking again. "A twenty?"

167

I elaborated on the lack of information the currency had provided. "But still, if he had taken it from a container, he meant it to be evidence."

"I think so, too. My question is, who killed him and why?"

I smiled. "The bill had fragments of fingerprints," I offered, "but we had nothing to compare them to. I'd gladly give it to you if you think you can find a match."

Looking at something in his imagination over my left shoulder, Sebastian, a tall good-looking man with an expensive cut to his dark hair, said nothing while he thought.

"You don't know who you can trust, do you?" In my head, waiting for an answer, I began counting, *one, two, three, four . . . eight, nine.*

He finally shook his head. "No, I don't. But I trust you."

"You should meet my husband," I suggested. "He's had that same problem, not knowing who to trust, even on his own team. But I don't know what else our investigation could tell you without comparisons or context, so I'm stuck knowing how to help you."

"Have you ever worked undercover?" he asked.

CHAPTER

27

"Oh, no." I scrambled to my feet. The wooden chair screeched across the floor and tipped over backwards. "Not me."

"I need someone – a woman – to go to a party and make a buy, chat a little. We're hoping to track down a contact for whoever is bringing this stuff in and sending back out guns and money," Sebastian said. "It's not even illegal to buy the merchandise."

"Not going to happen." Fists planted on my hips in defiance.

Sebastian stood up, maybe to maintain that eye-to-eye connection, or maybe out of pure courtesy, but he said nothing else.

"No, Lieutenant. I can't stop guns and drugs and cash from moving," I said.

"Look, counterfeit bags and sunglasses don't sound all sexy and grand, but selling them in this area is providing money for gangs and possibly terrorists in Los Angeles and worldwide."

He'd set the hook, and he knew it. I could feel the fisherman feeding out line as I burned up energy to swim away, only to be reeled back in again.

"Does your wife know what you do for a living?" I asked, reaching to pull my chair upright and slumping down in it like a criminal.

"What I do is not a secret in my marriage," Sebastian said, not following. "But she's not in law enforcement, so I don't tell her every little detail."

"Zach is – he's DEA, and I don't keep secrets from him," I said.

"So if you want to sell this little idea, you'll have to get him to buy into it first."

On the back of a business card I pulled from my pocket, I scribbled directions to the house. "Five o'clock. We're having hamburgers, I'm told. You can bring the beer. And yes, that is a test." I slid the card across the table and walked away, leaving him in the conference room, making my way out the front of the building instead of the side door next to the sheriff's office.

When I got home, Zach was working Waldo on a lead in the round pen. Enjoying the sunshine, I walked over to watch.

"He's smart," Zach said, nodding toward the Friesian colt we'd named Waldquinte in keeping with the dam's musical name Julaquinte.

But Waldo fit him just fine.

"He's had smart people to teach him," I said. "Is Amber around?"

"No, she went over to Cody's Randall's house," he said, chuckling. "She's gonna teach him to rope."

"What's he teaching her in return?" I asked, raising an eyebrow.

Cody was a new acquaintance Amber had made recently.

Zach cued the horse to stop, left him standing there, and came to where I stood at the gate. "I'm not worried. He's a good kid who walked out here to introduce himself when he came to pick her up." He flashed a grin and his holster under a lambskin vest. "They're going to watch a movie later, too. No doubt he'll bring her back unkissed, and she'll be mad at me for it."

"What a father," I said, giving him a kiss. "By the way, we're having a guest for dinner. A detective out of Portland."

"I see." He lifted his cap and wiped the sweat from his brow with his arm. "Do I want to know ahead of time what he wants you to do?" Zach asked, able as ever to see right through me.

I shook my head. "Nah, I think you should make him tell you."

❊

From the deck, Laser lifted his head and barked twice when Layne Sebastian pulled up to the cabin.

I came from the backside of the house to meet him. "Welcome to

Five Aces, Lieutenant," I said with a grand gesture. "Land of stars and mountains."

Standing next to a dark green sedan with Oregon plates, Layne no longer wore a sport jacket or a tie. "Please, call me Layne," he said, turning around one more time. "This is fantastic." He ducked his head inside the car again and produced two six-packs. "You didn't say what kind of beer, so I guessed."

"That'll do." I took them and nodded for him to follow me around the back of the house and inside. "Zach will be back in a minute. He had to go turn off the water for the horses."

In fact, Zach had put Waldo back and gone in to shower and change before Layne arrived. He'd also made his spicy hamburger patty mix ahead of time so it could marinate, and then gone out to the paddock to fill the troughs.

"How'd you find a place like this?" Layne asked, following me into the kitchen where I put one six-pack in the fridge and the other in a cooler in the corner. "And why'd you do that?"

"Some beer is better when it's cool but not chilled," I said. "I had nothing to do with finding this place – it's all Zach's doing." I heard boots on the deck outside. "Speaking of..."

The door opened, and the two men introduced themselves and began talking law enforcement as if I wasn't even there.

Turning away from them, I smiled, knowing they were sharing a sizing-up ritual I was to neither join nor interrupt. Soon the ego-fluffing and testosterone storm died down enough for me to hand each man a bottle of beer.

One would think I'd materialized from thin air, the way the pair looked at me, quickly recovered, and took the respective drinks I offered.

"I was just saying to Julie how fantastic this place is," Layne stated, again making me a bystander in the conversation and not a participant. "No peace and quiet like this in Portland, even where I live out in the suburbs," he said, walking toward the French doors.

Zach motioned for Layne to go on out on the deck with him, where they continued the conversation about the place.

While that might have seemed out of character to leave me out, I knew Zach was trying to decide whether or not he could trust our guest, something he found more difficult to extend to a stranger after his experiences with Pauly.

A short while later, I smelled the grill as it heated, so I knew Zach had made it to the point Layne could eat with us. So far, so good, I thought. I waited about ten minutes, then took the hamburger patties out of the refrigerator and went about setting everything else up for the meal.

Before long, Zach came in, got two more bottles and the meat, winked at me, and went back outside.

When the burgers were ready, the buns toasted, the table outside set, and I'd grabbed myself a glass of wine, we all sat down and passed veggies and condiments to personalize what looked to be huge burgers.

Layne swallowed and nodded to the table. "Great burger, Zach."

My husband, master of all things caloric, only smiled and nodded as he chewed.

"Listen, you two do this telepathy thing well," Layne finally said, waving a finger back and forth between us, "but really, have I passed the test yet or should I keep trying?"

Zach looked at me, then back at Layne before speaking. "Well, I understand you have something you want Julie to do, and I think I'm supposed to evaluate that request and offer my opinion."

I again pretended not to be there as Layne explained to Zach the whole story about the shipping cargo containers and counterfeit merchandise being sold to buy guns and pay for other gang-related business.

"We're concerned the money going back is funding an international terrorism group," Layne said. "And one of our undercover officers is probably the John Doe found up on the mountain here a few months ago – his disappearance shut us down hard. We're trying to find out where this merchandise is being purchased and where it's going, and mostly who's responsible for what goes back."

Zach nodded, then took a bite.

My patience snapped. "He wants me to go undercover to buy merchandise," I blurted.

"I get that you don't want to do it, really, but it's just a buy,"

Layne said, putting down his burger. "Look, Keith Hill wasn't married, but his parents are still alive. They've asked a few times, and I've told them he was still working undercover. They accepted that. I can't keep lying to them now that I know he's dead, but I don't want everything he found in this investigation to die with him, either."

Both men inhaled deeply and stared at me.

"What?" I asked, uncomfortable at the silence.

Zach shrugged. "It's a legitimate request, but it's up to you, J'."

Layne leaned forward. "Please? It's designer bags and movies and shades, like a damned Tupperware party. Ask some questions, buy a few things on my budget – no cash out of your pocket and you can even keep the merchandise."

Like I need a designer knockoff handbag.

"I'm not certified as a law enforcement officer in Oregon," I argued.

"Exactly," Layne said. "You don't have to be. I just need someone whose information I can rely on, and we don't have a woman on the team," he said. "And I trust you."

Zach probably felt more like a referee than a host.

"It wouldn't be a real undercover assignment, just go and buy a couple of items, ask a few questions," Zach repeated to me, as if I hadn't understood this the first or second time Layne explained it. He held up his hand to stop my response and turned to Layne, "But if she says she doesn't want to do it, I'm okay with that."

Sebastian would have argued with me till the sun went down. No one argues with Zach. The pair stared across the table, waiting on me to speak

Finally, I nodded in agreement to do it. The discussion was over, and we went back to eating.

※

"It's a sales party," Layne told me two weeks later as we sat in the corner of a small coffee shop for a briefing. "Like kitchenware or candles."

"Never been to either one, Lieutenant," I replied. "Not my thing."

"Just go in, browse, coo a lot at the great buys, and spend the money." He slid an envelope across the table to me. "There's two grand. Knock yourself out."

Looked like we were doing something illegal, I thought, so I swiped the money into my purse – a *real* Gucci handbag, Layne had pointed out earlier as his technician threaded the wire in my clothes.

That completed, he nodded approval of my highly decorated appearance, including fake nails and styled hair that would indicate I had money. Real estate or banking, or maybe just married a rich man who indulged me.

That was all fine, but the heels were killing me, even just sitting for coffee.

"Tell me specifically what do you need to know," I said.

"We need to know how this woman gets her product – how does she order it, does someone deliver it, how does she pay for it? Tell her you'd like to host a party for all your friends. After you spend some money, she'll talk."

I rolled my eyes. "Of course she will."

"You'll do fine," Layne said, trying to encourage me. "And we'll be in the building, just in case."

"Just so you know, Sebastian, the only reason I'm helping is because you lost a man in this operation."

He laughed. "You'd hate my wife. She's whimsical, sees the world colored like a shimmering rainbow. You, my dear, are as black and white a human as I've ever met."

"And you?"

"Lost somewhere in the eternity between, where most men are," he said. "I don't have to understand her, just love her."

"Smart man if you've given up on understanding the other gender."

So I went to the sale. I arrived well past halfway through, as planned. The showroom was nothing more than a hotel room with inventory spread on the two beds, waiting for buyers.

I complimented the hostess on the selection of handbags and sunglasses, even resorting to an exclamative phrase or two. I acted like someone who lived to impress others with what I owned.

Heck, I'd even driven Zach's Mustang to Portland for this gig – how ditsy was that?

Once we were alone, Lavonna, the hostess, volunteered all sorts of information about how she was making fabulous money, buying these goods online for pennies and selling them at a great profit.

"It's not illegal for you to buy counterfeit merchandise," Layne had repeated for me. "She's selling it as the real thing, only deeply discounted."

And I kept trying to not blurt out what was really on my mind – no wonder there are knock-offs, because who would pay a thousand bucks for a purse? Only people with more dollars than sense, I supposed.

I bought merchandise – a large handbag for my sister who thought she had to carry everything, a small purse for my niece, and a wallet and sunglasses for my adorable husband.

I hoped that whoever was listening to the surveillance got stomach cramps over this phony charm because it was certainly nauseating me.

Not quite an hour's work to spend a cool thousand bucks and some change, and I was back at the coffee shop. In the women's restroom, I'd changed out of the clothes, the heels, emptied my belongings from the borrowed handbag into my own.

"Keep the stuff," Layne said when I came to his table and handed him a paper bag full of merchandise I'd bought or borrowed. "That was part of the deal."

"I don't want them, Layne. Really." I handed him the change from the envelope, too.

He wiggled one eyebrow. "Take the real bag to your daughter – tell her it's a fake and see how long before she figures it out."

"Funny man."

When Vince brought in the tape transcripts of the party, Layne's expression was sheer elation.

Seemed like a perfectly planned encounter.

On the other hand, given how undercover work had gone for me in the past, there was still a chance that someone would die.

CHAPTER
28

Two weeks later, the dispatcher transferred a call from a lab supervisor at a hospital in Portland.

"We received final lab results for William Sells," the woman told me. "Serum lead levels were far above the toxic level."

"I'm not surprised since he'd been a plumber all his life."

The voice replied with a sharp tone of impatience, "We tested his blood daily during his admission, and the lead level began to rise sharply a few days after he was admitted." There was a pause. "He could not have poisoned himself. The nurses say he could barely lift his cup for water. I've already reported this to the police."

The very thought that Mr. Sells had a large dose of lead while he was in the hospital left me speechless for several seconds while I replayed my conversation with his son as we'd stood looking at the upheaval in the house. *Perhaps your father was exposed to lead in his line of work and here. His behavior could have a neurological history.*

"The son, Bob," I said, finding my voice again. "He came out here to see his father because I called him, showed him the house where Mr. Sells had been hoarding food, for lack of a better description. I mentioned then to the son the possibility that his father might have been exposed to lead while he was a plumber, or even just living in that old house."

"I see," the supervisor stated with all the concern of a cat. "You can explain those details to a homicide detective. My job is done."

With no more to say apparently, she hung up, leaving me listening to a few clicks and then a dial tone.

Homicide? Because of something I said?

I replaced the receiver and sat back, my thoughts interrupted by the squeak of the chair.

No choice but to wait for a call from an investigator from Portland, I decided. Which took all of about fifteen minutes – I hadn't even left the station.

"Detective Greerson, homicide," another female voice on the phone said. "I'm calling about William Sells."

"I figured," I mumbled. "The lab supervisor contacted me a bit ago. How can I help?"

Greerson explained how Sells arrived at the Portland hospital with what appeared to be a chronic but low-level exposure to lead, probably occupational as I'd suspected. But then as the doctors drew blood daily, keeping tabs on the kidney failure, they began to see huge spikes in lead and cadmium levels.

"So you're thinking someone poisoned him intentionally?" I asked.

"Can you offer any other explanation?"

I thought for a moment. "The son who came out here picked up a coffee cup. Maybe he took it from the house and gave it to Mr. Sells in the hospital. Some pottery glazes, especially from Mexico, have high levels of metals like lead and cadmium. Fruit juice can leach these from the glaze in great quantities."

"I can look into that."

"If the siblings took any of other belongings, it would be difficult to tell." I explained to her about the mounds of food.

"People really do that?" Astonishment thinned her voice. "Unbelievable. I'll check on this end. If you can, see if you can find something out there."

"You're looking to determine how he died, Detective Greerson. I'd be concerned, not that someone poisoned him intentionally, but that a family member is using something that could be causing accidental lead poisoning, too."

"That," she said, "is complicated, but I'll look into it."

❈

About the same time Amber started to school, Zach went back to undercover duty with the DEA, assigned to a group running a sting in the Portland area – one I didn't need or want to know details about.

Amber was still looking for a way this might get her driver's license early, but so far, it was a bust.

Lieutenant Sebastian called me at the station one morning in August to let me know how things had turned out in the prior few weeks with the smuggling investigation and the death of his detective. "Big funeral for Keith Hill," he concluded. "We just made up a date for his death." He paused. "You don't think that's cruel, not telling his parents the whole truth, do you?"

He asked as if he'd really wanted an opinion, so I gave him mine.

"I think the fact that you brought their son home is what matters most. Probably only confirmed the truth he was dead that they'd suspected and feared for a while," I said. "Making the situation as normal as possible for them is a very kind thing to have done, Layne."

"Thanks. All your reports and evidence helped a lot," he said. "We're hoping to make a slew of arrests soon – all the agencies, including the DEA. I hear Zach will be involved."

"Then you'll probably see him before I do."

I heard what sounded like a doorbell on his end.

"Listen, I gotta run, but I just wanted to say thanks."

"No problem," I said. "Take care."

I hung up the receiver and turned my attention to a burglary report.

❈

The next evening, however, stretched out in my recliner, relaxing muscles stiff from sitting in a patrol car most of the day, I received a call from dispatch.

"I wouldn't just give him your number," Bette Donovan told me, "but I have a Detective Xavier Richardson from Portland who says he needs to talk to you about Lieutenant Sebastian?"

"Sure, Bette, put him through."

A series of clicks gave way to a different sound on the line. "This is Julie Samualson," I said.

"Deputy, I'm not sure if you remember me, but we . . ."

I interrupted him, for the sake of efficiency. "Yes, at the station, when we talked about the shipping crimes and Keith Hill."

"Yeah," he agreed and then paused. "Something happened here that you should know about. Because I think the LT needs someone outside the department he can trust."

I waited for what had to be bad news, given his introduction.

"A woman died yesterday morning on the tracks at the Portland train station. The Bureau sent a young officer to notify the husband or family, based on her driver's license address. But when the kid got to the house and saw Layne, he freaked out. The woman was the lieutenant's wife, Trinidee."

"That's horrible," I agreed, but held my ground. "What do you think I could do?"

"Can you call him, just so he knows there's someone neutral he can talk to?"

"Xavier, why do you think I'm that person."

"Adam Barnes – the cop who went to Sebastian's house – smart guy, logged the vehicles in the driveway when he arrived. When Barnes left, we were still thinking this was an accident."

Despite not answering my question, I don't like where this is going.

"The preliminary autopsy report showed that she'd ingested," he paused, reading his notes, "sodium monofluoroacetate, whatever that is. It was a lethal dose. If the train hadn't . . . well, either way, she was going to be dead."

I stifled the expletive response on my mind. The chemical he named was a potent poison used for killing animals such as mice and coyotes.

"Later in the day, a witness came forward, saying Mrs. Sebastian was talking to another woman near the tracks," he continued. "The problem came when Barnes got his shit together and ran the plates for the vehicles at the house – the one was Layne's, of course, but the other was a red Mercedes-Benz belonging to Jason and Sarah

Gelhaus." He paused a moment. "The car suggests that Layne was not alone."

Wow, I didn't see that coming at all, but I suspected that "not alone" meant something besides drinking coffee.

The Blue Rule. Domino Hurley had mentioned it once – that people who wear a uniform tend to not stay married, unfaithfulness being a major reason.

I hadn't thought of Layne Sebastian as one of those men.

Then again, I hadn't considered it at all.

"The woman Layne's wife was seen with at the train station matches a description of Sarah Gelhaus," he concluded.

This just gets deeper by the minute.

"What is it you think I can do, Xavier?" I repeated.

"I don't know, but he'll listen to you," he said with a helpless voice. "Honestly, I just don't want him to make it worse, making a wrong decision, but he won't talk to any of us."

After a few more minutes on the phone with him, I hung up, not knowing much more than Layne's wife might have been murdered by a woman who was probably at the Sebastian house two hours later.

Then I remembered that Layne had called me the previous morning, and he hung up when the doorbell rang. What time was that? Early, not long after shift change. Was *she* the one at the door? I wondered as the conversation played back in my head.

I called the number Layne had given me when we were discussing the fake merchandise party.

"Sebastian," he answered. There was no life in his voice at all.

"Layne, it's Julie Samualson," I said, giving him a chance to escape talking to me if that's what he wanted.

It took a while for him to answer. "I guess you heard."

"One of the guys called to tell me about your wife, yes. He's worried about you, Layne. I'm so sorry," I said, pausing. "Sounds like you still don't know who to trust."

He made a sound that could have been mistaken for a chuckle by itself, but what I heard sounded less like understatement and more like desperation.

"Can I help?" I asked.

"How do you help someone like me?"

"I can listen if you want to talk. It's a place to start."

We agreed to meet where we'd had coffee before I went shopping for purses and information. He didn't invite me to his house, and that seemed like a prudent decision on his part.

He is still thinking – that's a good thing.

I made sure Amber was okay for the evening, then I got in my truck and drove to Portland, wondering why – what I could accomplish, and whether I might be getting involved in something that was over my head.

Layne was already sitting inside the coffee shop, a full cup in front of him. I walked by and ordered tea, then took it back to where he sat, away from the counter and the door.

"Thanks for coming," he said, then hung his head.

"Look, Layne, we're not best friends, but maybe it will help to talk to someone who isn't involved in any part of this, someone who can be objective. That's why I'm here."

He looked up at me. Dark circles under his eyes made him look like he hadn't slept in a week. Didn't look like he'd shaved that morning, either. One decision short of giving up.

I recognize that look. I'd seen it in the mirror a few years ago.

CHAPTER
29

"When the officer came to tell me about Trinidee," Layne began, but his voice broke when he said her name. He took a breath before continuing. "There was another woman at the house. Her name's Sarah Gelhaus. She and her husband used to be our neighbors, but they moved across the river to Vancouver a couple of years ago. She and Trinidee are friends." He swallowed hard. "Were."

I didn't ask what his relationship with Mrs. Gelhaus was – we'd get to that eventually.

"Why was your wife at the train station?"

"I don't know," he said, frustrated, as if he'd been asked that a dozen times already, and probably he had. "Trinidee never gave me a schedule of her day, so that wasn't out of the ordinary. That she was apparently ticketed to Seattle was a surprise, but not because I didn't know. Her office said she didn't have business there."

"So why do the police think Sarah was at the train station?" I asked again.

"I understand that a witness said someone who looked like her had been talking to Trinidee just before –" The attempt he made at swallowing sounded dry this time.

I nodded for him to go on, not needing those details.

"Sarah wasn't at the station, but by giving her an alibi . . . " Layne trailed off.

Finally we came to his dilemma.

"Sarah and I were friends, too. We'd been," he paused, trying to pick the right words, "seeing each other for a year or so. Sometimes she'd come over after Trinidee left for work." He squeezed his eyes shut to block out what was in his head.

No reason to ask, but I had to wonder – which woman did he see himself with when he closed his eyes?

Finally, the memory let go of him and he went on. "She was a few years older, not as pretty as Trinidee. But it was her strength and maturity that I admired. I had more in common with Sarah than my wife did, and our friendship blossomed over the last few years."

"Go on," I said. "Tell me about her."

"Sarah wasn't afraid to laugh. But it was her understanding and compassion that finally brought us close," he stared at me, trying to assess whether I was about to crucify him with his own words. "I didn't love my wife any less, but Sarah filled an empty hole in my heart and mind that Trinidee never wanted to see – the emotional side of being a cop. My wife expected me to be tough and in control of my feelings all the time."

He stopped talking when a couple came in the door of the coffee shop, turning further away from them as they walked by.

From his reaction, I couldn't tell if maybe he knew them or just felt guilty, but I waited, sipping tea.

Lowering his voice, he continued. "For weeks after I shot a teenager in Waterfront Park, I was a wreck, but Trinidee wouldn't discuss it – she refused to acknowledge how it affected me. She just said it would get better with time. I didn't want to wait – I had doubts and guilt I needed to vent, but I was really very alone," he said. "And then during the second week, Sarah dropped by to invite us to supper that night at their place – this was when they still lived next door. Without a word, she read the emotions on my face. She just came in and sat me down like a child on the couch, holding my hand until I broke, then she held me while I cried."

He'd needed someone who could accept how he felt, and I recalled Zach calling me one night in just such a desperate moment from Florida.

"Trinidee couldn't make the dinner date, so I didn't see Sarah again for a week, but she called one morning and asked if I'd like to have brunch, to see how I was doing. At the restaurant, we just looked at each other, and I knew. Nothing happened that day, but everything had changed." Layne's eyes met mine. "I know it wasn't right, and it was selfish and stupid, but I needed to feel whole. With her arms wrapped around me, I felt like a whole person again."

"Layne, I understand, and I know how dark and alone it can be without someone who can do that," I told him. "It's not my place to judge what you've done. I just want you to be able to make a rational decision what to do next."

"Screw rational – I don't know what to do at all, right or wrong. Even though I want to make this better for Sarah, it's not going to end up like I wanted."

Back to his dilemma.

"Bottom line – which is worse?" I asked. "Letting everyone find out she was in your bed when your wife was killed, or letting her be charged with Trinidee's murder and then everyone finding out you were sleeping with her?" I asked. It was a ruthless but simple question, followed by another. "Who are you trying to protect most – her or yourself?"

He winced, then nodded. "What about Trinidee's father? He's going to tear me to pieces for what I've done to his only girl."

"You really want my advice for that?" I asked. "Take it like a man. It won't be any better if you try to hide it or make light of it – not to him. You knew the price you'd have to pay – you only hoped you'd never get caught."

"Ouch." He tried to find a smile. "Yep, you're just black and white, aren't you, Julie."

"More or less." I shrugged.

"I envy Zach that." He wiped the tears that puddled in his eyes.

Maybe it's not so much that he envies Zach that I'm so cut and dried, but that I'm simply alive.

"Zach would say the same thing to you that I did," I said, taking a sip of tea that tasted like weeds dipped in warm water. "My advice is to save her. The people who find out Sarah was with you will find out one way or another. Some are going to condemn you, and some won't care. In the end, some will know you revealed an ugly secret to protect her."

He nodded just as his cell phone rang. All he said when he

answered was, "Yeah," then held it away from his ear.

I could hear a woman screaming from across the table.

"Calm down," he tried to say several times. "No, I'm not at the house. I'm –"

Before I could even ask, Layne was on his feet and heading toward the door, still trying to break into the panicked screams on the other end of the phone.

Never occurred to me not to follow him, even after he got in his truck, and I trailed him in mine. I wondered if I should call the police, but I didn't know where we were going, even if it was his house.

The ride wasn't long, ending when Layne skidded into a driveway on a cul-de-sac beside a red Mercedes Benz. I parked at the curb.

He reached the front porch before I did, wrapping his arms around a woman still wailing unintelligible words and pounding on the door. I took his keys from him and managed to get the pair inside, away from prying eyes of anyone who might have seen her standing there in hysteria.

I turned on the lights as he led her to the sofa, where she sobbed against his chest until he lifted her away gently to look at her.

"Sarah, what happened?" he asked, shocked at the blood from her lip, the bruising and scrapes on her face.

In the distance, tires squealed on pavement, sending her into another panic, screaming that Jason had followed her.

"You're safe here, I promise. No one is going to hurt you," Layne said, trying to hold her upright to take a better look – little more than raw nerves, chest heaving, and tears streaming down her cheeks. "Sarah, hon? Look at me, what happened?" he asked softly, lifting her chin. "Did Jason do this?"

She only nodded but pulled an envelope from a pocket and handed it to him.

He carefully pulled opened the flap and slid the contents out far enough to identify them. "Oh, God," he whispered. "Stay there. I'll be right back." He stood, taking in her disheveled appearance again, and it shook him, like a blow to the chest.

Going to the phone, he punched in a number and waited. "It's Layne Sebastian. You need to get to my house now," he said, then hung up. "Okay, Julie, now what?"

I shrugged, having taken a seat on a kitchen barstool.

Sarah, hearing that she and Layne were not alone, whipped around to see me.

I introduced myself, standing to extend a hand that Sarah did not take. I wasn't surprised.

"Julie's a deputy from Washington," Layne elaborated. "She was trying to help me figure out what to do next."

A dozen questions crossed her face, but she didn't bother to verbalize any of them. I guessed a few would tarnish my reputation, though she was wrong. But it wasn't a good time to debate the issue.

Layne went to the freezer and got a cold pack for her, walking back to where she sat. "Where did you get those photos? It might have something to do with who murdered Trinidee."

"You mean someone killed her?" Her eyes cut from Layne to me and back before she took the cold pack from him and put it against her face in a delicate motion. "Jason slammed that envelope down on the counter before he started hitting me and throwing things. I didn't even know what was inside, but when I got the chance, I grabbed it and ran."

"You did the right thing, Sarah," I said.

"I need to get cleaned up," she said to neither of us in particular.

While Layne nodded, I objected. "Let's get some photos first."

They both looked at me like I'd sprouted horns.

"Evidence photos," I stated again. "You need to make sure that whoever did this can never do it again."

At different times, they each nodded. I went to my truck for an evidence kit and camera, there for just such an odd emergency.

Inside, I took Sarah to a back bedroom and snapped a dozen photos, without having her remove any of her clothes. "I don't want to interfere with someone else's chain of custody, but if needed, I can testify and prove your injuries existed when we arrived."

"Were you with Layne?" she asked, trying to be polite, but there was thick innuendo in the word *with*.

"We were at a coffee shop," I said, "talking about what had happened to Trinidee, and how Layne could protect you."

"Protect me?" she echoed.

I nodded. "Apparently a witness described someone who looked like you, speaking to Trinidee just before she was killed."

"Me?" she repeated, an octave higher.

I heard the doorbell, then Layne talking to someone – whoever he'd called, I assumed, had arrived.

Their conversation continued, and I didn't mean to listen in, but the voices were loud enough to carry through the house.

I came out into the kitchen to where the pair stood, looking at what was on the counter.

Adam looked up when he heard me and discreetly reached for his gun in a motion I recognized. Very in tune with his surroundings, always on alert. Although he wasn't in uniform, the upright posture that appeared casual to most was not – he was not a man who would stick his hands in his pockets, even when he relaxed. Maybe he'd been SWAT at some time in his past.

"It's okay," Layne said, putting his hand on the younger man's arm, "Adam Barnes, PBP, this is Deputy Julie Samualson from Washington."

The same innuendo Sarah had shown crossed the younger detective's face – was I another of a string of women in Sebastian's past? But he nodded, shook hands with me before turning back to the photos on the counter. "Looks like you got caught more than once, Lieutenant. The question is, who took these and why?" He took out his phone to call someone else. When he finished, he explained to Layne. "Chris Bell – we'll need evidence bags and some better ideas."

A name I recognized, Chris Bell had worked on some of Portland's most publicized cases, and he had a talent for finding the invisible threads that held crimes together.

We waited for him to arrive, saying little, avoiding the photographs.

Bell arrived half an hour later, his mussed hair and slightly wrinkled shirt indicating either an intimate evening or a long stakeout had been interrupted.

"Looks like someone intentionally wants Sarah to take the blame," I said.

"It's the only thing that makes sense, if she was with Layne. With traffic cams, we might be able to track her car across the bridge from

Vancouver out here instead of downtown," Bell said. "But the question then becomes who – who would benefit?"

"Someone who would gain from Sarah going away for this crime," I said. "If her husband had copies of those photos, maybe he's most interested in seeing her in prison."

"Jason is a physician," Sarah told us. "He runs a stand-alone family practice clinic."

The three men nodded in agreement that it seemed reasonable but not definitive.

Plans began taking shape. We agreed that Sarah would follow me back to Vancouver to the hospital to be evaluated and treated for the injuries from her assault. Once a report was filed in Washington, her husband would be located and arrested by Clark County deputies.

Their plan sounded like a good start to me, so we left the men deep in a discussion of their next steps.

After Sarah registered as a patient, a nurse called her into an treatment room. To my surprise, Sarah asked if I'd accompany her. She was examined, taken to x-ray to see if she'd suffered any broken ribs, and brought back to her room. The doctor delivered the good news that nothing was fractured. He gave her a prescription for a mild pain reliever and discharged her. We waited in silence in a small room until a Clark County deputy came to complete the assault report.

He arrived and asked a hundred questions, but Sarah stuck on just one. "You'll go arrest him so I'll be safe, right?"

When he was finally done, we walked out into night to my truck. "We should leave your car here," I said, reiterating Bell's instructions. "Is that okay?"

She nodded.

"Come on, we'll know when Jason's in custody." For lack of any safer place, she agreed to go with me back to my house. "I promise, he'll never find you out there."

During the ride, Sarah sat looking out the window, an occasional tear sliding down her cheek. She jumped when my cell phone rang.

"Here's a break we could use," Chris Bell's voice said, though a little muffled. "The clinic here in Portland is owned jointly by both Jason and Sarah. With her permission to search it, we won't need a warrant. Same with the house for Clark County in Vancouver."

"That's good news. Hang on a second," I said, handing the phone to Sarah. "It's Bell."

He repeated his discovery and its implications to her in greater detail, and the request for her permission.

"Absolutely," she said. "I even have keys."

"Can you come let us in?" he asked. "We'll coordinate this with Jason's arrest and detainment in Washington."

She looked at me for approval. I nodded, and she passed on the word to him.

At the next crossover, I turned around on Highway 14 and crossed the Glenn Jackson Bridge to the address she gave me for the office.

"I'm curious," I said, "if the practice remained in Oregon, why would you move to Washington?"

"Jason had this complicated idea about paying less in taxes this way," she said, then looked down. "But I think the main reason was to get me away from the Sebastians. He was afraid I'd become more like Trinidee – want a job, to travel."

"Do you think he knew about you and Layne?" I asked.

She shook her head adamantly then hung her head.

"I'll tell you the same thing I told him – it's not my place to disapprove or judge either of you. My goal is for you to be safe and to not be charged with a crime if you did not commit it."

"There's no way I could have killed Trinidee. She was my best friend and –"

I turned to look at her in the dark. "But you see? Being her friend and sleeping with her husband sets you up perfectly for her murder, no matter what really happened. Somebody wanted you to take the fall for this. We need to find out who."

There were several patrol cars and other unmarked vehicles in front of the office where Sarah directed me. When I pulled in, Chris Bell came over to my side of the vehicle, and I rolled down the window.

"Ladies," he said as a form of greeting.

Sarah handed me a ring of keys from her handbag, and I gave them to Bell.

"I convinced a Clark County captain of Sarah's possible

involvement in the murder of a police officer's wife," Bell stated, holding his hand up to silence her argument. "Since Jason was not arrested for anything related to the murder, your consent to search the home and office in your own defense as a suspect for this particular crime is legal. Then because there will be no limitations of a search warrant, any other signs of criminal activity can be gathered, including the assault."

"And Jason?" she asked.

"If he's arrested at the house, the search is about the assault. But, if officers pick him up elsewhere, they can search the residence under the same premise as we are, that you give permission based on the accusation of Mrs. Sebastian's murder," Bell explained. "That's why we needed their cooperation – they will let him leave the house before arresting him. Based on what you told us, when our detectives search the house, we can then document the domestic assault as part of this investigation."

"We're going out to my place in Skamania County," I told him, "for her protection. Let me know after sunrise what you find in the office. We'll come back later in the morning."

He handed me a card. "Meet my contact at this convenience store back across the river, so she can sign a consent for the house search."

I backed out and returned to Vancouver where we met another patrolman. After Sarah signed a few papers, we headed east on Highway 14.

"Why are you being so nice to me?" Sarah finally asked.

Shaking my head at the silliness of the question, I responded, "There is no reason not to be nice to you. I'm helping Layne, by keeping you safe and more or less in custody, but I wouldn't do any of that if I didn't want to help."

"Even after. . ."

"What went on between you and Layne Sebastian was not one-sided. From what he told me before you called, he really needed someone who could listen to him and forgive him for doing his job, and you did," I said. "I know how much that can mean."

"Thanks for listening to him, and to me."

"Let's just get some sleep. Things will look different in daylight."

At the cabin, I parked in the drive and took Sarah through the front door so I wouldn't wake Amber when I opened the garage.

In the laundry room, I found a pair of sweat pants and a t-shirt for Sarah to sleep in, and a couple of blankets to use on the couch. She assured me sleeping on the sofa beat wasting time making a bed for just a few hours of sleep.

She went to the downstairs bathroom to change.

I trudged up the steps to our bedroom and peeled off clothes that, while comfortable enough, had seen a rough evening. In a camisole and flannel shorts, I crawled between cool sheets and closed my eyes, letting my mind throttle down into a dreamless sleep.

Until I heard the screams downstairs.

CHAPTER

30

Grabbing my duty gun from the bedside table as my feet hit the floor, I darted out the door and through the hall, whirling to the steps in time to see Amber's sleepy face peek from her room. I motioned for her to stay put and scrambled on down the staircase.

The screaming had stopped, which was more terrifying than when it filled the darkness. Dread congealed in my stomach as I thought about having left Sarah downstairs alone – I should have put her upstairs so I could protect her.

Two silhouettes danced in the shadows in the living room, trying to get away from each other.

I snapped on the light. "Zach?"

"Julie?" he blurted, whipping his head from one to the other, a woman on either side of him. "Who are you?"

Sarah pulled the blanket up higher under her chin, looking like a four-year-old woken from a nightmare.

"Crap," I muttered, putting the gun down. "What happened?"

"He came in and tried to –" she began.

"Yeah, I did," Zach interrupted at the top of his lungs and his vocal range. "I thought she was you!"

They both started yelling again and pointing fingers until I whistled and motioned for a time-out, hoping I didn't have to go stand between them to make the accusations stop.

"Sarah, meet my husband Zach Samualson," I said, feeling the tension melt out of my shoulders. "Zach, this is Sarah Gelhaus, who's kinda in the middle of a murder investigation that I don't think I have the energy to explain right now." I collapsed into the chair, hoping my heart rate would drop soon.

The pair studied one another for a moment, then shook hands and apologized for their respective reactions.

It was light enough outside to see shapes, which meant I'd been asleep maybe two hours.

Amber padded down the stairs to see what the commotion was all about, and I nodded for Zach to explain that he'd come home for the weekend and found a woman he intended to nuzzle and coerce upstairs to bed while everything was quiet.

"Wrong woman," Amber deduced. "And not quiet." She put her hands on her hips as if we were all idiots.

"I could fix us all breakfast," Zach offered, trying to make peace.

Three females shook their heads and headed back to their respective beds, leaving him standing alone in the middle of the room, probably wondering what he said wrong.

He didn't dally long before he followed me up to our bedroom, took a quick shower and climbed in beside me.

"So you're really letting a murder suspect sleep on our couch?" he asked, cuddling behind me. "That's novel. If you didn't want me to go to work, you could have just said so."

I smiled because it was hard to stay mad at him, especially when he was naked and snuggled up to me. "Remember Layne Sebastian?" I asked and felt him nod. "Layne's wife was murdered at the train station in Portland, and a witness identified someone looking like Sarah talking to her before she died. But Sarah had an alibi – she was in bed with Layne."

"Okay," Zach said in a drawn out manner, indicating he needed time to put everything I'd said into neat columns. "And the bruises?"

"I don't think Sarah's husband was happy when he got photos of the aforementioned alibi," I said, letting him draw his own conclusion to that.

"Have I told you lately how much I love you?" he asked, settling down in his pillow. In just seconds, his breathing changed, and I knew he was asleep.

✂

Several hours later, I left him sprawled under the covers and went downstairs.

Sarah was sitting in the recliner, legs curled up beneath her, blanked wrapped around her shoulders. "Sorry about the drama earlier."

I laughed. "I didn't know he was coming home. If he snuck up on me like that, he'd risk getting shot."

"We scared the daylights out of each other. I didn't think I was sleeping so hard, but I never heard him come in."

"If he was trying to be quiet, you wouldn't have heard him – Zach can move like a ghost when he wants to," I said. "How about some coffee?"

She followed me to the kitchen and took a seat at the breakfast bar while I went about a morning routine. While the coffee dripped, I was pondering breakfast when the dog trotted into the kitchen.

"Laser, where were you last night when everyone was awake?" I asked, stopping to add water to his bowl.

"Sleeping in the garage," a sleepy male voice answered, then yawned loudly. Zach came around the corner, convincing Sarah how noiseless he really was, even when he wasn't trying. He grabbed a mug and poured himself some coffee even though the water hadn't finished filling the carafe. "So, again, I do apologize for last night," he said to us both. "I guess next time I'll have to make a full identification before I –"

I interrupted him, unsure what his verb of choice was about to be. "How about you make us breakfast now?"

My reply was a raised eyebrow. "Horses first," he said, leaning to kiss my cheek. He turned and began chatting with the dog as they both went out the back door, headed to the barn.

"Wow, he really is that tall, isn't he?" Sarah shook her head.

Nodding, I poured us each a cup after the coffeemaker made its last sputters.

"I remember being that in love with Jason, once upon a time," she said, stirring a spoonful of sugar into hers. "We haven't been in years. It was just convenient to stay together, I guess."

I managed not to be rude enough to ask how convenient it had been to take Layne Sebastian to bed instead. "Had Jason ever been violent like last night before?"

She shook her head, but I wasn't sure if I could believe her answer.

"Julie?" a voice called from up above, more through the floor than down the stairs. "I can't find my riding pants."

I rolled my eyes. "Did you check the dryer?"

"Yeah."

"How about your bag?"

Silence.

Which meant I'd guessed correctly.

"Nothing like being psychic to a teenager," I said, lifting my cup in a mock salute.

"We didn't have kids," Sarah said, looking down into coffee. "I always thought I was supposed to be a mom. You know, soccer, ballet, cheerleading, band. A whole van-load of kids."

"And I never thought about it seriously," I replied with a shrug, evading the fact I'd lost our baby to a bullet. "Amber is Zach's biological daughter, but he didn't know about her until after we got married, when her mother had been kidnapped and was murdered. That's how maternity found me."

"That explains why she calls you by your first name."

I nodded. "It's not an ugly situation between us, but we both know I'm not her mother – no sense expecting her to call me that, which is okay. Amber's a good kid."

The phone rang, and Amber yelled that she'd get it. There was no question about that – I wouldn't even reach for it till the third ring.

"Teenage answering machine," I explained, "complete with announcements before and after the call is answered. So you didn't have children, anything else that you thought you were destined to do and didn't?"

A tilted head told me she was really thinking about the question, not just making morning conversation. "We didn't travel. Didn't have fun or relax, like lounging on a beach, dancing in the rain. Jason never just laughed."

"So here's some advice: Go do those things now," I said. "He kept you from enjoying your life, and you don't need him to have fun. As soon as they cut you loose from this wreck of an investigation, fly to Acapulco, bake in the sun, ride horseback on the beach, flirt with a masseuse."

"Yeah, if I don't end up in prison for a murder I didn't commit," she said.

I can relate to that in ways I don't ever want to explain again.

Amber came bouncing down the steps into the kitchen, where she grabbed a banana and then introduced herself to our guest with a handshake before grabbing something from the refrigerator and blasting out the back door.

In the distance, I could hear her asking Zach to take her somewhere. He peeked his head in the door and announced he'd be back in twenty minutes if I wanted to start breakfast.

I smiled as he disappeared again.

"What?" Sarah asked.

"Zach never relinquishes his kitchen to me unless he has a good reason. It's not that he minds me cooking, but our deal is that whoever doesn't cook has to clean up. He thinks I make a mess." I ambled to the cabinet nearest the stove.

"Coffee is about all I ever have in the morning," she said.

Retrieving two large skillets, I said, "Yes, but I'd bet that you didn't eat anything for supper, either, did you?"

She shook her head.

"I probably know as much about being in the situation you're in right now as anyone you'll ever meet, Sarah. I was accused of killing a deputy, and it went as far as a preliminary hearing before the case was dismissed," I said, stopping to look at her. "And I freely admit that I did kill him, which is very different, but I did it in order to save a girl's life."

"Amber's?"

"No, someone else," I said, thinking how many people had died because of me, then shaking the idea from my head.

"You're different than my friends, Julie," she said. "We began as neighbors to the Sebastians, so it was just a social expectation to like Trinidee. She was often lost in her own profession, much like Jason in

196

his medicine. In fact, he was better at holding a conversation with her than with me. Most of the time, I just went along with whatever she was babbling about, pretending to be interested, but I liked her, too."

"People stay together for a lot of reasons after they grow apart—what was yours?" I asked, taking nine eggs from a carton, breaking each into a cup before pouring it into a bowl.

"I was the trophy wife," she said, extending her arms for a pretend examination. "Maybe it's not so great now, but I sure didn't look this way to start with, either. Jason made me into someone to parade around to conferences and office parties, I think. He spent lots of money changing my appearance from plain to his idea of fantastic."

I shook my head. "I don't see that in you." From the refrigerator, I pulled two thick slices of ham, a Poblano pepper, green onions, and a bottle of buttermilk dressing to add to my ingredients.

She chuckled. "You can't change the fact that manure stinks, no matter how you alter its appearance. I suspect that's the other reason he moved me to Vancouver after I turned thirty, so fewer people he worked with would see me."

"There's nothing wrong with how you look or act, as far as I can tell," I said, washing and then shaking water off the pepper and green onions. On a cutting board, I began chopping them up and dumping them into the egg mixture. "As much as today is not where you wanted your marriage or your life to go, I think I hear you saying you're ready to walk away and to be happy as who you really are."

She shrugged. "More or less. But I didn't want Trinidee to die to get what I wanted."

CHAPTER

31

After we'd devoured the breakfast that Zach finished cooking for me, I drove Sarah back to her home for some clean clothes, then to a hotel to wait out the rest of the investigation.

Once she was settled, I left and called Layne Sebastian.

"I don't know what's happening with the investigation," he said, his voice dull and flat, not hiding his grief. "Funeral plans today, and Trinidee's father got to town this morning, so I need to talk to him."

Confess, he meant. Probably nothing in the world Layne had ever done would be as hard as facing his wife's father, with no way to hide his affair.

"Like last night, if you need something, all you need to do is ask," I said. "Otherwise, I don't want to intrude, so you won't hear from me."

Layne didn't need another woman showing up right now.

"Thanks," he said. "For helping. For listening."

We said goodbye and disconnected.

I called Chris Bell.

"The search of the physician's office by the Portland team netted us evidence I think will clear Sarah," he said. "But untwisting it in our favor is taking some time." He explained that they had found a message book on the receptionist's desk, showing five calls from Grady Reeves the day before the murder, and two that afternoon. "Coincidentally, Reeves is the witness from the train station," Bell said with deliberate emphasis.

"Ah, very interesting," I said.

"In the locked cabinet behind Gelhaus' desk, we also discovered several unmarked bottles of pills, and one of a fine white powder that tested positive for cocaine. Tucked into a brown envelope next to these was a pad of duplicate prescriptions for scheduled narcotics, every one of them for Reeves."

"How convenient to have a professional relationship with the only witness to the murder of his wife's lover's wife," I observed though the connections made my head swim.

Bell continued, "After technicians collected evidence, the last place I checked before they locked the office up was the medical files, and I found a folder for Grady Reeves, which was strangely thin for someone requiring such extensive pharmaceutical therapy, especially in comparison to those files around it."

Knowing the courts could not use healthcare records without one, Bell had requested a warrant directly related to the murder of Trinidee Sebastian, then waited for it so he could personally take possession of the chart.

Meanwhile, he said, Adam Barns had driven across to Vancouver to see Dr. Jason Gelhaus in the Clark County Detention Center, intending to accompany a Washington deputy to question him again about the assault and the photos he'd given to his wife.

"Barnes half-expected the doctor to be apologetic about the assault, to plead for his freedom or a chance to talk to his wife to straighten out a misunderstanding," Bell told me. "Instead, Gelhaus was still so agitated about his wife's affair, angrier still at being arrested for domestic assault, that he had some very unkind things to say about her, not to mention about the dead wife he said Sebastian deserved to lose. But he never mentioned killing anyone, even in his rage."

That was unusual, I thought. Slipping up about crimes during such a tirade was not uncommon.

"Now that he's free on bail, we're asking Dr. Gelhaus to come to Portland and make a statement about his wife's involvement with Sebastian, playing to his need to let her hang," he said. "Our plan is to let the media get word that Dr. Gelhaus had been detained on the assault, and that Sarah is being questioned in connection with the murder of Portland Police Lieutenant Sebastian's wife." He paused. "That will stir up a lot of sharks in the water, adding more stress to the doctor's situation. But at the same time, we're going to ask Grady Reeves to come make a positive identification of the woman he saw with Trinidee."

"You intend to get them together and see what happens," I said, now understanding the steps in motion. "That would be interesting to watch."

"Why don't you bring Sarah so I don't have to send someone official to get her, then you're more than welcome to watch," he offered.

Two hours later, I dropped off Sarah in an interview room away from where her husband would be brought in, then I joined Chris in his office while we waited for Gelhaus and Reeves to make their appointment times.

"The way I figure it, Reeves is the one who killed Trinidee Sebastian," Bell explained, setting the tape recorder on the coffee table. "He screwed up in the interview with us, but Adam and I both missed it the first time. Listen." He pushed a button.

"Well, on the morning of August 7th," a flowery, animated voice started, "I was at the train station, waiting to pick up a friend. I'd been there about half an hour, and the train was late, of course. Anyway, I noticed this beautiful blonde woman dressed in a gray A-line skirt, mauve blouse, and black spike-heeled boots, pacing back and forth. I'm sure it's the woman that died, I saw the photo of her in the morning paper."

A man who knows about skirt designs, I thought.

"She was talking to another woman over near where she fell."

Bell stopped the tape. "Reeves sort of pauses to see if we react, but we don't." He started the recording again.

"I wasn't close enough to hear what they were saying," Reeves continued, "but they seemed to be arguing over something the second woman handed the first. It was too small to tell what it was. Seemed like a lot of needless drama, so I went over to the restroom. When I came out, I saw the second woman hurrying toward the exit, and the blonde wasn't there. I didn't think anything else about it – I went to buy a soda, then my friend came and we left."

Bell stopped the tape.

I was stumped, trying to figure out what they'd missed.

"He says he saw the women talking over where Sebastian fell," Bell explained. "The only other witness we found says Trinidee Sebastian was talking to another woman just outside the restrooms. Grady's the only one who reports seeing the person he described as Gelhaus as she was leaving, and then he left, too."

"So the only way he'd know where she fell to the tracks is if he pushed her?" I asked, lost.

"No, if he'd pushed her in front of the train, the engineers would have seen them both," Bell said. "And we'd have found someone in the crowd who would have seen both Sarah Gelhaus and Grady Reeves – we did not."

Shrugging my shoulders, I indicated I gave up solving the puzzle.

"I think Reeves poisoned her, they argued about the disk with the photos on it. Then he watched her go out onto the platform, where she probably just collapsed onto the tracks."

Wow, that was some theory, I thought. "But why would he kill her?"

"I suspect it has something to do with Layne, though for the life of me, I don't know what," Bell said. "But I bet we find out when we get them together." He smiled a devilish grin.

A check of Reeves' criminal history had been informative to investigators. Reeves had a criminal record – possession of narcotics, and one conviction for sexual misconduct in California. The crime lab in Portland was able to match fingerprints on the photos Sarah got from her husband with Reeves' from that out-of-state arrest. These facts just added to the case against Reeves, though the actual motive was still unclear.

When everyone was ready, a young detective brought Reeves to an interview room, with its entry and windows facing the bullpen of detectives' desks and a few offices on the other side, where Bell introduced himself. After a few questions, Chris Bell asked Reeves to pick out the woman he saw with the victim from six photos. He identified Sarah with only a moment's hesitation. Bell then excused himself from the interview room to retrieve a statement form, which he'd intentionally forgotten to bring. He left the door open.

Bell went to his office, in plain view of the windows in the interview room, searching his desk for something.

My only part in this whole charade was to find Bell in his office and start a conversation that he couldn't escape.

In reality, we discussed restaurants in the Portland area, but it looked serious as I presented him with a stack of papers he thumbed as we talked.

Meanwhile, another detective brought Jason Gelhaus to a room just past the one Reeves occupied. "Have a seat here, Dr. Gelhaus. Captain Bell will want to take your statement personally. If you'd like, there's coffee right over there," he said, indicating an area across the bullpen.

Just as Bell suspected, Jason Gelhaus' curiosity was too much. The detective wasn't past the first corner when Gelhaus stood and took two steps into the main room, with the appearance of getting something to drink, until he looked over his shoulder for a second look – to be sure it was Reeves he'd seen.

The microphones in the room were working, the technician had assured Bell.

Only in the previous two years had the interview rooms been wired into the same system as the interrogation rooms, to record both video and audio as evidence for the identification of suspects. Adam Barnes observed over the closed-circuit monitors from another area, while Bell was in plain sight in his office, talking to me.

"What are you doing here?" Gelhaus demanded in a harsh whisper, as he stepped toward the doorway, struggling to keep his voice quiet.

"I'm here to identify your wife as a killer, Jason," Reeves replied, looking up with a fake frown. "These two women were arguing at the train station." He stood and took a step toward Gelhaus. "Sarah left, and the other woman is dead. Pretty simple."

"You saw it? You saw Sarah kill that woman?" Jason voice squeaked at the last word.

Reeves laughed, then lowered his voice an octave. "Your wife is too soft to kill anyone. But now you can get rid of her without any repercussions. Divorcing a wife accused of murder is simple and expected. You file on the grounds of adultery, the grievous mental cruelty you'd suffer during this trial and her conviction, and no one will think any less of you. She goes to prison, maybe even gets the death penalty," Reeves explained, his voice as smooth as honey. He stepped closer. "Once she's gone, we can be together, Jason. I told you I'd do something special for you. For us."

"You killed her?" Jason gasped, much less confident than when he came into the department. "For me?"

"Yes. After all these years, just the two of us, finally." Reeves reached out and touched Jason's cheek with his fingertips. "This will all work."

"You pathetic piece of shit!" Gelhaus bellowed, shoving Grady's hand away from his face. "You're framing my wife?"

Reeves held his fingers to his lips. "Jason, that's what's going to happen. And if you cross me instead, I'll tell the police you paid me to kill that woman and frame your wife. Paid me in drugs and cash all these years, hiding away our secret affair. You'll go down just as far as I do," he whispered. "Trust me."

Rage exploded in Jason Gelhaus, and he reared back and slammed his fist into Grady Reeves' face. Even as Reeves stumbled to the floor and cowered, Jason fell on him, pummeling him. It took three officers to subdue Gelhaus and escort him from the room.

Bell roughly helped Reeves to his feet, then shoved him into a chair, much to Reeves' dismay.

"Anything he says is a lie," Reeves whined, holding his broken nose. "Just hearsay."

Bell waved a video cassette – not the real one of the men's conversation, but a handy example. "No, it's hearsay if you testify you overheard me tell someone in this department that no one would blink if you had a very nasty accident before this ever goes to trial," Bell replied. "But your confession to Jason Gelhaus about killing Trinidee Sebastian is recorded, regardless what either of you says."

Barnes arrived to arrest Reeves, handcuff him, and read him his constitutional rights.

"Now are you clear on these rights, Mr. Reeves?" Barnes asked. "Because I don't want there to be any question on your part that you understand every word."

Reeves nodded. A drop of blood rolled down his upper lip.

"No, say it out loud for the camera – do you understand your legal rights?" Barnes asked again. "I can read them to you again, if you'd like."

"Yes, I mean no – don't repeat them," Reeves said, sounding stuffier with each passing minute as the tissues swelled. "I understand them."

Barnes made a visual cue for the recording to be completed. "You may think your lawyer will suppress the confession from this room, Mr. Reeves," Adam Barnes stated. "One might even argue about the permission granted by Mrs. Gelhaus to search the medical clinic. But a lawyer can't suppress the evidence I gathered from your house today with valid search warrant."

"You didn't find anything," Reeves said, but it sounded more like "Oo nidnt fine enyfing."

Barnes laughed. "I found several women's outfits – with several careful matches to what was in Mrs. Gelhaus' closet. And quite a lovely photographic studio – expensive cameras, computer imaging equipment, and copies of the photos of Sarah Gelhaus with Layne Sebastian – those same photos Dr. Gelhaus threw at his wife before he beat her in a fit of rage just like he was about to do to you. But you know what sealed the story for us, Reeves?"

The man in custody stared back at him.

Barnes beamed proudly, "The clincher is the bottle of sodium monofluoroacetate we found in your darkroom. No known photographic uses. No uses inside an occupied building. But it was the cause of death in Trinidee Sebastian, whether the train hit her or not."

"I didn't mean to kill her," Reeves mumbled under his breath. "I just wanted her to buy the photos and Jason's wife to take the blame for the affair. With his wife out of the way, Jason would have come to me."

✄

After all that, I drove home to find Zach waxing his Mustang in the garage.

"So how's your new friend?" he asked, leaning to give me a

quick kiss.

"All my friends are fine, and the man who killed Layne's wife is behind bars now," I said, picking up a rag to polish the chrome.

"You do manage to pick out some unusual people," he said, stepping out of reach when I popped the towel at him. "Did you help?"

I shook my head and recapped the conclusion of the investigation. Even though I hadn't been able to see him, hearing Jason's part of the conversation with Sarah wasn't a problem when she faced him in the holding area – it echoed through the offices and hallway.

"Sarah, I did not have anything to do with him killing Trinidee." His voice had quivered with clear animosity, without a trace of apology or shame, or awareness that if he spoke much louder, the officer standing guard would intervene. "But that doesn't excuse you having an affair with that cop!"

Sarah stared, arms crossed tightly across her chest, silent for a long moment. Finally she said, "You'll hear from my divorce attorney, Jason. I'll take everything, just like you intended to do." And she walked away from him without looking back when he began a loud denial.

Through the confrontation, Layne had sat slumped at his desk, rocking just enough to make his chair squeak beneath, but totally unaware of the brittle sound. His expression looked wilted, aging him a decade.

Sarah had marched straight toward Layne's desk, where she stopped next to him and blinked, inhaling to gather her resolve, or maybe just the energy to face him. "I can't believe any of this," she'd said, not looking at his face. Her eyes had focused on something in her mind, and she winced, then touched his shoulder. "I wish none of this hurt as bad as it does, Layne. The worst part is knowing that she's dead and that we're partly to blame. What I felt when we were together is dead now, too."

She'd pulled away her hand, hesitated only a moment before she walked away and left him sitting at the desk, unable to go after her.

Witnessing the goodbye was like watching a ship sink.

Safe though I was, it was devastating to know the losses.

Tears rolled down Layne's face, and finally he stood and pulled an envelope from his jacket. "Give this to Chris?" he asked, handing it to me and using the heels of both hands to wipe his face. "It's my resignation."

I'd nodded and watched him leave the bullpen before I went to Bell's office.

"If you think he's a good cop – if he's worth keeping – give him six weeks before you open this," I'd suggested. "He needs time to make sense of this, to grieve all he's lost."

Thinking how everything had ended, I didn't have words to tell Zach all the details, and I really didn't feel like I'd helped Layne at all.

But I knew I had come home to a man who loved me more than most people ever get to experience.

I leaned close for another kiss. "I'm gonna change clothes," I said, tossing the rag back where I'd found it. "Let's go for a ride."

CHAPTER

32

Unable to put Layne's catastrophe behind me completely, I wondered where he went when he left the Portland area. That he had left and it was a final decision was all Chris Bell would tell me a month later when I called to ask.

I could relate to having every single thing in my world ripped out from under me when my career ended with the New Mexico State Police. My choice – after months of recovery and then a year of self-defeating recklessness – had been to find a place to start over, thanks to Zach. I hoped that was what Layne had chosen, and that it was working well for him, wherever he'd gone. Our summer went on, a variety of shifts, teenager activities, Zach being gone for days or weeks at a time, and my working a dozen days a month.

Detective Greer from Portland left me a message one day, saying I'd been right about the glazed coffee cup being the source of the added lead poisoning Mr. Sells suffered in the hospital. Robert, his son, had taken the cup back home to his daughter, who'd bought it for her grandfather on a spring break trip. She took the cup back to Mr. Sells in the hospital, thinking that a souvenir from home would help. It hadn't, though I suspect it only sped up his death by a few days.

On a July weekend, Amber wanted to ride in a play-day, a rodeo-like competition with only timed events, several hours south in Oregon, so we got up early that Saturday morning with that very plan.

"I've been practicing barrels and poles," she told me as we gathered tack. "I was hoping Cody could go, too, but he has to work today."

Cody Randall was the new beau, though Amber hadn't really described him as a love interest, only as a friend. His family lived north on Wind River Road. Although my husband may not have known, Cody was a fraternal twin to Cady, just as Zach had been to Zoe. Cody was sixteen, and from the couple of times I'd met him, he seemed to be an okay kid, but I liked him better when I didn't think of him as Amber's boyfriend.

I'd hooked the trailer to my Suburban the night before.

She looked surprised when I led Rainier out of the corral. "You're going to ride?" she asked.

"Sure, and it's good exposure for the horses to be in public," I said. "Is there some reason I shouldn't?"

Rainier stepped up into the trailer without hesitation.

She shook her head as she led Denali inside and closed the divider. "I just didn't think you would ride yet. That's great." She stepped down, cocking her head toward the house. "Phone . . ." She took off running.

Zach, probably, I thought, wishing Amber good luck.

"Julie! It's for you!" she called a moment later from the door to the patio.

If it had been Zach, she'd have yelled that tidbit to tell me, too, I thought. Tossing my gloves into the storage compartment of the trailer, I headed for the house, not running.

Amber was still in the kitchen, glugging down orange juice from a quart bottle she apparently intended to finish off.

Picking up the receiver, I said hello.

The sheriff – not my husband – replied. "I hate to bother you on your day off, Julie, but we've been asked to aid in the search for a downed aircraft north of where you live. At the moment, we don't have any other manpower to spare. A team on horseback would be appreciated, I'm told."

I glanced up at Amber. "I can't go alone," I said, knowing his reply before he said it.

"You two had plans today, I know. Feel free to take her if that works for you. If not, if you can get your horses up there, I'll send up Seaver as soon as he gets free from the accident he's at," he said.

"No, that's great. Trailer's half loaded already." I scribbled directions to the trailhead where the search was being coordinated. "About an hour and a half," I said, then hung up.

"You can't take me to the play-day, huh," Amber said, wilted with letdown.

"Actually, no, but I'd like you to ride this search with me instead," I told her. "We're looking for an airplane."

"Really?"

I wasn't sure if her response was sarcastic, amazed, or continued disappointment.

"We don't ride alone for a number of reasons," I said, "and there are no other deputies available to respond right now. If you're game, we'll swap out a couple of packs and get going."

The altered plans seemed to be acceptable to her, so we headed back outside to exchange and add gear in the trailer.

"I don't get it," Amber said as I made the tack trades. "Why are we taking all this stuff?"

"Looking for an airplane means you might actually find it, and survivors," I explained as I rolled up two blankets each for our saddles. "It might be July weather here, but between the higher altitude and maybe being injured, having blankets for victims is the least we can do. Same with the tent and sleeping bags for us – we don't expect to get caught up there for the night, but it's much better to be prepared."

"You do this for every search?" she asked, watching me.

I nodded. "High protein and carbs, water, shelter. Yep, every time." I glanced up at the sky, looking for clouds. "I wish Waldo was ready for this. Neither he nor Julaquinte has been on a search, even as a pack horse," I said. "A real search is not the best time to train a new animal. All we need is a spooked horse running wild in a forest."

We went inside to change into something more suitable for a search than a rodeo, and I suggested a couple more items for her, including her hot pink t-shirt.

Amber wrinkled her nose in disgust.

"The idea is to be visible, not stylish," I explained.

From my closet, I added a hunter-orange fleece vest, grabbed a waterproof coat, and dug for a balaclava and gloves, just in case.

With that, we set off.

Every thousand feet in altitude we climbed, my ears popped like clockwork. In an hour, we reached the search coordinator's site.

"Good to see you, Deputy," a smiling woman in her fifties said, extending a hand.

"You, too, Mrs. Holland," I said, shaking. "This is my daughter Amber. She'll be riding with me today. Amber, this is Doreen Holland. She's one of our more distant neighbors up Wind River."

"I've heard you're quite a horsewoman, Amber," she said. "Glad to have you riding today."

"We were headed down to Oregon for a play-day this morning," Amber told her, "but this is more important."

Wow, Amber said that?

"I'll enter you two into the system and get you a map and route," she said. "We've got six teams out on foot already, so I'm going to send you through the canyon north, then east, I think."

We unloaded the two horses and saddled up. It took us about fifteen minutes to get all the gear tied down and ready. By that time, Mrs. Holland had a map ready for us, with our trail and those others marked.

"These are from Del Clinton's herd, aren't they?" she said, stroking Denali's neck. "Not many people ride Trakehners for anything but show and jumping."

"They're an accidental cross to a Quarter Horse. I've ridden a little English on him," Amber said, "but I don't like dressage. Dad says he's just as good a roping and penning horse as any Quarter Horse he's owned."

All of that was news to me, I thought, having given little thought to what a breed did or didn't do. Zach looked good on a big horse, so I assumed that's how we got the two we had.

I tested my radio, tucked it into my vest, pulled my gray Stetson down and climbed onto Rainier. Light as a feather, Amber mounted Denali, and we set off.

Away from the trail head, Amber asked, "How does she know where to send people?"

"Part of coordinating a search is knowing who will show up and how they intend to search. We're being sent through some easy territory first to cover ground, then we'll face rougher terrain than those on foot, because we have the horses."

"So there are eight of us so far?"

"No, she said there were six teams, which could mean anything from two to ten people per team. The more people, the farther they'll spread out but take the same track."

"You told the sheriff you wouldn't come alone," she said. "Was that some code for telling him I was with you?"

"No code," I said as we rode side by side at an extended walk. "He didn't have anyone else immediately available, and just like the other teams, no one goes out alone. You coming with me isn't unusual and it wasn't a secret."

The temperature wasn't unpleasant, but it was at least fifteen degrees cooler than at the house. Riding through the trees, it became too dark for my regular sunglasses, so I swapped them for my shooting glasses with yellow lenses.

"Those make you look evil," she proclaimed with an exaggerated sneer.

I stuck my tongue out at her.

We rode without talking for half an hour. Almost to the point where we'd turn off the trail to go east, I checked in with the base to advise our position and status.

"Every half hour," I said. "We need to know where we are, and in turn, we need to keep the coordinator up to date on our progress."

Amber just nodded.

"Not as much fun as running barrels, is it?" I asked, sensing her indifference.

"No, it's not that. I was just thinking," she said, falling behind me as the forest grew denser. "Can I ask you a question?"

"Of course."

"Cody's mom, Laura, she's pregnant again," Amber said. "But this time she's doing it for someone else. For money."

"She's being a surrogate, you mean."

"Yeah, that's the word," she said. "Is that right?"

"Right, as in morally, ethically, legally, maternally?" I asked. "I don't think I could be a surrogate, but that doesn't mean that a couple who wants a baby bad enough wouldn't consider having another woman carry the pregnancy."

"You and Zach wanted a baby, right?"

I considered my words carefully, not wanting Amber to question her place in our lives, if that were her intention with the conversation. "Yes, we did."

"Zach told me that you were pregnant when you got shot, and now you can't have babies."

I sighed. "That's true. But I wouldn't change what I did or why, and you were half my motivation to do it," I said.

"You two wouldn't pay for a baby that someone else carried, would you?"

She didn't quite have the legalities of surrogacy down – the accepting couple would pay a fee that included medical costs which legally negated the actual *purchase* of the baby – but I got her point. "We never discussed it, but I don't think it would be something we'd want to do," I said. "Why do you ask?"

"I don't think she should do it," Amber stated. "How can she just give up what grew inside her for all those months?"

"That would be difficult for me, I'd imagine, but I can't say." I checked my compass. "How far along is she?"

"About six months or so, I heard her tell a friend of hers. But she's already huge because it's twins."

"Like Cody," I said. "And like your dad."

"Did you know Zoe?" she asked, wondering about Zach's sister.

I shook my head.

"I sorta wish I'd been a twin," she said.

"Kinda lonely, being an only child, isn't it?" I asked, having wished for a little sister at one time. "We live in the situation we're born into."

"I guess so, but if you and Dad wanted kids," she said, reverting to the previous subject, "why wouldn't you adopt now?"

I turned in my saddle, trying to see what was on her mind. "Given our jobs and situation, that hasn't come up for discussion," I said. "I can't imagine going through that whole process, much less not working to stay home and raise a small child."

"Even if having a baby was what you'd planned?"

I stopped Rainier and turned him sideways in front of her, forcing her to stop. "Plans for a family? We really hadn't made any plans, but we have altered our lives as we've gone." Trying not to sound frustrated with where the conversation had gone, I added. "Laura can be a surrogate mother with all the planning that takes, but planning can't include every possibility." I reined my horse back to the path I'd chosen. "So it wouldn't have mattered if Zach and I had planned to have a dozen kids – now we can't. But we have you, and I'm glad."

"Why?"

"Because I couldn't take a baby on a ride like this, now could I?"

"But you took me," she said.

I smiled. "And I'm glad I have your company out here."

"That's not what I mean – you let Dad bring me into your new marriage."

"First of all, I didn't *let* him do anything – we agreed to do it if anything happened to your mother, before we knew she'd been murdered. You and your situation were different than adopting a child," I said. "Zach would never have dreamed of taking you away from your mother, or even Greg Hennessy, if you'd wanted to stay with him. But because you are his child, he loves you enough to want you to be with him. I feel the same way."

We came to a ridge that dropped off about six feet. I turned to skirt it, but Amber urged Denali over it, landing in a rustle of leaves and hooves thumping on solid dirt.

"That was quite a jump," I admitted, reining Rainier from following, "but I think I'll just go around there and take the long way down." I pointed at an outcropping. "We'll meet over there and climb out, then take a break."

"He'll make it – no problem," she turned to tell me.

"Yeah, the horse would do fine. The rider is a chicken about jumping."

I met her where I'd suggested. After our short break for a drink and to stretch muscles, I checked the map and confirmed our position with the GPS Zach had bought me, which was more useful every time I pulled it out for a new task.

Showing Amber where we were, I explained that we both needed to keep track, because that's what partners do. "If I should get hurt, for example," I said, "you need to be able to tell Mrs. Holland where we are, or even ride out for help and be able to come back to the same place."

She hadn't thought about that, I could tell by her expression.

We mounted up and rode along the base of a hill, scanning for wreckage, no longer in a deep conversation about surrogacy and babies, which I appreciated.

As we rode, I reached into my pack and pulled out a couple of protein bars, tossed one back to Amber.

"How can you eat these?" she asked, making a sour face when she opened it and sniffed. "They're gross!"

"I don't eat them because they're good," I answered. "We need to maintain our energy. While the horses are doing all the locomotion, we still expend calories riding. Plus, we're at a higher elevation than normal and it's colder, both adding to the demand."

She rolled her eyes and ripped open the wrapper to take a bite. "It's still disgusting."

The radio in my vest crackled with static, but I couldn't make out the message.

"Up the hill a ways," I said, pointing us off to the right for better reception.

Ten minutes later, I checked in again with Mrs. Holland.

"They found the plane, so you can return to base, Sweetie," the energetic voice advised.

I acknowledged the message and put the radio back in my pocket.

"That's that," I announced, stretching my arms toward the late morning sky, then checked my watch. "But I don't think we can make it to the play-day now."

"Can we just keep riding out here for a while?" she asked. "This is kinda neat."

I was surprised, but in a good way. "Sure." Handing her the map, I asked, "Where do you want to go?"

Amber studied the topographical map a few minutes, then pointed. "Let's go up to this creek, then we can cut back to the trail going west."

"Sounds good." I radioed Mrs. Holland to let her know we wouldn't be returning right away, and not to bother waiting for us.

I motioned for Amber to take the lead, and away we rode.

We'd made the far point of her ride and turned west back onto one of the hiking trails that cut through the forest. While they were more than fine for someone walking, at times we still found that the clearance was too low for a rider on horseback, so occasionally we had to divert around a tree or a stand of them.

Had we been walking on the trail as had so many people before us, Amber would never have seen the bag.

CHAPTER

33

Calling it a suitcase was not accurate, given its limp rectangular shape. It could have dated from a decade ago or possibly just a few months – initially it was difficult to tell.

Amber hopped down from Denali and handed her reins to me. "Let's open it."

"Wait!" I was startled to hear how loud my voice was in the quiet of the forest. "It looks rotted. If we try to dig it out here and open it, it may just all fall apart." I slid from Rainier's back to the ground. "Let's get it free of the dirt, wrap it up, then we can take our time when we get home."

Amber shook her head but smiled. "Always a cop, aren't you?"

I tied off the horses to a log and rifled through my pack for the one thing I was certain would work – a body bag.

Although it was in the hottest part of the day, the shade kept us cool as we dug in the soil around and under the canvas, eventually finding that a small root had penetrated the weave and disappeared inside.

"That'll complicate things," she offered.

"Not much," I said, pulling my knife from its sheath. "We just cut the root a few inches from the bag."

"Is that what you'd do for evidence?" she asked.

"In this circumstance, probably. Why?"

She sat back on her haunches. "Wondering, I guess. It's kinda neat watching what cops do with stuff to identify criminals."

I could tell she was considering what was inside the bag, which was more or less a small duffel made of a light-colored, heavy cotton, maybe twenty inches long and ten inches wide, but only about eight inches deep.

"What if it's a . . ." she trailed off, then looked around us as if someone might be watching.

"Too small to be a body," I said. But then I stopped. What if it *wasn't* too small? Who said a body had to be that of an adult? My stomach did a flip, rumbling the protein bar I'd eaten earlier. "Probably just someone's climbing clothes and underwear."

Amber's eyes met mine. She wasn't convinced either.

"Really, the odds of this being a skeleton, or even a part of one, are astronomically small. We're miles from nowhere," I said, trying to make the logic sound authoritative.

"Julie, we're less than half a mile from the trailhead where we parked," she replied, pointing a slender finger toward our destination. "If I wanted to hide something, this nowhere seems as good as any other."

"If you really drove into the wilderness then hiked this far to hide something, wouldn't you bury it?"

She stood up and scanned around us. "Nope. Besides, then you'd have to get rid of the shovel, but carrying this bag would only be weird, not suspicious. And maybe this was tucked inside a backpack or something to conceal it. To get rid of it, I'd just toss it under something. A bush, maybe."

"Where'd you learn to think like a criminal?" I asked, returning to the task of removing the bag from the soil and tree roots.

Ten minutes later, Amber helped me lift it just far enough to scoot a reinforced body bag beneath, then tie up the excess fabric. Though the whole lump only weighed a few pounds, I had to do some major rearrangement to secure it behind my saddle because Amber stated – hands on her hips – that she wasn't riding anywhere with that "thing" behind her.

"But you found it," I kidded her.

Just for the sake of thoroughness, I took out my GPS and logged the coordinates where she found it before we headed for the trail to get back to the trailer.

❧

We'd speculated on the bag's contents during the ride, but once we'd climbed into my Suburban, Amber fell asleep almost instantly.

I still envied her that.

After dropping off the horses and the trailer at the cabin, we took the "thing" – Amber refused to call it anything else – to the sheriff's department to open it.

I rolled a table outside to my truck to move it into the building. That activity garnered enough curiosity from the deputy who had been writing a report to follow me.

Amber was moving "it" to the table when he came out the door into the sunshine.

"What'dya find?" Mitch Seaver asked, giving my fifteen-year-old stepdaughter a lewd glance while her back was turned, which earned him a swift kick in the shin with my boot.

"Amber saw a canvas bag while we were crossing back to a trail after the search today," I explained. "So we thought it would –" I changed the words when Amber glared over her shoulder at me. "*I* thought it would be a good idea to bring it here to open, just in case."

Mitch shrugged. "I have plenty of work around here without digging up extra," he said. "Good luck." He left us to the soiled, rotted canvas bag.

We rolled the table inside.

"So do you really want to do this the easy way and just open it," I asked, "or go through the steps like it might be evidence?"

"You're asking me?" Amber blinked. "You'd go through all that, even thinking it's just underwear?"

I nodded. "If you want."

"Well," she said, drawing out the word as she thought for a moment. "It's been an adventure so far. Let's process it like evidence."

I laughed – she even had the professional slang right, so we set to work, nose-down in the procedures without even thinking about time until my phone rang.

"Hello," I said, sure it was Zach, who had probably gotten home and wondered where we were. I'd forgotten to leave him a note that we got diverted to a search or where we'd gone since.

"Tell me you're bringing fast food home for supper," he said. "I'm starving, and the dog refuses to share his kibble."

Hadn't considered food since our makeshift lunch either, I thought. "Yeah, we can do that. We got involved in the lab here at work."

"Somehow I didn't think the horses brought the trailer home from Oregon by themselves," he observed. "But being in the lab is a far cry from barrels and poles. Anything I need to know about?"

"Nothing that can't wait," I said. "We'll be there in half an hour or so."

As I disconnected, Amber stood, stretching her back, having collected samples of cloth, soil, tree roots, and the obvious contents inside the bag. She'd been viewing something through a microscope.

"Time to go home," I prompted. "Let's gather everything up for storage. We can come back tomorrow."

She'd been relieved – and so had I – that the canvas bag hadn't held human remains, though we did find bones from a small bird and several other items, including something crafted from twigs and feathers with twine and beads for decoration. She'd sketched the designs to research later tonight. All in all, it might have been a Native American collection of trinkets with one exception – a worn leather wallet, which I had not allowed her to open yet.

As we packed items into storage bins for safekeeping overnight, Amber asked, "So why not just see what's in the billfold and decide how old the bag is from that?"

"Two reasons," I said with a smile. "It's no fun to read the last chapter of a book first, right? We've come this far, so I'd like to continue the steps in order." I kept packing items, wrapping them in white paper for separation and cushioning as I went. "Second, we don't know if there's anything in the wallet to identify someone. If so, we don't know whether the person was the one who left the bag, whether he might have been a victim or even the perpetrator of some other crime. No sense calling him up to ask and blowing the element of surprise."

She nodded. "Thinking like a cop again."

"As if I can help it," I admitted. "Let's go home."

"You went to a search instead of the play-day, then kept riding and found a bag full of voodoo stuff?" Zach summarized as Amber set paper plates and napkins on the table.

We'd picked up burgers in town, and I gathered condiments from the refrigerator.

I wanted to hear Amber's version of the day, so I kept quiet.

"Not voodoo, Dad," she said. "But yeah, we were just riding along, and I saw this thing back under a bush. Julie wouldn't just open it out in the middle of nowhere, so we dug it up and took it to the sheriff's department lab for processing. I think it's really old, like maybe thirty years or so."

That's her idea of old?

She continued. "I got to take samples and check out stuff under the microscope."

I set the ketchup, mayo and mustard, lettuce and pickles on the table.

Zach glanced up at me, and I tried to hide the smile at how excited she seemed about the forensic evaluation.

"What kind of bird?" he asked, referring back to her listing of items in the bag.

Amber's animated descriptions of the day stopped. "I don't know. Why?"

I brought glasses of water for us all and sat down next to Zach.

"Because it might tell you more about the other items – different birds have different meanings in legends. Did you find a fetish?"

She scrunched her nose and looked at me for an answer, most likely associating the word with something deviant.

"He means a stone carving of an animal," I offered. "Yes, we found a crude one, a fox or wolf. I couldn't tell."

"That's what that was?" she asked.

I nodded and unwrapped my burger, knowing it would not taste as good as something Zach had created and grilled.

"And what is the purpose of all this investigation?" Zach asked her.

She beamed again. "I get to participate in the evidence collection, to see what really goes into figuring out a crime."

"Okay. You collected evidence," Zach nodded his approval. "What's your initial theory?"

"I think someone carried these things into the deepest part of the forest," she said. "Then she – it must have been a girl – couldn't find any answers in these gifts someone had given her, so she killed herself."

"That's quite a theory," he replied without sounding judgmental. "What makes you think so? You didn't find a body, did you?"

"No," she said, sounding a little disappointed. "But we might if we went back to look."

They both turned to me in anticipation of an answer.

"Let's see where this all leads," I said. "We still have the wallet, too. That doesn't seem to fit with a young girl."

"Maybe the girl stole it," they said together, then laughed.

"Fine," I relented. "We'll finish the contents of the bag on my days off this week, then if you still think we should go back to the forest and look for a body, we will. Deal?"

❧

Later that night, when Zach came to bed, he asked, "What is her real interest in this stuff?"

"I don't know. She really did just want to open it out in the woods, but when I suggested we should take it to the department and process it like evidence, she agreed," I explained. "She pulled fibers and trace particulates from the bag, drew the images so she could look them up. She has your artistic talent, too."

He smiled. I could feel it.

I snuggled closer. "I'm proud of her, of everything she did today."

"You think she'll go into law enforcement?" he asked.

"Maybe. I wondered about that when we were running from Pauly. Maybe not a badge, but she sure took to the evidence stuff. You think so?"

"Hope not. I don't want her to be a cop – it's hard on you,

physically, emotionally. Hard on your family."

"Sure, but can you see yourself being anything else?"

"Nope, but being a cop is no longer the first thing I am. I'd like to say my priorities are to my wife and daughter before the badge." He cleared his throat and moved his hand across my hip. "So how am I doing so far?"

CHAPTER

34

Although Amber helped me finish the preliminary evaluation of the bag she'd found on our ride, she was still convinced we should go back and look for a body. However, visitors interrupted any such plans.

Amber had stuck with her theory that the bag had belonged to a young woman who had kept the wallet of someone she loved. "I think she went out there with prayer charms to win the heart of a man."

"I can't argue your line of interpretation, but on the other hand, it could also be the remnants of a man's wallet after he was marched into the woods and killed by a woman," I countered. "There's evidence, but nothing to indicate context."

"Yeah, but my story is more romantic," she said. "Can Cody come with us when we ride back out there?"

I nodded. "We'll shoot for Friday."

"You're the best! I'll be home for supper." She tore off out the door to meet Cody as his rusty old pickup pulled in the drive.

"Or we might discover that a young girl's father dragged her boyfriend into the woods and broke him into firewood-sized pieces for acting like a teenage boy," I said to myself as I heard the truck fade away. "I can imagine that happening, too."

I'd just finished cleaning up our lunch dishes when Zach pulled in and parked.

"Look who I found at the airport," he announced as both his and my mother filed into the kitchen.

Warm hugs were passed around eagerly.

"We just thought we'd come spend a day or so," my mother said, patting my cheeks. "It's so nice to see you without bruises this time."

None that she could see, anyway. I didn't volunteer anything about the one on my hip from where Waldo had bumped me into the gate a few days prior.

I opened a bottle of wine, and we all went out to the deck to sit in the shade and enjoy the nice breeze.

"Where's Amber?" Vera asked.

"She's off with Cody again this afternoon," I explained. "A boy from up the road a bit. They're working on his roping skills in hopes of competing in a heading and heeling competition soon."

Zach inhaled sharply through flared nostrils. While he didn't have anything against Cody, I'd sensed before his disapproval of that teenage male influence – Amber was an example of what could result when adolescent hormones and poor judgment mixed.

"She ropes?" my mother asked.

"Not much out here she hasn't learned, Dagmar," Zach said. "She made it to country girl status in just a few months." He pulled himself out of his chair to get photos showing how his daughter had mastered so many horsemanship skills."We should all go for a ride tomorrow," he suggested. "We can borrow another pair of horses from the Clintons. He raises Trakehners and crossbreeds."

"Really? Is that where you got yours?"

Zach nodded. "Both Rainier and Denali came from his stock, normally Traks bred to Hanoverians and Arabians, but ours started as an accidental breeding to a Quarter Horse/Thoroughbred mix. It went so well with Rainer that they tried again and got Denali. Unfortunately, no one else wanted that mix, but I think it's great."

That was all Zach and my mother needed to carry on fifteen minutes about a horse breeding, complete with the bulging pages of the photo album.

While he regaled the mothers with stories about Amber and other horsemanship tales, I slipped inside to open another bottle of wine and to set steaks in water to thaw, for Zach to grill later. Then I took out potatoes to wash and bake, too.

I was wiping off the counter when Zach came in.

"Are you okay?" he asked in a low voice.

The question surprised me. "Yeah, I was just getting stuff ready to fix when we got hungry."

"You're not upset with their surprise visit?"

I stepped into his arms. "No, not at all."

"Good," he said. "Let's go fill those glasses again." He grabbed the bottle and was almost out the door when the phone rang.

We exchanged glances, hoping it wasn't somebody wanting one of us to come to work.

He set down the bottle and picked up the receiver. Amber was yelling, I could hear from four steps away.

"What's wrong?" he asked when there was enough of a break for her to hear him. More panic. "We'll be right there."

Zach hung up and took my hand, dragged me out onto the deck. "Gotta go – emergency up the road. Have some more wine," he told the pair of women, handing my mother the bottle he'd opened. And then he pulled me on around to the driveway and pointed me to the passenger side of my Suburban. "Cody's mom is in labor. The ambulance crews are both out on calls."

Enough said.

But I knew that Laura was carrying twins, and that if she were really delivering them now, it was early. Very early.

Thinking while Zach drove, I doubted delivering the premature infants would be the problem, but I had very little in the way of resuscitation gear for a premature baby, much less a pair.

My cell phone rang. "Samualson," I growled, not liking any of the possible circumstances ahead.

"I've requested an ambulance from Stevenson for you," Georgia told me from dispatch. "But I've got no one else to send right now. There was a multi-victim collision on Highway 14 east of Carson."

"I just hope we don't need a second unit, then," I said. "She's carrying twins."

The look Zach shot me had to be the same one I'd have seen on the dispatcher's face.

"Keep ya posted," I told her and disconnected.

"You mean . . ." He took a deep breath and nodded. "And what Amber said about these being surrogates is right, too?"

"That's what she told me," I said.

I hadn't been to the Randalls' place, north of our own by about ten miles. Zach had taken Amber up there several times and knew the way, which was why he was driving.

"Are you going to put her in here and transport her?"

"There's no room to deliver, no room to work on babies. I don't think that's the answer."

Relief colored his face as he made the turn off the highway. Maybe he was hoping I'd ask him to wait in the vehicle, but that wasn't going to happen. Still, it was amusing to let him wonder.

Ahead, the Randall home turned out to be two single-wide trailers set almost side by side but offset in length. Four dogs ran around the Suburban and leaped, barking.

I'll shoot the first one that jumps up and scratches the paint.

Zach parked, and I got out and stepped to the back of the truck for my response kit.

Three younger children hurried toward us, seemingly out of nowhere. Their exclamations were no more understandable than the dogs'. But two were grabbing me and pointing toward the door of one trailer, so I followed.

Inside, the house wasn't really dirty, but every available space was cluttered with crafts and pictures, magazines and books, and clothes.

"We're back here!" Amber yelled, which at least gave me a direction to choose.

Going toward her voice took some carefully placed footsteps, and I stumbled once when I stepped on some small toy. I hoped it was a toy – it looked like a mouse.

In the master bedroom, Laura Randall took up a good portion of the mattress, a sweaty and pale woman weighing about three hundred pounds.

Somewhere in my past, a partner had facetiously developed an absurd formula for determining a patient's weight inside a trailer house. Three hundred divided by the number of steps up into the doorway, times the number of turns the stretcher would need to make but could not negotiate, times whether the ambulance needed to return code one or code three to the hospital, divided by the number of people available to help lift.

Turned out to be a perfect three hundred calculation, which was just plain wrong of me to even consider, I knew.

Cody looked at me from his mother's side, where he sat, holding her hand.

"Julie Samualson," I said by way of introduction. "I'm Amber's stepmother."

The woman only nodded as a contraction began, gritting her teeth to hold back a moan.

"I'll need your assistance." I said to Amber, who only shrugged. "Go help Zach find clean sheets, towels, blankets. We'll need a lot."

"We don't need to boil water?" Cody asked.

Despite her distress, his mother smiled a bit.

"That's an old movie thing to get fathers out of the room," I said with a wink. "I won't be needing it." I scooted away a basket of clothes and knelt at the foot of the bed. "We've not met before, but I think we're about to become intimate friends," I told Laura as I opened my kit.

Women in labor, especially after the fourth or fifth time, have no modesty left.

Laura only raised her head to nod at me, then moaned again. "About every eight minutes, but I think I'm crowning," she said, aware of information I needed to know.

I had Laura bend her knees so I could peek under the sheet and see how she'd progressed. She was right – sort of. As the contraction pushed the babies downward, I saw three things that were disturbing – an umbilical cord, a tiny hand, and a lot of bright red blood.

With a single infant, a doctor might try to turn the sideways baby for a head-first delivery. But with twins, I doubted there was room, even if that were an option. With a cord presentation, every contraction would cut off the baby's blood supply from the placenta as the head engaged into the pelvic girdle. If the babies were identical instead of fraternal, they would share one placenta, putting them both at risk. Having had one set of fraternal twins – Cody and Cady – and this being surrogate twins, I presumed they were also not from the same egg, thus giving them each a placenta and amniotic sac separately. Wasn't a lot of good news, but the best I could find.

No matter what happened next, however, mother and infants were in big trouble. Only a surgical birth would save the twins. Without it, even Laura might die.

CHAPTER

35

Zach and Amber came into the bedroom with an armload of towels and sheets, and Amber returned to my side at the foot of the bed.

"Call University Hospital," I told Zach. I'm sure my look conveyed all the bad things I hadn't yet found words to say yet. "Get someone on the phone."

He lifted his cell phone, then shook his head. No signal. He turned and hurried back down the hallway to find a telephone.

"Something's wrong, isn't it?" Laura said, panting.

I nodded. "The baby trying to deliver first is crossways," I said. "What you feel is a hand and an umbilical cord." I didn't bother to explain the heavy bleeding I suspected was from one placenta tearing away from the uterine wall too soon. "Do you know if the twins are fraternal or identical?"

"Fra-fraternal," she stuttered.

Her lips were pale.

"There's not a lot I can do, Laura, but I'll try," I said. "You need to roll over, up on your knees and elbows."

"I ca- can't. My knee won't hold me," she said, panting through another contraction, which was much sooner than the eight minutes she had just told me.

Somehow, I wasn't surprised at either fact. Having her pull her knees up to her chest wasn't going to work either. "Cody, find us a couple more pillows, then. We can elevate her hips and tilt her to the left."

Cody scrambled to the closet in search of more pillows, and with both his and Amber's help, we were able to place them.

I pulled another pair of gloves from my pack. "Laura, I need to prevent this baby from cutting off the circulation through the cord," I explained, inserting two fingers into the birth canal to lift the pressure off the loop of umbilical cord. I could feel the pulse in the cord's two arteries, estimated it to be about eighty, which was much too slow. The baby whose cord was being compressed was in distress, and there was a very slight possibility it didn't belong to the baby lying sideways, meaning both babies were in serious trouble.

"Amber, get my stethoscope out of the bag, please?" I asked, trying to sound calm.

She dug in my bag and found it. Without asking, she pulled the earpieces apart for me. With my free hand, I moved the diaphragm around on Laura's pregnant belly, trying to hear the heartbeat of the other baby, which I eventually located in the upper left. It was thankfully almost too fast to count accurately, well over one hundred forty.

Zach yelled from beyond the walls, "It's a corded phone, I can't get any closer."

"Do you have someone on the line?" I called.

"From the emergency department."

Crap, last thing I wanted to do was yell bad news across a house. "Laura, how far along are you?"

"Thirty-two weeks," she said.

I took a deep breath. "Thirty-two weeks, fraternal twins, breech hand and prolapsed cord of the engaged infant presenting." I could hear Zach repeating every phrase I'd said, not having a clue what it meant.

"You got the pressure off the cord?" he asked.

"Yes, but the pulse is already slow, about eighty."

Zach repeated the words, said something else, and then he hung up, which told me exactly what I feared – there was nothing else they could tell me to do to help.

In the distance, I heard a siren.

"Zach? See if you can clear a path back here for a stretcher," I said.

Cody looked at me, almost as pale as his mother.

"What are you going to do?" Amber asked.

"Exactly what I'm doing now," I said, feeling the muscles tighten against my fingers against the pelvis as the next contraction began. At least the baby's head wasn't smashing them against the mother's bones.

At his mother's request, Cody went to help Zach.

"This was supposed to be a cesarean delivery," Laura whispered. "I've got genital herpes."

I hadn't seen any lesions, but then I'd been too overwhelmed by what I had seen to be looking for skin conditions.

"Nothing either of us can do about that," I said. "Surgery is where we're headed because you can't deliver these babies this way."

"Is there time?" After six kids, she probably knew the complications were both rare and potentially fatal for both the infants and her.

"I don't know, Laura. We'll have to get to White Salmon and let the doctors do their thing," I answered, but I knew the chances were sliding downward every minute she stayed in that house.

✄

Cody rode with Zach and Amber to the hospital behind the ambulance. The medic provided oxygen and started an IV, and he got orders for nifedipine, usually a cardiac drug, which seemed to confuse him until I explained how it worked for premature labor. But with that and the IV drip of magnesium sulfate, the contractions that had been smashing my fingers began to lessen in intensity.

We rolled awkwardly through the emergency room, gathering an entire ensemble of providers waiting to accompany the patient right up to the surgery room doors. There, the only non-hospital person who accompanied Laura further was me, maintaining the pressure relief. The OR staff moved Laura from the EMS stretcher, leaving me stretched over the foot of the operating table as a sterile sheet was thrown over her hips and over my head. The hospital team went to work to sedate her and prep her for an emergency C-section. I could feel her body relax as the anesthesia began to take effect, but despite the dozens of questions she'd answered before she became unconscious, having herpes had not been one of them.

"Uh, doc?" I asked, knowing my voice was muffled beneath the drapes. "I was under the impression this was a surrogate pregnancy, and she was supposed to have a scheduled C-section due to having genital herpes."

The room went quiet for just a moment, then activities resumed all around me.

Not being able to see, I could only feel and hear what happened over the next ten minutes or so. When the first baby was lifted from Laura's abdomen, nurses carried it away to a warmer and began resuscitation efforts that ended with a weak cry and words of encouragement. Next, I felt the second baby's arm being pulled through my fingers, the loop of cord removed.

"I'll have the nurse get you out of there shortly," the doctor's voice said.

Another team had taken the second twin, and I could hear bits and pieces as they worked to get it to breathe, to pink up, for the heart rate to increase – but there were none of the positive words I'd heard with the first baby.

Soon, a nurse lifted the sheet behind me and had me back out.

"You'll be sore in the morning," she said with sympathy, patting me on the shoulder.

I stood, my back and hamstrings in screaming cramps. When I removed my bloody gloves, two fingers were already dark red and bruised. "Might not even wait till morning," I grumbled.

"Good job," the doctor said, looking up from the surgical field.

When our eyes met, I understood – what I'd done was probably what got Laura to the hospital alive for a delivery.

Looking over at the two neonatal teams, I shook my head.

Both infants had pulses – signs of life. But I had to wonder if having a heartbeat was really the primary indicator that humans called living.

We left Cody with his father at the hospital. They both repeated how much they appreciated us coming to help.

Us, because the two people on the ambulance couldn't have carried Laura out by themselves – Zach had been instrumental in helping them. I had just been in the way, no matter where I tried to position myself, but I couldn't remove my fingers.

Amber asked about staying at the hospital with Cody, but she wasn't disappointed when I told her she should come back home. "Their family needs to be together."

Zach didn't tell her until we were almost back home that we had company waiting.

Truthfully, I'd forgotten both our mothers had arrived.

CHAPTER
36

Vera Samualson and Dagmar Madigan stayed for a four-day weekend, which included a nice afternoon ride Sunday. I borrowed two mares from Del Clinton, but we took our horses to his place to ride in the forest behind his ranch. Amber rode next to one then the other of her grandmothers, trading family tidbits, a few of which I hadn't heard.

Zach and I lagged behind, not pushing them any particular direction or speed. It was a nice break to ride together with Amber focused elsewhere. We didn't get to enjoy the ride in silence, but we did get chances here and there to talk quietly.

"How's Cody's mom doing?" Zach asked.

I shrugged. "She's still in the hospital, but two days after an emergency C-section, that's not unusual. I haven't heard about the condition of the twins, but they are both still alive."

"That's good," he said, then looked at me. "Isn't it?"

"Given that the one infant was in distress for so long, cerebral palsy or any other birth injury conditions wouldn't surprise me much." I looked ahead at the three riders, abreast in an open area as we skirted a meadow. "But he does have a heartbeat."

"You don't think his survival so far is a miracle?"

"Miracle?" I repeated. "What quality of life do you have if you're blind, deaf, mentally handicapped and crippled? There's no way to know yet what sort of deficits he might have."

Zach was trying to piece together some reply, but I continued.

"Most doctors try to convince parents that it's right to do

everything possible to keep a baby alive, no matter how premature. That all the efforts will produce a living human being," I said, feeling myself climb onto a soapbox Zach might not appreciate. "I've never heard anyone tell the parents of a premature infant with multiple birth defects that keeping it alive until it can breathe and digest on its own may only produce a growing body that breaths and digests, but that's all it can do, for the decades it's alive. Is that really a miracle?"

"So you think that they shouldn't have tried so hard to save one twin?" he asked.

"I'm saying there comes a point when someone has to ask, 'What are we really saving?' Zach," I replied. "We put down animals that cannot survive or that will not be able to function or even exist without severe pain, and we call that humane. But we can't draw that line with our own species without the decision being labeled barbaric or animalistic, ironically. Medicine has gotten lost in its own ability to provide technology without offering perception of reality or consequence."

He nodded that he understood my side of the debate, but not that he necessarily agreed with my arguments.

"And top it off that this pair of boys was being carried for another couple."

He looked at me. "You don't approve of surrogacy?"

"Regardless how I feel about surrogacy, I have to wonder whether one or both of the infants were exposed to an incurable viral disease from the birth mother, and whether the family who paid for this pregnancy knew about that, either before or now. Would they still want these boys now if they knew?" I shrugged. "And what happens if they don't?"

He didn't say anything while he extrapolated the consequences.

"Dad?" Amber yelled over her shoulder. "You guys are falling behind!"

With a look, we agreed to come back to our discussion later, and we urged our horses forward to the trio ahead.

❦

Zach drove our mothers to the airport in Portland Monday morning, and I promised to take Amber to see Cody on my lunch break.

I came home in a sheriff's department car, and we were almost ready to leave when a vehicle pulled up to the garage behind my cruiser.

Amber was already in the garage when I stepped from the foyer to see a man get out of the sedan.

"Can I help you?" I said, hand resting on my duty belt, easily within reach of my weapon.

"I'm Trent Fields," the man in his not-quite-perfectly tailored suit said with buttermilk smoothness he'd spent hours rehearsing. "I'm the attorney representing Laura Randall."

Nothing in my life involving someone else's lawyer ever turned out well for me, so I didn't reply.

He walked forward with an envelope in one hand, but when he put his polished shoe down on the cement just outside the garage, Laser moved from behind Amber and let loose a threatening growl, stopping the man in his tracks.

"I came to serve you papers," he said, swallowing so loud I could hear it, "in a lawsuit Mrs. Randall has filed for complications related to the delivery of her twin sons."

Laser took a step forward, Fields took a step back.

"All Julie did was try to help her," Amber whined, winding up to a verbal argument until I put my left hand on her arm to quiet her.

"Mr. Fields," I said, nodding. "Nonetheless, I suspect you are trespassing on private property, since I didn't invite you. And if you do not turn around and leave immediately, I believe I'd be within my rights to respond to your actions as a threat to the safety of my family. If that means having the dog chew your right arm off," I said as he took another step backward, "I probably won't have to feed him tonight. Laser?"

The dog answered me with a loud series of aggressive barks that echoed in the garage.

Trent Fields scurried back to his car, but he tossed the envelope on the ground. "I'll still report this as having served you," he said from behind his door as he slithered inside to safety from the dog.

"And I have a witness who says otherwise," I replied. "We'll see how that goes in front of Judge Harrison."

Fields slammed the car door and twisted the key, his eyes trained on me, my hand still hovering over my Glock, the dog at my side.

As gravel flew from his get-away, I heard Amber inside on the phone.

"Cody, what's going on? Your mother is suing Julie for trying to help!"

Great, now what was complicated is going to be even worse after I ran off a lawyer.

I stepped back into the kitchen.

Amber paced as far as the telephone cord would reach, listening then talking in shorts bursts. "That's just stupid, Cody, and you know it. How could she . . . It wasn't Julie's fault something bad . . . No! I don't ever want to see you again!" She slammed the receiver into the wall cradle, turning to me with tears spilling down her red cheeks. "They're suing everyone because the surrogate parents only want the healthy baby."

"It's an ugly situation," I said as she rushed into my arms to hug me, ignoring the metal on my uniform. "Money isn't the best reason to do something, and you can't always depend on people to do what they say." I hugged her tight. "But Amber, I'm not afraid of her lawyer if he can't even serve a subpoena without wetting his pants."

CHAPTER
37

When I retrieved the envelope tossed on the ground by the attorney, I read details that the lawsuit was indeed going to include everyone – me, the ambulance crew, the emergency room staff even though we didn't stop there, the operating room team, the doctors, and the agency that wrote the surrogacy contract. But nothing was mentioned about suing the parents who were supposed to receive the twins. Nor did the suit include Zach, which I found odd.

To demonstrate how stupid this whole charade really was, I considered suing the other parents, because had they not wanted a baby in the first place, none of this would have happened. That seemed to be the sentinel event, in my mind.

I hate lawyers.

As for the lawsuit, I was not concerned about my actions, except I assumed the legal process would take time I didn't want to waste on it.

"I guess this means you don't need me to drive you to see Cody now?" I asked Amber when she collected herself and wiped away her tears.

"As if!" she rebutted. "He can find someone else to rope with."

She'd stood up for me in her own way, which felt pretty good except that she'd alienated someone she had considered a friend.

I opened the refrigerator to pick something for lunch. "It's pretty slow today," I said. "Do you want to come with me back to the lab and finish up on that bag you found?"

She slumped into the barstool across from me. "Nah, not today. I'm too bummed."

We made ham and cheese sandwiches on whole wheat. I guzzled down a glass of milk, then went back to a patrol route that took me to the eastern edge of the county and back to the station. By the time I came in at a quarter to seven that evening, Trent Fields had been to the sheriff's department to find me, or better yet, to locate the sheriff to complain about how I'd treated him.

Wade Fordham was waiting on me.

"What's this crap about a run-in you had with a lawyer for the Randalls?" he asked, leaning into the squad room where I was finishing up some paperwork. "He says he tried to serve you papers."

Without even looking up, I replied, "Well, I didn't shoot him for trespassing."

"Considerate of you."

"Thought about it, though." I raised my head. "When Laura Randall went into labor Friday, Amber happened to be over at their place. The ambulances were both tied up with that collision on Highway 14," I said. "So Amber called me, and I helped."

"Attorney says you're being named as a responsible party because the adopting parents only took one twin. What the hell does that mean?"

"Laura was pregnant with two boys, presumably from an in vitro fertilization of the so-called adopting parents who contracted with her to carry them. I don't know what the contract might have covered as far as breach of duty, pardon the pun, of either party," I said. "Breech, because the first twin presented an arm and an umbilical cord. Both are pretty rare complications, and together even more so. Even though she was only about seven months, that infant wasn't going to deliver sideways. No matter what, they were premature."

"So why are they suing you, and us, by the way," he said with raised eyebrows and a sneering upper lip to indicate his disgust. "Something you did or didn't do?" His voice did not indicate any accusation, just a clarification of the details.

I shook my head. "The only way both babies and the mother were going to survive was an immediate surgical birth. I did what any other prudent licensed person would have done." I tossed down the pen I'd been using. "Happy to sit in front of a judge and explain that the only thing I'm guilty of is offering to help, which was just about the only chance any of them had at surviving."

He nodded.

"Who would be sued if no one had done anything to help and they all died, Wade. It's just crazy," I stated. "And it's not my place to decide whether or not doing the right thing was the right thing to do."

Wade chuckled. "You have such a way with words, Julie," he said. "Anyone can sue anybody over anything, so I guess Laura Randall's lawyer will get his fifteen minutes of fame with this case."

❧

Three days later, I decided it was time for Amber to open the wallet that had been inside the bag.

"Really?" She pulled on a sweater over her tank top. "I hope it's got something we can use to find the owner. That would be sweet."

I took her enthusiasm as a sign that she'd gotten past the funk of what Cody's parents were doing, although she'd refused to speak to him when he'd called the previous night.

"What if there's some identification in it?" she asked. "What will you do then?"

"Depends what it is," I answered as we walked to my truck. "First we run the name on any identification through the criminal databases, see if there are any records. Next we find out if that person is still alive. Then if nothing directs us to a crime, we can contact him or her."

If I'd tossed a bag that deep in the forest, I don't think I'd want someone to ring me up and ask who I was, but that was still many steps ahead.

"Did you hire an attorney?" she asked, changing subjects so fast my thoughts stumbled.

"For Cody's folks? No." I could tell she was still worried. "We'll wait and see what happens." I knew that Laura Randall's claim I'd done something wrong was worth about a million dollars to her. And that a sympathetic judge or jury might just award it to them. "But getting a case into a courtroom is much more difficult. In many cases, defendants like the hospital will offer a settlement."

"That's pretty silly, if you didn't do anything wrong, isn't it?"

I shrugged. "Lawyers go after the parties with the deepest pockets, so defending a claim – even a bogus claim – requires money and time and in some cases, bad publicity. What's paying a million compared to spending two million, win or lose?"

"Can they win?" she asked.

"She's charging me with consequences to negligence, but she didn't refuse my help, and I did not do anything beyond my license or anything wrong. If she can't prove I was negligent, and because she consented to my assistance, she really has no claim."

"How can you prove that?"

I smiled. "I learned the value of a tape recording a long time ago."

"You recorded everything that went on?" Amber sounded astonished. "Wow, I didn't know that."

"Not common knowledge, by the way. I don't want everyone around here thinking I record every word," I warned her.

We rode on to the sheriff's department without continuing that line of conversation.

Returning to the crime lab, albeit very basic as far as forensic testing, I unpacked the evidence we'd sorted, collected the results from various tests, and assembled everything on one table.

"We should have a drum roll," Amber whispered. "This feels like a grand finale." She put on nitrile gloves, then spread a white piece of butcher paper on the metal table. Taking the wallet from the evidence bag, she placed it on the surface and slowly opened the crumbly leather like a book.

The wallet held no driver's license or credit cards, but in the plastic sleeves were a library card, two ticket stubs to a circus – child and adult – and a photograph that was too faded to get details except it looked like three people, two adults and a child.

The library card was faded red or orange cardstock with a metal piece that had a five-digit number, though the card itself was barely readable. Facing the card was the photograph – faded to almost white and appeared to be melted to its plastic covering.

"I can't make out where this is from," Amber said, tilting her head back and forth as she tried to make out the imprint of the letters on the library card.

First I tried shining a light across it, to see if there might be an imprint shadowed where the typeset was done or where the name was typed. When this didn't reveal a readable image, I took a light wand from the cabinet behind us, then switched off the fluorescents overhead. By illuminating the card with different bandwidths of light, eventually the offset printing showed well enough to make out the name of the library.

"It's from Texas?"

The name of the library was visible at the top – Cross Plains Public Library, a Texas town I'd never heard of.

"What can you do with the photo?" she asked, holding it to the lighted magnifying glass.

I went through the settings on the alternate light source again, but none of the choices did more than bring up a vague outline of people. However, I wasn't positive that it wasn't the plastic that made this less than successful, yet it would take some craftsmanship to remove the photographic paper without ruining the image.

"Let's call and see where that card leads us first. Shouldn't be a problem to find out who it was issued to, assuming the library is open." I suggested. "I may have to enlist technical help with the photograph though."

Although I was about to wrap up our little project, Amber picked up a large pair of tweezers, reaching into a small pocket opening toward the middle of the wallet, pulling out a badly discolored piece of stiff cardboard.

I picked up the camera and took a few photos.

Amber sighed in frustration, then turned it over. "The ink looks like it was a transfer from another surface – it's all faded," she said. "Looks more like a design than writing."

Again, I produced the alternate light source wand, but this time I handed it to her.

She shook her head. "What if I break it?"

"You saw how I used it," I said. "Just do the same thing."

Tentatively, she took the wand and shined it onto the surface. After several attempts at switching the light frequencies, suddenly the ink lit up.

Muscles that had held me up all day suddenly felt like mush as I realized that what Amber had pulled from the wallet wasn't a thick piece of cardboard with a drawing.

It was a tattoo. On human skin.

CHAPTER
38

"What is it?" Her voice sounded far away, and I inhaled deeply to regain my focus in the office where we stood instead of the vast forest where the rest of a body might be hidden. About to speak, I flinched when my pager sounded.

Peeking at the display, I saw it was Zach and clipped it back on my belt. He could wait.

"What?" she repeated when I still hadn't spoken. "You look like . . ."

I swallowed. "I think that's a piece of skin, Amber."

The pink in her cheeks faded to the color of a dingy cotton t-shirt, and she yanked her hands away from the table. "But it's not very big."

She was right. Like folding a standard playing card in half, maybe – about two inches on each side.

"Can't be human," she countered. "It looks like leather."

I knew what she was thinking. "What animals do we tattoo with designs like that?" I didn't want to say aloud that human skin could be dried and tanned just like hide from a cow or any other animal. What was now a bit over two inches square could have been as big as maybe six inches each side before – I had no idea, really.

That very idea nauseated me.

"Now we have a reason to involve the department officially," I said, wondering if that would send us looking for a body, given the location where we'd found the bag.

Reaching for the wall phone, I dialed Mitchell Seaver's

extension.

"Yeah," he said, knowing the call came from inside the building, and not bothering to disguise the fact he was chewing.

"Hey, I need your opinion on something," I said. "Can you come to the lab?"

"I'm eatin' lunch, Julie," he mumbled around a mouthful before swallowing. "Can it wait ten minutes?"

"Sure," I said. What would six hundred seconds more be to a case that had probably been a crime before Amber was even born? I hung up.

"What's next?" she asked.

I shook my head. "No clue."

Clues are all you have. None of them make sense.

Questions whirled in my head. How had it been preserved? Could we get DNA from a piece of tanned human skin? What about fingerprints? Was the tattoo something we could trace or was it too distorted? Where would we start looking for the body it came from, given the only other identifiable evidence was from Texas? Was there a connection?

I stepped to where Amber had been working, to take a better look at the imperfect square.

Keeping the design centered and whole seemed to be the goal of the cuts surrounding it. Figuring out what it was supposed to be was not going to be any easier than tracking it down, I suspected. Didn't appear to be a flower, an animal, a word, or a symbol I recognized.

Amber looked up as Seaver swung himself around the doorframe into the room.

"You had a question?" he asked before pursing his lips.

"Remember the bag we found a few weeks ago? We've been going through it, just as if it were evidence from a crime scene as a little education," I explained. "Today we finally got to the last piece – a wallet. Nothing unusual itself, leather, folds in the middle. It contained an old library card from Texas, couple of circus tickets, a photograph so faded we can barely make out any details," I said, pointing to the table, "and that."

Seaver raised an eyebrow at my summary before he took two steps closer to examine more closely the contents I'd described. "You found this," he repeated, using his finger to make a circle in the air above the items, not taking his eyes off the square piece, "in that bag you brought back?"

I nodded when he finally looked up.

He deflated like a blow-up mannequin – far more than I had.

"I think I know . . ." Seaver looked up at the ceiling and blew out a deep breath. "Let me see if I can find a file." He looked back at me. "You haven't called anyone yet, have you?"

I was surprised. "No, who would I call and why?"

"Don't. If I'm right," he said, scrubbing his hands over his face, "that came from Doc Bishop's daughter." He hustled back out the door.

Amber broke the silence that hung in the room. "You mean this might really be a piece of someone?"

"Yeah, which isn't what I wanted to hear, either. Trust me."

This time, I bagged all the pieces myself, taking care to seal envelopes and mark them for evidence collection, stacking everything in neat rows in the cardboard box. Finished, I thought it would be better not to interrupt Mitch Seaver's afternoon again while he searched.

This ought to make for some interesting dinner conversation tonight.

We got in my truck to drive home.

"I still don't understand," she said. "How could that little piece be human?"

"You can tan and preserve hide from almost any animal," I said. "Even bodies in a swamp undergo a similar process due to the chemicals in the water."

"It's not a hide!"

"Actually, human skin isn't much different than the pig or cow hide that we make into leather, just less hair."

"That's gross, Julie." She crossed her arms and turned her head to peer out the other side, as if I were the criminal. "Why would someone do that?"

"Do what?" I retorted. "We don't know anything about it."

"It's disgusting that someone had it, much less that he carried it around in his wallet!"

Hard to argue that.

For someone who'd been revolted at the idea, Amber was certainly uninhibited about discussing it over food an hour later – a trait that again made me think she'd go into some medical service or law enforcement when she got older.

"The other deputy thinks he might know who it's from," she told Zach over his version of meatloaf and scalloped potatoes. She turned to me. "Isn't Dr. Bishop your boss?"

"Yes, but I never heard anything about his daughter," I said.

True enough, but I didn't tell her Seaver had called me not long after we got home, saying he'd dug out an old case file about Catherine Bishop, who apparently had dropped out of high school, became addicted to drugs and various other facets of a life that hadn't been expected to last long when she disappeared.

I confirmed with him that the library card had enough of the right letters to be her name typed on it, though I hadn't spent much time trying to read it, figuring the library could help us.

Seaver promised to get back with me when he found out more, but he confided that we'd more than likely have to re-open the missing person case.

I understood his desire to keep the situation under wraps until he was certain, but I wanted to know more myself about Catherine Bishop and her life before I told Amber, even though she'd spotted the bag that had started everything.

What would Boyd Bishop and his wife say, and how many years had it been since they'd seen their daughter? Did they have any idea what had become of her after she left – she presumably had made it to Texas – so what happened later?

"I wanted to claim that bag," Amber continued explaining to her father, "'cause I was sure that wallet had money in it."

"Finding money or other valuables isn't always a gold mine like you think," Zach said.

"Isn't it finders keepers?" she asked.

He shook his head. "Depends whether an item was abandoned, mislaid or unclaimed, and whether the owner intended it to remain his," Zach said. "For example, if you reported finding a bag of money, authorities would have to decide if someone just set it down and forgot to pick it up again, or maybe it fell out of an armored car when the door flew open. Or had someone buried it to prevent it from being stolen, then died before it was recovered?"

"Then I just wouldn't tell anyone I found it," she said with stoic teenaged defiance.

"If you lost your purse at school or a restaurant, wouldn't you want it back with its contents?" I asked.

"Sure," Amber replied, less convinced. "But I don't believe it would happen."

"You might be surprised what gets sent back to rightful owners with thousands of dollars in cash untouched," Zach said with a smile. "Nevertheless, with your purse, you would intend it to continue to be yours and thus have an expectation of return, so it would be considered mislaid." He took another bite.

"So if this bag had a hundred dollars in it, which would it be?" she asked.

"Depends," he said. "Who really owns the bag and what happened to it? Is there any evidence it was discarded, or was it lost or intentionally hidden? What if it really does hold evidence of a crime of some sort?"

She looked at me for help.

"We'll find out soon enough," I said. "At least there wasn't any money to worry about."

Just the skin we suspected had been cut from a woman who had been missing for two decades.

❁

Three days later, I sat in an office, crowded around an abused conference table with Sheriff Fordham, Deputy Mitchell Seaver, and Boyd Bishop and his wife Esmeralda.

Mitch's voice sounded kind and apologetic to the Bishops for this case raising its ugly head again. This was his first attempt explaining to the Bishops that the department investigation had been reopened.

"Deputy Samualson and her step-daughter were on a rescue recently, riding in the forest east of Mt. St. Helens," he said, "and found a bag."

The bag in question, the one we'd so carefully retrieved and brought back to the lab, had turned out to be little more than threadbare canvas held in shape by the dirt. Mitch had brought photos of it, hoping the Bishops might recognize it.

Neither spoke up.

"Although there was no real reason to treat the bag as evidence at that time, Deputy Samualson was demonstrating to her step-daughter how we process something like this, taking samples, photos, and the like." When he swallowed, his Adam's apple bulged. "The last item they examined was a wallet." He produced another photograph. "Inside was an old library card, two circus ticket stubs, a faded photograph of three people, and a small square of what is believed to be human skin with a tattoo."

Esmeralda Bishop clutched her husband's sleeve so tightly her knuckles turned white, but she did not speak.

Seaver continued. "We review cold cases once a year, so I recognized the design as being similar to your daughter's tattoo – the one on her left shoulder," he explained. Again, he presented the couple with a photo, an image that was very close to real size, appearing to be sort of a heart interlocked in a Celtic eternity knot of some sort.

"That's not it," Mrs. Bishop said, looking away.

But Boyd reached out and took the image, studied it, then shook his head.

I spoke. "Dr. Bishop, the skin may have shrunk or been distorted during its preservation," I said, avoiding the word 'leather' at least for now, "or over time from being carried in the wallet."

He shook his head again. "It's similar but it's not the same. Catherine's was smaller, delicate, not quite this shape." From his lab coat pocket, he pulled an old photograph of a young woman, shorts and tanktop shirt, bent forward washing a car, turning just her head toward the photographer. The tattoo on her shoulder was visible but not clearly. The image had lost some of its color, but from what little I could make out, Catherine's tattoo appeared to be two hearts interconnected, not a heart and a triangle.

The lines of the tattoo on the skin we had were thicker.

Mitch took a breath, probably to argue, but I beat him to the draw. "Did she maybe know someone who had a similar tattoo?" I asked. "Boyfriend, best friend?"

Both of them shrugged.

"Do you know where she had hers done, what year? Even knowing a city could point us in some direction."

The doctor frowned, pushing his eyebrows together. "It was in the summer of 1974. She went to some shop in a suburb of Portland. East of the river, I think."

He meant the Willamette River, which cut the city in half east and west. It left a large area to search for the sort of business that probably wouldn't have lasted twenty-two years.

"First time I saw it was two months before she disappeared," Dr. Bishop said, shaking his head in what I saw as disgust.

I nodded, wondering if our questions had accomplished nothing more than tearing open their old wounds.

"We'll see if we can get any sort of DNA or blood type from this that would help get an identity," Mitch said, although I'd voiced my doubt that either test would yield a usable result.

"Won't do any good," Dr. Bishop said, his hand covering his wife's, still gripping his sleeve. "We adopted her when she was a baby, so matching DNA to either of us won't help. And I made Ez throw out everything of hers years ago."

I understood he was trying to say we couldn't match the tattoo unless we found a body, and maybe not even then.

✄

"So that's the best you can do?" Amber demanded after I explained what had happened in the meeting. "No one's even going to try to find out what happened to her?"

"We don't know the tattoo was hers," I replied, "or even what it is."

"It's a Buddhist love knot," she announced as if I should have known that.

"Okay, but even so we doubt it is from her so the possibilities are endless. She could be dead or still living anywhere in the world," I replied. "I'm open for a reasonable direction to go if you have one."

"The library card?" She anchored her fists onto her narrow hips. "Did you check that?"

"Yes. The public library in Cross Plains, Texas, opened in 1979, which is five years after she disappeared from here. The card was issued in her name but wasn't used after the first eight weeks, during which she checked out seven books including *Scruples*, *The Holcraft Covenant*, and *If Life is a Bowl of Cherries.*"

"See? That's not the sort of stuff a homeless drug-addicted runaway would read."

"Have you even heard of any of those titles?" I asked.

"I can read," she retorted in sarcastic teenage fashion, "and I know who Erma Bombeck is, yes!"

I sighed. "Valid points, all. So what do you deduce from this information?" I pulled out a stool and watched her pace in the kitchen.

"You say the Bishops reported her missing in 1974, when she was nineteen. Old enough for a driver's license and a Social Security card," she said. "So either she was alive at least five years to be in Texas when that library opened or someone used her identity. She liked common stuff to read, or maybe it was the least difficult to find and get back out of the library with, so you should find out what she might have been reading here before she left."

"Good ideas," I said. "Keep going."

"I think she hooked up with someone who tried to get a similar tattoo," she continued. "It would be revealing if we knew whether that was before she left or after. The fact it looks like hers but apparently isn't makes me think it was some guy who beat her, until she eventually killed him in self-defense."

My past flashed backward in my head, stopping on the memory of the moment I pulled the trigger and shot David – a memory I'd hoped might someday be buried so far it never haunted me again.

Apparently not yet.

"Maybe so, Amber," I conceded. "Which means she might still be alive, but that still leaves us not knowing where or how to find her."

"You said she was adopted. If it was me," she said, "I'd go look for my real mother."

"There's a trail we might be able to follow if we can get her birth records opened," I said, standing up. "Thanks. Keep thinking. Who knows, we might find her yet."

"What about her reading choices here?" Amber prodded.

"Best I can tell, she didn't check out books from the public library here," I answered. "There are no school records, and Mrs. Bishop doesn't remember anything noteworthy."

"What about nearby towns to Cross Plains?" she asked, unwilling to give up.

"Amber, I'm afraid we could call every library in Texas without finding her. If she's alive and changed her name, then likely she will be using someone else's identity now, too."

CHAPTER
39

Because it was a good idea, I followed Amber's theory about finding Catherine Bishop's birth mother that same week, running into another moat and brick wall. Two months later when the records were opened, I learned that her birth mother, Robin Case-Matthews, died years before of cancer. Catherine would have been about nine. Doubtfully she would have started searching until she was sixteen when the Bishops said she found out she was adopted, and maybe she never found out who her biological mother was. When I interviewed Robin's husband, he denied knowing she had given a baby up for adoption before they married, some six years after Catherine had been born.

I tried searching the national criminal databases for all variations of Catherine's name and date of birth, to no avail. Searching for someone who never wants to be found is difficult.

Disappointment wrinkled on Amber's face when I let her in on the lack of progress. "Did her mother have any other children?"

I shrugged. "I didn't think to ask her husband, but that's a good idea."

And it was, but it led nowhere, too – no half-siblings.

The case remained almost as cold as it had been for the last two decades.

✳

Despite the attempts we made at matching pieces of the puzzle created by items in the bag, months passed without any sort of step forward or backward in the case.

Zach was gone for work several weeks at a time, which left Amber and me evenings to discuss the case. I could tell she was determined to find some answer, and I followed her suggestions, chasing any lead until it was exhausted.

We'd even taken the horses back out to where she'd found the bag, and in an afternoon, searched an area almost a mile square around it without finding any other clues.

For a class project, Amber wrote a paper on the science of the investigation based on this case, which earned her a hundred plus ten points for her photographic supplements. Still, there was no sign of Catherine Bishop.

In early October, the lawyers took sides and battled in a courtroom about who should be responsible for the calamity that had been Laura Randall's pregnancy, delivery and the survival of the twins. Judge Harry Harrison, a stodgy-looking man whose appearance belied his advanced age, finally threw out the suit against everyone except the obstetrician who was supposed to have been following the surrogate pregnancy after having performed the implantation, for failure to assess and document the potential for communicable diseases prior to pregnancy or at the time of birth.

While the adopting family had adequate legal right to the healthy baby per the contract, they chose not to accept custody of the other. Their decision, while not the most ethical, perhaps, still proved to be in their best interest as the second infant's condition worsened, first with pneumonia, then with signs of both ocular and central nervous systems herpes viral infection. Although treatment had begun at his premature birth, the infant had developed a severe reaction to the acyclovir regimen, which had to be stopped.

"You mean the baby caught Laura's herpes?" Amber asked while we prepared supper one evening.

I nodded.

"Will he be blind?"

Blindness was one of many likely consequences, rolling on toward death. "Probably so," I said. "But even worse, because the delivery was extremely compromised, I suspect that he also underwent a long period where too little oxygen reached his brain."

"That's why the contract parents didn't want him, isn't it?"

"It's not like choosing from the last two puppies in a litter when one is a runt, Amber. Both sides of the argument have valid moral points for their choices," I said, "From where we stand, there are a lot of wrongs, none of which add up to making a right."

Amber stopped chopping peppers and looked at me. "And Laura Randall will have to keep this sick baby, won't she?"

I nodded. "Sad to say, but if she doesn't take him, he'll end up a ward of the state until he dies," I said, thinking to myself what a blessing to him that might be.

Three weeks later, I wondered if I'd cursed myself with such a bleak thought when a stranger came to tell me Zach was dead.

CHAPTER

40

When Amber and I returned to Washington in mid-November, the cabin didn't seem so much a home as an empty shell – a physical example of how I felt after we'd had Zach's funeral in New Mexico on the sixth. The next two weeks we'd spent in Albuquerque were a blur – a wild, desperate, chaotic disaster, like a spinning tornado that left our lives uprooted in shreds. I felt like a flood had crashed through and washed away everything with meaning.

Amber had been at school when a stranger in an expensive suit and tie, polished shoes, and government-issue mirrored sunglasses came to the cabin door the last day of October – Halloween.

I was pissed that the DEA had sent a stranger to deliver a death notification, not someone I knew, or at least someone who worked with Zach. The one partner my husband would have entrusted to perform such grim duty was dead. Zach hadn't been the first to tell Domino Hurley's wife, either, but I forced Zach to leave my hospital bedside to go see Roni because he was the only one who could tell her the real story of what had happened, and she needed to know the truth.

I understood that.

The stranger at my door had given me nothing. I didn't even get truth from him.

Among his many words, all I heard was "Suicide," which the stranger had said without any emotion at all on his face.

I don't know whether I said "Bullshit" aloud or just in my head, but it echoed like thunder in a canyon.

Dying by one's own hand was an emotional cliff where Zach and I had each stood at different points of our lives, waiting for a moment of courage or cowardice, desperation to jump or even to be knocked off by fate. Not often had we spoken of those feelings to each other, but I knew only one instance in his life when he'd put his gun to his head and considered pulling the trigger.

And I know what stopped him.

I remember thinking those exact words as the stranger in the doorway kept talking, before I interrupted his droning monologue. "No, tell me how he died."

He repeated that Zach had committed suicide.

When I pressed for more information, the stranger repeated the vague explanation that sounded carefully scripted by someone else. Someone who didn't really know Zach. The veracity of the story was like cheap fabric. Each time it was washed, more color rinsed away until it was gray and streaked. I suspected if I pulled hard enough, it would rip.

I tried, but the more questions I asked, the sketchier the information became, until the nameless stranger quoted nonsense to me – words not meant to protect me from the grief, but to shield me from the truth.

For all his secrets, I knew Zach Samualson well enough to realize he would have died for any of a thousand reasons, but he would not have killed himself. Hearing the words, for the briefest moment, I contemplated the possibility that he might really have committed suicide. But I could not – would not believe it. In my broken heart, I knew that, although he might be dead, there was no way he would have taken his own life, no matter what. A lot of other things might have happened to him, but not that.

Maybe after everything I'd survived in the past, I wasn't all that surprised to hear the impersonal bad news about my husband's death – just the reason he was dead.

The bland emotionless face spoke smooth rehearsed phrases that were meaningless in light of the overall message.

"Hearing you talk," I said, feeling my face grow red, "I suspect that the government has finally created robots to make death notifications."

Then I'd slammed the door in his face.

When he had the gall to knock again, I loudly gave Laser an order to kill – the dog didn't know any such command but barked fiercely just the same.

The stranger hurried to his car, leaving my questions unanswered and my emotions boiling in a stew of anger and grief.

I stood motionless, staring at the door until my chest burned, triggering me to take a breath. Alone, save the dog, I trudged to the window seat of the cabin and bawled until Amber came home from school.

When I tried to tell her, tried to get her to sit down and listen, she rebelled with a rage I had not yet been able to summon. She yelled at me for crying as I wiped tears from my eyes that no longer even rolled down my cheeks but just puddled and blurred my vision.

Trying to repeat what the man in the suit had said, I choked on the words.

"You're lying!" she yelled and ran outside.

I wished she'd been right. I wished I had the energy to go after her.

From the kitchen window, I watched her bridle Denali and swing herself up to his back without a saddle. I understood her need to run away as fast as possible, and that in time she'd come back.

I picked up the phone to make calls that had to be made. I'd started with my mother, hoping for some sort of wisdom or strength. Next came Zach's mother. Telling Vera Samualson she'd lost her son was the hardest thing I've ever had to do.

I'd been on the phone to Eric Rader, a friend and ex-boss from my days in the New Mexico State Police, because I didn't know who else to call, when Amber shuffled back inside. When I hung up, she put her arms around me, and we cried together.

Although I'd steeled myself all along for the possibility that Zach could die doing what he loved, I felt brittle and cold. The next day, while Amber and I made plans, I barely had strength to open my eyes each time I blinked. But as the news really sank into my soul, as crushed as my heart was, I was positive that no matter what his death had looked like or what someone wanted me to believe, suicide had not been Zach's intention.

Amber and I agreed the memorial service should be in Albuquerque, much like what Zach had planned for her mother and grandmother.

Zach's mother had wanted the services to be in the Catholic Church where she went.

"It's not church," Amber announced in a flat voice after we hung up with Vera. "I want it to be whatever you think Dad would want."

"Funerals and memorials are for us, for the living," I responded. And as much as the next words were unbelievable to me, I continued, "It's a way for us to celebrate the life we shared with him and to say goodbye."

And we cried again.

Once those plans and travel arrangements had been made, I no longer had the energy to deal with the doubt and resentment quivering in my soul by Zach's death. I couldn't think clearly enough to overcome the lack of logic, to make sense of my unanswered questions and demand answers.

Had it not been for my mother, flying to Portland that afternoon to help us, nothing would have been planned at all.

Two days later, sitting in the front pew of the church in Albuquerque, I tried hard to remember my words to Amber about celebrating his life as I listened to Zach's friends who stood to talk about him. Words about him like integrity, loyalty, and friendship brought more tears to my eyes because I could see that others had loved in him the same qualities I had. That they would miss him.

Some of his friends and coworkers spoke to me afterward, sharing snippets of Zach's life I might not have known otherwise, but then they were all gone.

After Amber and I returned to the cabin, my anger at what had happened bobbed up and down, but my questions continued to be ignored. Fighting the government to get the truth was more effort than I could rally.

Perhaps Zach and I did something right, teaching Amber how to grieve the death of her mother, because she was the only thing that kept me going those days when I felt like crumbling to dust. Still, sometimes seeing Zach's green eyes blink in her pretty face could make my heart skip a beat, but I held on to the one living part of him that I had left.

I understood better how my mother must have felt, looking at me after my father was murdered.

Not having a biological child myself, I was left with the daughter of others in a complicated matter of circumstance and death. I tried to remember that she'd lost both of her parents and her grandmother, all within a year or so, without being able to say goodbye. Some days, Amber's anger erupted with painful truths like the fact I wasn't her "real" mother. There were times the best we could do was agree that we both missed Zach. Somehow, grief kept us leaning on each other, but in reality, we had no one else.

Parenthood was difficult for me because I tried to make everything black and white, straight-edged, rigid and permanent, befitting my own personality. Amber's world was multi-colored and pliable like blobs of Play-Doh. I wanted to guide her away from all the problems I'd faced as a teenager, but our worlds wouldn't mesh and she refused to follow. Still Amber and I had pulled ourselves together to go on with living.

No matter what I expected – rational or not – the world didn't stop turning just because my husband was dead. And I resented that it hadn't, at least for one tiny moment.

But by mid-November, things had become so difficult for Amber, she asked to go back to Albuquerque and stay with Zach's mother during the holidays, to live there for the rest of the school year in the spring. I believed her move was a desperate attempt to leave a place where she could not escape the memories, though I was less sure if it was my presence or his absence she felt she had to leave.

Watching her board a jet should have been sad, but I couldn't find an emotion or reaction for it.

And then I was alone.

CHAPTER

41

Empty. Some days that was the best I could do. There were a lot of moments that much worse whispered my name. For the first time in a couple of years, I felt that gnawing urge to do what Zach had called prowling: finding dangerous situations to skirt, hoping to feel fear because there was so little other emotion left.

Work and taking care of Five Aces, Zach's name for the hundred-acre property where he'd built the cabin and barn, filled my days and zapped my energy though December.

Although I'd gone many days or weeks, or longer without seeing Zach, both before and after we were married, facing the fact that he wouldn't ever come home again felt like I was being slammed into a brick wall, and it left me as broken as I'd ever been.

But just a few days after New Year's, another stranger knocked on my door – a driver from a shipping company, with a box propped on a dolly, waiting for my signature. I just about dropped to my knees when I saw the address to me.

In Zach's handwriting.

Another mystery box – like the one he gave me at Christmas before we got married? Maybe. Only this came from a dead man.

Why now? Had Vera kept the box and waited to send it? Had it been lost in transit?

I signed for it, but the box itself ignited more questions and no answers, including the fact that Zach's mother hadn't shipped it – the return address was somewhere near Seattle, Washington.

I considered waiting to see if Amber came back during spring break, but it wasn't addressed to both of us, and I didn't know what to make of that.

Putting the box on the kitchen counter, I used a paring knife to cut the tape along the edges. I realized Zach would have had a tantrum if he saw me torturing one of the kitchen utensils in such a manner.

The box wasn't stuffed almost past its capacity like the first one he'd presented me, but it was full. The first thing I picked up was an envelope.

Addressed by hand to me, my heart pounded too hard to peel the sealed flap – I put it down until my hands stopped shaking. Gaining control again after a few deep breaths, I reached into the box and pulled out two t-shirts from Seattle and Portland. A sweatshirt from the zoo in Point Defiance – a place we'd gone together once. The image on the front was an otter.

What had Zach said when we were there? That he'd like to be reincarnated as an otter because they have so much fun.

Tears filled my eyes.

I pulled out two music CDs and few other knick-knacks, then a small box. I lifted the lid to find four handmade pieces of white chocolate candy – which had been my favorite until Anthony Bock had drugged the pieces before sending me a box when I was in the hospital. So many years ago, it seemed. There was a small card inside the lid, in Zach's neat handwriting – *Some things you'll always love...*

Debating whether or not to have one, I put the chocolates aside and dug deeper past more souvenirs to a white box about the size of a picture frame for a 5 x 7 photo, a bit over an inch deep. When I picked it up, I found the box was heavy and not balanced.

Taped shut, I had to use the knife again. Pulled off the top and found...

A pistol? In a sealed evidence bag.

Not Zach's, neither the Sig he carried nor the Kimber I'd given him for his birthday, still upstairs in his top dresser drawer.

This was a Taurus, a small-caliber model Zach would never have used.

Without realizing, I shoved the gun and its wrappings back inside the larger box just to get it out of my hands.

Why on earth would there be a gun in here?

In plastic.

In a box shipped to me from a dead man?

The questions made my pulse pound in my ears.

My attention returned to the envelope again. Turning it over, I recognized the return address on the flap was the street where I grew up.

I scrambled to the bathroom, barely in time to puke in the toilet. Finally, weak, pale and sweaty, not knowing what else to do, I threw everything back inside and carried the box upstairs into a locked closet in the office.

Then I tried very hard to forget it.

CHAPTER

42

The next stranger at my doorstep in early March stood beside a man who was anything but.

"Julie," Nolan said when I opened the front door. He stepped forward to hug me though he was obviously a little stunned at the pale, thin woman I'd become. He did not ask how I was.

Nolan Forester, FBI special agent, ranked in the list of last people I expected to see. Not those I hadn't expected to see anytime soon – those I never expected to see again.

He held the hug tightly and whispered in my ear, "Julie, I was so sorry to hear about Zach."

As if seeing Nolan wasn't enough, hearing words of sympathy in a moment of surprise caught in my throat, and the best I could do was nod.

He finally released me and took a step back. "I'm sorry to barge in like this, Julie. This is Special Agent Jamie Gordon," Nolan said, motioning to the man beside him. Maybe he said something else, I don't know.

Facing a man I was sure I'd never met, some weird connection sparked as I stared into dark eyes every bit as haunted as my own. Eyes that saw exactly what mine saw.

A physical sensation like an electrical current hummed in my skull when he took my hand to shake it.

"Julie, there's something we need to talk to you about," Nolan said, breaking the spell.

I blinked, gathering my wits and manners, and invited them inside.

We could have sat in the den, but without direction from any of us, we ended up at the dining room table, gathered around the end. I offered to make coffee, but they both declined.

I sat, and we exchanged looks around the table again.

"Mrs. Samualson, I need to ask you some questions about your husband," Gordon began.

Suddenly my brain recognized more implications to this conversation than I knew how to interpret.

I looked at Nolan. "Is this official FBI business?"

"Not exactly."

Maybe I held an irrational prejudice of all federal agencies, lumping them together into the same basket I'd shoved the DEA, where Zach had proudly served despite the problems. Like feeding its own to a pack of wolves led by a rogue DEA agent running a drug ring who then somehow walked out of jail with multiple state and federal charges against him. That monster had murdered Amber's mother and erroneously another young girl thought to be Zach's daughter, and then Zach's partner. Had it not been for Nolan Forester's help – as a friend, not as an FBI agent – I'd probably have lost my husband during that clusterfuck of inept bureaucratic action.

Nolan was the only government agent from my past in whom I'd retained any trust at all. It was the man I trusted, though, not the agency that employed him.

Now he'd brought someone into my home to ask questions about Zach. Questions that were "not exactly" official FBI business.

Questions that stunk like roadkill on a hot day.

The silence was awkward, but I volunteered nothing as I stared at Nolan.

"Mrs. Samualson," Gordon said, trying to get my attention.

I waited another moment before turning to him, sitting across the table from me. "I think you know way too much about me to maintain the illusion of formality. Just call me Julie and quit wasting your breath."

He nodded and sighed as if I'd already tried his patience, yet he hesitated. "When was the last time you were outside the country?"

"We took our daughter to British Columbia last summer," I said, not liking the fact that he started with a family matter instead of just Zach.

"Overseas?" he clarified.

"Germany in 1989, after the Berlin Wall fell. But if you know enough to ask me, you already know the answer." Now my patience was beginning to fray.

"You were born in Germany, correct?" he continued, attempting to sound casual.

"Only because they wouldn't let my mother onto the U.S. military base to deliver her baby," I retorted. That complication had been difficult for my father to sort out before bringing my mother and me to the United States.

"Did you receive any packages from Zach when he was away on assignments this last year?" Gordon asked.

A wild leap of topics.

I had to weigh whether or not he already knew the answer to this, and so I offered a purely semantics response. "No. Zach didn't send any packages while he was on an assignment."

"Are you sure?"

"Sure of what?" *I'm sure I'm telling you all I intend to...*

The agent almost rolled his eyes, I could tell. "Did he send anything here before he died?"

Nope, not before he died, Mr. FBI. I dare you to ask me if he sent me anything after.

I shook my head, wondering what sort of fishing expedition this was. No matter what Agent Gordon was fishing for, I was feeling very much like the bait.

Bait always ends up dead, something in my head screamed. My defenses jangled my brain on higher alert than it had been in four months, though I wouldn't have thought anything could stun or surprise me, especially after what I'd found in the box that I was so careful not to acknowledge even existed.

I kept my face the emotionless blank left by Zach's death, an expression that had begun to feel permanent already.

Gordon was about to ask another question when I interrupted him.

"Look, I've put up with all the government crap I intend to about my husband. You can tell me what you want to know and why, or this discussion is over," I declared, leaning back and crossing my arms in defiance.

Gordon looked at Nolan, who shrugged.

"I said I'd bring you to meet her. I never said this would be easy," Nolan said to him. Then to me, he continued. "I don't know all the connections to this, but I don't think Zach committed suicide."

CHAPTER
43

Nolan's words bought my past with Zach into sudden mental focus, and I savored the moment. I really didn't care whether my face gave away the distraction, as much as I treasured the memories, which had become harder to recall – a "normal" reaction to grief that I hated. Though he was well beyond the statement that derailed my thoughts, I held up a hand, interrupting him mid-sentence. " ... didn't commit suicide?" I blurted.

Nolan shook his head.

"What proof has anyone really shown that he did?" I demanded. "For the last four months, I've sat in this house, wondering what proof there was he had committed suicide as they insisted, because I didn't get a body to bury – I was given an empty coffin. No, let me rephrase that," I growled, "I had to *pay* for an empty casket to bury. But no matter what they told me, I never believed Zach killed himself. What is this all about?"

I realized that I was standing, towering over my two guests. Yelling.

"Julie, please sit. There is a lot of conflicting and misleading information circulating without any proof. Evidence exists but makes little sense outside its context," Nolan said.

Government bullshit. I knew all about that.

"'Truth that is different than the sum of its facts,' I believe you once said," Jamie Gordon quoted me from the lawyer's notes when I'd faced charges for the murder of Deputy Matthew Shannaker in

Michigan.

Turning on Gordon like a viper, I leaned across the table toward him. "Who *are* you? How did you know that? What do you have to do with anything related to Zach?"

Jamie Gordon did not back away. "I'm trying to find out whether your husband was involved with my wife's death."

"How dare you!" I shrieked, pointing to the door. "Get out!"

"Julie!" Nolan stood and took my arms, turning me to face him. "I know you're upset, and I haven't handled this well. But listen to me. During Zach's last assignment, he was on a case that might have crossed paths with Jamie's wife, Rebecca Nelson. She specialized in computer and accounting forensics at a large insurance company."

I took a breath and nodded for him to go on with his explanation.

"The facts say she was in Seattle. The DEA was there on a case of international drug dealing. There is no proof that she and Zach ever met. However, they both died in ways that don't make any sense. Deaths with no bodies. Bad explanations."

Gordon continued. "I apologize. I didn't mean to imply your husband caused Becca's death. Authorities told me she was on some small plane that crashed outside of Denver, nineteen days later than when your husband died in Seattle," he said, then paused. "I'm looking for the truth about Becca, just like you are about your husband."

"What has any of this got to do with me? I don't *know* what Zach was doing. I certainly don't know anything about your wife," I argued. "Why are you here?"

Jamie Gordon reached into the inside pocket of his black leather jacket and pulled out a wedding photograph, holding it out.

Intending to dismiss it, I glanced, then blinked and looked more closely.

My own mother would have sworn it was me standing beside the groom, who was undoubtedly Jamie Gordon. The bride had slightly darker hair than my own, shoulder length, but otherwise was a dead ringer, pardon the pun.

When I raised my head, his eyes locked with mine, and behind that practiced calm expression, I saw a man whose world had shattered into as many pieces as my own. Electricity zinged the base of my skull again.

Just as quickly, Jamie broke the connection and looked away, almost as if he were embarrassed that I could read his thoughts. If I really looked that much like his wife, I could only imagine what was going through his mind.

"I heard about Zach," Nolan continued, "but not until several weeks after his death."

"So, how did that come to involve me?" I asked again.

"I'd just gone back to work when I heard about a drug enforcement agent who'd taken his life in Seattle, a reported drowning with the body never being recovered," Gordon began, only to be interrupted.

"You heard he drowned?" I asked, dismayed he knew more than I did.

His response was just a shrug. "That's what I heard. The scenario seemed as unlikely as Becca dying in a plane crash when no identifiable remains were returned to me."

"When Jamie began looking into Zach's history, he came across information about you and the incident in Florida, so he contacted me. He told me about Rebecca, but when I saw her photo, I just about fell over. I knew it wasn't you, but it was so close."

There was no debating that, I thought, handing the photo back without looking at its recipient.

"Had Jamie not been with the Bureau, I wouldn't have contacted you. But then when we dug deeper, this isn't the only jagged connection in the story, Julie," Nolan stated. "Not only were Rebecca and Zach in Seattle at about the same time, Jamie had been stationed at Holloman AFB in Alamogordo when you worked there. It's just too coincidental not to mean something, but I don't know what."

Bewildered, I sat down again. "Alamo?" I was too surprised to be angry.

"I was the officer on duty for the surveillance at the base the day your – you – he – your husband – I mean your – " Jamie's stammer unnerved me out of being speechless.

"The day David Wesley slit my throat," I finished for him. "The day I shot him twice in the chest and killed him. Yes yes yes, *that* day. I remember it." In a response I still could not always control, like a knee jerk to a doctor's hammer, my hand went to the scar across my throat, tugging up my collar.

Jamie nodded at my outburst but continued. "Despite my commanding officer's orders not to interfere, I called 911. After the gunshots. I should have done the right thing sooner. I'm sorry."

I shook my head and considered what he'd said. "That's great. I don't know whether I should thank you for finally calling or shoot you for waiting so long."

Maybe I was kidding, but he couldn't be sure. Regardless, my words hung in the air between us all while I glared at him.

"Look, there is a lot of this story you two need to discuss and figure out. Off the record," Nolan said, breaking the silence. "Things I should not be involved in. I promised Olivia that I wouldn't stay, but I didn't think you'd speak to him if I didn't come."

"You're right," I stated but didn't take my eyes off Jamie.

"So, if you wouldn't mind taking him to his motel in Stevenson when you're done talking, I have a flight to catch back to Michigan."

Jamie opened his mouth to disagree to their arrangements, to being left with a woman who'd just threatened him.

Nolan chuckled. "Trust me, Jamie, if she really intended to shoot you, I'd already be dragging your body back to the car."

With a half-smile, I shrugged a non-committal agreement.

We walked with Nolan outside to his rental car. Jamie retrieved a thick briefcase from the backseat.

Nolan hugged me and whispered in my ear, "I think you can trust him, Julie, but make him earn it."

I smiled and kissed his cheek. "It was nice to see you, Nolan. Tell Olivia I said hello."

He nodded, shook Jamie's hand, and climbed into the car. "Good luck."

Two of us, strangers, waved as Nolan drove toward the gate.

I wondered if Jamie Gordon was as terrified as I was.

CHAPTER

44

Jamie followed me into the house and placed his briefcase flat on the table where we'd been sitting, but he hesitated before reaching for the locks.

"I was about to fix lunch. Will you join me?" I said, trying to be a hostess and find something else to do or say besides the previous discussion about our respective spouses, most of which had really freaked me out so far.

"That's kind of you, yes."

Motioning for him to sit at the breakfast bar, I pulled out a large resealable container with leftover chili I'd made the day before, poured it into a pan to reheat, then started on a grilled sandwich to cut in half.

I could feel him watching me.

When I picked up a knife to slice a tomato, he reached across the bar and put his hand on mine, wrapped around the knife. "God, this is so eerie. That," he said, nodding to my right hand beneath his, "is the only thing I see different. Becca is left-handed. You're like mirror images of each other." His voice faltered, and he let go of my hand, but I don't think it was because he wanted to.

A flashing thought went through my head about how much more I'd have looked like her when I cut and dyed my hair before going to Florida a few years ago. "I'm sorry," I said, not knowing what else to say.

It's not as if he had any physical resemblance to Zach I could compare. Jamie was probably a little over six feet tall, with a hard runner's body, thin and gaunt. He shaved his head but wore a trimmed goatee. His eyes were dark brown, like bitter chocolate.

Jamie watched as I finished slicing the tomato for the sandwich. "I'm sorry. I had no idea how hard it would be to look at a stranger and see her."

"I can't imagine. So she's left-handed. What else is different?" I held my arms out and spun around.

He squinted, studying me. "She wasn't as thin, but you're more muscular, I think. You've lost weight since your husband died, right? Eating because you have to, because someone makes you," he said. "I see myself shrinking, more in my head than my body, maybe. As if I'll disappear completely before it stops hurting."

It won't ever stop hurting.

I nodded. I felt something similar. Sleepless in a bed where there had only ever been Zach and me. Exhaustion had led to sleep, but hunger did not return to its previous norm.

Slicing cheese and layering ham onto the bread, I then placed the sandwich on the griddle and stirred the chili.

He waited until I'd turned my back to continue. "Her eyes were not that same color of blue as yours. Hers were more a hazel color, but she wore blue contacts often. You move in some of the same ways, like with the knife."

Peeking over my shoulder for just a glimpse, he looked like someone had slugged him in the chest with a bat.

He swiveled the bar chair to look out over the deck. "Beautiful place here."

Change of subject.

"Thank you. It was a surprise. Zach bought the land and had the house built before we got married." *Before he even knew for sure I'd be a part of his life.*

"Tell me about him," Jamie said, gazing out toward the barn.

"He was with the Houston PD before going to DEA. His –"

"No, Julie, I don't want a dossier," he interrupted, turning back to me. "Tell me about who he was to you. I need to understand all of these pieces before I can face what I suspect really happened."

"Which is?" I said, feeling anxiety race through me at being asked to paint an image of Zach for someone who wouldn't understand what was on the inside. To me, my husband was something totally different from what other people saw.

"Later," Jamie said, dismissing my question. "Dig through the facts and see what *you* think happened. You might not see what I do. I could be wrong. I hope I am."

I flipped the sandwich to brown the other side, letting the silence build for several minutes. "You think either of us can really be objective about these so-called facts?" I finally asked, turning off the burners. I ladled chili into bowls and then cut the grilled sandwich in half, using the spatula to slide each onto a plate, scooting the dishes across to where he sat at the bar. "I want to know the truth because what I've been told makes no sense. I want to know why I'm being lied to about my husband."

He pulled the food closer. "Problem with finding the truth, Julie, is we might not like it very much."

"Damn sure don't like the lies," I said. "I don't know about you, but I think I deserve to know whether my husband really did kill himself. And if he did, I need to understand why." I took a bite of the thick red chili. I tried not to think about what I could have missed in Zach's life that would leave him on that edge again. Although I was almost certain, a tiny doubt always raised its head to say he *could* have taken his own life.

Jamie picked up his sandwich, sighed, then put it back down. "You're right. I suspect I won't like the truth about Rebecca, but I need to know. I think she was doing something illegal. Moving money out of the country for someone, maybe."

"You really believe that?" I asked, taking another bite to hide my surprise.

"She was a forensic accountant, an expert at tracking hidden money. That was her job, right? There's no reason to think she couldn't find better ways to move or hide it, if that was what she was doing," he said, stirring his chili absently. "According to Treasury, no one has reported any large sums of money missing, so I suspect it was a criminal's."

"That doesn't make any sense," I said, trying to picture what he described.

"I know. If she was stealing money, it wasn't out of necessity," he explained. "Her parents are wealthy. She'd lived off a generous trust fund since she started college and stands to inherit millions." He looked down and corrected himself. "Stood."

Instead of answering, I took another bite of the grilled ham and cheese sandwich and chewed.

Finally, he did the same, but he was telling the truth about his weight – the food held no interest to him at all. He ate to be polite.

I swallowed. "Can I ask you something," I said, unsure how to word the question, but knowing he wouldn't like it.

He looked up and nodded.

"You talk about Rebecca in both the present tense and past tense. Do you suspect she is alive?"

"Without a body, who am I to dispute the government's report that she was killed?" he asked. "There's no evidence to the contrary, or so the FAA politely pointed out – there was a crash, she was a passenger, and all souls aboard died. Their facts leave me hanging between a truth I hate and a suspicion I can't live with. Either she's really dead, or she's a thief and maybe even a traitor."

CHAPTER

45

"So let's work the case like it was ours to solve." I said, taking another bite of chili. "Even where we're missing information, we may be able to speculate,"

"Nolan told me that you were a good investigator." Jamie paused to take a spoonful.

The muscles in his jaw flexed as he chewed the hearty chunks of beef in the chili, but within seconds his eyes opened wide and he gasped.

I slid off the stool to reach into the fridge and tossed him a beer, which he opened and gulped.

"Holy crap! If I hadn't just watched you heat this up and then take two bites," he croaked, taking another drink, "I'd swear you'd poisoned me."

I tried to hide a grin when beads of sweat broke out on his forehead. "I forgot to warn you. I make it hot."

He finished the beer, holding the bottle up to the light as if he were surprised it was already empty. "You could have just shot me, really," he muttered, wiping his mouth and then his forehead with the paper napkin I'd provided.

"Wouldn't have been nearly as satisfying." I pulled out two bottles of cola this time, holding one up. "Milk works better, if you'd rather."

He shook his head, his eyes still watering when he took the drink. "No, this is fine." He cleared his throat. "Man, that's just cruel."

I smiled innocently and took another bite, clearly not saying aloud that I didn't taste anything out of the ordinary, before I opened my can.

He scooted the bowl away. "As I was about to say, Nolan told me a little about how you work a case. Even second-hand, it sounded intriguing."

"Just a different way to look at things."

He took a more careful bite of the sandwich, leery of a hidden jalapeno, perhaps. "No, you make that sound too simple. Profiling doesn't –"

I interrupted him mid-sentence. "The FBI thinks its Behavioral Science Unit is great, and profiling is no doubt a valuable tool. The evidence may indicate a certain type of person committed a series of crimes, but what use is it if the profile points to a white male in his forties with a blue collar job, a female companion who thinks he's domineering and neighbors who think he's a recluse, if he's a statistical anomaly."

"How many deviations from the normal serial killer are there, statistically?"

"Who's counting, but how many does it take?" I asked.

"Okay, but in this case, we don't have anyone's behavior to evaluate. There's not even a crime scene, so there's no idea what the crime was, only missing bodies." He shook his head. "It's like a black jigsaw puzzle with a thousand pieces, most of them missing."

Not a bad analogy, I thought. "How do you work a regular jigsaw puzzle without seeing the picture on the box?"

He shrugged. "Start with the edges. Group like colors."

"Then that's how we start. Separate the edges and find the corners, group the colors, and then take one piece and keep trying it with the others until two fit."

When he'd finished the sandwich, I apologized again for the chili as I collected the plates and bowls. "I'm just used to making it like I always have. No one here to complain."

"What about your daughter?" he asked, indicating a family picture over the fireplace.

"She's Zach's biological daughter, but not mine. After Zach's death, Amber moved back to Albuquerque for the rest of the school year," I said. "It's been tense between us since Zach died."

Jamie went to the table and opened his briefcase while I loaded the dishwasher, but I caught him staring at the framed drawing on the far wall, drawn to it.

"That's you, isn't it?"

"One of Zach's hidden talents was drawing me in places I'd never been. He bought that mare for me before I –" I couldn't finish. The words hung in my throat like fish bones.

Jamie turned back to me. "Nolan told me how much you loved Zach. That you risked your life for him more than once."

Although there were no tears, emotions strangled me, again leaving me unable to do more than nod.

"That must be extraordinary. I loved Becca, but I don't think she'd have put her life on the line for me. I'm not sure she would have grieved for me if I were dead."

I took a drink, hoping to find my voice steady. "Zach always said that love is about how much you give, not how much you receive. He loved me a long time before I let myself love him."

"Maybe so, but it doesn't mean you don't want to be loved like that in return."

There had been a time I hadn't wanted Zach to love me. Now I spent my nights thinking how so many of those wasted moments might have changed everything, had I not been afraid to open my heart. It's possible that any one of the nights he'd spent with me could have created a completely different future for us both. All I knew is that I would have given just about anything in my past to be somewhere other than without him today.

Now, Zach was gone, and standing in my dining room was this man I could add to the list of people I blamed for today being what it was. What would have become of us all, had Jamie Gordon called the Alamogordo Police an hour sooner? Or had he not called at all, as he'd been ordered.

No sense in mentally rewriting the past – any minute change could lead to something worse just as easily as to something better. Same with regrets about all the choices.

Jamie and I both took a moment to tuck away our emotions, to find something tangible and believable in the present to anchor ourselves, and then we began sorting the files he'd brought.

I took an hour to familiarize myself with the facts and suppositions Jamie's files revealed. I dug out a pack of index cards and colored markers, scribbled notes, drew arrows, rated the validity of the various facts and theories to decide a place for each on the table, and make connections to others. Some were marked as true and others as questionable. Two were marked as invalid unless further evidence came to light to substantiate them. One was actually false.

The next time I looked up, it was time to feed the horses. My back was telling me I needed a break as loudly as my head was.

"Come on," I said. "We need some fresh air."

Jamie followed me through the laundry room to the garage where I pulled on my barn boots. I tossed him an old jean jacket, and grabbed another for myself.

Laser lay asleep on the deck next to the hot tub as we walked by. "You're getting lazy," I told him. "Go chase a rabbit."

Maybe out of guilt, the dog stood to stretch and trotted behind us to the barn. Or maybe he was hoping I'd go for a ride, which seemed to be his favorite pastime as much as Amber's. He was nearly nine now, his youthful energy slowing down, but he still stood guard for me nightly, and I appreciated his company.

Sliding open the door of the barn, I pulled a pair of leather gloves from my jacket, then picked up an armful of alfalfa hay – one of the most perfect and easily identifiable odors of nature, I thought as I continued out the back door to the paddock.

Maybe I'd expected Jamie to offer to carry something heavy, do the manly thing. He wasn't dressed in the stereotypical FBI suit, tie and shiny shoes. He wore dark jeans, a black polo, loafers. He'd pulled off his leather jacket for lunch. It was warm in the sunshine, but he looked chilled, pulling the denim closed up to his neck and stuffing his hands in the pockets.

"You have any problems keeping a place like this going by yourself?" Jamie asked as I went through the gate into the paddock. He stayed outside.

"No, not really. I pay a neighbor to bale hay for me during the summer, which pretty much keeps me going for the year. We swap chores."

I heaved the alfalfa over into the feeder, then shook it apart for the four horses that appeared behind me. I stepped out of their way, and I made introductions for Jamie to Julaquinte and her colt Waldquinte, as well as Denali and Rainier, the pair of geldings we'd bought from the Clintons.

As usual, I had to explain the historical music references of the names of the Friesian pair. The mountain names everyone figured out, even if not everyone had heard Mt. McKinley called Denali

"Wow," he said, looking around us again. "Is there anything out here you don't have?"

"Besides my husband?" I asked with a frown. Coming through and closing the gate behind me, I headed toward the barn without waiting for him.

"I'm sorry," he called, following me. "I just meant it seems like such a perfect place to live."

I was going to elaborate, explain how perfection was now meaningless without Zach.

Until I heard squealing tires and an impact of some sort out on the highway.

Maybe I left him standing there wondering, but his hesitation didn't last. In only a few strides, he was running next to me. That wouldn't be hard. A third grader could outrun me. I headed through a stand of trees to where our – my – driveway met the pavement, knowing that if I found anything, I'd have to climb over the fence when I got there.

Anything turned out to be Del Clinton's old farm truck, nose-down in the ditch where my mailbox once stood. Del's nine-year-old granddaughter Courtney was behind the wheel, trying to climb out the window, probably because the door was jammed shut.

Before we made it to the fence, I sent Jamie back to the house for my cell phone and my truck – I'd have first aid gear in it, which I'd need, looking at the blood all over Courtney.

So much blood, and yet other than a small cut on her forehead from the steering wheel, I'd guessed, I saw no source for it.

When she saw me, Courtney's hysteria doubled, shrieking that I needed to come, I needed to call 911.

I didn't think the truck crash was that serious, and I wasn't sure

911 was necessary.

"... tractor... Daphney..." she screamed, eyes wide, panting in terror as she crawled out of the window and launched herself at me.

My blood chilled, raising goosebumps. No matter how I interpreted those two words, it was bad news.

"Okay, Courtney, we're going there right now." I pulled her to me, and she held on so tight around my neck I could barely breathe. I heard the Suburban coming up the driveway. "Here comes my truck."

Jamie stopped, and I carried Courtney to the passenger side to get in, motioned for him to turn left, and he sprayed gravel as he accelerated onto the asphalt.

"Two miles, take the right just past a log sign for Clinton Ranch," I told him, then dialed my phone. A calm voice answered. "This is Deputy Samualson. I need an ambulance to the Del Clinton's on ..." I hesitated to point up ahead for Jamie. The voice said she knew where that was, what was the emergency? "I don't know. One of Del's grandkids showed up at my place, covered in blood – something about her sister and a tractor."

"On their way – let me know if you get an update or want the helo."

"Put it on standby, Geo, I don't think this is good."

"Will do – ambulance ETA is 18 minutes. I'll see who else is close to come help."

I pushed a button to end the call and shoved the phone in my jacket pocket as Jamie wheeled into the Clinton's driveway in a controlled slide.

"Where, Courtney?" I asked.

White as snow, she pointed a trembling hand back past the house toward the barns.

Jamie followed the road, not bothering to stay off the grass in the corners, coming to a hard stop twenty feet from an old man, a riding tractor, and the body of a little girl.

Peeling Courtney away from me and leaving her in the seat, I hurried to the back and grabbed my first response kit, pulling on nitrile gloves as I ran to Del.

What I found him holding took my breath.

Del was in the same condition as Courtney, speaking words –

though his voice was hoarse now – that made no connected sense. Long past screaming.

Out of the corner of my eye, I saw Jamie grab Courtney as she tried to run to us.

I nodded at him. She didn't need to see any more of this.

No one needs to see a child like this.

"Ambulance is on the way, Del. We'll take care of her."

He looked at me, eyes wide, as if I were some apparition that had magically appeared.

I carefully lifted Daphney's jaw to help her airway, hold her head still between my knees, and reached for my phone to prop it against my shoulder.

The 911 dispatcher answered.

"Geo, we're gonna need the chopper for a seven-year-old female who's been run over by a mower. If they can pick up some O-neg blood, it'd be good."

"Will do."

I tossed the phone back into my pocket.

From a packet, I pulled a space blanket and asked Del to spread it over the little girl's body to help conserve heat.

Part of me was still a paramedic, though I hadn't actually worked in an ambulance for a couple of years. But I had no fluids to start an IV and help replace the blood loss. I had no oxygen. The best I could do is to maintain her airway, keep her breathing, and stop the bleeding.

I told Del to go sit with Courtney, and to send Jamie to help me.

Had to tell him twice, actually, before he nodded and stumbled as he got to his feet.

After getting Del and Courtney settled into my truck and wrapped in blankets, Jamie rushed to where I knelt. "What can I do?"

"If you're squeamish, I just need you to come take her head, hold her jaw open like this," I demonstrated. "If not, she's got a lot of nasty bleeding that needs to be controlled."

"Head it is."

We carefully traded places, and I set his hands on her mandible to lift it forward slightly. "That's it. If you hear or feel gurgling when she breathes, let me know." Our eyes met. "Or if she stops."

Daphney hadn't shown any indication of being conscious, which was more or less a blessing but not necessarily a good sign.

In the distance, I could hear sirens. Not the ambulance yet, but another deputy. Maybe even Doug Logan, who was an EMT.

Oh, yeah, that would be very good.

Peeling open trauma dressings and stretchy gauze, I covered wounds that were bleeding profusely, finding it hard to support shattered limbs with one hand and wrap with the other. I put pressure on an arterial bleed that started when I moved her lower leg, which left me just one hand.

More hands. Oh, please hurry...

My purple gloves were slick with blood, which had also dampened my jacket cuffs. I could smell the coppery odor, along with the exhaust from the tractor and a hint of horse manure, hanging in the air around us.

I looked at the pale limp body, the only real signs of life her breathing and the expanding blood stains on the bandages. "No, damn it," I whispered. "You can't have her yet. She can't die here in front of them."

Jamie raised his head, maybe to look at me or to say something, but my phone rang.

Unable to let go to answer, I scooted a bit to let Jamie dig in my pocket.

"Julie Samualson," he said. "I'm here with her. Tell him to go left around the house past the barn and up the hill. He'll see us. Not good." He hit a button with his thumb and tossed it back in my pocket.

Our eyes met again.

A new wave of determination rippled through my chest.

The Skamania County sheriff's car skidded up beside my truck. The driver came directly to us as I heard another car skid in the gravel turning in the gate.

"Holy Mother of God," Sheriff Wade Fordham whispered, and crossed himself as he dropped to his knees opposite me. "Mitch's right behind me. Doug's gonna land the chopper at your place in the meadow and bring the team over. I don't know what we can do to help, but here we are."

I nodded toward my kit. "Grab some gloves, Wade. Help me hold this." When he was ready, I put his hands around a bloody dressing.

Mitch Seaver's car whipped in beside the sheriff's car, grabbed another first aid kit and came running. He knelt, took a deep breath and set to work.

I gave him a turn at holding the artery in her leg. Wade and I went back to bandaging and splinting what we could.

Finally with enough hands to have accomplished that, we were able to roll Daphney to one side to check her back, which gave us a more places to put dressings against the massive muscle damage to her buttocks and flanks, full of grass and mud now. Nothing to do about that.

The sheriff looked up. "Are we doing the right thing?" he whispered, and maybe not even to me.

I didn't even pause. "Doesn't matter, Wade. If it's her turn to die, nothing we do will matter."

CHAPTER
46

The ambulance arrived a few minutes later. Paramedics started two IVs and intubated Daphney, getting her ready for transport to the helicopter I'd heard approaching. Because he was farther away, Doug had brought the helicopter crew to the scene. Law enforcement had stepped back to let the medical team take over, and hands blurred as they worked.

I'd removed my gloves, and dumped my bloody denim jacket into a heap near the sheriff's car.

When they were almost ready to go, I interrupted the flight nurse. "Her sister needs to say goodbye," I said, pointing toward my truck.

"We don't have time," the nurse announced.

I took a step closer and lowered my voice. "If Daphney dies on the way to Emanuel or before her family gets there, her sister will have lost her only chance to say goodbye. I didn't want her to see what we did, but she gets thirty seconds before you get in that ambulance or else."

Three uniformed men with guns stood behind me in support of *or else.*

The nurse nodded, but she rolled her eyes at my demand as she turned away.

"We'll meet you at the ambulance," I said, heading to my truck. Inside were two shivering people who barely held each other together. "Del, Courtney, they're getting ready to fly Daphney to the hospital in Portland. Would you like to see her for a second?"

They both nodded.

I picked Courtney up from Del's lap, unsure he could carry his own weight, much less hers.

Walking them toward the ambulance, I explained to Courtney, but loud enough Del could hear me, what the situation was. "They gave Daphney some drugs to make her sleep and put a tube in her mouth to help her breathe. She can't talk, but you can touch her forehead, and tell her you'll see her at the hospital."

The little girl in my arms leaned forward and whispered in my ear. "It's my fault. I backed over her with the tractor!" And she wrapped her arms around my neck again, sobbing.

"Courtney, listen. I can't promise you that Daphney will be okay," I said, "but everyone is working as hard as they can to help her. It's really important that you tell her you love her. She'll hear you, even if she can't talk."

She leaned back, her broken-hearted brown eyes searched mine for truth. "Can I tell her I'm sorry?"

I wiped her cheeks. "Yes, you can. I think that would be very brave of you."

The flight team and ambulance crew carried the backboard toward the gurney sitting outside the ambulance, and I put Courtney down. When they put Daphney on the gurney and strapped her down, several of them stepped away so Del and Courtney could approach.

"I love you, honey." Del touched her hair. "We'll be there when you wake up." He stepped back.

Courtney let go of my hand and moved forward, bending down close and whispered, "Daffy, I'm sorry. I didn't mean to do it. I love you," then she kissed her sister's pale forehead.

Even the flight nurse, who intended to slap me with the value of the golden hour, wiped away the tear that slid down her cheek.

"That's great, Courtney. Let's let them go take care of her, okay?" I prompted. "We can watch for the helicopter to take off in a few minutes."

Courtney took a giant step backward, watched them lift the gurney into the ambulance for the brief transport to the waiting helicopter. When they closed the doors, Courtney took off running toward the barn.

Almost out of nowhere, Jamie scooped her up as she bolted by like a wild hare.

She struggled, but her fight was gone before I could even catch up.

Without a word, Jamie shook his head at me and took her on into the barn.

Nothing I could add to that, so I returned to Del.

"We were feedin' hay, and I just turned my back for a second," he said. "Court' had been driving the little tractor around with the trailer for me this afternoon, with Daphney riding on the back. I was throwing hay over the fence when I heard her screaming."

He buried his face in his hands, and I held him while he suffered the same sort of guilt-ridden sobs Courtney probably did. They'd have to console each other later, no matter what the days ahead held for them.

In the distance, I heard the helicopter lift off and barely got a glimpse as it banked back to Portland.

Finally Del gathered his composure a bit.

When I offered to keep Courtney, he politely declined. "I think we need to be together." He also refused Doug's offer to drive them to Portland. "I'll need my truck once we get there anyway. I'll be okay for now. I don't have a choice."

Jamie returned hand in hand with Courtney, whose face was red from crying.

I followed her inside and helped her pack a bag for their stay.

She had some questions, and I answered as honestly as I could. She needed a little hope, but not empty promises.

I wrote down my cell phone and home numbers for her in a little notebook. "Keep this, and if you have questions or just want to check on things here, you can call me. I'll look after the animals until you get back home. And I'll get the truck out of the ditch and make sure it's okay, too." It was just an old work vehicle for the farm, so it wouldn't be needed anytime soon. "You did a great job coming to get me."

She nodded, but tears kept leaking down her cheeks.

We went outside, and I put her bag in the newer pickup next to Del's small suitcase. When Courtney was buckled in and the door closed, I asked, "Del, why'd you send her down to get me?"

"Our phone's been out all day. I knew you'd have a cell and would come help. You'll never know how much…"

I needed him not to break down in tears again. "Go be with Daphney. Drive carefully. Call me if you need anything. We'll take care of things here."

He took a deep breath and climbed inside, buckled up, and drove out through the gate to the highway and out of sight.

I looked back to see Mitch, leaned over next to the sheriff's car, vomiting. He'd held together as long as necessary.

"Thanks, guys," I said when he came back. What else was there to say?

"Julie, what you did –" Wade Fordham started.

"No, we all did. It means everything to me that no matter what, Delbert and Courtney don't have to think every day that this is where Daphney died. She might, but it wasn't here."

We shook hands all around as I introduced Jamie, leaving off his FBI credentials. The deputies and sheriff went back to wherever they'd been, though I figured the sheriff had come from his house to help.

Back in my own truck, Jamie drove us back down to my driveway where we assessed what to do with Del's truck. Not a minute later, the rancher from north of Del's place drove up on a New Holland tractor with more attachments than a Kirby vacuum cleaner.

Without a word, he tossed out tow chain for us to hook up, and the tractor pulled the pickup out of the ditch without any effort. He crawled out. "Don't know as I ever met you, Mrs. Samualson, but I knew your husband. I'm Lonnie Reynolds."

We shook hands.

"If you can take even days feeding the horses, I'll take the odds. Harold Cummings will see to the rest of the chores as they need doin' including working on this old truck. Our wives will clean up the house," he said, then winced a bit. "And I hate to ask, but we'd all be obliged if you'd see to that tractor and stuff, please, ma'am."

I nodded, understanding. Otherwise, the neighbors would take care of things as long as needed.

"Everyone doing a little gets a lot done," he said and climbed back into the tractor cab and turned back up the highway, leaving me alone with the stranger who'd appeared at my door earlier.

CHAPTER

47

I drove Del's old truck back to his place, and Jamie followed.

With his help, I unhitched the little trailer and pushed the oversized lawn tractor toward a water faucet and hose, and began spraying off what I tried hard to pretend were not pieces of little girl. I also tried to pretend that what ran down my cheeks now and then weren't tears.

Jamie went to find blocks so we could tilt the tractor and wash beneath the mower deck, then he took the hose from me and handed me a crisp white handkerchief. "Go sit down, feed horses, something else."

No argument.

Having fed for Del before, I knew his schedule and what needed to be done. First I finished putting out hay, even though I had to carry bales around to several corrals by hand. I turned on the water at each trough I came to, then circled back to check them and shut the faucets off. I checked all the gates and took a head count before I figured Jamie had finished the grisly task. Last, I shoveled manure where the accident had occurred and spread it around to help the blood break down more quickly with the added bacteria, then I picked up one more armload of straw used in the stalls to put over the manure, and tossed a couple of buckets of water over it.

That was all the outdoor chores I could think of, and Jamie was done with the tractor, so we pushed it into the shed, locked up the place. I checked the house for anything left out that might spoil, grabbed the trash from the kitchen and took it out to the garbage can.

Jamie drove us back to my place. We hadn't spoken in more than an hour, and yet nothing seemed to need saying.

He parked my truck in the driveway. In the garage, I pulled off my boots, leaving them along with the shock of the last few hours. We scrubbed, using the utility sink.

I went inside and grabbed us each a beer. He followed me out onto the back deck, and we collapsed into the chairs in the afternoon shade. It was cool, but I didn't feel much except exhaustion.

"Some hostess you are," he finally quipped.

"Shut up and drink your beer," I said with a half-smile, relieved the tension was finally broken.

"Never heard anyone talk to God like that before," he said before tilting the bottle up again. "Saying that she couldn't die there."

"I believe that it's not up to me who lives or dies," I said. "I just didn't want her to die at the ranch. And what were you praying?"

"Me? I was praying she wouldn't die. Praying I wouldn't throw up. Praying you'd tell me what to do next." He emptied his beer. "Saving lives was never a career goal for me. I always knew it wasn't as simple as it looks on television, but I'm proud to have been with you today."

I didn't know how to respond to that.

"The deputies knew you'd lead," Jamie said. "That you'd tell them what to do next."

"Doug's brother and nephew were hit by a drunk driver a couple of years ago. Zach and I saw it happen. I got out and stayed with them; Zach chased down the driver." I thought back to that day, to the same fatigued muscles and adrenaline-emptied sensation I felt now.

Damn, I miss Zach so much. I closed my eyes, remembering how he'd held me that night.

A hand took mine, and I squeezed it tight. I knew it wasn't Zach's, just like I understood Jamie knew he wasn't holding Rebecca's hand. For a moment, it didn't matter. It was just comfort.

Then the moment was gone, like a flash of lightning, leaving an imprint of the touch on my soul instead of my retinas.

❧

Jamie looked out to see the sunset illuminating the top of Mt. Hood in the distance as I drove him to Stevenson. "I don't remember seeing that before."

"Magic mountains. Sometimes you see them, sometimes you don't."

"You're from New Mexico, so how'd you get to Michigan and then here?" he asked.

"Go back one step further – my family lived near Seattle when I was little. When Dad got out of the navy, we moved to Albuquerque. I transferred with the state police to Alamogordo, and you know about why I left there. Michigan had the first reasonable job offer when I was ready to leave New Mexico, so I went there."

"What about Zach?"

I smiled. "He grew up in Albuquerque. When I left for Michigan, he showed up now and then to visit. Until the cabin was finished and I agreed to live here, I don't think he had a permanent address. He went wherever the DEA dropped him next." I missed Zach's now-and-then appearances, but it was a trail of memories I couldn't let myself wander. "What about you? Where are you from?"

"Grew up in Phoenix, joined the air force. I met Becca in Alamogordo," he said, "and I hated her at first."

A look kept him talking.

"From my point of view, she was a typical rich snob looking down her nose at a blue-collar kid like me," he said. "First time I met her, she was investigating a bank theft, interviewing everyone on base who had an account there. I reported as ordered, entered and snapped a salute and held it. She ignored me. Sat at her desk and finished writing something, making me wait nearly ten minutes before she finally looked up and said, 'I'm not in your silly air force. Sit down.'"

"You saluted for ten minutes?" I laughed. "My father told me not to enlist because I had to use all five fingers to salute an idiot."

"I saluted a few of those idiots, though I know what you mean."

I pulled into the motel parking lot, following his finger-pointed directions toward the right room. I gave him my phone number and told him to call in the morning to make arrangements when he was up and around, and that I'd be out feeding horses around seven.

Jamie had picked up a second car rental in Portland, which made sense if Nolan intended to drive back. But he'd made Jamie leave it at the hotel before they came to see me, though I hadn't asked why. Nolan probably thought it would be easier to get me to talk if I had to take Jamie back to his vehicle.

I drove from the hotel to the sheriff's office to see if anyone had heard from Del Clinton.

Georgia offered to call and see.

"No, no news is probably the best we can hope for," I admitted. "Daphney could be in surgery a long time."

"From what Mitch told me, it sounded awful."

"Awful doesn't even come close, Geo," I said, patting her on the shoulder. "Thanks for your help, though."

I checked my voice mail and found nothing important, so I drove home to a dark, quiet house where the memories and ghosts whispered in my head when I closed my eyes. No sense going up to the bedroom – I'd be awake all night unless my brain had something to distract it. As much as I hated it, falling asleep in the recliner with the television on was the best drug I'd found. Didn't always work all night, but usually I slept longer than with any pill I could take.

In sweats and a comfy t-shirt, I settled into my recliner with a blanket and a little pillow. Picking a news station, I tucked myself in for the night, closing my eyes – searching for the mental state where all my concentration was focused on ignoring the television and thus the other iceberg thoughts on my mind.

My body must have overridden my brain's need to process the last day's events. I was still groggy when Laser woke me with a couple of sharp barks which were followed by knocking on the front door. I glanced at my watch and blinked.

Crap! It was almost eight o'clock!

I wasn't a very good substitute rancher starting like this. I hurried to the door and let Jamie in with barely a greeting, excused myself upstairs to change clothes and brush my teeth, then hustled back down and swung into the kitchen.

"Have you heard from the hospital?" he asked as I came back

into view. "There was a piece on the news this morning about Daphney."

I slid to a stop on socked feet. "You remembered her name?"

His voice was sober. "I'm not likely to forget what happened yesterday anytime soon."

"I need to get over to Del's and feed," I said, grabbing my boots from the foyer.

"It's good you got sleep. Anything I can do to help?" he asked, taking a banana from the hanger on my counter. While I pulled my boots on, he peeled it, then held it out to offer me a bite.

I stood up, staring at him with what was likely a more stunned expression than either of us expected. It was something I suspected he had once done out of habit, and maybe it was my appearance or something completely different, but he realized it was a mistake as soon as our eyes met.

Leaning forward, I took a bite, trying to break the spell.

He opened his mouth to say something. Something I wasn't sure I was ready to hear, so I pushed his hand and the banana up to his lips, effectively excusing him from speaking.

He took the next bite, then turned away from me.

Embarrassed?

He was hard to read, I thought. Like French or Italian – I could see the letters and words, but they didn't make sense.

"You have other plans today besides the chores?" he asked as I motioned him to follow me out to my truck.

"I'm on call for the ME's office until five."

"Why that?"

I turned the key and pulled away from the house. "Why what?" I asked, reaching for the banana and taking another bite, then giving it back.

Yesterday I threatened to shoot him. Today I'm swapping germs with him. Why, indeed.

"I'm just curious. You could do just about anything you wanted. Why would you choose to do what medical examiners do?" He took the last bite, then rolled down the window to throw out the banana.

"No, save that for the compost pile," I interrupted. "No sense wasting it." I drove, trying to think of an answer for his question. "I worked as an office manager or some bizarre title Dr. Katz made up for over a year when he first hired me, putting together the computer systems and filing papers. The investigation part fell in my lap one day because I had skills that were just what he needed, but I like it. I like finding answers for people who've lost a loved one." I turned into the driveway at Clinton's. "Why the FBI?"

"I didn't choose it. I suspect it was Becca's father's doing. His daughter was too good to be married to a low-ranking military officer," he said, looking out the window. "Sometimes I wonder if I could have said no."

"That's kinda scary." I parked near the barn.

"Julie, this is all scary," he said, opening his door and stepping out. "People disappear all the time. I don't mean to sound insensitive, but making someone like Zach disappear is not a big deal. Making a wealthy man's daughter vanish should have huge ramifications. Thomas Nelson seems he couldn't care one red cent less she's gone or that no one is looking. That's what's scariest to me."

I unlatched the wooden door, and we went inside the hay barn.

"Have you tried to discuss this with him?" I asked.

"He told me at the end of December, and I'll quote, 'You leave this alone, Jamie, and you'll live comfortably.' He didn't have to say 'or else.' The emphasized word was 'live' and not 'comfortably.'"

I nodded in agreement that it did seem weird that a father would be so uninterested in finding answers to what happened to his child, especially when he had ample means to search. Perhaps there was some clue there we could follow.

Setting to work, it didn't take long to figure out why Del used a tractor to move hay around. I decided the flatbed truck next to the barn was a better option than dragging bales or trying to use the wheelbarrow. After making sure it would start, we loaded nine bales and a couple of buckets of grain on it. Jamie drove while I pushed off and cut baling wire, then dumped out oats for the eighteen horses in three different fields.

Head count is nineteen – there's a brand new colt in the third pasture.

No great horsewoman, I called the vet. Last thing we all needed was the Clintons to come home to a dead colt. Everything looked fine, per the vet's questions I could answer. The colt was up and walking, nursing, and attentive to his surroundings. Mare looked well, too, so we agreed he'd stop by on his way home.

Jamie walked with me as I checked the water tanks.

"You mentioned the breed name but I can't remember," Jamie asked on the way back to the barn. "What's their purpose?"

"I couldn't remember it either for a while. Trakehners are a warmblood bred initially for the cavalry of the Prussian army."

"Does that mean there are hotblood and coldblood breeds?" he asked as though I made up the term.

"Yes, there are. Think of it as a scale. Draft horses are coldbloods, like Clydesdales – stout, gentle, powerful. Hotblood breeds are fast, temperamental breeds like the Thoroughbred or Arabian. Warmbloods are those bred to get the best traits of both. Most often Trakehners are ridden in dressage or jumping."

"So it's not a matter of geology or weather?" he asked, still not sure I wasn't joking.

"No. This entire breed," I explained, leaning on the corral fence, "was almost lost during World War II, when the Russians closed in around Trakehnen. The breeders evacuated about eight hundred horses by train and on foot. Fewer than a hundred survived the flight, but because of that, the breed survived."

"That's quite a tale. You have a couple of these, don't you?"

"They're not purebred, but they are from Clinton's stock," I said as we went in the barn. "They're a grand ride, if you're up for it."

"Maybe later," he said, turning away from me, again shutting off the connection.

I apologized for delaying our morning start on the information we needed to dig through regarding our respective spouses.

"I'm just glad you could sleep at all. I didn't fare nearly so well last night," he confessed.

"Most nights I don't sleep, either, Jamie. I sort of understand."

"Usually I just can't stop thinking about the possibilities of what happened to Becca. But last night was different. Every time I drifted to sleep, I felt that little girl's arms hugging me as she sobbed. I sat here with her, and we cried together." He dropped down on the bale, unembarrassed by his words. "In fact, yesterday I met the first two women in my life who fought a valiant battle. I'm not sure which of you I like better." He smiled.

"You know, I was thinking about driving to Portland later and checking on them. Would you like to go?" I checked my watch. "And I wanted to invite you to the debriefing today, too."

"Debriefing?"

"Critical incident stress debriefing," I said, sitting beside him. "For only those people who were involved – me, you, Wade, Mitchell, Doug, the medics, and maybe Georgia, the dispatcher. It's just a chance for people to hear everyone else's piece of the story, say what the worst part of it was for them, to believe that the feelings involved with something so awful aren't really so abnormal. I really think it's a good process."

He shrugged.

"Not biting, I guess. Cops don't normally like it. It's too touchy-feely."

"Those people know you. Who am I supposed to tell them I am?"

"No one here cares who you are, Jamie. The guys who came to the scene will remember you kneeling in blood and horse manure right next to them, fighting to save a little girl's life. Everyone's heart was broken yesterday, so don't think they'll expect you to be any different today, no matter who you are."

"I don't think I can talk about how much it ..." His voice cracked.

"Hurts? It's okay to say it. I hurt, too. Dying kids rip our hearts out. It doesn't get any more human than that." I stood up and offered him a hand. "Come with me. I promise, other than telling them your name, you don't have to say another word unless you want to. Let's go to the debriefing, then we'll go to Portland."

His fingers squeezed mine. He looked up at me, and I felt that eerily electrical connection again.

I couldn't tell if he saw me, or if he was lost in seeing his wife.

But I see what's playing in his mind almost as clearly as he does.

CHAPTER
48

As late as I'd been getting over to feed the Clintons' livestock, my four horses stood at the gate waiting on me, stomping impatience for their morning meal when I finally got back to them. I hadn't much more than finished that chore when the sheriff's department called to send me on a prisoner transfer to Vancouver. Being the only female available made me a necessary chaperone with another deputy to Clark County.

I apologized to Jamie, who asked me to call him when I got back, then drove away.

The other deputy and I returned to Stevenson just before time for the debriefing to start, and I circled by to pick up Jamie at his hotel.

"I still don't think I should come," he argued, but he got in my truck anyway.

Two hours later, we left the debriefing at the hospital conference room, headed for Portland to see how Del and Courtney Clinton were doing.

Daphney was still in critical condition, but she was stable.

"She's a fighter," Del told us, though I suspected his words were faith and hope, not medical fact. He'd aged a decade overnight. "I'm glad you both came to check on us."

Courtney and Jamie took a walk down the hallway from the waiting room.

"She won't say a thing to me," Del confessed to me. The shock must have showed on my face. "Nah, I don't mean she won't speak, just that she won't talk to me about what happened, or about going to get you."

"Could be she's still searching for the words, Del," I suggested. "It's hard realizing you're responsible for such devastation, much less talking about it to someone you think blames you. Maybe she thinks not talking to you about it will save you that pain, too."

He nodded.

"Give her a little more time."

"I can never thank you enough for what you did, Julie."

"You don't have to thank me. All of us, we did what we could," I said. "You have a new colt, by the way. Might be something you can share with the girls. I'll see if I can get a photo to bring back."

"That'd be good, yeah," he said, head hanging.

"You know, this isn't your fault." I put one hand on his forearm.

"If it's not my fault," he argued, "then it's hers, and I can't let her face that." He nodded down the hallway at Jamie walking back with Courtney.

"You need to get past feeling that, just like she does. It was ugly and it's a tragedy, but it was an accident. Look ahead, Del. Looking back can't change what happened."

✄

The sunset had not been as beautiful as the evening before. Although it was almost dark as we drove east on I-84 from Portland, enough color remained to cast the top of Mt. Hood with purple tints.

"I can see why you'd like this part of the country," Jamie said, watching a barge on the river. "It's rugged but not desolate like New Mexico."

"Rainy season can be a little depressing, but nothing like winters in Michigan."

"Nolan showed me around the Traverse Bay area. There's snow on the ground in piles," he said as if that would surprise me. "Snow was generally not a problem in Phoenix, so I never thought about what happens to it when it gets plowed off the roads or parking lots anywhere else."

I only nodded. My surprise wasn't how much snow was on the

298

ground there, but that he'd met Nolan in Traverse City.

"You're not living in Alamogordo now," I said, "so where is home?"

"Ended up in Virginia after we got married. After I got into Quantico with her father's connections." His voice was sharp with sarcasm. "I hate it there. I'll stay as long as I have to, but I'm not a happy government employee. It's an awful lot of bullshit wrapped in overpaid official hierarchy that encourages criminals to search for better ways to find loopholes instead of enforcing laws. But obviously that's not how the government likes to portray itself to its taxpayers."

Pretty accurate, I thought. "What exactly did Rebecca do?"

"She was a forensic accountant. The insurance agency she worked for contracted with banks and companies handling stocks and bonds to trace stolen and laundered money."

"How?" I asked, wrinkling my nose, not sure exactly what I wanted to ask. "How does one move money – hide it, launder it? How do you chase it? Balancing my checkbook is about as far as my financial savvy goes."

He raised his eyebrow, maybe waiting for me to say I was kidding – I wasn't.

"Starting simple," he began, "if I had a counterfeit twenty-dollar bill, it has no real value and it's a risk to me as long as I have it. I need to exchange it for something else of value, so I walk into a convenience store and buy a candy bar for a buck-fifty, get back eighteen dollars and some change, making a hefty profit and reducing the risk by washing the useless paper out of my hands. The money I have left is safe."

"And the candy bar, to boot. Okay." That sounded easy enough if counterfeit money was your trick.

"Bigger operations launder money because you can't just buy a candy bar with a hundred grand and keep the change, but it's the same theory," he said. "You have horses, so let's try that. Let's say I breed horses as my show business and deal in drugs for profit. If I had twenty grand in cash from selling crack, I can't just go throw it in my bank, right? So I 'buy' breeding rights to a stud from someone who appears to take my money. In return, that someone else 'buys' a registered horse from me and pays me eighteen grand, so now I have lost two grand of dirty money, but I have clean income for 'services' no one can ever truly prove were provided or not. Ten percent is about average."

"But does the money really exist? Where does it go?"

"In this case, it doesn't matter if it's currency or bank balances. To track it, you look for the obvious places money goes without actual product changing hands. If I bought forty tons of hay, then someone could actually measure how much is in the barn, right? How does the government disprove my claim that someone trained a dozen horses for me or that the stud fee I paid yielded no foal? How does the IRS prove that a dead horse isn't worth a certain amount of money if there's a pedigree?"

I nodded. "So you look for intangible assets for money laundering. That makes sense. But how do you move money if you intend to steal it?"

"Usually money has to exist to be laundered. It regains a legitimate history by being funneled into actual income. On the other hand, you can steal cash, or steal it at the moment it becomes an electronic blip in a bank somewhere on its way to somewhere else. But the catch is you have to know where it is at a given moment and to have a place to hide it when you steal it."

I thought about money tracks, making them, erasing them.

That led me back to why Rebecca was reportedly dead, but I still could not find any connection to Zach.

I pulled up to get my mail at the driveway, having forgotten that Courtney had knocked down the post and mailbox yesterday. Yet it was standing, straight and uncrushed, where it was before she plowed it over.

Neighbors, I thought.

I checked the box, took the usual handful of junk, and drove on to the house.

"What do you think she was doing in Seattle?" I asked.

"Tracking money moving out of the country, best I can guess."

"So can we track that money?"

He shook his head. "No idea where it came from or where it was going. And her boss claims she wasn't doing anything for them in Washington. If it wasn't work, I have no idea why she would have gone there."

Inside, I grabbed us each a soft drink and followed Jamie to the living room.

"That," he said, indicating the stereo setup and Zach's choice of supersonic speakers, "is some serious music equipment."

I hit the power button on the remote next to my recliner, and a CD booted up to play something by Tangerine Dream, and the music filled the open room like a recital hall with thick base and haunting mid tones.

Smiling, I let it play a few moments as we sat, then turned it down so we could talk.

"Thanks for asking me to go to the debriefing," he said, finally bringing up his attendance. "That was really powerful, to hear other people express the same sorts of feelings I have – helplessness, self-doubt, anger."

"And grief," I added. "Even though Daphney is alive, there's a huge sense of loss for her and her family, especially because the girls' parents died in a car crash a year or so back. Sadness that this ordeal could likely go on with glimmers of hope for weeks and end with her dying yet."

"I'm still in awe of what you did, Julie. How you stayed composed, from the time you heard the crash. I reacted. You responded. It's not the same thing."

I couldn't think of anything to say, so I took another long drink.

"Could I tell you something?" he asked, staring at me.

No. Oh no.

I nodded.

"You're an incredible woman. I'm sorry I didn't drive to the hospital in Alamogordo to see you that evening. I wanted to. Maybe I should have."

"Trust me, I wasn't much company that night. In fact, I wasn't much of a human being for more than a year after that, so you really didn't miss what you think you see now," I said. "And given half a chance, I probably would have shot you then."

He smiled. "That's what makes you so unbelievable. You survive and then you save other people in a perfectly selfless way."

Without answering, I shook my head.

"I don't know anyone who'd've done what you did to save Kim Katz."

I finished the cola, trying to be unperturbed. "Anything else about me Nolan told you?"

"He gave me quite a briefing. 'Objects in mirror are larger than they appear,' and so on."

"Lovely." *Maybe I should shoot Nolan instead.*

"But what I wanted to say was that I look at you and I feel *something.* I don't know what, exactly. Some of it is how much you look like Becca, but another part of it is like seeing ..." he shook his head, struggling for the words.

"Like looking at your reflection in a broken mirror." I finished it. "You see the shattered image of yourself in my eyes."

His expression brightened. "I don't even know what that means, but it's exactly right."

Yeah, I know.

"Don't get all this mixed up, Jamie. You might be thinking how easy it would be to just close your eyes and touch her again," I said. "It doesn't work like that. Even if Rebecca is alive, you're not going to find the woman you think you loved. Whoever she was then, I suspect she's gone." I stood up, certain I needed something else to drink.

He got to his feet at the same time, putting us face to face, much closer than I'd meant to be. Unsure how that had happened. Uncomfortable. "No, that's not what I feel," he said. "It's scary that you look like her, but I still feel drawn to you anyway."

"Emotional upheaval is no reason to – " I intended to go on.

"I'll leave."

And I let him.

Then I spent the rest of the night wondering why.

He was smart, funny, had a heart he wasn't afraid to show, and he'd made a genuine effort to help me with the kids of a total stranger. Integrity, if not guts.

I couldn't deny I was attracted.

What was I so afraid of, besides everything I'd listed and more?

Kicking back in my recliner and clicking on the television, I dozed, exhausted by the new anxiety a stranger had brought to my world. Between his losses and mine, all our unanswered questions, I didn't want to think about an attraction to someone grounded in mystery. Was it worse to find each other in the middle of the questions, or after we found answers we hated?

My alarm went off at seven, so I crawled out of the recliner, stiff with insomnia and other sore muscles. A hot shower would be good, but it was senseless to shower before feeding the animals, so I dressed and fed Laser, who stopped to gobble a few bites before he followed me into the utility room. I hit the garage door opener, then tiptoed on the cold cement to my muck boots and propped myself against the car, pulling the first one on as the door raised.

"You sleep okay last night, boy?" I asked the dog when he came trotting out to join me.

"Not a wink," a voice answered from behind me.

I whirled to find Jamie, sitting on the hood of his rental car, feet dangling, as the garage door came to a stop.

Laser growled but made no move.

Jamie held both arms away from his body, clearly recognizing that I'd reached for a weapon on my hip. I just wasn't wearing it.

"I didn't want to wake you up this morning, but we need to talk. Something happened."

Unable to speak until my heart quit pounding, I slid on my other boot and a jacket, then motioned for him to follow me toward the barn, not waiting to see if he did so.

He caught up and kept pace. "You don't make any effort to look beautiful in the morning, do you?"

Offended, I ran a hand through my hair.

"You misunderstand. Your lovely sleepy eyes and untamed tresses make you more beautiful than makeup ever could."

I'm a lot of things physically. Beautiful isn't one of them. Especially first thing in the morning. My cheeks blushed in the cool air.

"Flattery will get you nowhere," I mumbled, unable to think of anything else to say. I kept walking.

"Not flattery, Julie. You're honestly who you are, and you don't try to look like anybody else. I think Becca actually tried harder to look like you than you do."

"That doesn't even make sense." I cocked my head to look at him as I walked. "You said something happened."

"Last night, after I got back to the hotel, I found out something that makes me think Becca knew about you. Her mother calls me to talk when she's alone and drunk, which I previously found annoying. She called me around midnight in one of her nastier moods, and one of the things she accused me of was making Becca change her appearance."

I shrugged in confusion and frustration at whatever point he was trying to make.

"Because she's always neck-deep in a bottle of gin, I never thought to question Becca's mother about her before," he said as I opened the barn door. "But after what you and I talked about yesterday, and hearing her mother saying Becca had been altering the way she looked, I looked at family photos on my laptop from her teen years. She didn't look much like you when she was in high school or college."

Feeling lost, I made a circular motion with my hand for him to keep going.

He sat on a bale of hay, so I sat next to him, waiting for the rest of the story.

"Before she and I met, her hair was the color of, I don't know, wet sand on a beach. After we got married, she bleached it lighter and let it grow."

I still was missing his point.

"Becca had her nose and chin done one holiday when she said she went home to see her parents. She supposedly went to see them every Christmas for two weeks without me," he said. "Last night, her mother told me they hadn't seen Becca during the holidays for more than four years. Becca told them I insisted we go see my family, but she told me she went to see them and didn't want me to go."

"I don't understand, Jamie."

"Rebecca went *somewhere*," he stated, sounding as if he were still arguing this in his head. "I think she went to a plastic surgeon and began looking more like you, but I didn't know what you looked like. All I knew is she was changing. It was subtle, and I thought it was just a rich-girl vanity thing. Only it really never made *her* more beautiful.

I mean, it wasn't unattractive, but like with her nose, it wasn't a change that I thought made her prettier. Julie, I think she either wanted to become you, or she wanted you to be the person someone thought she was."

"How would she even know who I am?" I asked in increasing astonishment of the conversation.

"She spent time in Alamogordo. Maybe you gave her a speeding ticket," he said, smiling.

"Like I'd remember?"

He dragged his hands over his weary face. "Why you? Why her? If there's a connection, where is she in it?"

"With her dead, we may never know."

"What if she's not?" he asked.

I shrugged. "What if? So we go back to the storyboard. Add in the new information and see what we get. Maybe we can design a better hypothesis of what the ultimate goal would be for her to look like me and disappear."

"If that doesn't work, then what?"

"You'll give up if you don't find the answer on the third day? No, keep digging. There's got to be some key that holds it all together." I stood and pulled on my gloves to feed. When he didn't move, I offered him a hand.

"Come on, I think we should go for a ride today."

He stood up and shook his head. "I haven't been on a horse since I was a kid."

"So?"

Jamie looked out over my shoulder into the sunshine beyond the door "My brother was thrown and hurt really bad when we were young." He swallowed hard. "I'm afraid of horses."

That took some amount of courage to confess, I thought, reaching to touch his shoulder. In response, he put his hand on top of mine. Our eyes locked.

I couldn't think of anything to say. I didn't want to move, but it seemed more like a game of chicken than of intimacy.

A horse whinnied that breakfast was late again, breaking the spell.

I turned away first.

Without his help, I threw hay out to the four horses in the split corrals, and we walked back to the house.

"I'm stunned by what we've concluded," he said, continuing the conversation. "Changes what I was thinking."

"Okay, tell me what your original theory was."

Inside, I washed my hands and started to fix breakfast without even asking if he was hungry, leaving him to keep talking.

"My first thought was she had found someone else, and she knew her parents would be angry if she just walked out on me," he said, "not because they are overly fond of me, but her father's invested a lot of favors in my career. So if she disappeared, maybe she thought I'd be blamed, and she could live abroad until I'd been forgotten in a prison somewhere. But to do that, she'd need money, so maybe she was stealing it."

"No one suspected you in her disappearance?"

"They told us she died in a plane crash," he said. "Besides, I was in training at Quantico for three days prior to her supposed death. Hard to suspect an FBI agent who's playing a hostage on the other side of the country."

Before I could reply, my pager went off in the other room.

CHAPTER

49

I returned from the call after noon, and I found him sitting on the back deck.

"Enjoying yourself?" I asked. I peeled off my windbreaker and sat down in the chair next to him.

He didn't even open his eyes, but the smile was proof he liked where he was.

"Good. I'm going to run up for a shower," I said. Instead, I kicked my legs out and relaxed, letting the sunshine warm my skin.

"You're not getting wet," he said after a few minutes.

"Just enjoying the breeze."

"Well, I don't want to sound rude, but you smell like dead people," he said, raising an eyebrow. "Anything interesting?"

"Interesting, just not terribly exciting," I said. "By the way, Del called the department this morning, said Daphney is having more surgery today. They intend to take out part of her intestines and a kidney. It's iffy whether she'll lose that leg, but they're doing all they can."

"Anything we can do?"

"They're setting up a blood drive in town tomorrow, if you want to donate. And there's a trust fund for her medical expenses, too."

He nodded.

Finally I got up and went to shower.

When I came back downstairs, he was tossing a salad.

I pointed to the bowl. "None of that stuff was in my refrigerator,"

I said, swiping a carrot.

Jamie laughed. "There's nothing in there but beef, milk and beer."

"Yeah, meat, dairy, alcohol – three of the four food groups, right? I make coffee for caffeine."

"That does make four," he agreed, shaking his head. "One way of looking at it, I suppose. I eat out rather than cooking for myself. One of my favorite places is a soup and salad buffet chain back east."

"Unless I'm stuck in town, I don't eat out. Sometimes I don't bother eating here." I took a cherry tomato this time. "So tell me something about you. You mentioned your brother, what about your family?"

"My father was a math teacher, died of a heart attack about ten years ago. My mother keeps books for a small art gallery in Scottsdale. My brother is two years older than me, and I have a younger sister who's a nurse in Denver."

"What does your brother do?"

"His head injury was so severe, he lost his sight. He suffers from frequent seizures without medications, but if he takes enough to control them, he's just about unconscious. He's been in an assisted living home for years. He does paintings, and my mother's sold a few at the gallery."

"You said he's blind, but he paints?" I didn't mean the response to sound incredible, but I was surprised.

"Because he had sight during his childhood, he has a concept of color, so someone sets up his palette where he knows where each color is. They're abstracts, but he's really had some great pieces. He says he paints what he sees when he has seizures."

"Wow, that's intriguing. I can't imagine what I'd do if I couldn't see."

"Same thing Daphney will do if she loses a leg," Jamie said. "Adapt."

I shook my head. "Five little letters in a word doesn't make it simple."

"No, it doesn't," he said, then paused as if watching a memory. "I spooked my brother's horse and it reared. Watched him fall and get stepped on, so I had a very good idea what was going through

Courtney's mind the day before yesterday. And probably today. And tomorrow."

"That's what you told Courtney when you took her in the barn?"

He shook his head. "When we talked at the hospital."

"Thank you. For doing that."

"Sometimes sharing is the best thing to do with bad experiences."

I guess I knew that, having shared my experiences with Kim Katz and Amber.

Jamie slid a plate across to me. I wondered if I'd find a jalapeño or something else in my salad. I stabbed a forkful and took a bite.

"I called and talked to Becca's father today," he said. "We didn't discuss whether his only daughter might have done anything wrong, but he said if I wanted to dig my way through and find a better answer, he'd do what he could to help me. I didn't tell him about you. I don't want anyone to know just yet. Surprise can be a powerful weapon."

I nodded and took another bite.

My phone rang, and I excused myself to answer.

"Julie, someone called to identify the body you picked up at the campground this morning," the medical examiner told me. Dr. Bishop's hoarse voice made him sound decades older than he really was.

"Really? I wasn't aware we'd gotten any hits off the search for missing persons."

"We didn't. This guy's father called, said his son had been hiking up here over the weekend, never came back home. Described him well. They'll be in to claim him this afternoon."

"Any word on cause of death?"

"Not yet. I'll finish the autopsy, and the labs will be back tomorrow," Bishop said, "I don't see anything on exam to suggest foul play. Probably heart. Great detail on your report, though. I appreciate it."

"Let me know if you need anything else."

I disconnected.

"That was quick," I said, returning to the breakfast counter, feeling something didn't fit. "Someone's already identified that body I picked up this morning."

"Why is that unusual?"

"Because *we* didn't know who he was."

Head tilt.

"No idea at all. No car, no wallet, nothing," I said. "The body was found in a tent near a popular hiking trail along a river north of here, but no car to get there. Not wearing hiking clothes. I was anticipating having to do DNA and wait for some sort of match to make an ID." I stretched my hands over my head before picking up my fork. "Back to Rebecca's father. So he's willing to help if he doesn't get his hands dirty, I take it."

"More or less."

"Could her father have been involved in helping her disappear?" I asked.

"Right now, I could believe the Easter Bunny dragged her into his den to make her vanish."

"Okay, I'm a little skeptical of that suspect, but there are a lot of possibilities. So if Mr. Nelson is involved or even just knows what's happening, why would he encourage you to investigate now when he clearly made threats before?"

"Either he thinks the information has become safe enough I won't find anything, or it's a setup so I disappear, too."

Ouch. I reached back to the dining table and picked up more index cards and began writing out our newest theories.

"And just for the sake of argument, if he's not involved, why the change of heart to let you spend his money?" I asked.

"I can't think of a good reason," he said, playing with the salad instead of eating. "It doesn't sound like he believes there's anything to find. Then again, how much can I really spend?"

"Gotta have a plausible theory for the card," I prompted, "whether or not it's true or even reasonable. How about pressure from his wife?"

Jamie shook his head. "I think she's a bottle of gin away from a rehab center. He doesn't care what she wants and never has, from what I can tell. That's why she gets drunk and calls me."

"So let's say that she's been nagging him and he's tired of it. If he lets you dig, then he can get you both off his back. Show that even the FBI boy married to their daughter can't find any proof something is wrong, so he'll have her committed."

"That's as good a reason to fill in as any, I guess."

When I finished the salad, I strolled back over to the dining room table, looking over the maze of connections. We posed more questions neither of us could answer, and I made more cards for our growing spider web on the table. At some point, I just had to walk away, so we wandered to the deck in the shade.

Even outside, I found I couldn't sit still, so I got up to check the hot tub while we talked. My sore muscles were dying for a dip.

"Don't suppose you have a swim suit?" I asked.

"Didn't bring one."

I offered to find him a pair of shorts or something as I flipped the cover off, which spooked Laser into retreating to the other end of the deck.

Jamie followed me upstairs and stood while I dug through drawers in the office until I came up with a pair of shorts.

"They're big, but there's no diving anyway," I said with a grin, holding them out for him.

The large drawing Zach had done of me had absorbed Jamie's attention. "A shame he was wasting time with the DEA," Jamie said. "I'd pay a lot of money for that."

Unsure how to interpret his response. I pointed to the bathroom next door and left him to change and went to my own bedroom to dig around for a bathing suit. I waited long enough that I heard him go back downstairs and out the door.

I stopped in the kitchen and poured us each a tumbler of lemonade.

Jamie was relaxed in the bubbling water up to his neck, his eyes closed, when I came out.

Deliberately not looking at me?

I sat the glasses down on the tray and slid into the water. A sigh escaped as I settled into the heat.

"This is the final straw. I may never go home now," he muttered to himself. He smiled and opened his eyes. "You said Zach had all this built before you ever saw it?"

"I'm sure people questioned his sanity, putting things into place for us. While he waited for me to come to my senses."

"Do you think you'd have met him and fallen in love in different circumstances?"

"Like David not trying to kill me?" I asked, not trying to hide the sarcasm. "Hard to say. In my head, I've played out just about every possible 'what-if' you could imagine. It's infinite, better, worse or the same. Doesn't matter, I can't change it." I took a sip of lemonade and then drifted back on how many hours we'd bubbled away here together, Zach and I, until the memories began to hurt with his absence.

"Why do you still cover your neck?" Jamie asked. "The scar's barely visible."

Apparently he hasn't seen my back.

I paused, struggling to keep my hand from covering it. Why, indeed? "It's not what I want people to see," I said. "Like having acne as a teenager. Suddenly you wake up one day and it's better, but you still habitually compensate for the embarrassment with every blemish later."

"Well, women might, yes."

I tried not to roll my eyes at his remark. "Why did you think Rebecca was having plastic surgery?"

"Because she could afford it," he answered bluntly. "Like I said, she bought a different looking face than the one God gave her. I assumed she thought it was more attractive, whether I did or not."

This had struck a nerve, so I waited for him to continue or change the subject.

"She didn't care what I thought about that or much else. I finally saw that her opinion of me was much like her father's – I was way below her standards in the military and she was tired of the novelty of slumming, so Daddy helped her improve my station in life. If not more financially rewarding than the air force, at least having a husband who was an FBI agent was intriguing to her friends or whoever she tried to impress."

"She worked, too," I countered.

"She did because her job sounded mysterious and powerful to people, and because it irritated her father," he said. "Can we talk about something else besides her for a while?"

I shrugged.

He sipped lemonade and finally put the glass down. "I didn't come here expecting to like you. In fact, from what Nolan had told me, I figured you wouldn't even talk to us, much less offer to help. And I find it most disturbing that nothing I had presumed about you was correct."

CHAPTER
50

We soaked for half an hour, then I had to move again. I got out and dried off, slipping on my jeans over the bathing suit and pulled on an oversized sweatshirt. Jamie did the same, and then he came out with me to visit with the horses.

It was a beautiful day, mid-sixties and a light breeze.

Often in the afternoons, I took time to interact with the horses. Their winter coats were still thick. Julaquinte especially loved to be brushed. Waldquinte, the colt, was still a goofy and sometimes unpredictable youngster with what could only be described as a sense of humor. Waldo'd never once bitten me, but his favorite stunt was to lip-nibble me when I wasn't paying attention, or to grab gloves from my back pocket and frolic around the paddock, wanting me to chase him.

While this friskiness wasn't always an endearing trait in him, I found it a sign of his intelligence and disposition, and as we worked on new skills, he caught on quickly.

"Why so many when it's just you?" Jamie asked, cautiously rubbing Julaquinte's neck over the fence while I brushed away the dust that gave a reddish hue to her black coat.

"Sentiment, I suppose. Zach bought her for me, and she was already bred, so we've got Booger there, too," I said, pointing to the black colt. "We bought the two geldings from Del when we first brought Amber here for her and Zach to ride. Taking care of four isn't much harder than two. I need to make more time to ride, but other than the searches last summer, we haven't been off the place in months."

"Search?"

"Rainier's a good trail horse, so I've taken him on search and rescue rides for lost hikers and a plane crash once with Amber where we took Denali, too."

"Anything you won't do?"

Julaquinte tried to nuzzle him but he stepped away from her.

"I've yet to jump out of a perfectly good airplane," I offered. "Other than that, I've taken my share of risks."

"Was the Harley one of those?"

"I never thought so," I said, after a moment of thought. "It was an escape I bought for myself in Alamogordo. A very me-oriented way to take myself out of work mode."

The two motorcycles had been parked in the garage, untouched since Zach died.

"When I was younger, I had a motorcycle. Living on base, I had a sport bike, like most post-adolescent boys. Fortunately, it never ended up buried in a car or a guard rail somewhere, but I doubt it was because of any smart choices I made."

"You'd have been one of those kids who'd make a run at passing my bike, just because it was going the same way on the highway." I laughed. "Go fast, die hard."

"Young and stupid," he nodded. "What kind of risks did you take, then?"

There were plenty of them throughout my life, but I hesitated. Jeremy McNeely had walked away from me after learning those details. I shook my head. "Not ready to have that conversation with you yet."

"Fair enough. What do you do for fun?"

"Fun?" It sounded like a foreign word I struggled to define, especially without Zach. "I hike. Sometimes I grab a tent and go spend the night out in the middle of nowhere to listen to the silence. You?"

He smiled. "I jump out of perfectly good airplanes just for the hell of it. I shoot a lot, but I don't hunt. I scuba dive and sometimes spelunk."

The very thought of feeling trapped underwater made me shiver. Zach had wanted to get us kayaks last summer, but the idea I might end up upside-down, unable to right it, made me veto that idea. Scuba diving, losing a mask, held a similar fear I couldn't explain.

"Which of those won't you do?" he asked, having seen something flash on my face.

"Scuba. I'm not afraid of the water, but I'm terrified of not being able to breathe." The very thought made my heart beat faster. "Maybe I drowned in a previous life. It's irrational, considering I've never had a bad experience."

"It's one of the biggest primal fears. Are you afraid of dying?" he asked.

I shook my head. "Jamie, I've had plenty of experiences with dying and didn't really like any of them, but I can't say it scares me. Mostly I'm not all that keen on finding out what comes immediately after." I didn't continue.

Surely Nolan had told him that I'd faced death, but he didn't need to know I'd gone looking for it intentionally, nor that I'd found it repeatedly.

Or that I'd recently felt that same urge.

I finished grooming the mare, but I could feel Jamie study me again as I put up the brushes in the tack room. He followed me back to the house in silence.

On the patio, I undressed back to the bathing suit and slid back into the hot tub.

"There are so many things I want to ask you," he said when he joined me, "but it would seem like an excavation of your past. That's not what I want. But I also want to share parts of my life with you when the time is right." He took my foot and wrapped his hands around it, caressing it. "One day."

"How long are you going to chase this?" I finally asked when my brain found a brief moment to function as Jamie switched from one foot to the other.

He shrugged. "I'd like to have answers. I'm on leave from the bureau indefinitely, only because it allows me to have indirect access to some resources I might need. After that, I'm resigning. I never wanted to be a cop of any sort."

"Dare I ask what you want to do?"

"Write."

"Write?" I echoed. "Books? Music?"

"I finished a couple of historical fiction manuscripts I'd like to see published. I like the research and the creativity, so I write. I never told Becca because I didn't want her father buying my way, but I have an agent, and there's a nibble or two on the first one."

"I don't think I could write, even fiction. I could give Stephen King nightmares."

"There's a market for that, too," he said with a chuckle. "It's persistence, a little luck. Having the right puzzle piece at just the right time. I just like being in my head where I get to make the rules."

"Must be hard to make a living writing to start out – not having a set product you can create to make a paycheck every two weeks."

"Thanks to Becca's life insurance, money's not a concern for a while. I mean, I'm not wealthy by any means, but ..."

That seemed to embarrass him.

I understood. Between David's life insurance, Zach's inheritance that had paid for the property I lived on, and his life insurance, if I managed the money right, I'd never have to work again. But I still did. I just hadn't considered a new career lately.

When we first came to Washington, Zach had asked me if I wanted to do something else, saying I could do just about anything I wanted. Considering all the options, I came back to what I'd done in Michigan because I like it. Different here only because I'm a county deputy, too, not just an employee of the one-man medical examiner's office – the best of both worlds. I'd been happy, taking care of things when Zach was gone, helping with Amber as she grew into a charming young woman. What else could I want?

Until news came about Zach. Everything changed in that moment, and what I wanted most, I couldn't have ever again. I'd become a widow twice now. I didn't like the moniker.

"I don't have to worry about money, either," I said, "but I need to work."

I'd rather struggle to make a living and have Zach.

"Did you ever see yourself starting over with someone new?" Jamie asked, switching to the other foot again.

"It's not time." I shook my head. "Might not ever be."

"I swore I'd never get involved with anyone again."

"Never is a long time," I countered. "But I understand. You don't rush into something similar after you've lost something so special."

"It takes a while to remember that the pain was still worth all the time you had, if it was good." He let go of my foot and floated closer to me. "I just don't want to waste time I'll wish I had cherished later."

And he leaned forward to kiss me.

Gentle. Asking instead of taking.

Not the always-soul-shattering kisses like Zach's, and I wouldn't have liked it if they'd been like that.

As I reached to touch his face, close to mine, just fingertips on his skin, a not-quite-polite throat-clearing cough echoed around us.

My physical reaction was hidden somewhat by the bubbles. No one had ever walked up to the house unannounced before without Laser intercepting.

Except for this morning when Jamie was standing next to the garage.

I scanned discreetly for the dog, not wanting his surprise to get someone shot by the disheveled man who stood at the side of my house, holding a pistol loosely at his side.

CHAPTER

51

"Mrs. Zach?" the stranger said, closely watching as Jamie slid away from me back to the other side of the hot tub, "I need your help."

"Okay," I said, sitting up a little more. "You know who I am. Will you tell me your name so we can talk?"

His eyes roamed wildly, perhaps trying to assess and prioritize threats and allies, then finally settled back on me. "I'm Kenny," he said, then cleared his throat. "Kenny Underwood. They're going to arrest me for killing that man, but I didn't do it."

My lungs inflated in fear, almost causing me to float.

By name, I knew who Kenny was. Stories circulated through the department about him. Although I didn't think I'd actually ever seen him before, he looked like the perfect scary stereotypical psychopathic killer from any horror movie of the last three generations.

Doesn't even need a hockey mask.

My throat made a hollow sound when I swallowed. "It's nice to meet you, Kenny. Maybe it would be easier for us to talk if I got out of the hot tub," I offered. "We could go sit at the table, and you can tell me what's going on so I can help you."

He shrugged, stomping his boots as if he were standing in an ant bed.

"It would also make me feel better if you'd put the gun away," I urged casually.

He pulled it behind his back. "You can't have it!" he yelled.

I felt four fingers and a thumb squeezing my foot in a caution I didn't need.

You never face down an aggressive dog. You don't challenge a bear or a wild cat. What is the right answer for disarming a known mental patient with a gun?

Whatever works.

"Kenny, I don't *want* the gun. I am asking you to put it somewhere safe, like in your pocket," I suggested with no alarm in my voice. "You trusted me enough to come here, and I want to help you. I need to trust you a little, too."

He spent a minute finding the correct pocket of his oversized parka to put it in.

I really didn't feel he was threatening us so much as he was just out of his mind in paranoia and panic. "Let me get out and go get a towel, okay?"

He looked at me and nodded.

I eased up to my feet and stepped up to swing them over the side one by one, turning my back on him, walking to the little cabinet where I kept towels. I didn't rush, but I dried a little and wrapped it around my shoulders as I walked to the table.

"Let's talk, Kenny. Come tell me what's wrong." I waved for him to follow me.

"Everything's wrong!" he shrieked, holding his head between his hands as if trying to keep it from exploding. "I'm crazy so no one ever believes me, but they'll believe my brother when he tells them I killed that man. I don't want to go to jail again, but no one will believe me!"

I motioned again for him to sit across the picnic table from me. "I want to help, Kenny. Come and tell me which man you're talking about."

Only one man had been found dead in the last week that I knew of – the one I'd picked up just hours ago near the trail. I was sure he hadn't been shot, so I worried less about the gun in Kenny's pocket.

Kenny's eyes darted from me to Jamie and back.

"I'll stay right here if that's okay with you. This feels way too good to get out," Jamie stated as Kenny made a wide circle around the hot tub.

"That man is not your husband," Kenny declared, looking over his shoulder at Jamie when he got to the table.

"Zach died, Kenny. Did you come to his funeral service in town?" I didn't think he had, but who'd been counting homeless crazy people? Certainly not the devastated widow – me.

"Mr. Zach will be mad," he stated more emphatically, turning to where I sat. His eyes were still wild and only focused on me occasionally.

"Zach is dead."

He shrugged. "Mr. Zach will be mad if you kiss him again," he insisted, pointing at Jamie.

"I'll remember that. Tell me about the man who was killed, Kenny. Which man?"

"You were there," he insisted, finally sliding onto the bench across from me. "This morning. I saw you put him in your truck."

"At the trail to the waterfalls?"

He nodded. "I didn't kill him."

"Kenny, I didn't think *anyone* killed him. It looked like he had a heart attack or something. How was he killed?"

"Shots."

"What kind of shots?" I felt like I was having a conversation with a three-year-old.

"Like doctors' shots." He sounded exasperated, too.

"With needles?"

He nodded like I was the three-year-old here. "My brother said he'd tell the sheriff I did it, and they'd just lock me up." He clammed up, literally – both hands clamped over his mouth.

"Did your brother tell you not to tell anyone?" I asked.

He hesitated, nodded, hands still in place.

"Okay, Kenny, it's not telling me if I guess, right? You just nod yes if I'm correct. Can you do that?"

More hesitation, another nod.

"You saw your brother today."

His eyes got bigger, but no nod.

"You saw him yesterday."

Nod.

Wouldn't take long for me to run out of questions like this. I thought back to the scene. "You were near the trail today."

Another nod.

How could Kenny get from town out to the where I picked up that body?

"Your brother took you there yesterday and left you."

Nod.

"So he knew the dead man was there in the tent?"

Some thought first, then a nod.

"And when you saw me take the body, you wanted to talk to me, but you were afraid he might be watching you."

Sort of a nod. Close enough.

"You walked here so I could help you."

Another nod. He'd walked about twelve miles to get to my house.

"Kenny, did you touch the man who was dead?"

"No, ma'am!" he blurted out between his hands. "I peeked inside the tent to see what was stinking, but I didn't touch that man."

"That's good, Kenny." Luckily, if he were telling the truth, there would be no fingerprints or other trace evidence to say he had. "Where have you been living?"

Questions turned away from the dead man, so Kenny began answering me again.

He told me he'd been in White Salmon at a church shelter, but they made him leave after thirty days. For a while, his brother had let him stay at their parents' old place east of Carson. Until yesterday when he took Kenny to the trailhead and kicked him out.

I nodded as he talked.

As a deputy, I'd heard that no one wanted Kenny around these days. He'd spent most of his adult life in and out of psychiatric hospitals for paranoid schizophrenia. Before Zach and I moved here, Kenny's parents had picked him up from a yearlong admission, hopeful that he'd be stable for a while. Five days later, deputies found Mrs. Underwood's body in her garden, strangled with a piece of rope. Kenny was sitting on the barn floor next to his dead father, very much out of touch with reality. He'd claimed he hadn't killed them. But his prints were all over the ax handle. He was covered in blood – some of it his father's, some his own.

Kenny had spent several more years in the mental hospital as lawyers threw his case from desk to desk, and then he was turned back on the streets when the facility closed. Even the justice system failed him by refusing to prosecute. Without a job, he couldn't buy the drugs he needed to treat his mental illness. Without the drugs, he couldn't possibly hold a job.

"You should stay somewhere you'll be safe while I look into this, Kenny. Is there anywhere you can think of where you'd feel safe?" I asked, hoping to let him find a solution that would be suitable to his psyche.

Watching him go through the possibilities was like watching a genius calculate a physics equation on an abacus. Finally, he made a proposition. "Could you put me in jail, but not for killing that man?"

I considered that. That would give me time to go check the dead man's autopsy and records, and put Kenny where he'd get a few meals and a shower, which he really could use.

"Okay, I'll arrest you for trespassing on my land. Then later, I'll drop the charges. Deal?"

He understood the criminal justice system pretty well for someone who seemed to be struggling with his common sense at times.

He doubts most of mankind, so why on earth does he trust me?

"In order to arrest you, I have to take your gun," I explained.

He pulled it from his pocket, and it became obvious to me that it was a piece of wood, carved like a common semi-automatic, charred by fire to a black shiny finish.

"I can't have a real gun, but sometimes it makes people leave me alone," he explained, putting it on the table in front between us. "Can I have it back when you unarrest me?"

I nodded. "How about we leave it here, so it doesn't get lost in evidence somehow. I'll go change clothes and get my handcuffs, if you'll wait."

"Yes, ma'am," he said politely.

"Is there anything else you can tell me about this man who was killed?" I asked.

"You should ask my brother's wife," he concluded, then stood up and extended his hands for handcuffs I didn't have. "She can tell you everything."

Whatever that meant, I thought.

323

I went inside the cabin, wondering what the hell had just happened – the whole event seemed totally unreal. I pulled on my jeans and tucked my own weapon into the waistband, put on a sweatshirt, and grabbed the cuffs from my duty belt.

When I walked back out onto the deck, Kenny stood exactly where I'd left him, hands still extended for me.

❃

Supper was ready when I got home.

Jamie had probably spent most of the afternoon, wondering the very same thing as me – what the hell . . .

I peeled off my jacket and put my gun and cuffs away. "Today has been one of the freakiest days of my life, not counting those where I almost ended up dead," I qualified. There had been worse. "So let's see if I can put this in a nutshell."

"Nuts indeed. Is he really as crazy as I gathered?"

"Absolutely. Long history of mental illness. Kenny was accused but never charged with killing his parents a couple of years back."

"Oh, wonderful. So you sat and had a little chat with him, thinking he had a gun in his pocket?"

"Jamie, what's nuts is that I think I believed him all along. The medical examiner hadn't found any obvious cause of death yet, but thanks to Kenny, I managed to catch Dr. Bishop before the body was released today," I said, explaining how the tale got weirder. "The man who identified the victim wasn't his father. Not related at all. He's a demented old man who claimed the body was his son, who is actually on a tour of duty overseas. He was set to have the body cremated today. Immediately."

"I don't understand." Jamie set two plates on the counter, followed by serving dishes of food I was sure hadn't come from my pantry or freezer, including pork loin and mushrooms, scalloped potatoes, and a bowl of green beans that at some point I'd have to confess I wouldn't eat, even at gunpoint.

While Jamie dished out food, I tried to explain what had almost disappeared in the fires of cremation. "Initially, a lot of pieces to a puzzle seemed unrelated. But because of what Kenny told me, we

324

reviewed every millimeter of skin of the body, which was again a John Doe instead of Major Raymond Davis. The doctor eventually found one tiny needle mark in the macerated decaying skin under the left arm. Toxicology will be several days on the tissue, but it substantiated Kenny's story of the injection." I inched my hand out to take a plate.

"What about the old man?" Jamie asked, keeping the food out of my reach.

"We questioned Davis' father, Jacob, about why he thought this was his son. He said someone from the Army called and told him his son's body had been recovered at the waterfall, told him what he was wearing and such, so he identified the body. Caller ID on his phone showed the number was blocked."

"So someone exploited his confusion to expedite release of the body for cremation to hide the evidence of a murder." Jamie's summary was spot-on.

He still did not push my plate toward me, and I could feel my stomach rumbling.

I nodded. "Add to the mix a man who says he'll be framed for the murder, someone with an obvious mental illness history and accusations of killing his parents. It all adds up to someone getting away with this murder but having scapegoats, if necessary."

"Any leads?"

I laughed. "Even better. Remember Kenny said we should ask his sister-in-law about the man, right? We brought her down, and after a little legal prompting, she identified the body as Hugh Dexter, the man she's been having an affair with for over a year. She'd told her husband she wanted a divorce last week, making Ben Underwood the number one suspect. So after bringing him in, Ben explains he told Kenny about his plight of marital unbliss and swears Kenny went off in a rage to kill Dexter. Had to be Kenny, he insisted, because wasn't the body found in Kenny's tent?"

"In Kenny's tent. How would he know that? Did you?"

I shook my head. "Kenny said he'd been staying at his parents' farm until Benny dumped him at the trailhead. He told me he didn't touch the dead man inside it, but I didn't ask if it was his tent. Because it was, his DNA and prints are all over it. Mixed in plain sight with his identical twin brother's."

"Twins, as in their DNA would even match?"

"Exactly. Making it easy to point to Kenny, if we were looking. A backup plan," I said. "But besides the other evidence and statements, a pet project I've been working on will probably point to one twin brother and not the other. Brother Ben is a nurse at a local long-term care facility, giving him access to syringes, needles and various drugs." I paused. "This particular facility has had a recent outbreak of resistant Staph infections thought to be caused by a healthcare provider who is a carrier of the bacteria." I gave up being subtle about my hunger and picked up my utensils, hoping this would prompt Jamie to feed me.

He ignored the universal signal for hunger and motioned for me to continue.

"The mucus spray I sampled in ample quantity from the body and sleeping bag will show *Staphylococcus aureus*, which can be readily isolated from many other pathogens by a culture. And guess who has a cold?"

Jamie nodded.

"By sampling Ben's mucous then running a DNA comparison on the bacteria, we'll be able to determine if the strain is a match. If Kenny isn't a *Staph* carrier, we can presume he didn't commit the murder." I reached to pull a plate toward me, but Jamie didn't let go.

"How did you figure all that out?"

"I didn't. The microbes I collected were a fluke," I said. "Kenny showed us pieces no one else had seen or even been looking for. We just shuffled them around until we saw the picture more clearly. I suspect that if Ben's conviction for this murder flies, they might even consider charging him with his parents' murders. It's possible the blood they thought was Kenny's was really Ben's. I'm inclined to think maybe Kenny's telling the truth that he didn't kill them."

Jamie came over to where I sat, took my fork out of my hand before I had a chance to stab something. Pork, him – I didn't care.

"If you can solve that in twelve hours, I'm sure you can help me figure out the rest of our puzzle. Can I have another kiss?"

I considered the question. "Okay."

He looked around then leaned closer. "You didn't bring Kenny back home for dinner, right? I clearly got the impression he doesn't like me doing this."

I shook my head. I couldn't pull away from him nor did I want to.

The kiss was not desperate or demanding. Not soft or teasing. A kiss that said there was more to be had, but it wasn't rushed. It was just two people finding each other physically.

Two people wanting to be wanted again, but afraid.

The kiss ended, slowly letting go. It wasn't a wow kiss. It was the sort that left you with a soft sigh when you replayed it in your head.

"I promise I won't forget you are not her," he whispered.

"Was that like Rebecca?" I asked.

"No. A very good no." He smiled. "She didn't like to kiss. I think you do."

He leaned forward for another.

After a long, slow kiss, I snatched the fork from his hand. "Now, stand back or risk permanent injury," I play-growled and stabbed a mushroom.

"Note to self: Do not stand between Julie and food when she's hungry," Jamie mumbled, returning to his own barstool.

"Add addendum to Jamie's note: Julie won't eat green beans."

"Damn, I debated getting squash or something else."

I laughed, stabbing another mushroom. "Did you find a single fresh vegetable in my kitchen? Fruit? I know you've been sneaking out to the grocery store." I flaked away a piece of the slow-cooked pork and took a bite. "Mmm, this is great. You actually fixed this in my kitchen with stuff I own?"

"Threw it into the slow cooker. Takes about four hours."

"I have one of those?" I asked.

"Yes, you do. Maybe you didn't know that the box thingy under the stove is called an oven? It's used to cook food, too."

Obviously he'd seen that I used it for storing cast iron skillets.

"You'd make a wonderful wife," I said in a dreamy voice and took another bite.

"Men usually try to get a mate in bed before marriage," he stated.

"You suggesting I might not like it?" I said with my mouth full.

He shrugged. "Don't mistake this for male insecurity, but one should always allow for such a possibility. I'm not six and a half feet tall, you see, and a guy makes suppositions."

"You're over six feet, whatever that supposition really means," I said. "I'm more concerned that I look like your wife – it's frightening, at least to me."

"I find it weird, but not so scary. I've learned that there's far more to you than what I see," he said. "But just for the record, I never sleep with a woman before the first date."

When supper was done, I helped Jamie clean up the kitchen despite his protests.

"I said I didn't know how to use this stuff, not that I couldn't wash it and put it away," I argued, still teasing him about my lack of culinary skills.

"Do you expect me to believe that your tongue-melting chili magically appears in your refrigerator?"

"Zach outfitted this kitchen for his cooking talents, not mine. The best thing I ever made for dinner was reservations, but I haven't starved yet." I had been the creator of a few family favorites, but I really missed how Zach could throw anything on the grill and make a meal of it.

Jamie took the towel from my hands when I finished. "As much as I'd like to stay, I think it's probably a good time for me to go back to the hotel now."

I was surprised. "Why?"

We hadn't worked much on the dead spouses project, owing to other issues.

"Because, after hot-tubbing and the kisses, given what's been on my mind today, I can only be a gentleman for so long."

"And what's been on your mind?" I fluttered my eyelashes innocently.

He stepped toward me, nudging me back into the corner of the countertop, leaned forward and whispered in my ear a lengthy detailed description. When he was done, he stepped back to see my reaction.

"Oh my…" I think I blushed. "I guess we can't be doing *that* before a first date. Or at least not that one thing, you know, with the butterscotch sauce."

He laughed. "I like you Julie." He leaned forward for another kiss, soft and tender. "It scares me that I like you this much so soon."

"So soon after losing Rebecca or so soon after meeting me?"

He kissed me again. "Both."

He closed his eyes when he kissed.

So he wouldn't see his wife?

"We could pretend this was our first date tonight," he suggested, flipping off the overhead lights, leaving us in the flickering light of the fireplace. "I did get the butterscotch."

Part of me wanted him. Wanted him to do all the things he described. Wanted to feel his breath against my bare skin. Wanted to feel reckless and wanted and physical.

And part of me didn't want him at all because he wasn't Zach.

Jamie touched my face.

"This isn't what I expected." It wasn't – I'd hated him when he walked through my door, asking questions.

He moved back slightly. "Raise your hands, like this." He brought his palms up between us, facing me. I did the same, putting mine to his, but he shook his head. "No, as close as you can get without touching."

We separated. Slightly.

"You can feel that, can't you, like electricity? It's hard to describe, but you know what I mean. You felt it when you first saw me at the door. The first time we touched. Maybe you can't explain it either, but you feel it."

I closed my eyes and held still, letting that electric sensation zap through me until it was gone. When I opened my eyes, I was standing in my kitchen alone, listening to my heart pound.

CHAPTER

52

The phone rang hours later. It was no surprise – I hadn't even bothered to stretch out. I answered.

"I think I should apologize for tonight," he said.

"No, you shouldn't. I don't know what I'm supposed to feel, what I want. Why should you be any different?"

"Doesn't mean I should act like a high school girl, teasing the football captain then changing her mind and running off."

"I wasn't complaining," I said.

"You deserve to complain. All these feelings," he said, pausing. "I felt like I was being watched by a ghost."

"Mine or yours?"

I hesitated. We could keep talking about that electricity and ghosts, but I had to tell him. "Jamie, when you and Nolan first arrived, you asked me a question, and I didn't answer quite honestly. I think I need to do that now."

"Okay."

I heard him shift his body. More attentive.

"You asked if Zach ever sent me anything while he was on assignment. The answer to that is still no," I said, carefully choosing words. "Before we lived together, he wrote letters and gathered trinkets for me that eventually he had delivered here for our first Christmas together in 1995. It was the most wonderful gift I'd ever imagined, reading cards and figuring out souvenirs he'd collected for several years. But he didn't directly send it while he was on assignment."

Jamie said nothing, and the silence felt ominous.

"I got a similar box of stuff in December," I said, then paused. "After Zach died."

"You what?" he repeated, maybe not sure he heard me correctly.

"It upset me," I said. "When you asked, I didn't know what to tell you, because it seems so impossible."

"Why did you lie?" Jamie demanded, his voice hot with anger, setting me on edge. "You should have told me the truth!"

Why is that box so important?

"Tell you? You came to my house, demanding I answer your questions like every other hotshot federal agent when all I've gotten from anyone in the government about my husband's death is bullshit and more unanswered questions," I argued.

"That's no reason to interfere with an investigation."

"See? You still call it that, even though you're on your own," I said, but there was no reply so I kept talking. "I had no reason to trust you when you showed up, no reason at all to cooperate. But I did not lie to you. I answered your exact question accurately – I never received anything from Zach *while he was working*. You didn't ask me whether I'd gotten anything from him since he died."

The response was more silence, followed by a click as the connection broke.

One thing about cell phones – you can't slam the receiver down when you're angry.

A dream. I knew it was a dream. At first, I didn't want it to end.

Hands caressed me like silk draped over my skin.

Whose hands?

I wanted them to be Zach's, so desperately that I could feel tears on my face in the dream. I cried, much as I had the first night after the stranger had shown up with the news of Zach's death, when no one could see me sobbing against his pillow.

The hands in the dream changed to Jeremy's, but the physical feeling did not stray from the sensual, which disturbed me even more.

I'd missed Jeremy before he showed up, as much as I hated him for leaving again.

And they changed again to David's hands. I never wanted to remember anything about him, though the dream brought back the feelings I'd once had. But when the hands became Anthony Bock's, anger and terror raced through me. This was not part of my life, neither memory nor fantasy, and I struggled to make the dream go away.

Leaving only Jamie, and I remembered the kiss.

The dream returned to the soft luscious feel of hands on my body. Wanting.

When I woke, unsettled, I found my face damp – not surprised to find I really had been crying in my sleep.

I rolled over and punched my pillow.

Undeniably, I was attracted to Jamie. Certainly physically, but also emotionally. Almost unnaturally attracted, like a moth to a flame. I considered whether I pursued the feelings because by solving his mystery, I might also find answers of my own about Zach. I could not shake the sense something at this very moment wasn't right.

How do I get on with my life, not knowing what really happened to you, Zach? Where do I find the answers?

In the box.

Three words popped into my head, and as much as I wanted to ignore them, they would not go away.

I tried again, but sleep wouldn't come. Instead, I went to the office. Using my keys to unlock the closet door, I pulled the box into the light and sat on the floor beside the cardboard cube full of trinkets and letters I couldn't wrap my head around, wondering what else was inside that held answers. What had Zach sent that made Jamie ask about it? How did he even know about the box? I began to pull out items, one at a time, sorting into piles of things that held no mysterious meaning, those that might, and those that I did not understand at all.

When the phone rang, I didn't answer it. I didn't bother to see who was calling – it would have been no one else but Jamie.

I kept pulling stuff from the box. Not knowing what it meant, I came back to the question of why I got it after Zach's death. What would I have stirred up if I'd called the shipping place and asked who sent it? Had the box been lost in shipping for several months, or maybe the postal center Zach chose had decided it was full enough to send? Shipping might have been requested on a certain date. By whom? Was that something Zach's lawyer would have set in motion?

I had lots of questions. I was simply afraid to guess any answers.

I flipped through envelopes and small packages, finding only one that was dated after Zach's death, which made even less sense but clearly a mystery. A plain envelope, it had been the one on top – the one that had sent me running to the bathroom – was postmarked from Whidbey Island two months after the funeral. It was mailed to this address, but I hadn't pulled it from my mailbox, which made me wonder how it had been delivered and who had retrieved it, then how had it ended up in the box?

Taking a deep breath, I studied the return address on the back, the street where I'd lived in my childhood. Only the number wasn't the same – this would have been the house across the road. The name surfaced in my memory. Benjamin S. Hyden.

I remember as a kid, we made fun of the mailbox – Ben Hyden.

Been Hiding?

The envelope had been sealed but empty.

I thought my heart would explode before my head ran out of arguments about that.

After I'd spent another hour going through the items, two other things had no explanation, besides the empty envelope.

A small antique key, a little over an inch long, hanging from a long gold chain – like a necklace. Didn't appear to be expensive, but there was no lock to match it.

And a box holding a clear evidence-style bag with the compact semi-automatic in it. Not Zach's duty weapon. Whose? I couldn't run a history on it without the risk of triggering something I couldn't explain, like the fact it was used in a crime, given the spent bullet and casing in a smaller bag I also found. Distorted from its original shape, the bullet appeared to be of the same caliber as the gun, but I couldn't tell for sure.

I leaned back against the wall, rubbing my face, wondering what it all meant. Why would Zach send me a gun that had a history I shouldn't explore, or should I? Did the gun and bullet go together? Had someone been shot with the bullet? What did the key unlock? Why the empty envelope from Whidbey Island?

Had Zach sent it at all? If not, who had and why?

The clock beside the bed read 4:38. No wonder I couldn't make heads or tails of this stuff, I thought, but I didn't get up.

Questions whirled around in my head.

Special Agent Jamie Gordon, Federal Bureau of Investigation, sat at the top of my unresolved issues list. In just a few days, I'd discovered some likable qualities in him, despite his employment with the FBI, and I'd developed a sense of trust I hadn't thought possible after Nolan Forrester left him here.

But Jamie thought I'd violated that trust by withholding an answer to a question he'd asked in the first few minutes after we met. However, based on Jamie's reaction on the phone tonight, there was something in that box I needed to protect, even if I wasn't sure what it was or why. I'd have to keep looking.

Why did I tell him about the box?

That thought was replaced by another - why had Jamie Gordon come here? Nolan had been right – I wouldn't have talked to a stranger without his introduction, but for all the interpretation of the puzzle, I got the feeling Jamie wanted something from me besides the truth regarding his wife.

The links connecting Jamie, Rebecca, Zach and me were bizarre, unbelievable. I was a doppelganger for the wife of the man who'd barely saved my life from my first husband and a serial killer, and my spouse and Jamie's were said to have been in Seattle for two separate reasons, both reported to have died under questionable circumstances.

My head hurt. I got up and went to the kitchen for a glass of water.

Laser got up to follow me and lapped from his dish.

"Where were you when Kenny Underwood showed up this afternoon?" I pretended to scold him. "Letting strangers sneak up on me like that. You should be ashamed."

Laser came to me and leaned his head on my leg in apology. Age was creeping up on him. I scratched his ears.

Going from police dog to a family companion hadn't kept him

active and strong, but Amber had fallen in love with him immediately, and they'd become inseparable. But then she left for Albuquerque. Did dogs really miss their people? Maybe, but I knew Laser missed his job, because on occasion when I'd come home in a patrol car, he'd made an effort to get in.

Checking my calendar, I wasn't scheduled for duty for another three days, though I was on call for the medical examiner in a few hours.

I thought about going out to feed the horses just for something physical to do. Still dark outside. Of course – it wasn't even 5 a.m. yet.

Instead, I walked to the dining room table, to the dozens of index cards and photos spread out. Why was I at the middle of so many connections? Maybe not me, I thought, but my appearance. What was the purpose for that? What were the real crimes here? Money laundering? Multiple government alphabet-soup agencies saying they investigated two deaths without any results or bodies. Were there crimes committed that I could go to jail if convicted because someone thought she was me? Was reasonable doubt enough I didn't?

And another thought crossed my mind – even though I didn't know exactly how, I certainly had the computer knowledge to learn to steal money, even if, or maybe especially because I didn't have the kind of money that would pay to move offshore. All my money was accounted for, already taxed, including Zach's inheritance and the life insurance. No reason to think hiding or moving it would benefit me. Perhaps that small amount could feed a small third world country for a few months, but it wouldn't buy weapons of mass destruction.

But Rebecca had money.

Or more specifically, Jamie said, her father did.

Stacks of papers and cards with arrows and theories littered the table. Ideas drifted off when I tried to focus on them, lost in lack of sleep. Still, the connections seemed to involve me.

I heard a car pull onto the gravel road to the cabin.

Trying to make up for earlier, Laser gave me a warning bark.

With a sigh, I pulled the carafe from the coffee maker to fill it with water.

Laser was waiting at the door when I let Jamie in.

335

"I didn't figure you'd go back to sleep."

"Would it have mattered?" I grumbled, closing the door behind him. "You'd show up here anyway, right?"

"I saw the lights on," he said. "Look, I'm sorry I hung up on you. I didn't want to say something wrong."

Not knowing how to answer that, I returned to the kitchen to finish fixing the coffee. He followed me. I pointed to the table. "Whoever is in the middle of this web is the key," I said, not acknowledging it was me. "I have many more questions."

The key. There was a key in the box. What did that mean?

"What if you became Becca?" he asked. "What if you showed up as her, defied the feds to explain."

I tilted my head in confusion. "What would that accomplish?"

He shrugged, but I suspected that he really had an idea in mind.

"That would surely get someone's attention, wouldn't it?" he said.

Not for long. One set of fingerprints would prove I wasn't her. *Or would it – could he have gotten my prints and altered the federal databases?* I ignored that possibility in lieu of worse ones. If I showed up as Rebecca Nelson, would someone kill me and make me disappear to cover up a secret? No sense trying to discuss that yet. At least until we knew who *they* were. "The big question is, who would it piss off the most and why?"

"Let's go to Seattle and retrace her steps," he suggested.

We let that idea hang in silence until the coffee maker hissed its last drops through the basket. I selected two mugs from the cabinet and poured coffee in them both. From the refrigerator, I pulled out a green bottle of creamer and topped off my cup, then replaced it.

No need to offer it to Jamie – he drank his coffee black.

I shouldn't know that. He's still a stranger.

He wrapped his fingers around the cup but didn't drink.

"No," I said. "I won't pretend I'm her, not even to help you find out what happened to her."

"Even if it means finding out what happened to Zach?"

I shook my head, but the enticement tickled a doubt. "Nothing on the table even hints that they met, much less that their deaths were connected," I said. "I want to know the truth, but not by becoming her."

After a moment, he nodded. "Julie, I know there's a lot more to figure out, and we can get to that later. That's not why I'm here." Leaving the cup full, he walked around the breakfast bar to where I stood. "I came for something else."

Close enough I could smell his warm skin. Shampoo on his hair.

He leaned forward, barely breathed against my ear. "I want to learn how you feel, Julie." And he lifted my hair away from my neck, trailing the slightest touch of his lips down my neck, making me shiver. "I want to feel your skin against me."

I closed my eyes, maybe not breathing.

Jamie moved close enough I felt the heat between us, closer still until our bodies made contact, creating a sensation of electricity where skin met skin. Teasing, making me want to feel his fingers touch me. "I don't want to waste any more time in our lives, Julie. We could have everything."

Warnings that had clanged together in my head suddenly fell still. I was torn – wanting everything he offered, yet fearing to take a step or risk losing the chance.

Jamie caressed his hand from my cheek down to my neck, fingers making my skin burn, turning my face upward to meet his.

We stood, foreheads touching, eyes closed, just a moment from whatever came next, surrounded by silence.

Broken by a distinct two-stage click I immediately recognized – the hammer being pulled back on a Kimber .45.

CHAPTER

53

My eyes popped open in surprise.

Zach?

Zach!

My husband stood behind Jamie, whose eyes were squeezed shut in fear.

However Zach had appeared in the kitchen, it had been as soundless as the shadows.

"What did I tell you about kissing other cops?" my husband asked in an amused voice.

I shoved Jamie out of the way to get to Zach, a thousand questions to ask, but nothing came out as I clung to him. Tears streamed down my face.

Jamie turned his head to peek over his shoulder, to see what had really happened, perhaps surprised that he wasn't on the floor dead.

Zach's gun was still pointed at him, left handed. The other arm held me tight.

No one moved.

For months, people told me Zach was dead. Told me I should move on. And as wrong as it had felt, I'd begun questioning whether he'd really take his own life, whether I needed to believe that and believe in a next step. Now, wrapping my arms around him was the only way I could believe he was alive.

"Mr. Gordon has some explaining to do," Zach said, letting go of me long enough to remove a pistol from the back waistband of

Jamie's pants, then motioning him to the chair on the other side of the bar. "Sit."

As directed, Jamie made his way to the other barstool, not speaking. Zach's weapon remained pointed in his general direction.

The gun Zach had removed now lay on the cabinet, and I waffled on the idea that Jamie was supposed to be carrying it – he was an FBI agent – but without a holster, I suspected he'd carried it with a specific goal other than duty in mind.

Fear won the mental debate.

I picked up my spoon and used the handle to scoot the weapon far out of Jamie's reach.

When I moved back into the crook of Zach's right arm, he flinched.

"I'm okay, Julie. It's still healing," he told me.

Pulling away, I yanked up Zach's shirt, finding dark, dimpled skin with an elliptical scar around it on his right side, lower than the previous knife scar. On around on his right flank, another longer surgical incision had left its mark on what had been a perfect back.

I wanted answers.

So many more questions, but Zach pulled me close to him again. "I'll explain later." He looked up again. "So start talking, Mr. Gordon."

"I don't know what you mean."

"Come now, you make up a story about your wife dying and tell so many people, and eventually someone is not going to believe it. Let's start with how you intended to get the money out of Canada."

"What money?" Jamie's eyes bounced from Zach to me and back. "I have no money there."

Zach shrugged. "Fine. I'll just call the FBI to come get your sorry ass out of my house and let them –"

"No, wait!"

"Wait?" I demanded, feeling Zach holding me in place by the collar of my shirt. "You lied to me?"

Jamie hesitated.

"Or I could just let her beat it out of you," Zach suggested, still amused. "Because it certainly looks like she would."

Outnumbered and outgunned, Jamie still chose not to speak.

"Let me see if I have these details straight, then," Zach said. "You wanted out of the military, and this incident involving Julie was likely going to end your career anyway. Then you met Rebecca, stunned at her money and how much she resembled you, Julie. And the high-society girl was happy to go slumming just to drive her father crazy. You talked her into getting married, hoping to get access to her money."

Jamie looked up. "To her father's money. But he wouldn't give it to us – not one dime. Instead, he told her to earn her own living, but he arranged for me to get into the FBI, a huge favor someone owed him, he said."

"Where does Nelson's money come from?" I interrupted.

"Interests in oil and gas, energy stuff," he replied.

"Was it legal?" Zach asked.

"How the hell should I know?" Jamie barked, then backed off when his outburst earned a frown from Zach, still holding his gun. "Most of it was, I guess. But Becca found one shell company from where he'd been shifting profits, so she began to steal from it. *Because* it wasn't legal, she said." He leaned back as if two wrongs canceled each other out.

"You don't get off that easy," Zach prompted. "Keep going."

Jamie sighed. "Rebecca captured assets and moved the money to a Canadian bank account she'd set up. Nothing huge, just five or ten grand at a time out of millions. No one complained. I mean, if it wasn't a legal business, Nelson wouldn't report it, right? And it should have been her money anyway."

I scowled, becoming angrier by the minute but not about how or whose money they stole. "How'd this involve the DEA?"

"I don't know. I never heard from her after she arrived in Seattle."

Zach picked up the story. "Rebecca used forged documents to start an account in a Vancouver bank in your name, Julie. The plan, according to Jamie, was for Rebecca to impersonate you and to withdraw the money from the bank in Victoria, and to leave a trail of crumbs as you with all the proper documents. From there, they would meet in another country, leaving you as the scapegoat."

Still confused, I got madder with each new twist.

"The Department of Treasury had been tracing the thefts and suspected she was about to make off with the stolen money from the bank account, which they thought was in Vancouver," Zach continued. "Because we already had a team in place when she left Seattle going to Victoria instead, Treasury asked us to intercept and follow her after she crossed back into Canada to get the money. When she arrived at the branch bank, she was to be given counterfeit money with a tracer."

Jamie said nothing.

Zach moved the pistol to his other hand and kissed me on top of the head. "As she approached the bank, I guess I looked like a good body guard to her, so she asked if I could just walk with her, saying she thought someone might be following her because she was about to pick up a large sum of money. I think she knew Gordon was around somewhere."

He paused until I nudged him to go on.

"We were walking down the street toward the bank when someone shot her, then me."

Silence hung in the kitchen like smoke from burned bacon.

"I went down, unable to give chase, so the shooter got away," Zach finally said, shaking his head.

Still shaken, I wrapped my arms around him again, just to feel him breathe.

"I don't get it. When Rebecca didn't come home," he said to Jamie, "you never asked anyone at her office where she was or when she'd be back. After two weeks, the FBI told you it had connected her with you, since she'd kept her family name. You jumped at the idea she was on a jet that crashed, because it left no traces of her or your crimes."

Jamie shrugged and looked away.

"Her death meant you got everything, but you weren't satisfied with her life insurance and the money her father would have given you, were you?" Zach asked. "You wanted the money she'd stolen, too."

"How much did you really get for her life insurance?" I demanded.

The answer was an easy two million dollars.

"You weren't happy with that?" I asked, resisting the urge to slap his face. "So you thought you'd talk me into just taking a ride to British Columbia, so I would walk into a bank and make a withdrawal for you?

"Then he intended to kill you," Zach concluded. "Isn't that about right, Mr. Gordon?"

Anger vibrated through my body.

"What happened to you?" I asked Zach.

"Bullet hit a renal artery, dropping me like a rock. The shot that hit her broke her neck."

Jamie sat motionless, speechless. He didn't ask about her, and I hated him even more for that.

"Next thing I knew, I was in a hospital." He stared hard at Jamie. "By the way, Mr. Gordon, you assumed Rebecca intended to share that money you'd talked her into stealing, but I guess you wouldn't have known that she only had about five thousand dollars Canadian and a single one-way ticket to Amsterdam in her bag, under an assumed name for which she had a passport and credit cards."

Jamie shook his head. "Once she was safe with all the money, I was supposed to join her in Brazil."

Zach smiled. "She didn't want you to join her. You were being scammed just like you were scamming her. She had stolen money she tucked away in places she never told you. Altogether about fourteen million. All she wanted was a reason to get out of the country without you, so the plan for her to go to Canada worked perfectly. You thought all the money was in Canada, but she'd only left enough there to collect and fly to Europe," Zach said. "But you followed her up there and figured out she was going to leave, so you intended to take the money. Your first shot missed and hit her, but I wasn't dead, so you couldn't grab what you thought was all that cash. How ironic that neither of you gets a dime."

Seething, I twisted back toward Zach. "They told me you killed yourself, that your body wasn't recovered."

Zach pulled me closer still. "I'm sorry, Julie. I didn't want to do this, but by the time I was awake again, everything was already in play. Then no one thought it would go this long." He wiped away a tear that crawled down my cheek. "I didn't think you'd believe the suicide story, no matter what. But I sent the box, just in case."

"The box?"

I pulled away from Zach and leaned on my elbows against the breakfast bar, rage building exponentially until my temper unraveled. "Why the charade?"

"Mr. Gordon could have collected her life insurance from the supposed plane crash and gone on his way, but he didn't. When he accepted the story about what had happened to Rebecca without any proof she was dead, the feds decided to see how deeply he was involved in her crimes, too. Sure enough, he got greedy and wanted the money he still thought she'd deposited in Canada," Zach summarized. "The bank, by the way, provided a caller with an account balance big enough to entice him, even though there was really no money there." He turned to me. "The only way he could get it was to convince you to go make the withdrawal."

I just couldn't find the words to begin the tirade dammed up inside me.

"Mr. Gordon, just so you know, Rebecca isn't dead," Zach said.

Jamie looked up, but his expression was more of boredom than caring about her.

"She's in a Seattle hospital," my husband continued. "They charged her with a handful of high-powered crimes, including the felony theft, but there's no sense taking it to trial. She can't move, can't even breathe on her own. It's a prison of her own making, more or less. Even though you pulled the trigger. "

Jamie's head hung again.

My thoughts came back to me – screw the money and the criminal charges, the DEA lied to me about Zach committing suicide!

"You let a bunch of heartless bureaucrats convince your daughter that her father didn't care enough to come back to his family," I said, turning to face Zach, on the verge of pounding my fists into his chest. "That one lie might not matter to anyone else involved in this case, but it does to me."

"Julie," Zach said, pulling me close again. "Amber is just fine. I was in Albuquerque at the ranch while I recuperated."

I pushed myself away. "You told her but you didn't tell me you were alive?"

"Actually, I tried to, but I guess you didn't figure it out," he said. "In the box, there's a key – it goes to the locket I bought you for Christmas. You couldn't open it, remember? With the key, you could. I'd left you a note inside. I'm sorry."

"What did Jamie want with the box?" I asked.

"The gun he used to shoot Rebecca and me was in it. If you'd run the serial number, it would have come back to him," Zach said. "I suspect that if you hadn't given him that gun tonight, he'd have drugged you or maybe even killed you for it, even without the extra money he thought was in Canada. He was going to Brazil in four days, one way or the other." He pulled the ticket folder from his hip pocket and dropped it on the counter.

So many clues I'd ignored because I didn't understand, because I'd been so wrapped up in a blanket of grief. Tears burned down my cheeks, and Zach pulled me close again.

The door to the garage opened, and Amber came running to me, giving me a hug. Half a dozen people in black clothing, agency abbreviations on their backs, surrounded Jamie and handcuffed him.

I paid them little attention as they led Jamie Gordon out through the garage, until I looked up to find Nolan Forrester and Layne Sebastian standing in the kitchen, which left me flustered.

"I am so sorry," Nolan said. "We never thought the sting would go so long before Gordon came to you. He knew Zach had survived the shooting and had sent the gun to you, because no one had come after him about it. That's why the suicide was staged and dated a week later than the shooting." He grinned. "I wasn't sure what to do when you denied receiving another box, but we let it play out, which snowballed into a much longer operation than we ever thought."

"And you?" I said, turning to Sebastian.

"Zach recruited me into the DEA when I left Portland," he said with a shrug. "I was with him in Seattle."

"Layne's probably the only reason I'm still alive," Zach stated. "He identified Gordon."

And finally it occurred to me, the one man who had tried to tell me the truth – Kenny Underwood. *Mr. Zach won't like you kissing him.*

"You've been here, watching," I said to Zach, slugging his arm as

I fought back more tears.

"Since Nolan brought Gordon up here, yes. I stayed at the Underwood farm until Kenny came back. He caught me sleeping in the barn one night," Zach said. "We've become pretty good friends."

Friends with a crazy man.

I guess that made perfect sense.

CHAPTER

54

"So even Kenny knew you were alive! That's just wrong, Z'," I said when I finally calmed down. "What about the murder at the trail?"

"Absolutely unrelated to this, but I had faith you'd figure out it wasn't a natural death when Kenny talked to you."

"Julie, I'm sorry we couldn't tell you," Amber pitched in. "It's been awful not being able to talk about Dad being alive, so the best I could do is not talk much at all."

Tears streamed down my cheeks again, joyful tears finally, knowing Zach was alive. That our family was whole again.

The house was finally empty of criminals and law enforcement except Nolan.

"I didn't want to go away," Amber said. "But when Grandmom Vera called, she promised everything would be better if I came to Albuquerque, but I swear I didn't know till I got there."

Duped by everyone, even my mother.

"After being shot, I was in a Canadian hospital for three weeks before they moved me to Seattle," Zach continued. "Despite surgery and dialysis, I ended up losing my right kidney."

"You couldn't tell me? I'd have been there with you," I repeated, like a child who'd been abandoned. "Instead, some robotic idiot came to tell me you'd killed yourself?"

Who was I kidding – I hadn't calmed down yet. Might be weeks.

"Like I said, the trap for Gordon had already been put into play before I had any say, but it was slow. I went to New Mexico to hide and recuperate because we knew he would eventually come to you to get the money, or at least the gun."

Nolan strolled over to the dining room table, looking at the dozens of index cards I'd marked and laid out, evaluating clues and ideas. "I knew we couldn't let you go too long or you'd solve the case," he said. "Looks like you got close."

"Close to what? Figuring out that Jamie wanted me to get the money from a bank?"

"No, to figuring out that Rebecca was stealing money from dozens of her company's clients as well as her father's accounts. That would have led you to Canada and eventually to Jamie wanting you to retrieve the money, which wasn't even there."

I remembered the day he'd dropped Jamie Gordon into my life, how I'd felt like bait. The feeling boiled up in my stomach again.

"We wouldn't have let anything happen to you," Nolan assured me. "That little girl getting injured was a tragedy, but it was enough diversion to let you trust Gordon, which is exactly what he needed to happen."

"Tonight was the end of the line, though," Zach said. "When you told him about the box, he packed before he came here, presumably to convince you to go with him or kill you."

I swallowed hard, understanding more how much trouble I'd been in without even knowing.

Amber came over and hugged me. "I missed you so much. Now we can be a family again."

Outside the bay windows, the sky began to lighten, though it was still hours till sunrise. Somehow, the dark shadows on my soul began to lift, relief from the depression of believing in Zach's death.

"I'm so sorry, Baby," he said again, pulling me against his body. "But I do have a complaint."

I jerked back, about to yell that he had no right to complain about anything that had happened, but he silenced me with a finger on my lips.

"You didn't wear that sexy red dress at my funeral like you said you would."

EPILOGUE

June 1998

On Saturday afternoon, Zach took Amber to a penning competition, a time-limited event where three riders cut three like-marked cattle from a herd of thirty and drive them into a small fenced pen. It was something all three of us had done, but they had hoped to catch a third rider at the arena since I couldn't go.

Late that evening, I heard the truck pull in toward the barn to unload the horses.

Amber came in through the garage, looking as limp as a potted plant left baking in the sun.

"I know Dad wanted me to help him with the horses," she told me, reaching into the refrigerator for water, "but I'm just exhausted."

Instead of asking how they did, I held the back of my hand to her forehead. "You don't have a fever, do you?"

She rolled her eyes. "No, I just need a nap."

With the bottle of water and her hat, she dragged on through to the stairs and clomped up them in what sounded like slow motion.

Through the kitchen window, I saw Zach walking toward the house from the barn, talking to the dog trotting at his heels. Before I could finish loading the dishwasher, I heard him come through the garage door.

"What's up with her?" he asked. "The longer we were out, the more listless she got."

"She says she's exhausted," I repeated, wondering how an energetic teenager could be that way after just a few weeks of summer working two days a week on trail rides with Del Clinton and one day sitting with his granddaughters Courtney and Daphney.

Daphney was still in a wheelchair, which meant that getting her around to errands in town was more than either she or Del could manage yet, so Amber stayed with the girls for the afternoon while Del tended to shopping and other matters.

Zach shook his head. "I don't get it."

I shrugged. "It was tough coming back and getting caught up again the last two months of school. She's keeping up her chores and stuff, so who can complain if she says she's tired now and then?"

About to say something else, we heard a loud thud above our heads.

"Amber?" he called.

When there was no answer, he whirled around toward the stairs, taking them two at a time ahead of me, hobbling as fast as I could on crutches.

In her room, Amber's pale body lay crumpled on the floor.

"Amber?" he yelled again, patting her face.

When he looked up, I was already dialing the phone for an ambulance.

CPSIA information can be obtained at www.ICGtesting.com
Printed in the USA
LVOW08s0520271113

362880LV00001B/9/P